CAGED NO MORE

Caged No More

Molly Venzke

a production of
www.traffickinghope.org

ISBN:
ISBN - 13: 978-0692575727

Cover Design by The Refinery for CAGED NO MORE (Movie)
Adapted by Unmutable Creative
Actors Featured On Cover: Cassidy Gifford (photo by Trevor Boyd),
Loretta Devine, Kevin Sorbo, Alan Powell (photos from movie)

Overall Book Cover Design by Unmutable Creative www.unmutablecreative.com
Back Cover photos by Ike & Tash Photography www.photomelatasha.com
Interior Design by Lisa Garrison

Caged No More is a 2nd Edition

1st Edition published as:
Caged by CreateSpace Independent Publishing (May 2011)

Printed in the United States of America

This book is dedicated
to the millions of children around the world
whose lives have become not their own.

You are not forgotten.

Please hold on to Life...

We're coming to get you.

ONE

"DIS DA LAST TIME I'm gone make dis trek out to Maringouin," Aggie said. "And in da snow at dat! What kinda devil done possessed dis state o' Louisiana and made it snow? And while I'm askin, what ol' black Cajun woman drives herself from Lafayette to da tiny po-dunk town of Maringouin in all dat possessed snow? I'll tell you what kind. A crazy one, dat's what. I swear I'm gone kill myself drivin in all dis snow."

There was no one in the car with her, but Aggie always talked out loud. In her house, in the car, or in the middle of the Olde Tyme Grocery on West Saint Mary Boulevard. Even before Harold died over ten years ago, Aggie's thoughts generally flew right on out, unedited from her mind to her mouth. Only on Sundays, which Aggie called *la jour de Bon Dieu,* or the Good Lord's Day, did she practice restraint. And on this late Saturday night, she had at least fifteen minutes until the clock struck midnight and her discipline had to kick in.

"Good ting no one else crazy as me to be out on da roads at dis God-forsaken hour. *Chooooh,* it's Mardi Gras weekend, too! Dat's why da streets are bare; all dem heathens are still celebratin da holiday. Da night's still young for dose folks. Well, now I guess it's a good ting Macy *did* call me when she did. A few more hours, and I'd be havin to worry about all dose drunks slidin around tryin to smash into me. Well, all I'm sayin is, I'm not gone do dis again. Dis da last time she gone call me in da middle of da night cryin, needin someone to come save her—*and* her little girls—from dat awful man.

"And she not even making any sense dis time. What did she mean 'he done sold em?' Sold what? Ha! What else dat greedy man got to sell, anyway? He already sold anyting worth of value my girl Macy ever had, he so up to his eyeballs in debt. I told her dat she needed to make dat good-for-nothin get a j-o-b. Den maybe he don't have to hock anyting dat's not nailed down.

"I'll tell you what I'm gone do...I'm gone march in dere and tell dat girl she gettin outta dat house, and dat's just gone be da way it's gone be. I told her once, I told her a million times, dat boy *canaille* and a cheat. I'm gone pack her up with her li'l baby girl, and she gone come live with MaMa Aggie. I'm tellin you, I'm not gone do dis again."

As Aggie turned her '95 Chevrolet off of I-10 east and onto LA-76 west toward Maringouin, she had no idea the irony her words held. This would be the last time she made this drive, but for much different reasons than she ever could have anticipated.

"And I know none a dem roads are gone be cleared. Dis town so small, I bet dey don't even own a plow, or even at da very least, salt da streets. I tank *le Bon Dieu* I don't live here. All da poor ol' women like me'll be havin to pour out da entire pantry of Epson Salts all over da sidewalk just so's dey can make it out to da mailbox without breakin a hip."

In truth, even if Aggie did slip and fall, the chances of her breaking a bone were slim. She was strong as an ox for her stout, 5-foot frame, and she only boasted her age so other people would feel compassion and give her assistance. She figured since she'd made it on the planet over 67 years, she might as well use her age to her advantage. Plus, it gave her the opportunity to talk to folks as they carried her groceries, helped mow her lawn, and walked her across the street.

The snow was barely dusting the streets, but for this Cajun woman who could count on her fingers the times she had seen snow, let alone drive in it, there may as well have been ten inches. She slowed down to a crawl as she entered the small town of Maringouin. As she turned onto Landry Drive, gradually making her way to her destination on Lions Ave., she chuckled at the number of families who were out in the snowfall.

"Dose mamas must've woke dem babies right out dere beds just so dey could see dis snow," she said. "Well, I guess I'd pro'bly do da same ting if little Skye and Elle had been sleepin at my house dis night. If da *Bon Dieu* gone bless da South with snow, ya gotta get out in it, cuz if ya sneeze, ya gone miss it."

Aggie was surprised at how a paper-thin coat of white snow could improve the appearance of the worn-out neighborhood. Blanketing over the thick, mossy patches on the roofs, and trimming the windows and door frames with a look of cleanliness, the snow offered this particular street a much-needed facelift.

"Too bad da sun's gone come up soon and melt all dis away. Dis house almost looks like a decent place to live." She pulled into the driveway of a small, one-story home, her wheels sounding pops and crackles over the frozen grass.

Aggie was half expecting to hear chaotic sounds seeping from the house, a party, an argument, or at least a television blaring questionable programming. But there was just a strange, quiet calm. She noticed Jack and Macy's car was gone, and from the lack of tire tracks in the snow, it must have been gone for a while. She breathed a sigh of relief knowing she wasn't going to have to confront Jack. Not only was he conniving, but he was also a brute of a man. There's no way he would allow Macy to pack up and leave, without a fight, that is. And Jack was no stranger to hitting a woman. Macy could attest to that.

Aggie lumbered out of her car, feeling the stiffness of the hour-long drive. "Dis da last time I'm gone do dis," she mumbled under her breath once more. "Aggie, you best be takin it careful gettin down out da car, else you slip in all dis snow."

Slowly, she climbed the narrow porch steps, cautious to test each one's sturdiness before trusting it with the fullness of her weight. And once she arrived at the front door, she noticed it was slightly ajar. She entered the house saying, "Girl, what you tinkin keepin dis door open with all dis snow and it being so..."

Her words trailed off as something just did not feel right. What was that smell? Burnt metal? Bleach? Rotten food? Sour alcohol? It was a noxious mixture of it all.

"Macy?" she called out. There was no answer.

The hair stood up on the back of her neck as she rushed into Macy's bedroom. She wasn't in her bed, so Aggie checked her bathroom. Vacant. Next, she tried the kitchen, which turned out to be the source of the horrible smells. Covering her mouth with her hand in hopes to keep from gagging, she scanned the wreckage. One end of the kitchen looked like a chemistry lab with glass vials, empty pill bottles, and deeply charred saucer pots. In the sink was a heap of unrecognizable, rotting food, and on the floor tile in the opposite corner, it looked as if someone had vomited...a few days ago. Aggie's heart sank down into her stomach.

"Macy, you in here?"

A soft moan came from the girls' room, and Aggie hurried to respond. When she opened little Elle's bedroom door, she found Macy crumpled on the pink carpet beside Elle's empty bed. Half dressed in a t-shirt and men's boxer shorts, Macy looked as white as the snow falling outside, and the blue hue of her lips brought panic to Aggie's chest.

"Macy girl, Aggie's here," she said as she knelt by her side and tried to cradle her. The stench coming off her body was sickening. "Can you hear me, *Sha?* You here?"

Aggie could see Macy's nostrils flaring with each breath; even so, her breathing seemed quite labored. She pulled a blanket off Elle's bed and did her best to wrap Macy's torso with it. Macy let out another soft moan.

"Mama Aggie? Did you come, after all?"

"Aggie's here, *Sha*. Talk to me. Tell me what you took?" Aggie could tell Macy was trying to muster up some kind of urgency, but she was barely finding the energy to speak. "Mama Aggie, Jack sold them. Right now. He's selling them. They're gone."

"OK, now, you listen to me right now. You tell Mama Aggie what you took. And how much of it did you take?"

"I don't know. I don't know." Macy whispered between shallow breaths. "It doesn't matter anymore. They're gone now, and they're not coming back. The bastard sold them. How could he do that? What kind of person does that? And now we're all gonna rot in hell." She slipped out of consciousness.

"Macy! You gotta stay with me, *Sha*!" Aggie patting her cheeks. "Macy, you gotta wake up. You gotta stay with me, and den we'll get back whatever it is Jack done stole. Ain't nothin worth losin your life over. You hear me? Macy, you gotta keep with me." The older woman attempted to sit Macy up but even as emaciated as she had become, Macy's dead weight and tall body was difficult for Aggie to maneuver.

"911! I gotta call 911!" But she had left her cell phone in the car. "Lawd, it's gone take dem too long to get way out here." Aggie pulled a pillow off the girl's bed, trying to make a comfortable place for Macy to lay. As she scooted her onto the makeshift bed, the young woman emerged again into consciousness.

"Mama Aggie. Are you still here?"

"*Bebe*, I'm right next to you."

"There still might be time. I don't know. But there might...you've got to...listen to me, Aggie...I'm all done, Aggie, all done...and I deserve it. I've been a terrible mama to the girls, so blind to everything. I should've seen it; I should've seen it. How could I not have seen it? I deserve to die and go straight to hell."

"Macy, I don't wanna hear you talkin like dat."

"It's ok, Mama. I know I deserve what I get. But not the girls; they're innocent. They don't deserve a single bit of it. Mama Aggie, please, I'm begging you. Get the girls. Will you promise me to get the girls?"

"You not makin any sense, *Sha*. Of course I'll get 'em. When Skye gets back from her boardin school, I'll get her. And where is Elle? I'll take her home with me right now."

"That's just it, Aggie!" Macy's desperation flared. "You don't understand! How could he do it?" and she fell back onto the floor half-moaning, half-crying.

"Macy, you gotta get yourself clear in da head, and tell me what you mean."

"Mama, it's all on his laptop," she whispered. "That idiot forgot to take his laptop." And she almost drifted off again, but then she shot up and lunged forward to grab Aggie. Her whole body shook from the effort as her eyes locked into Aggie's. "Mama, don't you let the police get that laptop. *You* take that. They won't know what to do with that laptop. Do you understand me? *You* gotta take that laptop and use it to get the girls back. Promise me."

"What're you talkin about? Where's Elle? Is she with Jack?"

"Promise me!"

"OK, baby, I promise you. I'll get da girls. I'll take da laptop. Aggie'll do whatever you need. Don't you worry bout a ting. I gone take care of all of it. Now listen, Macy, I'm gone get my cell phone to call for help. I left it out in da car. I'll be right back, though, so you rest here and Aggie be right back."

"Wait! No, wait, Mama. Take the laptop with you right now. You take that thing out to your car before anyone else can get it. Mama Aggie, you hear me? You've got to take it right now! It's in the kitchen. Give me your word; promise me that you'll take it right now!"

"Yes, girl. I promise I'll take da laptop. Trust me, we'll get all dis worked out as soon as we get you some help."

"Nobody can help me now." Macy whispered as she melted to the ground and slipped out of consciousness.

TWO

AGGIE KNEW THE MOMENT she stepped back inside the house, Macy was gone. The absence of life could be felt. And when she approached the door of the girls' room, she saw the proof of it. She'd seen the expression of death many times before, on her mama, both her younger sisters, and on her own husband, Harold, when he died in his sleep over a decade ago.

She stared at Macy, suspended between the knowledge of death and the deluge of its pain. "Funny how death looks da same on ever'body," she breathed. "All different faces, but somehow it still looks da same. How dat?" But instead of an answer to her question came the reality of her loss, an engulfing wave of grief so powerful Aggie had to clutch onto the doorframe to keep from collapsing under the weight of its rush.

She staggered in toward Macy and crumpled beside the dead woman. From deep within her gut arose a wail of emotion unlike anything Aggie had ever felt, a silent heave of sorrow much too profound to be vocalized, though her mouth was open wide. She wrapped her arms around this woman who was the closest thing she ever had to a daughter. Aggie kissed her hair and her cheeks, and clung to her body that had not yet grown cold. She wished she would have waited to go to her car rather than be absent when Macy let out her last breath. Aggie had been in the room when Macy, as a baby, had taken her first breath; she had aided in her delivery. Aggie felt the injustice, that simply by a matter of moments, she had missed her final one.

"Aggie shoulda stayed with you, *Sha*. I'm so sorry you had to go alone. Aggie shoulda been right here with you." Those words paved a way for the tears and the cries to spill forth, and for the next many minutes, Aggie wept as she rocked Macy back and forth.

"Oh, my baby, why'd you wait so long to call your Aggie? Why'd you wait so long?" she whispered to Macy, stroking her hair. "I coulda come here sooner and saved you from dis. You know Aggie woulda come to help you. And now how'm I gone live without my Macy girl?" She rocked and rocked as she groaned in sorrow.

Aggie was unsure how much time had passed when she began to hear the faint sound of sirens in the distance. Her grief gave way to her protective nature as she became acutely aware of how unpresentable Macy would appear to the medics. Even in death, Aggie felt obliged to preserve the dignity of this beloved girl she had helped raise.

With great care, she released her embrace and slowly straightened Macy's body across the pink carpet. She found a clean pillow on the bed, placed it under her head and began to smooth down her clothes. As Aggie straightened Macy's shirt, she was shocked at how bony she had become; even through the white T-shirt, her ribcage could be seen. She covered her body with a blanket, and dedicated herself to ridding the rank smell of vomit out of Macy's hair.

By now, the approaching sirens were quite loud. Aggie rummaged through a child's dresser to find a hairbrush. Taking it into the bathroom, she wet the brush and massaged a bit of shampoo into its bushy bristles. Macy's hair was thin and straight, so it was easy for Aggie to brush out the knots and gather it to one side of her face. Outside the emergency vehicles announced their arrival to every house along Lions Ave.

"*Bon Dieu,* you'd tink dey'd turn dose sirens down. Dey're gonna wake up da whole neighborhood and make dis whole ting a three-ring circus."

Aggie walked to the front door to meet the medics and police officers. As the ambulance and cop car pulled into the front yard, their rotating lights illuminated the entire block as they reflected off the freshly fallen snow. Alternating colors of blue, white, and red streaked in every direction as the men and women emerged and crunched their way toward the house. As she welcomed the officers, she saw that already, the folks who had been out playing in the snow had stopped what they were doing to watch the activity.

"Tank you so much," Aggie greeted. "Tank you for comin so quickly. She's right in here." Making sure to close the front door from the outside onlookers, she then escorted the team into the room where Macy's body lay.

The next several minutes seemed surreal to Aggie as the paramedics tried their best to revive Macy. She stood just outside the room and watched them work. There were three of them, one woman and two men. The woman was constantly checking Macy's vitals while one of the men injected something into her arm. The second man began to warm up the defibrillator, and even though several attempts were made to shock Macy's heart back to life, all were futile. Eventually, they stated the inevitable, and pronounced her dead on the scene.

A police officer touched Aggie gently on the arm and asked, "Ma'am, I need to ask you some questions, can we sit down in the front room?"

"Yes. Yes, of course," she replied absentmindedly, keeping her gaze fixed on Macy's face. She could hear her mind telling her body to address the officer, to turn around and start walking toward the front room, but her faculties had grown deaf and dumb. Leaning against the doorframe, she lingered until the medics covered Macy's body with a white sheet. It wasn't until her face was fully hidden under the cloth, that Aggie could manage to peel her eyes away.

"Ma'am?" The officer once again addressed her. He had been waiting, politely giving Aggie a bit more time.

"Yes. I'm sorry. Yes," Aggie said in a daze. "Questions. Of course, you have questions. Let's go sit in da front room. Would dat be alright?"

Smiling, the young officer nodded and allowed her to lead him. They both began to take a seat, but no sooner had Aggie sat down than she shot back up. Even in her shocked state, she was a Southern Cajun woman through and through, and this DNA offered her the ability to shift into hostess at any given time, regardless of how dire the circumstances might be.

"I'm sorry, sir, where are my manners?" Aggie said to the policeman as he sank down into the broken-down sofa. "Can I get you and your fellow officers sometin to eat or drink? You must all be freezin, comin out on a night like dis. And Mardi Gras weekend at dat! Would you like sometin hot to warm your belly? It wouldn't take but a minute. I could look in da kitchen..." and then her words trailed off as she remembered her own revulsion upon entering the kitchen earlier. No, to find anything edible in a wreck like that would be impossible.

"No, no, no, no, no," the officer said as he took her arm in his hands and guided her to rest in the chair opposite the sofa. "Please, ma'am. We're just fine, and you don't need to worry about us at all. It's very late, and I can see you've been through a lot. The EMTs will take good care of...well, of the woman in that room, and I just have a few questions I need to ask you. This isn't going to take very long, and then we'll all be done here. OK?"

Aggie could see this man was trying to be as sensitive as he could. He had caring, dark brown eyes and a smooth, round baby-face, the kind of face that stayed exactly the same from birth to adulthood. She sighed deeply and replied, "Yes sir. I want to help in any way I can."

"Wonderful. My name is Officer Mark Landon. Can you give me your full name?"

Aggie: My given name is Agata Prejean, but ever'one calls me Aggie.
Mark: Alright, Miss Aggie, do you live here?
Aggie: Oh no. I live in Lafayette. 311 Bellot Street in North Lafayette.
Mark: Lafayette? How did you get all the way out here tonight?
Aggie: Well, I drove my car, Officer.
Mark: All the way out here in the snow? You're a brave woman. *He opened up an oblong spiral notebook and began to take notes.* OK. Let's start from the beginning. Can you tell me the name of the victim, and how old is she?
Aggie: Her name's Macy DuLonde. Before she married, it was Macy Bacchus. She only 34 years old, still just a chile.
Mark: And what is your relationship to her?
Aggie: I worked for her parents from, O Lawd, let's see, from 1963, I believe it was, until dey both died in 1995. Paul and Jenny Bacchus were dere names. Dem's good folks, da Bacchuses, real good folks.
Mark: How did they die?
Aggie: A horrible car accident. Dey just gone to a birthday party for a friend, and on da way home, dey got in a terrible wreck. Four

people died right dere on da road dat night, and one more a few days later in da hospital. It was just heart-wrenchin. Macy girl was just startin her first year at LSU when all dat happened. She got so broken up, she never did finish school.

Mark: So you worked for the Bacchuses. What did you do?

Aggie: Mais, sir, da only ting a black woman could do back in da 60s. I was da Bacchuses' maid. I tended to da home every day for over 30 years. *Choooh*, I practically raised little Macy myself; she even calls me 'Mama Aggie.' But dey's wonderful folks, the Bacchuses. Dey treated me and Harold like we were part of da family; even had us over for every single holiday. I didn't know just how much Ms. Bacchus loved me til she died, cuz she put it in her will to pay off Harold and my house and my salary for five more years.

Mark: Wow. That was very generous. And who's Harold?

Aggie: Oh. I'm sorry, Harold was my dear husband. He died in '99, God rest his soul. Can't believe it's already been so long since he went to be with le Bon Dieu.

Mark: I'm sorry to hear that, Miss Aggie. He paused for a moment as he jotted down the facts. So, Macy...how long had she been using drugs?

Aggie: (*sighing*) At least six or seven years, maybe ten, maybe even more. She met dat awful Jack less'n a year after her parents died, and from da start, I knew he just wanted her money. But she was so broken, she couldn't see straight, and convinced herself dat he loved her.

Mark: Is she still married?

Aggie: Yes. His full name is Jack DuLonde.

Mark: And they have daughters?

Aggie: Yes sir. Dey have two beautiful girls, Elle is 10 and Skye is just 15.

Mark: What do Jack and Macy do for work?

Aggie: Ha! Nothin'! Dat man just hops from job to job while he leaches off Macy's inheritance. She used to do secretary work til she had da girls, den she stayed home with dem. But for da last few years, I could tell da money had run dry. At da end of da summer, Jack got into sellin horses, but I don't know too much 'bout dat. It did provide da money for Skye's schoolin' though.

Mark: Do you know where Jack and the girls are right now?

Aggie: Dat's just it. I don't know where he is or where Elle is. Last ting Macy said is dat he took her, but I don't know what she meant by dat.

Mark: Wait. I'm getting confused. Which girl did Jack take?

Aggie: Elle, I tink. (*remembering*) Oh, Lawd have mercy! I remember now. I know what Macy was talkin about. Of course. How could I forget? Elle is on her trip to see her sissy.

Mark: Where is her sister?

Aggie: Dis last summer, Jack and Macy both decided to send Skye to an art school in Europe. It was supposed to be a great opportunity, a place where Skye could grow. It was Jack who came up with da idea, and Macy was against it at first, it was too far and too long for Skye to be away from home. But den, all Macy wanted was for her girls to wind up better off dan her, so she finally agreed. She'd do anyting for dose girls. Elle'd been missin her sister so much, Jack and Macy gave her a trip to see Skye for a Christmas present. Dat's where dey is, I'm sure of it. Jack is takin Elle over to visit her big sissy.

Mark: Why didn't Macy go with them?

Aggie: Oh Lawd, no. Macy don't fly. She never could get herself over dat silly fear of flyin. But I told her she should've gone with 'em. I don't trust dat Jack as far as I can throw him.

Mark: Do you have any reason to believe there was foul play that might have lead to her death?

Aggie: (*pausing for a moment to think about this question*) I don't know, Officer. She been gone for a while now.

Mark: Gone? Where has she been?

Aggie: No, I mean, gone in her head. She just not been in full reality. She and Jack were motier foux most of da time, just crazy. I mean, don't get me wrong, Macy is a precious girl, and she did da best she know to do. She takes excellent care of dem girls, but she was just gone. Maybe it was da drugs. Maybe she never got over da death of her folks. I dunno.

Mark was busy writing down as much as he could of what Aggie was saying, when another officer, who had been standing in the room listening, interrupted their conversation.

"Hey, Mark. Check out this picture. What do you make of this?"

"Seriously, Zach? Can you not see I'm working here?" Mark was irritated.

"No, really. You've got to come and look at this picture here on the wall. Did you not notice who these people are?"

Mark went over to look at the photo, and Aggie could see the surprise on his face. She didn't need to get up. She knew this house like the back of her hand, and she knew exactly what was in the frame the men were staring at because she'd hung it there herself. It was a picture of Macy and Jack, shortly before they had been married. The one next to it was one of Macy and the girls, and the one next to that was of Macy and Jack on their honeymoon in Hawaii.

Officer Mark removed the picture from the wall and brought it over to Aggie.

"Miss Aggie, do you know who this man is?"

Aggie's face turned sour. "Yes, I do, and except dat Macy gave birth to two precious girls by dat man, I wish none of us had ever laid our eyes on him. He's a wicked, awful man."

"Miss Aggie," said Mark, sitting back down on the couch. "This man is Richard DuLonde, one of the wealthiest and most influential men in New Orleans. He has a reputation of being one of the most generous philanthropists in Louisiana."

"Ha! Dat is *not* who you tink it is. Dat's Jack, Macy's husband, and I've known him since he finally convinced her to marry him over ten years ago. Dey already been livin together for years and had one daughter together. It took her fallin pregnant with her second baby dat finally made her crazy enough to commit to him. I guess he started out nice enough, but it wasn't long before he so drunk all da time, he never knew which way was up. And he da one who got Macy started on all dose drugs. She never shoulda gone and married dat man."

"But this looks exactly like Richard DuLonde. The same dark hair, the same blue eyes, the same face shape...and they even have the same last name. Don't you find that to be a little odd? Even the slightest bit coincidental?" Mark asked.

Aggie just shook her head and said matter-of-factly, "I'm telling you, dat's Jack."

"All I'm saying is this guy is a dead ringer for the guy," Zach said.

"Miss Aggie," Mark asked, "did Jack ever mention a cousin, a brother, anything?"

"I'm tellin you, dat *peeshwank* Jack could not be related to nobody like you describin. I'm sure of it. He don't have a speck a righteous blood in his body! Dat boy *canaille*," Aggie announced. She was getting riled, which always brought out the Cajun in her. "Dat *capon* so full o' da devil, he'd sell his own children just to save his-self."

Barely had the words escaped her lips that she heard Macy's pleas ringing in her ears. 'Skye's not coming back home from school. Right now, he's selling them,' she had said. 'It's all on his laptop; I found it all out on his laptop.' And then, 'Mama Aggie, please, I'm begging you. You have to get the girls. Please, get the girls.'

A panic gripped Aggie's chest as she tried to make sense of it all. Aggie was having trouble catching her breath, as the room began to spin on an axis, quickly shrinking in on her.

"Miss Aggie! Miss Aggie, are you alright?" Mark's voice sounded a million miles away. "Medic, can you come in here, please?"

Within minutes she awoke, only now she was lying on the sofa, breathing into an oxygen mask, with a cool compress on her face. As soon as her eyes opened, the medic began reassuring her that everything was just fine, she had simply fainted, probably from the trauma of the evening, but suggested Aggie think about resting here a bit before heading out in the snow again.

"Miss Aggie," Mark said quietly as he knelt down next to the sofa. "I've got enough information from you for now. Can you give me your number so I can call you in the next day or so to get anything else I might need?" He handed her a cool bottle of water as he talked to her.

Aggie took a long drink, halfway wishing it was vodka and that she hadn't decided to support Harold in their early years by going sober with him. She recited her phone numbers to Officer Mark, laid her head back, and closed her eyes.

"We'll be here for quite a while, gathering all the evidence we need," whispered Mark. "You just rest a bit here, Miss Aggie, and I'll wake you up once everyone is heading out. I'll even escort you to Lafayette if you need me to."

Sleep enveloped Aggie as she felt Officer Mark covering her with a heavy blanket.

THREE

"HAROLD, I WISH YOU WAS HERE. I know it's been a long time since you've been gone, but I'm still mad as hell at you leavin me here all by myself. Now, you hear dat? You just made me curse...on *le jour de Bon Dieu* at dat. *Choooh*, I'll probably have to spend two more weeks in Purgatory just for cussin on a Sunday. Well, Hal, I'm tellin you right now, I have half a mind to slap yo face once I get up dere, just cause you left me here by myself for so long. I can see it now: I'll walk through dem pearly gates, check in with St. Peter, slap you upside da head, and den have to go right back down to Purgatory. Well, I'm takin you with me. You hear dat? You're gone go right back down dere with me. And dat's just gone be da way it's gone be."

The first hints of daylight were beginning to glow in the east as Aggie drove along I-10 back towards Lafayette. Still quite groggy from the early morning's events, she was very grateful Officer Mark Landon had kept his promise to escort her back to her hometown. His gesture offered her the luxury of mindlessly following behind the lights of his car, with full confidence she would return safely. The roads were still icy and slick, and Aggie was not at her best.

"Well, at least da snow has passed. I got dat to be tankful for. And, looks like it's gone be sunny today. I bet all dis snow'll be melted by mid-afternoon." Aggie sighed, wanting to keep her conversation going, even if it was simply to give a break from thinking about Macy. "I might as well just go to early mass dis morning. No sense tryin to go to bed for a bit and *den* get myself ready for church. When I get home, I'll just cook myself some *couche-couche*, get dressed, and head right back on out. It's not my usual mass, so I'm gone have to get dere early if I'm gone get my pew. Oh Lawd, Aggie's not gone be happy if folks be sittin in my pew. And after da night I just had, I cannot be held responsible for what's gone happen if folks be takin up residence in *my* pew."

She drove in silence for a bit, amusing herself with the scenario of ordering people out of her pew, knowing full well she would never do such a thing. And then, at the first pause in her thoughts, images of Macy began pouring in. Aggie was glad she had her driving to keep her from giving herself fully to the grief.

Losing Macy was so much different from losing her younger sisters, or even her husband. This was her child, maybe not blood-born, but certainly soul-born. And once she and Harold had given up hope of ever having a baby of their own, she allowed her roots of attachment for Macy to burrow into the deepest soil in her heart. Aggie had raised that little girl, changed her diapers, taught her how to go on the potty, kissed her knees when she fell off her bicycle. She was the one who sat with Macy and helped her with her schoolwork. Most days, it was Aggie who picked her up from school or cheerleading practice. Aggie even traveled with the family and helped get Macy settled into her LSU dorm room. All of these memories formed a bittersweet montage in Aggie's mind as she drove into Lafayette, silently weeping.

"Lawd, it's just not right to bury a child," she whispered as a prayer. "Dat's not da natural order a tings. She shoulda laid me to rest; not me doing it for her. Lawd, it's just not right."

Macy's affections for Mama Aggie were wholly reciprocated, especially after the death of her own parents. She deferred to Aggie for everything a daughter would, and often left her girls to stay under Aggie's care for weeks on end, particularly during the summer months or when Macy's drug habit would take a drastic turn for the worst. Aggie was the only grandparent the girls had known, certainly the most stable and trustworthy adult figure, and they all loved her dearly.

As Officer Mark Landon drove into the heart of Lafayette, he pulled over to the side of the road, motioning Aggie to park beside him. Rolling down his window, he asked, "Miss Aggie, do you think you can make it the rest of the way home?"

"Most certainly, Officer Landon," she said. "You've gone far above your call a duty tonight. Tank you for helpin me with ever'thin and for bein so kind. I'm gone be fine da rest of da way."

"Alright, ma'am. If you're sure."

"I'm sure."

"Great, then, I'll be in touch with you in a couple of days. By chance, do you know how long Jack is supposed to be gone?"

"I'm sorry, Officer, I don't know exactly when dey left, or when dey're comin home," Aggie answered. "I do know da trip was gone take a couple weeks, total."

"OK. If you see or hear from Jack, will you call me immediately?" he asked as he started to roll up his window.

"Yes sir, I will." she said, and began to drive away. The memory of Jack's laptop, the one Macy made her put in her car right before she died, leapt in her head. *Bon Dieu, am I committin a crime havin dis ting? Should I turn around and give it to the police?* "No," she answered herself. "Macy specifically told me not to let da police get it. Why would she say dat?"

Her mind began to revolve around her many unanswered questions. With no reasonable answers, she felt a deep pit in her gut, and she promised herself that finding those answers would be the day's priority after she returned from Sunday mass.

IT WAS LATE AFTERNOON THAT SUNDAY EVENING before Aggie woke from her nap. As she opened her eyes, the grogginess gave her a few moments of peace, until the tides of her memory began to come in. The first wave brought in Aggie's precious last minutes with Macy how she felt in her arms as she rocked her and brushed her hair. The second wave washed in the realization of death's finality. Aggie allowed it to come over her, once again springing forth a fresh stream of tears. She rolled to her side and curled up her body, hugging a pillow as she wept for several moments.

A soft rap on her bedroom door brought Aggie out of her grief.

"Auntie?" a voice said gently. It was Leona, her late sister's daughter, who now lived across the street from Aggie. "Auntie, are you alright?" Leona rushed to Aggie's side and threw her arms around her.

Aggie welcomed the embrace, thankful for the opportunity to share the emotional burden with someone she could trust. As she cried and shared the events from the prior night, she felt herself relax into the safety of her niece's presence, and Leona's silence was proof that she truly understood Aggie's pain. More healing than any spoken words is the quiet reverence of a dear friend.

After Aggie's tears finally dried, Leona said, "Auntie, can I make you something to eat?"

"Oh, chile," she answered weakly, "I don't tink I could eat a ting."

"Then at least let me make you some of your favorite coffee." And before Aggie could answer, Leona was making her way to the kitchen. "Just take your time, and I'll be in there waitin for you with a warm cup for your belly."

Aggie relaxed back into her pillow and breathed a prayer of thanks to God for sending Leona over to her house. Aggie loved having her niece living nearby. She was so much like Lou-Lou, Aggie's younger sister, and her frequent visits soothed any pangs Aggie felt from her sister's absence. The whistle of the kettle and the smell of fresh brewed coffee was what Aggie needed to give her impetus to lumber out of bed.

At the sight of her aunt, Leona couldn't hold back any longer. "What time did you get home last night, Aggie? Why didn't you call me so I could've gone with you? Girl, you never should've been drivin by yourself in all that snow! You know Uncle Harold would never've let you do that."

"Well den he shouldn't've died on me. He's no longer da boss a me."

Leona chuckled, "Was he *ever* the boss of you? I don't think so."

Aggie took a long sip of her coffee and enjoyed the sensation of hot swirling liquid as it filled her stomach. She then realized just how famished she actually was.

"Did you say you were gonna make sometin to eat, too?" Aggie said with a smile.

Leona went to work, not even needing to ask Aggie what she wanted. In a matter of moments, she'd have whipped up the best *couche-couche* in Lafayette. As Aggie watched Leona buzz around her kitchen, her mind wandered into anxiety: the fervent pleas from Macy, the girls, the laptop and a panicky feeling of dread.

Almost instantly, Aggie's hunger and fatigue were replaced by a sense of urgency to find out anything she could about whatever Macy was trying to communicate. She jolted out of her seat and began looking through some baskets of papers on a side table. Her new panicked state alarmed Leona.

"What's wrong? What are you looking for?"

"Some letters...emails. Skye's emails. I can't remember what da name was of dat school in London dat she's goin to right now. She's been sendin me emails, and I sometimes print dem off to read 'em. I gotta find dem!"

Aggie was flipping faster and faster through the stack of papers, and when she couldn't find what she was looking for, she darted over to her secretary in the corner of the kitchen. Frantically, she rooted through every cubby, every drawer, and came up with nothing.

"Where are dose letters?!" Aggie was on the brink of hysteria.

"Auntie, please." Leona came over and put her hands on Aggie's shoulders. "Please come sit down and eat your corn meal. I promise I'll help you with whatever it is you're looking for."

"No! I have to find 'em now! I have to get to my baby girls and tell dem about dere mama! It's gone be terrible for dem to hear it from dat Jack! He gone take Elle to see Skye and he gone tell dem dat Macy died. Dey need to know I'm here for 'em...*I gotta find dose letters*!"

"Listen to me, Aggie. You need to sit down and eat something, and get yourself together. It all can wait just a few minutes while you get your mind clear. I'll sit here with you and together we'll figure this thing out. Please."

Aggie knew Leona was right. She nodded and allowed herself to be led to the kitchen table. Leona gave her a few minutes to start eating before she began asking the questions burning in her mind.

"Now tell me again everything Macy said last night."

"She wasn't makin any sense at all. She was a horrible mess when I got dere, Leona; she must've been shootin up for days. Why didn't she call me sooner? But she was so crazed, makin me promise to save da girls from Jack, and she kept sayin sometin about Jack goin to sell sometin. Jack is tryin to sell what? She even said he was 'goin to sell her.'

Sell who? She wasn't makin any sense. And den she made me promise to take Jack's laptop—dat all I needed to know was on dat laptop—-and she made me put it in my car before da police came. I just can't figure any of it out!"

"Okay, okay, Aggie, let's think about this for a minute." Leona was attempting to keep Aggie from getting herself too worked up. "Where are Jack and Elle right now?"

"Don't you remember? Jack and Macy gave Elle dat Christmas present to go visit Skye at her new school."

"And Macy didn't go with them?"

"Lawd, no. You know dat girl never got over dat silly fear o flyin"

"So she let Elle go by herself with Jack?"

"Yeah."

"Out of the country? With Jack?"

The look on Leona's face was almost enough to make Aggie vomit the little bit of food she'd just eaten. Setting down her fork, she took a deep breath, but the pressure in the room was beginning to swirl around her.

"You not sayin anyting," Aggie said. "What are you tinkin'?"

Leona just shook her head. Again, Aggie took a deep breath, somehow knowing a bomb was about to drop.

"Aggie, did you happen to watch the news last night?" And without waiting for a response, Leona went on, "There was a lead story about a woman from New Orleans who was just caught tryin to sell her daughter to a pimp."

Aggie aggressively shoved her plate away from her, and exclaimed, "*Macy would never do such a ting!!*"

"No, no, no! Of course she wouldn't! I'm not sayin that. But Jack? You know that man never paid any attention to those girls except to slap 'em. And Macy used those words, right? She said 'Jack is going to sell her'?"

Aggie nodded and pointed to Jack's laptop that she'd taken the night before, "Yes. She said dat everyting I needed to know was on dat ting right dere."

"Have you fired it up?"

"I tried last night when I got home, but da stupid ting is dead, and I didn't even tink about dat when I was dere. I was too busy tendin to Macy."

Leona picked it up and tried to turn it on. She inspected the port for the cord. "Do you mind if I run over and see if we have a power cord for this?"

Aggie consented, and as Leona rushed out, she was glad to have a few minutes alone to breathe. Her chest felt like she was wearing weights of lead, and every inhale was an effort. Sitting back in her chair, she closed her eyes and prayed, "Lawd, please show me what I'm supposed to do."

As she reached for her coffee, a thought entered her mind to do a bit of research herself before Leona came back. Several years back, Macy had given Aggie a PC and had sat for many hours with Aggie as she taught her how to work it. An amazing world opened to Aggie as she got her DSL connection hooked up and was first introduced to one of her now most favorite friends: Google. Aggie had learned more in these last years than she had in her entire life, combined. At her every whim, her Google friend could deliver to Aggie any information she wanted... and now with her new computer with wi-fi, in just 0.28 seconds.

Receiving that computer had been a day of freedom for this Cajun who only had the opportunity to receive an education until 13 years of age. Then, her father had died, and Aggie's mother was forced to work full time, sometimes even two jobs simultaneously. Aggie would stay home and take care of her youngest sister, Lou-Lou, until Lou-Lou started elementary school. By then Aggie was almost 16, so she got her first job as a maid to ease the financial burden for her mama. It was just after turning 18 that she began the long-term employment as the Bacchuses' maid.

While she never second-guessed her choice to go to work, she did regret her lack of education. Ever since Macy showed Aggie how to work the computer, she rarely missed a day to peek through that window to explore the vast and complex frontier outside her state of Louisiana.

"Let's see what Mr. Google can teach me today," she said as she powered up her desktop computer. "I wish I could remember da name o' dat school Skye's gone to!

"What's gone to happen to dose girls now? Who's gone watch over 'em? I can't let dat *bon rien* Jack care for 'em. He'll just ruin 'em. And what if he don't ever let me see 'em? Well, I don't care. MawMaw Aggie is gone have her place in dem girls' lives, and dat's just gone be da way it's gone be." These thoughts fueled her fire to find out what Macy could've been talking about.

After a moment of thinking what words to Google, the name "Richard DuLonde" popped into her head. "What was all dat talk with dose police about Jack lookin like someone named Richard DuLonde? I wonder if dem officers were onto something?" she said as she Googled his name. Aggie gasped at the pictures of this man that now filled the screen. "*Chooooh!* It's Jack! It looks jus' like him! How dat?!" For minutes, she sat stunned in disbelief at the resemblance. She had to dig deeper to get to the bottom of it. Although there were many profiles listed about Richard DuLonde, she clicked on her other favorite resource, Wikipedia. She knew they would list a birth date, and possibly, a family history.

"Well, look at dat *lagniappe...*" said Aggie. "Ol' Jack has a twin brother."

She continued to read the full Wikipedia profile of the man. It included his success in several businesses, as well as an expansive list of generous contributions to the city of New Orleans since the Katrina disaster in 2005. *How can a person look identical on da outside but be 'xactly da opposite on da inside?* And for the first time since she received Macy's late night phone call, Aggie began to feel the slightest glimmer of hope.

FOUR

ELLE COULDN'T HAVE BEEN HAPPIER. In all of her ten years, she could not remember being able to spend this much time with her daddy. Even when he was at home for longer than a few minutes, he was normally much too busy to pay attention to her, let alone play with her. He had work to do on his computer, or he had something important to watch on TV, or he had business to take care of on his cell phone. Many times, Elle would try to sit next to him as he talked and texted away. Being in the same room with him was better than nothing at all. And if she stayed perfectly still, he usually wouldn't yell at her or push her away.

But it had already been three days, and she had been with him almost nonstop. They had flown on the airplane together, walked side by side all throughout the streets of a Greek city that had a name Elle still couldn't pronounce, eaten some delicious new foods together, and met a lot of new people. They hadn't gone to see Skye yet, but her daddy said they'd go to play with her in a few days. Elle didn't care. Even as much as she missed her big sister, she knew they'd visit her soon, as it was the whole purpose of their trip. Right now, she was content to revel in the attention from her father, daring to believe that maybe he loved her at last.

And today was even more special, because he was taking her to buy a very special dress. He had told Elle that since the day they arrived in Greece, almost every person they'd met made a point to mention how beautiful Elle was. It was true that she noticed whenever her daddy introduced her to new people, they always seemed to pay special attention to her, looking her up and down, and talking favorably about her. While she couldn't understand their language, she definitely knew the conversation was primarily about her. Feeling embarrassed by such consideration, Elle wished she knew how to speak Greek, or at least that her father wouldn't speak so softly in the ear of his interpreter. She wanted to know what exactly was being said.

Her daddy told her these Greeks had strongly suggested Elle enter a beauty pageant for young girls that just so happened to be starting in a few days. All she had to do was walk up and down a fashion runway, smiling and wearing a beautiful dress, and she might possibly win all sorts of money and fun prizes. He seemed very eager for her to enter the contest. At first, Elle was hesitant; she'd never done anything like this before, and she'd always felt awkward about her appearance. While she knew she was pretty, as folks always commented on her curly red hair and the single deep-set dimple on her cheek, she was also very petite for her age. All the other boys and girls in her 4th grade class were easily two or three inches taller than she was. They sometimes would tease her about being the "baby of the class."

On the other hand, her daddy had never treated her like this before, so attentive and loving. She certainly didn't want to do anything that might stop how he had been acting toward her. Not wanting to disappoint him, Elle agreed to enter the pageant. And if truth be told, Elle would've probably consented to do almost anything her daddy asked of her.

So today, Elle's dad was taking her on their very first shopping spree together. One of the locals had told him about a special boutique that carried beautiful dresses and matching shoes for young girls. But first, he had told her they needed to make a stop at the doctor's office. It was early morning when Jack and Elle began walking the streets of Thessaloniki, Jack leading the way as he followed some directions he had scribbled on a small piece of paper.

Elle: Daddy, why do we have to go see a doctor? I'm not sick or anything.

Jack: You need to have papers from a doctor to be in the pageant.
Elle: Why?
Jack: That's just how they do things here. The doctor will give us papers that will verify that everything's intact.
Elle: What do you mean, 'intact'?
Jack: Uhh, that everything is in the right place and as it should be. The better report we get from the doc, the higher the—well, the bigger the prize you'll get when you win.
Elle: That's funny; they have different categories for how healthy you are? That's so weird.
Jack: Well, we're in a different country. Who knows why they do what they do here?
Elle: Do you really think I'm going to win?
Jack: (*chuckling*) You just stand there with a big smile, and for sure you are gonna get a big prize.
Elle: But are you sure the other girls won't be older and prettier? I'm only ten, and everyone back at home still teases me that I look like I'm just a kid.
Jack: Don't worry about it. I know what I'm doing. Trust me, this is a kind of contest where the younger you look, the better the chance you'll bring in the highest score.

Elle smiled broadly at his words. Never before had he expressed such confidence in her ability to do anything well. She looked up at her daddy, but his face was focused forward. Jack seemed to be in a hurry, and Elle had to almost run to keep up.

Elle: How come we haven't met any other kids yet? I haven't even seen any girls my age around here.
Jack: Well, there'll be plenty of girls to meet in the beauty pageant. I'm sure you'll find one of them to be friends with.
Elle: And then, as soon as the contest is over, we'll go and see Skye?
Jack: As soon as the contest is over.
Elle: I can't wait to see Skye! If I win prizes I can bring some for her, too. She'll be so excited to see us.

After walking through the narrow streets for nearly an hour, they came to an archway in the middle of an alley. Elle thought it looked more like an entrance to a cave than a doctor's office, but her dad turned into the opening and waved Elle to follow after him. They walked down a set of musty-smelling stone stairs, stopping at the dark bottom. There was a sole wooden door at the dead end, and by the light of a solitary light bulb, Elle could see there was some lettering in Greek painted on the door. Her father checked the paper he was holding to confirm they had arrived at the correct address.

"This is it," announced Jack.

"Really?" asked Elle as she listened to her voice echo up and down the stairs. "Are you sure, Daddy? It looks kind of old and dirty."

"This is the right place." Jack looked down at his daughter sternly. "Now I want you to listen to me. Whatever the doctor asks you to do, you do."

"What do you mean? What is he going to ask me to do? I'm not going to have to get a shot or anything, am I?"

"I don't know, but whatever he asks, I want you to do it. No whinin' or complainin'. Just do what he says. Don't worry, I won't leave you alone with him, because I need to make sure he doesn't try anything fishy, but even if he needs to give you a shot, I want you to just do it, O.K?"

Elle was beginning to feel uneasy. What did he mean by 'fishy'? She nodded in agreement.

"That's a good girl," said her father, patting her head.

The door creaked open into what looked like a very old basement clinic, and Elle wondered how many people had come here to meet with a doctor. And if they were kids, did they feel as scared as she did? This room was nothing like the bright, sterile clinics her mom or MawMaw Aggie had taken her to back in Louisiana. There was no friendly lady behind a desk to greet people, no place to sign in, and the six or seven chairs scattered about the waiting area were all dusty and mismatched. There was absolutely nothing hanging on the walls, not even a magazine rack. Elle wondered when the last time those smooth cement walls had been painted. And it was also very quiet; the only sound was a very muffled drone of a radio or television spilling in from some unseen back room.

A short, barrel-chested old man entered the room and looked from Jack to Elle, then back to Jack again. Using the same paper with the address written on it, Jack read off a request in Greek. He stumbled over the language and must have pronounced something incorrectly because the doctor let out a gruff, condescending laugh. But he nodded his head and held out his hand for payment. Jack shuffled through his wallet and counted out the proper amount into the old man's small, fat hand.

After stuffing the bills into his front trouser pocket, he motioned Jack and Elle to follow him into a back room, which was even less fancy than the waiting room. It held one oblong wooden table, one wooden chair, and a small chest of drawers. The doctor pulled open the top drawer and picked out something that resembled a hospital gown. He tossed the thin robe to Jack and motioned for Elle to take off her clothes and put it on.

Jack handed it to Elle. "I think you understood what the doc said."

"Umm...Dad, isn't he going to leave so I can undress?"

"Elle, he's a doctor. He knows what you look like."

Elle's cheeks flushed bright red, both from embarrassment and from her father's sudden harsh tone, and she felt as if she could throw up. At this, the doctor exploded with another demeaning laugh and motioned for her to get on with it. She turned her back and did her best to remove her shirt and jeans and cover herself with the robe as discretely and quickly as possible.

She obviously wasn't moving fast enough because the doctor briskly crossed the room, picked her up under her armpits and plopped her down on the table. She could smell a stale, sour smell of tobacco on his breath as he bent over to pull a small light out of his pocket. He shined it into her eyes, her ears and her mouth. He seemed to linger as he peered down her throat, and Elle thought it seemed as if he was counting her teeth. His fingers felt all along her neck, and then he motioned for her to lie down. The table was too short for her entire body, only long enough for the span from her head to her knees. When she lay back, her shins and feet dangled toward the floor.

The doctor pulled open her robe and with rough massages, he examined her adolescent breasts. Elle let out gasp as she felt this foreign man touching her with such inconsideration for her modesty. Her eyes filled with tears as he continued downward with his ugly hands poking and prodding into her lower abdomen, looking at things he had no business looking at. Through a haze of tears, she saw the doctor nod his head toward her father as if to approve something. He motioned for Jack to follow him out.

"You can get dressed now," Jack said to Elle, as he left the room.

Alone with her mortification, Elle cried as she tried to understand why they had really come here to this dirty office, and why her dad just sat there and allowed that yucky man to touch her in such a violating way. In her disillusionment, Elle began to wish they'd never come to Greece.

FIVE

JACK AND ELLE WALKED IN SILENCE from the cellar-like doctor's office. By now the young girl's embarrassment had morphed into anger towards her father, and this fueled her steps to the point she had no problem at all keeping up with his brisk pace. Her mind was rehearsing the many words she wished she had the courage to say to him. How she didn't want to be in this stupid beauty contest, how she wanted to see her sister right now, and how she hated the way he didn't even care for her enough to protect her from that fat, disgusting doctor.

And as long as we're being for real, Elle vented, *how come you've never cared about me before now? You've never so much as stepped foot in my school when I was in a play or something. And why don't you ever spend time with us? Or even remember our birthdays? And what about the time I saw you hit Mama? Yeah, you didn't know I saw that, did you? Well, I did. I saw it, and I cried all night in my bed, and you never even noticed. I hate you for that.*

At the notion of her mom, Elle almost burst into tears. She had never been this far away from Macy before, and she missed her desperately now. Even during the summer months, when she and Skye would go stay with MawMaw Aggie, her mom was still just a phone call away. Every few days, MawMaw would let them call home so they could connect with their mother.

Elle's homesickness grew all the more at the thought of Aggie. Elle wished her MawMaw had come on this trip with them; she wasn't afraid to fly on an airplane and Skye would've given anything to see her. Plus, there was almost nothing bad in the world that MawMaw Aggie couldn't hug away. Whenever Elle was upset, all MawMaw had to do was open up her big arms and Elle would come running. She'd sink into the softness of Aggie's bosom, as she listened to her grandma whisper wonderful things in her ear. "*Mon Sha*," MawMaw would say. "Why you sad? What you got to be so long in da mouth 'bout? You blessed, *Sha*. You beautiful, you funny, you gots da brightest red hair, and you da smartest girl I know. And on top o' dat, Aggie love you more'n life itself." And then she'd kiss Elle's neck until it tickled so much she giggled.

Elle thought she'd give anything for a hug from MawMaw Aggie right now. *MawMaw would never have let that doctor even get close enough to touch me. She'd've whipped the snot out of him!*

"Why're you lookin' at me like that?" Jack's annoyed voice brought Elle back to the streets of Greece. It wasn't until he said something that she realized she had been scowling at him.

Elle didn't answer; she only looked ahead and kept walking. Now, her anger swelled against herself for her inability to speak her thoughts, to stand up for herself.

"Look," said Jack. "If you're gonna give me an attitude, then I can slap your ass right back on a plane to Louisiana and you won't be spending any time with your sister. Is that what you want? Here I am, trying to make a great time for you, and what thanks do I get for it? Do you have any idea how much money all this is costing me?"

His words were like a smack in the face, and Elle could feel the guilt rush in as she began to think her daddy was fully justified to say what he did. After all, he had gone completely out of his way to take her to Greece just so she could spend time with her sister. He was giving up at least two weeks of work, and Elle knew very well how important work was to him. Plus, this was by far the most extravagant gift her parents had ever given her. Usually birthdays, and even Christmases, would come and go and the only thing she or Skye would receive was an apology from Macy for the lack of money. Elle could not begin to imagine how much this trip was costing her parents; at the very least, she should be grateful.

"Oh, Daddy, I'm so sorry," she said, her eyes filling with tears. "You're so right! And I am very grateful. This is the best present you and Mama have ever given me, and I'm loving every minute of it...I just didn't like that doctor, is all."

"Well, how in the hell was I supposed to know what he needed to do for us to get your papers? It's not like I'm a psychic or anything."

"I know, Daddy. I'm so sorry, and I promise I'll be good from now on. Please don't be mad at me. I won't complain about a *thing*, and I'll do my very best to come in first place in the beauty pageant. I'll do whatever it takes to win those prizes for you. Please don't be mad, OK?"

"Now, that's my girl," Jack said, smiling. "That's exactly what Daddy likes to hear. And just in time, too, because we're here."

"Where?"

"This is the store where we're going to buy your dress for the contest." And with that, he walked into the small boutique.

Elle had been so consumed with her own thoughts, she hadn't noticed that all their walking had taken them to a street containing several shops, lined in a row. In fact, she had almost forgotten about the big shopping spree her dad had promised her early that morning. Her childlike joy was restored as she followed in behind him and gazed around at all the beautiful dresses hanging throughout the store.

Elle wondered why everything in Greece seemed so small. The restaurants were small, the streets and cars were small, and this shop was so tiny it could've fit inside Elle's living room. And instead of the racks offering several different sizes of the same dress, like the stores back at home, these only held one dress of each kind, in whatever size that happened to be.

No one was in the shop, so Jack opened and closed the door again so the dangling bell on the doorknob would sound again. A young woman came out of a back room and kindly said something in Greek to Jack. Elle wasn't sure why, but her Dad seemed surprised to see the lady. He quickly looked around the entire shop, and even craned his neck to try and get a glance into the back room, its door now standing ajar. Jack was looking for someone else to wait on them.

The woman spoke again to him, this time slower and more deliberate. Jack took out the paper he had used to communicate at the doctor's office and read off the one sentence written on it. Unlike the doctor who had laughed at his broken Greek, this woman did not find his words the least bit amusing. Her welcoming smile dissolved into a frown as she crossed her arms and glared at Jack.

A silent moment passed between the two adults, and Elle wondered what was happening. *Why did the woman all of a sudden have such a mean look on her face? Didn't she know we were here to buy a dress from her?*

But Jack didn't seem to care; he simply repeated his sentence.

Finally, the lady spoke back to him, again in Greek, and from her gestures Elle could tell she was asking him where something or somebody was. To answer her, Jack motioned to Elle.

The woman's expression went from disapproval to shock as she looked down at the young girl. Elle thought she'd try to win her approval by giving her an eager smile. The saleswoman's attention returned to Jack. With one eyebrow arched, she locked eyes with him and took a few steps toward him. She leaned nearer in until her face was only a few inches away from Jack's, and then she spit.

Elle gasped and even Jack seemed caught off guard. The woman sprang back, and began yelling loudly, mostly in Greek. But Elle could also hear her attempting to say a few words in English. Her arms were flailing as punctuation marks to her message as she pushed by them so she could fling open her front door. She motioned violently for them to leave, shouting accusations at Jack the entire time.

As he paused for a moment to wipe off his cheek, Elle noticed a very familiar expression on his face. He was going to hit this woman, Elle was sure of it. That's the same look he had on his face that night she saw him beating her mom. Elle tried to ask her dad if they could just leave, but she couldn't make the words come out of her mouth. She felt a pit in her stomach and she squeezed her eyes shut, much too afraid to watch him lash out at this young woman.

It seemed like an eternity as Elle listened for Jack's fist to make contact, but the lady started yelling "Police! Police!" and then something else in Greek, which Elle assumed was the equivalent to "police". Before Elle knew what was happening, her dad yanked her by the arm out of the dress shop, hoisted her up over his shoulder, and as fast as he could, sped down several streets. He kept looking back to see if anyone was coming after them, and only when he was certain they were not being followed did he set her back down on the narrow street.

Jack flipped open his cell phone and made a call. The person must have picked up almost instantly because Jack began yelling, "What in the hell are you tryin to pull? Are you tryin to screw me over? Because if you are, I'll kick the life out of you, and I won't even think twice about it.....(*Elle could hear the muffled sound of someone on the other end.*) I did! I went to the dress shop you told me to go to, I said the sentence you gave me, and the bitch in there spit at me! (*Elle heard laughter from phone*) Are you playin me? Is this some kinda joke?! Cause I will mess you up!"

Jack began pacing back and forth wildly as he listened to the person on the other end of the call. He continued his rant:

"I'm telling you, that's exactly what I did. I went into the store, this little bitch came out, and she—(*the person on the other end interrupted him*).....I don't know, she was probably about 25 or 26......What?! Well, how the hell was I supposed to know she wasn't the right person?....Son of a bitch! I had a feeling she wasn't the right one, but I looked around, and there was nobody else in there. What am I gonna do now? She's already seen me and the girl; it's not like I can just go back in there. She was yelling for the police!.....Is there anyplace else I can go? I still have a few days til the deal......OK, I'll call you later." Jack sat down on the ground to catch his breath.

Elle was thoroughly confused at all that had just taken place. Actually, nothing that had happened this day made any sense to her 10-year-old mind, and she didn't know what to do other than sit down next to her father. She could tell he was extremely upset, far too angry for her to dare ask any questions. She decided her safest bet was to quietly wait for him to cool down, and then surely he would explain everything to her.

SIX

WIL WAITED IN HIS CAR FOR A MOMENT contemplating whether he should tell them today. With his departure date only a few weeks away, his opportunities to break the news to his parents were slipping away. Today might be a hard enough day for them, and the last thing they'd want to hear is that he was going back in the special forces. Besides, tomorrow night was a very special event for his mom and dad, and Wil wanted to do whatever was needed to make it all they wanted it to be. It was the least he could do for his father, who completely paused his entire life to walk with him through these past six months of recovery and rehabilitation.

As soon as Mardi Gras is over, and we've all settled down, I've got to talk to them about what I'm going to do next, thought Wil. *I love my dad, but I can't let his fear of me getting hurt again stop me from what I know in my heart I'm supposed to be doing.*

Having made this decision, however, did not make the sick feeling in his gut go away. His mom would cry, his dad would worry, and this tore him up inside. In addition, what if his dad saw this choice as a rejection to his offer of a business partnership? If only Madison was still here. Everything would be easier if she was still alive. Just the thought of her made Wil's breath catch in his chest. He needed to get out of his car.

Grabbing the large bouquet of purple Tiger Lilies, Wil jetted out of his Range Rover and welcomed the brisk cold air that hit his face. It felt good to fill his lungs with the icy air. He bounded up the steps to his parents' late-19th century mansion in the famous Garden District and walked inside the entryway.

A smell of lingering smoke hit Wil's nose and he chuckled, knowing exactly what went down this morning. Because of the unusually cold temperatures, his mom would've pressed his dad to build a wood fire in the fire place. Dad would've countered with the idea of simply using the gas fireplaces throughout the house. Wasn't that why he paid so much money to get them installed anyway? But Mom was not so easily won, especially when it comes to a wood-burning fire, so she would've filled the firebox with the proper kindling and wood, maybe even threatened to light it herself. Dad would've stepped in, complaining that she was going to burn the house down, even though he knew only a little bit more than she did when it came to building a fire. Inevitably, he would've lit the wood, but forgotten the timing on when to open and close the flue. The entire drawing room would've flooded with smoke, causing Dad to cuss and Mom to giggle at his cussing, which would only make him cuss more.

Wil's dad's footsteps sounded on the hardwood floors, going towards the kitchen. Wil met him there.

"Why didn't you wait until I got here?" Wil teased.

Richard smiled. "Don't even start in on me. You know your mom. She had to have the fire."

"I can't blame her; it's hard to believe how cold it is today! Did you hear it snowed a few inches in Lafayette, and even in Baton Rouge?" Wil set the flowers on the counter next to a family picture. "Maybe these will help with the smell in here."

Wil picked up the framed picture to gaze at his sister. His heart burned at the sight of Madison's smiling face. If only his pain could will her back to life. It was the last photo taken of the entire family, right before Wil was set to leave on a mission to the Middle East, and right before Madison's cancer came back with a vengeance.

Wil had seen many atrocities at his young age and had faced situations that he probably would never speak out loud about, but nothing could come close to the sheer torture of being away from his family while Madison's teenage body was ravaged by cancer. This young man who had given his life to save and protect others could do nothing to rescue the people whom he cherished the most. The best he was able to manage was a short leave to make it home right before she passed, and he could never forgive himself for his failure of Madison dying on his watch. In his mind, Wil knew there was nothing he could do, but this knowledge was not in a language his heart could understand. And he carried that guilt with him as a talisman.

Today was the three year anniversary of Madison's death, and in honor of her, Richard and Lottie threw an annual Mardi Gras ball to raise money for her foundation.

Rich: It's hard to believe it's already been three years.

Wil: I know. It seems just like yesterday. How's Mom doing today?

Rich: Actually, she's doing really good. You know she's the epitome of the steel magnolia. *Richard takes the picture and gazes at his daughter*. I imagine today will always be a hard day, but I tell ya, throwing this benefit every year to fill Madison's fund definitely keeps her mind busy.

Wil: Mine, too. So is everybody ready for it?

Rich: Are you kidding me? Your mom has made it her full-time job to make sure I'm ready.

Wil: I bet she has! So what's your costume? You guys always do it right.

Rich: Wait. Your mom hasn't told you the theme yet?

Wil: Dad, you know I don't care about any of that. I'm there to get a job done.

Rich: (*smiling*) I'll let her tell you...and don't ask how I got talked into this one.

Wil: Ha! Now you got me curious!

Rich: Is your team ready?

Wil: Completely.

Rich: I really appreciate this, Wil.

Wil: Dad, it's the least that I could do. And hey, all my training's gotta count for something, right? Have your guys been able to track the source of the emails?

Rich: Not really. They are from a fake account built at a public library here in New Orleans, so they could be from anyone. And I haven't told your mother about them, so don't mention it to her, OK?

Wil: Got it. Are you sure you want to have Mom host this thing with you tomorrow night?

Lottie bursts into the kitchen in a Scarlett O'Hara dress.

Lottie: (*in her best Scarlett voice*) Fiddle-dee-dee! Why on earth would anyone not want to host a ball? *She notices the flowers.* Oh, is that beautiful bouquet for little ol' me? *She swoops around to grab the Tiger Lilies, and gives Wil a warm hug. Wil kisses her on the top of her head.*

Wil: I love you, Mom.

Lottie: Aww. Madison's favorite. She would've loved these. Thank you so much, honey.

Wil: (*looking at her costume*) So what the heck is this?

Lottie: Why the surprise? Hasn't your father told you about our costumes?

Rich: I thought I'd give you the honors.

Lottie: Have you at least told Wil what he and his team will be wearing?

Wil: What?! Are you crazy? What's she talking about, Dad?

Lottie: Since we're all going to be at a civil war era mansion, what better costumes are there than *Gone With the Wind*?

Wil: Alright...but what does that have to do with me?

Lottie: I'll be right back, sugar, with your costume.

Wil: Dad. I did not sign up for this.

Rich: If I have to go as Rhett Butler, the least you can do is be my wingman.

Lottie pranced back into the kitchen and bestowed a garment bag from a Chicago costume rental company. Wil lost his words as she unzipped the bag, giggling all the way. She pulled out a Civil War Confederate costume, complete with hat, shoes, and medals of honor. Richard laughed at Wil's stunned face and walked over and gave him a big bear hug. "It's just once a year, son. Let's rally together for Lottie DuLonde."

Wil took the costume and said, "Only for you, Mom. Only for

you." And the beaming look on his mother's face made it worth how uncomfortable this costume would be.

"Don't worry, baby, you won't be alone," she said. "I got costumes for all your security guys, too."

And before Wil could protest, his dad said, "Come on, let's go into my office and go over the plan for tomorrow night."

SEVEN

"*MAIS, OUI.* I GOT DIS ONE CHANCE to get in da place tonight, and by God, I'm gone get in. Dis outfit is my ticket, and dat's just gone be da way it's gone be."

Aggie took a last look at herself in the mirror. She hadn't worn her old maid uniform since the Bacchuses had died. For sentimental reasons, even if only to one day show her old work clothes to Skye and Elle, she had stored the uniform in her closet all these years.

Her reflection spun Aggie's memory back in time. The crisp, white uniform, a one-piece dress. The thick, dark-beige stockings. Her hair smoothed back to the nape of her neck. Every workday, Monday through Friday, this had been Aggie's normal wear. She laughed at the sight of herself.

"*Choooh!* Too bad my face don't look as young as da last time I wore dis. Hal, you remember dis? You were still here da last time I had dis on. And look here at all dis extra fabric. I didn't know I was dat much bigger back den. Looks like ol' Aggie needs to be eatin more pork boudin to fatten her up! Hal, how many toilets you tink I scrubbed in dis? How many pots o' gumbo you tink I cooked?"

"Way too many, Auntie Aggie."

Aggie screamed and jumped from surprise at the sound of Leona's indignant voice. Her heart was beating so fast, she had to sit down on her bed.

"Chile, you tryin to send me heaven?"

"All I'm sayin is you scrubbed way too many toilets and floors in your time. Those Bacchuses should've hired help for you to clean that big house, at least paid you more, and not taken advantage of you."

"You hush, girl!" Aggie replied sharply, "I will not allow any words of disrespect to be spoken about dat family, at least while I'm alive! Dey gave me an opportunity when nobody else did. Dey treated me and Hal like family."

"Hmm. Family don't get paid to scrub toilets."

"Dat's right!" Aggie pointed her finger at Leona and laughed, "Family do it for free. I got paid, and was happy to serve 'em. I bet you didn't know dat after dey died, dey put it in dere will to not only give me five full years of my salary, but also dey paid off dis house. Completely! I never had to work another day in my life."

Leona saw she was proven wrong, but she was not willing to fully relent. "You got lucky. There are thousands of other black women around you today who don't have the same story."

Aggie softened. "Chile, it was a different time then. You're right, but I didn't have da options you have today, and I'm tankful da good Lawd blessed me with dat family. Sure, I wish life would've been different then, just as I wish we'd be farther along today. But wishin can't change da past, so let's keep our eyes forward to progress." Anxious to change the subject, she added, "Did you bring da shoes?"

"Yes, I brought the shoes." Leona handed over a pair of white nurse shoes.

"Dis gone make da look complete!" Aggie said as she began to lace the shoes on her feet.

The night before, Aggie and Leona had stayed up past midnight researching Richard and Lottie DuLonde. Without a means to power up Jack's computer, it was their only lead. After reading of his generosity to an array of charities over the last ten years, Aggie thought this man might help her find out what Jack was up to, if somehow she could just get a moment with him to plead her cause. But Leona was quick to point out that a man of his social status would not be the easiest for an old, black, Cajun retired maid to approach. Perhaps if she persisted enough, she would be able to manage an appointment with a secretary or someone who could help her reach Richard.

But it was already Sunday evening, and Macy had been so urgent. Aggie couldn't risk taking the time to go that route. So Aggie redirected her energies toward Lottie DuLonde, thinking maybe she'd be easier than Richard to make contact with. Her full name was Charlotte DuLonde, maiden name, Grande. She was the great-granddaughter of Charles Grande, founder of Grande Energy, and had lived her entire life attending Louisiana's most elite schools and social clubs. The DuLondes only had one son, now an adult, and Lottie spent much of her time working with local charities. In fact, in 2009, Charlotte DuLonde was named "Woman of the Year" by a prominent New Orleans organization.

Wanting to know more about this woman, Aggie had clicked on the link to the article about Lottie receiving that award. As she had read the interview with Lottie, Aggie's confidence grew in this woman. She would most definitely be willing to help her. In the article, Lottie shared how she'd grown up knowing such prosperity, she never considered the fact that other people were not also enjoying as blessed a life as hers. She had always taken her wealth, and all the privileges and ease that came with it, for granted. She commented she was ashamed to admit it, but not until Hurricane Katrina hit New Orleans in 2005 did her eyes become open to the people living every day in lack and need, people who were right under her nose.

Lottie told the story about how an experience during the aftermath of Katrina had altered her life forever. Her gardener, an employee of the DuLonde family for over two decades, had become her close friend. This gardener, her grown daughter, and her twin grandchildren lived in the 9th Ward and relied completely on public transportation. Consequently, when the hurricane evacuation orders went forth, this family had no way to properly vacate their house before the storm hit. When the levees broke and the flooding violently coursed through their neighborhood, all four of them were trapped in their home. The waters swiftly rampaged through their house and rose to the ceilings. For five days in the unbearable Louisiana summer heat, this family was stranded in their attic, without food or clean water, as they waited for someone to rescue them.

By the time help finally arrived, all four of them were severely dehydrated, especially the 3 year-old twins. They were taken to a makeshift hospital shelter, where Lottie's gardener was then able to contact her. Lottie drove to the triage, and ended up staying for the next several days, 24/7, offering her help in any way she could. Lottie shared how heart-wrenching it was to see so many families who, because they had no means to leave New Orleans, had been caught in the wake of the disaster. In the end, both of her gardener's precious grandchildren had died.

Lottie told the interviewer that as she and Richard stood through the double funeral for those two children, who just a few weeks prior had spent the day at the DuLonde's, running around the house and swimming in their pool, they realized how selfishly they'd been living their lives. Up until this point, they'd never really considered how people outside their social sphere managed their lives; they'd simply been focused on building their own dreams and fortunes.

"Not that there is anything wrong with cultivating wealth," Lottie was quick to point out. "It's just that until this point, Richard and I hadn't learned the true purpose for wealth; which we now believe is to help people. We promised each other we'd never become so short-sighted again. Obviously, we can't help everybody, but we can help the ones who, for whatever reason, cross our paths." Then the article went on to give a very impressive list of Lottie's contributions, not only of money but also of hours upon hours of community service to many local organizations designed to equip and empower children and young women.

And then Leona had hit the goldmine. She found an online newspaper article reporting about an elegant Mardi Gras Ball hosted by the DuLondes. The event was to be held at the Nottoway Estate, and the guest list included 100 of the most up-and-coming business owners of Southern Louisiana.

"That's it!" Aggie had announced. "I'm gone go to dat ball and find a way to talk to dem. I know once dey hear my story, dey will help me." And no amount of protesting from Leona would convince her otherwise. So it was no shock that this morning, Leona arrived all guns a' blazin'.

"Listen, you don't have to do this," Leona said. "I don't think you should be doin this. You're gonna get yourself arrested, and then what good would that have done for Elle?"

"I'm gone do dis, and dat's just gone be da way it's gone be."

"But what if—"

"Chile, I ain't got time for what ifs. I made a promise to Macy, and dis da fastest way to keep dat promise. Tink about it, Leona, what are da chances dey'd be throwin a costume ball less dan two days after Macy... (*she couldn't bring herself to say the words*). And dat Richard is Jack's twin brother?! What kinda coincidence is dat? Well, I don't believe it is. It's *mon Bon Dieu* makin a way for his favorite Cajun to save her girl, dat's what it is."

"Do you think you're gonna just walk in to that party and nobody's gonna notice you don't belong there?"

"I called up dat Nottoway Mansion and pretended that I was special staff for dis event. Da woman told me she'd been gettin all kinds of calls from da extra people who'd been hired just for dis one night. So I'm just gone pretend I'm one of dose folks."

"Alright," Leona persisted, "Let's suppose all that works out. You're gonna be workin...do you think you're gonna be able to just walk up to either Richard or Lottie DuLonde and talk to them? And then what? What're you even going to say?!"

"Da Lawd's gonna go before me, and open up da way. And den He's gonna fill my mouth with da right words."

"What if they don't help you? What if they have you arrested?"

Aggie smiled. "Den you gone come bail me out and we'll tink of what to do next."

Leona knew she'd been beaten and smiled back at her courageous auntie. "You crazy."

"I'm not da least bit crazy...I'm Cajun."

At this, they both burst into laughter.

"Now help me get my coat on so I can get on da road. It's gone take me a couple hours to get to dat Nottoway."

Leona led her into her coat and walked with her to her car. "You sure you don't want me to go with you?"

"*Choooh!* Dat would be way too suspicious. No, I can do dis."

"Then you've got to promise me to keep me updated through text?"

"You got Auntie Aggie's word on it."

Aggie gave her a hug and loaded herself and Jack's laptop into the car. As she drove away, she noticed Leona standing near the road, watching until her car was out of sight.

As Aggie drove along I-10, she chuckled at the absurdity she found herself in. “I wonder who’ll all be in dat place tonight? What you tink, Hal? Dere’s gone be more money represented in dat room tonight den either of us have ever imagined. *Chooooh*! How dis ol’ Cajun girl gone act around folks like dat?” Then she giggled. “I’ll just have to remember what you always used to say: ‘Ain’t no matter how much a person makes, dey still sit down to use da toilet.’ Dat’s what I’ll tink about if I start gettin nervous.”

At least at this point, Aggie was not nervous at all; she felt happy about how smoothly everything had worked out thus far. But she was also aware that the first part, getting ready for the evening, was the easy part. The rest of her plan, once she arrived at the Nottoway Plantation, was much sketchier. While she played out in her mind the many different ways by which she would catch the ear of either Richard or Charlotte DuLonde, she really had no idea what she was about to walk into. Aggie had been to Mardi Gras events before, but she had never experienced a high society event of this caliber.

In addition, she’d never worked a job besides her time as the Bacchuses’ maid; she didn’t know the first thing about how to make herself an effective—and anonymous—part of a systemized staff. She wondered if she would be able to blend in with the rest of the workers. But there was one thing Aggie knew she had going for her; she was a hard-working Cajun woman, very resourceful and scrappy. She knew the odds for success were against her, but she didn’t care. If anything, her underdog status only served to fuel her determination. Come hell or high water, she was going to make her case known to the DuLonde family.

EIGHT

AGGIE PULLED INTO THE ENTRANCE of the Nottoway Plantation off LA 1 South, along with three other cars. Aggie's relief that she was arriving with other staff was squelched as she realized every car was being stopped at the gate. There was a small white building with a side window, much like any check-in point at an upscale country club, and the person inside was talking to each driver, making them show identification before allowing them to enter. Aggie began to panic.

"Hal! Do you see dis, Hal? Dis a *mal pris*! What'm I gonna say if dey ask me questions? You know I'm not any good at lyin. I'm gone get myself caught before I even get in!"

Aggie tried to regain her composure, as she inched her way up in line. She thought of Macy, of the girls, and knew she could not afford to lose her confidence, at least for their sakes. She took a deep breath, and pulled forward to the man in the window. As she put down her window, she smiled her sweetest Southern smile. She spoke very slowly, as she attempted her best Louisiana non-Cajun dialect.

Aggie: Good Afternoon, sir.
Man: Good Afternoon, ma'am. You on staff tonight?
Aggie: Yes, sir. I'm part of da staff for da DuLonde Mardi Gras Ball. I was told to arrive by three o'clock.
Man: Yes, ma'am, can I've your name please?

Aggie: Why, sure. It's Agata Prejean. Do you need identification?
Man: Yes, ma'am.

Aggie handed the man her driver's license. She pretended to be calm, looking forward as if this was an every day procedure for her. He paged through the many pages on his clipboard, and then paged through them again. Knowing her name was not going to be listed, she tried to distract him.

Aggie: Can you please tell me where to park my car? Of course, as staff, I want to make sure the guests have the best parking. I'm assuming we won't be parking in our usual spot?
Man: (*not seeming to have heard her*) Miss Agata, your name is not on da list for da staff. And I was given very strict orders not to let anyone in here tonight dat was not on dis list. I don't mean to *faire la misere*—excuse me—I mean, I don't mean to cause trouble for you, but-
Aggie: *Dit mon la verite'!* (Tell me the truth!) You cajun, *Sha?*
Man: *Oui, oui! Je reste au Bayou.* (Yes, I live in Golden Meadow)
Aggie: Go to bed! *Mon Defan Nanan reste au Bayou.* (My godmother, now deceased, lived in Golden Meadow) *Choooh!* It's a small world, isn't it? *J'ai gros couer pour le Bayou.* (I have a special place in my heart for Golden Meadow.)
Man: I've never wanted to live anywhere else.
Aggie: Dat's Cajun country! Why'd you ever want to move? Listen, *Sha,* I don't know why my name's not on dat list, 'cept maybe it's 'cause I just got da call to work tree days ago. I know Miss Lottie DuLonde's maid, she a Cajun too, by da way, and she heard I needed work. So she gave da recommendation for me to Miss Lottie DuLonde herself. Please, if I don't show up tonight, my friend will hear it, and dat'll be two Cajuns you gone make da misere.
Man: I don't know, Miss Agata. Dese *Texians* (anyone who doesn't talk like a Cajun) run a tight ship. 'Specially tonight, I don't know why, but dere's a lot of extra security. I've never had to be so careful 'bout lettin folks come in here.

Aggie: *Sha*, you tink *dis vielle* (old woman) gone cause trouble for da DuLondes? What could someone like me do? 'Sides, I'm gone be too busy passin' a mop all night long!

Man: *Alohrs pas!* You a good ol' Cajun woman; I know you'd never cause any trouble. But maybe I should put a call into Wil DuLonde just to make sure? He da point man for da night.

Just then, the driver in the car behind Aggie's impatiently tapped her horn.

Aggie: *Chooooh!* You don't want to make ever'one late. If I know anyting about Wil DuLonde, he don't like folks bein late.

Man: Alright, alright! Go on through, but don't talk bout dis to no body.

Aggie: *Merci!* Not a word...We Cajuns gotta stick together!

Aggie quickly pulled forward before the man had a chance to change his mind. The road was a straight paved road, with centuries-old trees evenly lining the way on each side, and she wondered when she would actually see a glimpse of the famous mansion. At the end of the road was a large lot, and Aggie parked along a far edge. Because of her extended time with the gatekeeper, the people who had been in the cars ahead of her in line had already gone in to work. So Aggie decided to wait in her car until, hopefully, there would be a small group of employees in the following cars that she could walk in with.

"*Mon Dieu, Mon Dieu, Mon Dieu*, I am in dis ting over my head. Once I get in dere, what to say? What to do? I don't know a ting to do! You gotta make a way for dis *vielle* and help me to get to a DuLonde tonight."

As she sat in her car, a minivan parked a few spots down from her car. Four women, all dressed in white and obviously employees, unloaded from the car. Two of the women appeared to be in their 40's and 50's. Aggie breathed a sigh of relief, knowing she wasn't going to be the only older woman working that night. The fear had crossed her mind that if all the other employees were young, she most certainly would stick out in the crowd. Looking at these women, Aggie was sure she'd be able to blend in. Granted, at age 67, she was far their senior, but she also knew she didn't look a day older than 60, if that. With her smooth, shiny, dark-mocha skin, she definitely had a complexion that worked in her favor as she was often mistaken for a woman in her early to mid-50s. Tonight, she knew now was the time to act like it.

"*Mon Dieu*, did you make it so all dem women pulled in here just now?" she said, smiling upwards. "I bet you even made sure to have dat good ol' Cajun boy at the gate, too, didn't you? You sure are showing me dat you're on my side. Well, let's just be keepin it dat way, OK?" Aggie felt a deep peace envelop her heart, and she knew she was closer to finding out what exactly had happened to Elle.

NINE

ELLE LAY IN HER HOTEL BED, looking up at the ceiling. Once again, her dad had left her alone in their room for most of the day. She hated sitting around in this foreign place all by herself. In her mind, she counted how many days they'd been away from Louisiana. Tonight was the sixth night without her mom, and Elle was feeling the pangs of it. Her dad only let her call home one time, and that was on their layover in New York City, so she hadn't been able to talk with anyone about the things that had been happening. He'd let her send texts, but told her an international cell phone call would be too expensive.

Also, she was feeling very confused about her father. As long as Elle could remember, she hoped and prayed that her dad would spend more time with her, or notice her more, or talk with her more. She remembered how jealous she was last August when Jack took Skye with him on the trip to Europe so that he could enroll her into her new school. Every night, Elle would cry herself to sleep, half because she missed Skye so much and half because she was envious of all the amazing adventures Skye was probably having with their father. Her mom would sleep in her bed with her, stroking her hair, and whisper how much she loved her until Elle fell asleep.

Now that she was on her first big trip with her father, Elle was very disappointed. Other than the first few days of activity, which included that awful trip to the doctor and the lady who spit on her dad, she had mostly been confined to her hotel room. Jack would bring up breakfast for them in the morning, then maybe they'd leave for a couple hours. But even then, those outings were all about him talking to other men, always through an interpreter, and mostly in low tones to keep her from hearing. After that, he'd bring her back to stay in the hotel while he went back out, Elle never knowing exactly what time he would return. The only ways to fill the time were to watch shows on the television, most of which were not in English, or to read the *Little House on the Prairie* books MawMaw had bought for Elle to read on the plane. Normally, Elle would've gobbled up the books, but in this Greek hotel, her mind kept getting distracted by thoughts of her dad.

Elle was beginning to think her dad was not a very nice man at all. Before spending this amount of time with him, she'd been able to make excuses for his outbursts in the home. Maybe he'd just had a bad day? Or, maybe he wasn't feeling well? Since his interactions with her were usually so few and far between, Elle had chosen to believe that he probably acted much better when he was with other people. Rather than blame him for his meanness, Elle had assumed that she was the reason for it. She probably was doing things that irritated him, and if she could just work out how to be the right kind of daughter, then she was sure he'd treat her with more kindness.

But now Elle was seeing that he treated everyone like he treated her and her family, with the exception of some of the men he was trying to impress. And even that attitude could change in a heartbeat if the person didn't give Jack what he wanted. He'd erupt, swearing at the guy and trying to use his force to get results.

She wondered if this was why MawMaw Aggie never seemed to like Jack. Even when he walked into the room, sometimes Aggie'd just go about with what she'd been doing and never acknowledge his presence. This behavior always surprised Elle because it was completely out of character for her MawMaw. She talked to *everyone*, even to herself, and even to people who had already died, like PawPaw. She could meet a person in line at the check-out and before she'd paid her bill, Aggie would know that person's name, age, job, all of their kids' names and their grandkids' names. Aggie loved every person she met. Except Jack.

Elle had never actually heard MawMaw speak badly about her dad, but there were times, late at night, when she would hear MawMaw and Macy talking intensely in the kitchen. Even though they would keep their discussions to whispers, once Elle overheard MawMaw urging Macy to pack up the girls, and for them all to come and live with her. At the time, Elle assumed it was just for a long visit, but now...maybe MawMaw was meaning for them to live with her forever? What did MawMaw know about Jack that Elle didn't?

But if her dad was so bad, then why would he be spending so much money for Skye to go to her special school? And why would he have brought Elle to come and visit? Elle's mom had made it seem like the visit was Jack's idea for a Christmas present, but maybe the truth was that she was the one who had set it up, and was just trying to make Jack look like a good dad?

Nothing made any sense to Elle. She had so many questions that didn't seem to have any answers. She couldn't wait to be with Skye so she could talk with her about all of this. Skye always had the right answers Elle needed, and in just a few more sleeps, she'd be with her at last. Elle wished it could be sooner, that they didn't have to wait until the stupid beauty contest was over on Friday afternoon. She hated that her dad was making her do that. She probably wasn't going to win anything anyway, so what was the point? But it was too late now, because her dad had already bought her the dress.

The day before, he'd gone back to that same store, and apparently had a much better time. He'd come back to the hotel with a beautiful, dark pink satin dress that went all the way to the floor. Elle had never personally worn something so soft and silky before, and she loved the way she looked in it. The dress was fancy with thick satin ribbon straps that tied behind her neck, and a small pink flower right in the middle of her chest that had thin, pale pink ribbons curling down from it. When Elle asked about the lady who'd spit on him, her dad said she hadn't been there that day. Elle thought that lady was lucky, because if he had seen her again, he probably would've hit her.

As Elle lie on her bed thinking about the dress, again she could feel the conflict in her heart. If her dad was all bad, why would he have bought her such a pretty new dress? Why was he so proud of her as to have her enter a beauty pageant? And why did he believe so much in her that he kept saying he really thought she'd win? She wasn't sure what to believe: who was good, who was bad, or who could she trust?

Her restlessness got the better of her and she began to pace the room. She noticed there were several people walking up and down the sidewalks outside, and as she went over to gaze out the window, she saw the strangest thing. There were four young men all laughing and walking in a group, but the one in the middle was blindfolded. He seemed to be having fun though. *This is a strange city,* thought Elle. *I can't wait to get to London and be with Skye.*

TEN

GALEN HATED THE BLINDFOLD. He could have managed walking through the streets of Thessaloniki with his hands tied behind his back, but once his friends added the blindfold, Galen was everything but comfortable with the situation. What started out as a light-hearted birthday party hosted by his brother, Nikkos, had now shifted into a bullish prank.

Galen: Come on, guys. You can take the blindfold off now.
Nikkos: Hey, little brother, that's half the fun!
Galen: For all of you, maybe, but not for me. Aren't we supposed to be doing what I want to do for my birthday?
Nikkos: Trust me, Galen, in a few minutes from now, you'll be doing exactly what you want to be doing. In fact, I'd venture to say there'd be nothing else on the planet you'd rather be doing than what you're about to do.

At this, George and Artimas laughed.

Galen: Can you at least tell me where we are? Or even a hint about where we are going?
Nikkos: I can tell you this; you've never been here before.
George: And it's something you've never done before.

Artimas: (*shocked*) Wait a minute—are you guys serious? This will be Galen's first time?
George: That's what Nikkos said, and he knows him best.
Artimas: Unbelievable. (*to Nikkos*) Is that really true?
Nikkos: Tragic, but true.
Artimas: (*to Galen*) And you're 17 today? That's so embarrassing! What's the matter with you? I think I was 14 when I came here for the first time.
Nikkos: Which is exactly why we're doing this. No brother of mine is going to go through his 17th year without experiencing this at least once.
George: But aren't we paying for the whole night? (*chuckling*) Surely, he'll be able to do it more than once.
Artimas: I still can't believe that the man is 17 and he's still—
Nikkos: (*interrupting*) Arti...shut up!
Galen: Can someone please tell me what you're talking about?
Nikkos: Only one more block, and the secret prize'll be revealed.

All the young men laughed, save Galen. The more Nikkos and his friends talked, the more anxious Galen became. And from the sounds of the loud music spilling out from each open doorway they passed, Galen was fairly certain they had come to an area of town he'd never been. Not because he was unaware of it, nor afraid to go to it, but because he felt the behavior of the men who chose to venture into this part of Thessaloniki was beneath him.

Galen considered himself to be a gentleman, a Greek philosopher, an intellect. Standing crammed shoulder to shoulder next to a slew of men in a hot, muggy space as girls in disgustingly skimpy clothing danced and writhed on a metal pole was not Galen's idea of fun. It was base and degrading for both the women *and* the men. Nikkos had repeatedly attempted to sway Galen to join him on his self-indulgent trips into the red light districts of Athens or Thessaloniki, but Galen had always refused.

Galen: Alright, Nikkos, you got me. I know where we are. You finally got me to come with you on one of your sex escapades. You know I hate this kind of stuff.

Nikkos: I told you guys he'd never come here without the blindfold.
Artimas: Why not?! This place is heaven! How can you do anything but love every minute of this place? What's your problem, Galen, do you not like girls or something?
Galen: Of course I like girls.
Artimas: Because if the problem is you don't like girls, I'm sure we could find you something you do like.
George: Yeah. I've never looked around for one for myself, or anything, but I'm sure we could find a guy for you to be with.
Artimas: Ha! We sure could! Nikkos, how come you didn't tell us your little brother was not into girls?
Galen: (*angry*) Shut up! You know that's not what I mean. Of course I like girls; I just don't like girls like this.
Artimas: (*sarcastic*) But that's what we meant. We could find you the kind of girl you do like. Like, how about a guy who is dressed up all nice and pretty so he looks just like a girl?

Indignant, Galen tried to kick one of them, but his blindfold handicap got the better of him. The guys all laughed at his futile attempts.

Nikkos: OK, guys, leave him alone. Besides, we're here.

Galen felt them entering what he assumed was a strip bar. blindfolded, he was able to feel the thumping bass rhythm of dance music vibrating in his chest. And as they pushed deep into the mass of people, he could smell the foul sweaty men as they cheered whoever was on the stage. Yelling over the music, Galen said, "Alright! We're here. You can untie me now!" But Nikkos continued pulling him by the arm, winding him through the crowd.

Galen sensed they were now on the outskirts of the audience.

"OK," said Nikkos. "We're going to be walking up some stairs here in a minute."

The music grew fainter as they ascended the spiral staircase, and once they came to a landing, Galen could only hear the dull, muffled pounding of the music from the lower level. He brother released his arm.

"Good evening," greeted Nikkos. "This is my little brother, and for his birthday, my friends and I want to give him a special treat. Can I see your menu?"

Menu? thought Galen. *Are we in a restaurant above the club? This is great! While we eat, it will give me time to talk these guys into getting out of here and moving the party someplace else.*

He felt George and Artimas step forward to where Nikkos was, and he heard them whispering and laughing as they looked through the menu. He couldn't decipher their exact words; he'd just hear a phrase now and then: "Oh! He'd like that." or "No, that's a bit too spicy for Galen."

"I think we've made up our minds," he heard Nikkos say. "How much would this be for the entire night?"

"The *entire* shift?" asked a woman.

The guys burst into laughter. "Yes," said Nikkos. "We want to treat my brother to a whole night of fun. It's his first time here and we want to do it right."

The woman snorted as she giggled, "The full shift will be 200 euros."

Nikkos: What?! Are you joking? We're not going to pay that kind of money. I can get twice as much for half the price in Athens.

Woman: You're not in Athens, Love.

Nikkos: Well, maybe we should take our business elsewhere.

Woman: I run my house just like the others here, and if you want, you can go take a look at their menus. You're going to find the same prices. You want just a hole? Then you go to Athens. You want a night of delicious dessert? You come to Thessaloniki. Your choice.

Artimas: (*interrupting*) We don't need to buy the whole night.

Nikkos: Yes we do. I know my brother. It's going to take him half the night to think about it before he makes his first move.

Artimas: (*laughing*) Then, let's see what else she's got.

Woman: Why don't you tell me how much you want to spend, and I'll give you your options.

Nikkos: I've got 150 euros.

Woman: 150? Well, I have the perfect one for you. Sounds like your brother over there needs someone special, a bit younger.

Woman: (*giggle-snorting*) One of our more experienced girls would eat him alive. How about this pretty young thing? She's one of our newer girls.

Nikkos: (*after a pause*) I like her. It's a deal.
Woman: Is he going to take off the wrist ties and blindfold? Because if not, there's an extra charge for that.

Galen felt his heart pounding in his chest as he began to understand where his brother had taken him. This was much worse than spending a few hours in a strip club; Nikkos had led him up into an actual brothel. He felt helpless. What could he do about it now? If he refused to go in, they'll never let him forget it. They'll call him a coward, and maybe announce to all his friends he was still a virgin, that he didn't even like girls. But there was no way he was going to lower himself to touch a dirty whore who has been with countless men. That was the vilest kind of woman.

"Brother, we are here!" Nikkos announced. "For your birthday, we have given you the best possible gift. And while you might not thank me for it right now, you'll be singing my praises tomorrow."

The moment Galen felt his wrists freed, he tore off his blindfold. It took a bit for his eyes to adjust and to be able to focus on his surroundings. The room was dimly lit by red bulbs, with chairs lining the walls. The woman standing in front of him was an ageless wonder with her thick, pasty make-up and tight polyester clothing; either she was in her 40s and had experienced quite a thorny life, or she was around 70. Galen couldn't decide. He wondered what disgusting secrets she was hiding behind her garishly made-up face.

Looking Galen up and down, the old woman smiled and said,"Follow me, Love."

Galen stood still for a moment contemplating his situation, trying to find a win. What's the big deal if he just went along with it? They'd never know what really happened back there. He wouldn't even have to touch the woman, and Nikkos would never know the truth. And then he wouldn't have to put up with their constant ridicule. Resolutely, Galen motioned to the woman to lead the way.

She began to walk down a thin hallway when she sensed more than one man following. Turning on her stiletto, she directed her voice to Nikkos. "Are you coming too? Because if so, there's an extra charge for that."

Nikkos patted Galen on the back and whispered some last minute brotherly advice in his ear before retreating to George and Artimas. As

Galen looked back at the trio, he noticed several other men beginning to wander into the waiting area and peruse the sex menus. He couldn't believe he was now to be classed with such deprivation.

Galen continued to follow the woman, passing under the industrial lamps with red bulbs hanging from the ceiling. Each room's door was decorated with a poster of a naked woman in a pornographic pose. After seven or eight rooms, the hallway ended with four final doors. It was noticeably darker at this point, and these doors were different from the previous ones. Each was fastened on the outside with a padlock. The woman rummaged through her pockets and pulled out a ring of keys.

"What are the locks for?" Galen asked. "I'm certainly not doing this if you're going to lock me in there all night."

The woman looked at him as if this was the first time anyone had asked her that question. "Oh, Love, the locks are only for the girls' protection while they rest. You boys got here a little early, so I hadn't had a chance to unlock the rooms yet."

Galen looked at her suspiciously. "If it's to protect your girls, then why is the lock on the outside?"

The woman giggle-snorted and replied. "Well, we wouldn't want our prize girls to get away, would we? Now you stay out here a moment until I'm sure she's ready."

Galen didn't think it was possible to feel any more uncomfortable than he already was, but the sight of those outdoor padlocks did the trick. He couldn't understand why a prostitute would allow herself to be locked inside a room, even if it was for her own protection. What if there was a fire, or a flood or a freak earthquake? It made much more sense to him that the highest level of safety would be achieved from locks fastened on the inside.

He heard the woman whispering inside the room. There was silence for a bit and then Galen was pretty sure he heard a slap, followed by a barely audible moan. Did someone just get hit in there?

The woman reemerged, smiling crookedly at him, unaware of the fuchsia lipstick smearing her front teeth. "She's ready for you, Love. Have a wonderful evening." And she motioned him to enter the room.

If he had a guarantee that Nikkos and his friends would be out of sight by now, Galen would have exited the brothel that very moment. But fearing their accusations of failure, he crept into the bedroom.

The first thing Galen noticed was the bars on the window. The room was small and sparse, a chair in the corner, a toilet and sink slightly left of the barred window, a small table next to the bed. And then he saw the girl. She was everything he was not expecting. Not that he knew exactly *what* he was expecting, but whatever that was, she was definitely not it.

She seemed dazed as she sat at the edge of the bed, like she wasn't quite awake or tuned into reality. And she was younger than Galen had envisioned. *Much* younger; maybe fourteen or fifteen? That was the age of his sister, Dimitra, and this girl looked similar in stature. What was a girl like this doing in a brothel? Shouldn't she be in school?

A blue satin camisole hung from her thin frame, gathering at her waist, so Galen couldn't see if she was wearing anything else below that. Her hair was long and very dark, curling past her shoulders.

He was at a complete loss about what to do next. So he did nothing, but stand there transfixed on the young girl, hearing his heart beating in his ears, or was that the dull, thumping music from below? His answer came when the girl looked up at him, and their eyes locked. He was definitely hearing his heart. Never before had he sensed such diverse emotions coming from a young girl. Her crystal blue eyes pierced him with hatred and scorn, yet at the same time, fear and hopelessness. She was like a caged animal, eyes wildly helpless.

This girl is obviously not in this place because she chose to be. And by the look on her face, she certainly doesn't want to do what she thinks I've come here to do. So then...who is she and why is she here, and more importantly, how did she get here?

Galen dropped his gaze. He couldn't figure out how to feel. Pity for this young girl, who for some unknown reason, was locked in this stifling room? Anger at the people who put her here? Shame for allowing himself to become a part of this degrading business? Maybe none of these. Maybe all of these. Galen wasn't sure.

The girl scooted herself back so her straightened legs could rest on the bed as she leaned her back against the wall. Her eyes had become dull again, and almost robotically, she brushed her hair away from her face and opened her legs. Galen's face flushed when he saw her, and he felt his natural male instincts quicken.

Disgusted at himself, he spun around and crossed over to the open window. Feeling the crisp, chilly winter air, he held on to one of the vertical bars with one hand and raked through the top of his hair with the other. He brewed over what to do next, his thoughts ping-ponging in his head.

He was resolute to not have sex with that girl. It was wrong. Period. And she looked no older than his own sister! Galen would murder the man who would so much as touch Dimitra with a lewd hand. When Nikkos comes here, does he buy girls like this? This young? She can't be here on her own volition; she's got to be a victim of some sort of sick joke.

Who is this girl, and how'd she get here? Where are her parents? Surely someone must be missing her? And why is she locked in the room like this? She's a prisoner here, forced to do, god only knows what! Burning with indignation, Galen no longer cared what sort of abuse he would have to take from Nikkos and his friends for not touching the girl.

He darted for the door but as his hand grabbed the doorknob, he had this realization: *If I leave, that old wench certainly isn't going to give me my money back, and as soon as I'm out the door, she's just going to sell this poor girl to somebody else. The least I could do is wait the night out and give her a break.*

Galen quietly shut the door and turned to the girl. For the first time, he noticed the redness of her left cheek. That sound he heard before he entered the room was someone getting slapped. That old bitch had hit her! Anger burned in his chest.

From the corner of the room, he slid the chair closer to the bed and sat. His eyes were now level with hers, but she refused to make contact. He began to speak softly to her.

"I know this might be different than what you are used to," he said. "But I don't want to do anything to you tonight. Your entire shift was paid for, so you can just rest, or we could just talk, or something..." His words trailed off. He could tell the girl could hear him, but by her blank stare, he wasn't sure she understood what he was saying.

He leaned forward and gently pushed her feet together. Shaking his head 'no', he said, "I don't want to do any of that tonight. But I don't want that woman to bring in anyone else, either. I've paid for your whole shift, so you can just go back to sleep. You look like you could use it." Still, she gave him no response.

"Do you know how to speak Greek?" he asked her. "Are you Greek?"

She seemed confused. He spoke very slowly and asked again, "Do you know how to speak Greek?" No answer. "Do you know any Greek at all?"

Galen could see by the way she had curled up on the bed that she was beginning to become very frightened. This was probably the first time anything like this had ever happened, and she didn't know what to do or how to respond. Also, he was positive this girl couldn't comprehend a word he was saying.

Where was this girl from, and how long has she been here, and worse, what horrific things have been done to her? Galen didn't even want to know.

He began to stand up and move toward her. Habitually, she shot up and started to spread her legs again. "No, no, no, no," he said softly, again shaking his head. "None of that tonight." He tugged at her pillow and gestured for her to lie down. Still confused, she obeyed. Then Galen spread out the threadbare blanket over her body and motioned for her to try to go to sleep.

He pushed his chair as far back as he could into the corner. He hoped his distance would help the girl relax. He leaned back in the chair and stretched his legs forward onto the concrete floor. *I may as well try to get comfortable,* he thought. *It's going to be a long night.*

ELEVEN

WIL STOOD FOR A MOMENT to take in the view. He'd been so 'on task' since the moment he arrived at the Nottoway Plantation, that he hadn't yet given himself the opportunity to broaden his focus beyond his mission at hand. He breathed a deep sigh and looked out from the magnificent balcony of Nottoway. Being raised in an affluent family, he'd been around opulence all his life, so there weren't too many houses that could impress Wil. When he was about 8 years old, his parents bought their late 19th century Garden District home. But even with its 5,000 square feet of bedrooms, sprawling outdoor balconies, library and ballroom, plus a 2-story carriage house, it paled in comparison to the home he was standing in now.

The majestic Nottoway Plantation was more like a blazing white castle that seemed to defy all superlatives. This home had 53,000 square feet of living space, 64 rooms, 6 interior staircases, 12 hand-carved Italian marble fireplaces, and incredibly intricate plasterwork throughout the rooms that boasted 15 ft. ceilings and 11 ft. doors. As Wil stood on the main floor outdoor balcony, he felt dwarfed next to the massive 3-story high square columns that served to help hold up the enormous structure. He scanned the property, which in full, encompassed 100s of acres, and wondered what it would've been like to grow up in a place like this.

Time to focus, he reminded himself. There was too much work to be done.

Bounding down the great outdoor granite staircase of the White Castle, he strode to meet his friends at the Fountain Courtyard, just south of the mansion. He chuckled at the sight of them in their costumes and wondered if they felt as odd as he did in his Confederate officer costume. On one hand, he thought it was pretty cool to be accurately dressed in the era of his present surroundings. The existing owners of historic Nottoway had been meticulous to preserve the authenticity of the site, and to walk the exact paths of former young men who had served in the Civil War—in almost the exact same clothes—was a bit eerie. On the other hand, if Wil had lived in Louisiana during this time, would he have worn the uniform of a Confederate? Judging from his values of today, he would've been in great conflict with the ideals for which the South was fighting.

Weeks ago as Wil had read up on the history of Nottoway, he learned that three sons of John Randolph (the man who built Nottoway) had fought in the Civil War; the eldest son was killed in battle. These very grounds had been occupied from time to time by hundreds of soldiers, from both sides of the war. Now as he briskly walked into the courtyard and saw a dozen of his friends in their Confederate costumes, a sight surely to have been seen by the 1863 soldiers, he felt a strange kindred to these ghosts of the past. As a former American soldier, Wil understood only too well the minds, the passions, and the nightmares of the men who had gone before him.

Using his best commanding voice, Wil yelled, "Atten-tion!"

The guys simultaneously turned to Wil, laughing and greeting him with handshakes and high-fives. The group of a dozen young men, ranging in ages from 20-28, were all close friends of Wil. A few he knew from high school athletics, a couple were close family relatives, and the rest were former fellow Army Rangers.

Matt: Well, I guess it's clear who the man in charge is. Check out that officer's hat! How come your costume is so much better than the rest of ours?

Wil: Because I am the man in charge, and besides, who paid for all of your costumes?

Matt: Umm...let's see...your dad?!

Wil: (*laughing heartily*) Ha! Well, you got me there. But at least I didn't cheap out on you and make you wear the $19.99 version with the plastic pants. These costumes are legit. Mine more than yours, though.

Tyler: So what's the plan for tonight?

Matt: Yeah, are we gonna get food outta this deal, and more importantly, are there gonna be any single ladies present this evening?

The guys laughed and started teasing Matt about his inability to succeed whenever he asked a girl out on a date.

Wil: Hey, I never said you'd get a date by helping me out, but I can guarantee you'll get a big ol' Southern dinner. Plus, if you want to stay after and hang for beers—and all the leftovers I'm going to steal from the kitchen tonight—I reserved a couple extra rooms in the mansion for us. It's pretty cool, 'cause the guy who built this place actually built separate living quarters for his sons, and those are the rooms I got for us.

Matt: Dude, how cool would that've been to grow up with your own part of the house? Me and my brothers would've torn the place up.

Wil: Well, he did have eleven kids, I guess he had to do something with them all. Wait til you see the inside of this joint. Seriously, the dude spared no expense. In the basement, he even built his kids their own private bowling alley.

Tyler: What?! Is it still there? Can we play a couple rounds?

Wil: Are you kidding me? First of all, it's not still there; it's a museum now, but even if it was, do you think they'd let us bowl with 150-year-old balls and pins?

Tyler: True that.

Wil: The guy who owns this place would never let us mess around with the antiques; although, I'd be the same way if I was in charge. The only reason we're getting the kind of free access tonight is because, one, he's a friend of my dad's—

Matt: (*interrupting*) Hello?! Who isn't a friend of your dad's? He's the epitome of "the guy who knows a guy."

Wil: And two, my dad has the cash to cover anything that might get slightly damaged.

Matt: Ya think?! He's one of the richest guys in Louisiana!

Tyler: Dude, you gonna be a smart ass all night long? 'Cause I can take ya down right here in front of all these guys.

Matt: Whatever.

Wil: Ok. Let's get serious for a sec. First of all, thanks so much for helping out. My dad and I really appreciate it, and know you could've gone to any one of a thousand Mardi Gras parties tonight, so it's cool you're here.

Matt: Hey, this is just Monday; we'll still be able to make the grand finale of Mardi Gras tomorrow. Which by the way, if any of you guys wanna ride down with me to New Orleans to see all the parades, I got my parents' Expedition. It's gonna be fly.

Wil: That will be fun. We'll talk about that after we're done with tonight. Anyway, I gotta fill you all in on what's been happening with my dad over the last few weeks, and why I've asked you guys to be here tonight. I know I'm probably just going overboard, but I don't want to be stupid either.

For the past month or so, my dad's been getting some bizarre, anonymous emails. Without going into too much detail, whoever's sending them is asking for large amounts of money, along with threats of violence if my dad doesn't pay up. Some of you already know this, but for those of you who don't, my dad has a brother named Jack who basically disappeared off the face of the earth when he was about 20. Dad's tried to get in touch with him over the years, but the guy's a real loser, probably a big drug dealer and into who knows whatever else, and he's never wanted contact. We think the person who's emailing Dad is somehow linked with Jack; probably looking to get back money my uncle owes him. Obviously, all of this is on the D.L., but you need to know this info to be on guard for tonight.

Once the newspapers printed a story about this party tonight, the emails got more frequent. It's been so frustrating because

I've been working with one of my dad's FBI friends, and as we've cased out the incoming mail, the addresses are always different. And now it looks like they're sourcing from public computers in various libraries, so we can't get a handle on any particular location.

I'm almost certain whoever is doing this isn't going to show up tonight, but on all fronts of my parents' social activities, we've been taking extra precautions. And this is where you guys come in. These grounds are huge, and by no means secure. Anybody could just walk right off of highway 405 over there and come in. So what we've done for tonight is this: First, we've bought out the entire plantation for today and tomorrow; all the rooms, all the venues, and all the tours will only be for the group of about 300 guests who'll be coming tonight. Besides those guests, the only other people who'll be on site will be Nottoway staff.

Last week, all the guests were mailed special gifts to be worn this evening. It's a gold lapel pin that's a doubloon with a fleur de lis.

Matt: So who's all coming tonight? And are any of their daughters single?
Tyler: Shut it, Matt...don't anger the beast. You might be his oldest friend, but—
Matt: Hey, I'm family. Blood runs thicker than water, bro.
Tyler: Yeah, and we're gonna see all that blood of yours in a second here if you don't shut your cake-hole.
Wil: (*chuckling at his friends*) I brought one of these gold doubloons for each of you guys.

Wil pulled out an envelope from his outer coat pocket and poured 12 pins into his hand. They were bright 14-karat gold doubloon coins, about an inch and a half in diameter. He passed them out, giving one to each of the guys.

Every person here tonight will have one of these. You guys can pin it on your costume, too. Some of the ladies might be wearing them as necklaces or bracelets, but everyone has to have this visible on their person to get in tonight.

Tyler: What about the staff? How will we know if they're real staff or not?

Wil: Right. Good question. All the staff has been pre-approved by me, and two weeks ago, they also received one of these pins in the mail, only theirs aren't real gold.

Matt: Are these ones you gave us real gold?

Wil: Are you kidding me? Not a chance.

Tyler: So, do you have specific places you want us to patrol?

Wil: Well, yes and no. Like I said, I really don't think there'll be any action to speak of tonight. The chance that the scumbag who's been emailing my dad would actually have the balls to come here tonight is next to nothing. But because of the nature of the threats, we just can't take any risks. Really, all I need from you guys is to be extra sets of eyes. I'm going to be interfacing with all the staff on many different levels tonight to make sure all goes as planned, so I'm not going to be able to keep track of all the people coming and going. What I need is for all you guys to pair off—

Matt: Dude, if we walk around all night in pairs with these light blue costumes, everyone's gonna think we're gay.

Wil: (*to Tyler*) I swear, I'm gonna kill him before the night's over.

Tyler: No worries, man, I'll help you hide the body over there in the Mississippi.

Matt: Hey!

Wil: ANYway, as I was saying, I want you to split up, walk around and just keep your eyes and ears open. Before everything starts, I'll give you all radios so we can be in touch throughout the night. Your first priority is to check to make sure everyone you see has one of these doubloons on. And I mean, for the entire night. If you notice anyone without the gold pin, politely ask them to show it to you. If they can't produce it, then radio me and I'll come and meet you. Stay with the person until I get there. Otherwise, just stay alert. For you, Matt, that means no booze until the deal is over. And for all my rangers, please remember this isn't some covert op that you have to get all intense about. Tonight's just a party with a bit of heightened security. The last thing my dad wants is for any of the guests to feel something might be up. Does everyone have their cards with the agendas?

As the guys took out small cards from their pockets, Wil continued:

Real quickly, the guests will arrive at 18:00. They'll be greeted and escorted to the main floor of the mansion, which is actually the second floor. They'll get drinks and hors d'oeuvres there, and they're allowed to be in the White Ballroom, the Gentlemen's Study, the formal Dining Room, and the balconies. At 19:00, everyone will be taken to the Randolph Ballroom, and that room is south of the mansion, just a short walk. Everyone'll be seated, and dinner will begin at 19:30. Look for me, and I'll make sure you guys know where to sit. At 21:30, you can see on your card, several things will be happening. Dancing back up in the White Ballroom, poker in the Gentlemen's Study, candlelight tours of the rest of the mansion, and brandy in the dining room. The party will go until exactly 00:00, in true Mardi Gras tradition, and not a minute later. We realize that technically it's the night before the end of Mardi Gras, but my parents want to do everything to give the folks a vision of what next year's ball will be like if they do decide to form an official krewe.

I gotta go and meet with the Nottoway staff, but I've already debriefed Tyler about everything, so if you have any questions, he can field those. (*to Tyler*) Right now, if you walk up to the main front balcony, there's a gal named Suzy who'll be ready to show you and the guys around the entire mansion. She'll be pointing out the rooms we'll be using for tonight, so you'll know if people tonight are starting to stray off the beaten path. You cool?

Tyler: As a cuke.
Wil: (*gesturing to Matt*) Make sure he doesn't steal anything.
Matt: Hey!

Laughing, Wil began to stride back to the mansion to meet with the staff, but not before he gave Matt a quick head-lock and pretended that he was going to throw him into the courtyard fountain. All the guys cheered Wil on, and continued to razz Matt after Wil let him go. Before he was out of earshot, Wil yelled over his shoulder, "Oh yeah, and don't forget to have fun! It's going to be a great party!"

TWELVE

AGGIE HATED LYING. It was the one thing she'd be sure to get a whipping for when she was a little girl. "Da Prejeans never lie," her PaPa would say gently as he'd unhitch his belt. "We may be a lot of tings, but we ain't liars, Agata. I do dis 'cause I love you, *Sha*." And he'd whip her butt with his belt. Never hard enough to leave a lasting mark, but definitely enough to sting and draw tears. Aggie'd crawl up in her PaPa's lap and cry while his big arms engulfed her in a way only a father's arms could. He'd speak softly, right into her ears, telling her how much he loved his girl.

But in this situation, Aggie knew lying would be a necessity, especially now that she'd heard about those gold doubloon pins the staff was required to wear for the party. She had to get herself one of those pins! She wasn't sure how just yet, but she knew she wouldn't last very long inside the mansion without one.

In the parking lot was where Aggie had learned about the doubloons. Aggie introduced herself to the women who had gotten out of the minivan, and began a conversation with one of them, the oldest-looking one. Her name was Judy, and as they were walking up to the staff entrance of Nottoway, Judy gave Aggie the run down of the evening.

Judy: How long have you been working here, Aggie? I don't remember ever seeing you at any mansion events.

Aggie: Dat's 'cause this is my first time. I'm a last minute add for da big party tonight. I know Miss Lottie's personal maid, and she told me Miss Lottie was worried about there not being enough cleanin' staff for da night. I told Bessie, my friend who works for Miss Lottie, dat I'd be happy to help out. So Miss Lottie told Bessie to tell me to show up in my white uniform and get to work!

Judy: Wow, that was lucky for you, wasn't it? I've gotta say, I'm looking forward to tonight. I've heard the DuLondes are great people.

Aggie: Bessie says dey da best she ever worked for.

Judy: So, this is your first time to Nottoway?

Aggie: It sure is. And I know we just met, Judy, but is dere anyway you could show me where to go? I wanna make a good impression, I really need da money. Plus, I gotta live up to Bessie's recommendation.

Judy: Why, I'd be happy to. We all need the extra money, nowadays, don't we? Just stick with me, and you'll be fine.

Aggie: *Mais,* I'm just part of da cleanin crew, Sha, so I just wanna stay invisible.

Judy: Ha! I understand. I'll show you what you need to know.

While Judy was leading Aggie into the staff room, Aggie did her very best to not look around at her surroundings like a tourist. She knew she had to act as professional as possible, even though she had never experienced anything remotely close to the grandeur of Nottoway. They entered a women's staff lounge that had small lockers for all the employees.

Judy: My locker is right over here, and you can just share mine for tonight. You'll want to keep all your stuff in here, and I'll lock it up tight. *After putting her own coat and purse in the locker, she took Aggie's coat and placed it on top of hers. She then took out her gold doubloon pin from her purse.* They're being real sticklers about these doubloons tonight. They told us every staff person has to have one of these pins on their uniform or they'll be sent home. Where's yours? Make sure it's pinned somewhere where it can be easily seen.

Aggie: (*lying*) Uhhh...da pin. Yeah. Bessie told me about dat. I'm supposed to get mine from Miss Lottie. Why we need it?

Judy: I'm not sure, they're just for the DuLonde's event. It's pretty unusual, but everybody was told to make sure we have it on our person at all times.

Aggie: I'll make sure to get mine right away.

Judy: Great. Now let me show you around.

Aggie: All I need's for you to show me where da cleanin supplies are, so I can get to pushin a mop through dis place.

Judy: (*smiling at her*) Aggie, I don't think you need to worry about living up to your friend's recommendation. You're gonna do just fine.

They walked out of the staff locker room and Judy took her to the several locations of cleaning closets. After Aggie had quickly gathered enough supplies, she asked Judy to show her where the public restrooms were so she could start there. On their way, Judy informed her that Mr. Wil wanted to meet with all the staff at four o'clock sharp in the White Ballroom. There they would get all the remaining details for the evening's event, and she would not want to be late for that. Aggie thanked Judy for her help and then urged her to go and clock in before her boss thought she was late. Once alone in the bathroom, Aggie closed and locked the door.

This bathroom, like most of the ones Judy had shown her, was a single room bathroom, and Aggie was thankful for the seclusion. She sat down on the toilet and took a deep breath as she attempted to adjust to her surroundings.

"*Mon Dieu, Mon Dieu*," she whispered. "What has Aggie got herself into dis time? Dis just too much for ol' Aggie to take care of. I'm gone get myself caught and put up in jail, is what I'm gone do! Oh, *Mon Dieu*, you best hide me tonight, or even better, make one of dem gold doubloons appear right now in my hand!"

She chuckled at herself, trying to order God around like she was fit to be his boss. She knew God would have his way, whatever way that was, and she was just going to be happy with the lot she was given. She took in another deep breath hoping it would calm her down a bit. The peace she had felt in the parking lot was short-lived because from the moment she heard of the doubloon pin, anxiety had set in.

She checked her watch. 3:20. A little over one half hour until she needed to be at the staff meeting with Wil. Without a pin, Aggie knew she needed to stay out of sight, and was hoping she would be able to hide in the bathrooms until then.

Aggie waited until 3:58 to exit her bathroom sanctuary and try to find her way to the White Ballroom. Surely, if she was one of the last people to enter the room, she'd be able to sneak in and hide behind the full staff. Having no idea where the White Ballroom was, she listened for the sound of voices to hopefully guide her in the right direction.

She started back the way Judy had taken her, and luckily, happened to catch sight of a few people walking up a large flight of dark wooden stairs. She sped over to the stairs, not wanting to lose sight of the people. Aggie noticed the simple structure of this particular staircase, concluding it must've been built solely for the purpose of the servants to move from floor to floor. As the stairs wound upwards, Aggie made sure to leave a safe distance between herself and the other staff. Once at the top, Aggie continued to follow, all the while keeping her head bowed to prevent making eye contact with anyone. She didn't dare venture her eyes away from the floor until she was safe in the White Ballroom.

She watched as the hallway's oriental rug gave way to pure white hardwood floors. Assuming she had reached her destination, she remained crouched down until she found her way to the very back of the room and chose her place behind the largest man she could find. Only then did she feel safe enough to look up. And when she did, the sight before her took her breath away. She'd seen online pictures of the famous Nottoway White Ballroom, but even in their splendor, they didn't compare to the real thing. For the first time since she'd stepped foot onto the plantation, she allowed herself to drink in the view.

Everything around her was stark white: the 15 foot walls, the ceilings with the most intricate plasterwork Aggie had ever seen, the Corinthian columns, the extravagant hand-made archways, the velvet curtains flowing ceiling to floor that framed huge windows, and even the expanse of the hardwoods. The gorgeous wood floors were painted brilliant white and were polished to perfection.

Mon Dieu, Aggie thought. *How many slave girls did it used to take to mop and shine dis floor by hand after a party? I'm glad I wasn't alive den to know dat answer! Choooh, dis da most beautiful ting I ever did see, though. It's like a little piece a heaven itself. I don't tink I'd ever get tired at starin at dis white room, even if I lived here for a hundred years.*

The only color variances from pure white were the gold trimmings accented here and there, and the oil painting of a Civil War-era woman which hung above one of the double fireplaces. The frame of the portrait, the supports of the crystal chandeliers, the frames of the large mirrors, the edges of the white velvet antique couches, and a few other decor items were bright gold. These golden touches only served to accent the regality of this one-of-a-kind White Ballroom. Lost in the breath-taking beauty that surrounded her, Aggie had momentarily forgotten herself and why she had come here. That is, until she heard Wil call the meeting to order.

The sound of his voice caused Aggie's heart to leap in her chest, and she quickly found her place behind the large man she had appointed as the visual barrier between Wil and herself.

Wil was a very handsome young man, tall with dark wavy hair and crystal blue eyes, just like Skye. Aggie was taken aback by the resemblance between these two cousins who had never met each other, never even knew of each other's existence. How much different the girls' lives might have been to have had a relationship with Wil and his parents, people with such a great reputation of strong character. Aggie felt a fire burning on the inside of her, as her passion was renewed to free Elle from whatever danger that evil Jack had put her in, and get the girls away from him forever.

Aggie listened carefully as Wil outlined the schedule of events for the evening. Here, in this White Ballroom, the costume ball would begin. The guests would arrive around 6pm for pre-dinner drinks and socializing, and precisely at 7:15 Richard and Lottie DuLonde would welcome and address the crowd, first from inside the White Ballroom and then from the outdoor balcony, for all the rest of the guests.

That's all Aggie needed to know. She was fairly certain she'd be able to stay out of sight until 7pm; the staff would be too pre-occupied with their preparation to notice a stray. Then, hopefully right before they addressed their guests, she'd be able to speak to either Richard or Lottie DuLonde. There was no reason to wait until the end of the evening, especially if that meant she would have to try and stay hidden until then.

Wil briefly mentioned the subject of the gold doubloon coins and introduced a few of his friends, all dressed in Confederate Soldier costumes, and explained they would be helping out with security for the evening. He then asked if anyone had any questions.

While a few members of the staff were getting their questions answered, Aggie thought this would be a prime opportunity to sneak away. The people were sensing the meeting coming to its close and were beginning to rustle around, so Aggie assessed it would be easy for her to slip out and hide somewhere until 6pm. Bending down a bit, she turned to exit.

"Excuse me, ma'am!" Wil's voice called from the front.

Instinct told Aggie to resist the temptation to look back, but she failed to heed the warning. She turned her gaze to the direction of Wil's voice only to find his steely blue eyes focused directly on her. She froze like a statue, unable to move or even think what to do next. With every step Wil took toward her, Aggie knew she needed to be doing something, planning something, but she was utterly caught off guard and dumbfounded.

"Hello," Wil said as he now stood next to her, his height against her small frame further commanding his authority. And still Aggie stood, silent and motionless, gaping up at his face.

Not understanding her intimidation, Wil tried to soften his approach by holding out his hand. "Hello," he said again. "I'm Wil DuLonde, and I don't believe we've met, which is unusual because I was supposed to have personally met everyone who was working tonight. What's your name?"

Aggie could tell by the look in this young man's eyes, that he probably could smell a lie a mile away. She was going to have to try anyway, "I'm Agata Prejean, and I was just goin to get my doubloon pin. I'm so sorry, Mr. Wil; I didn't put it on yet. I could just run down now and get it and come right back up here. Please don't send me home; I really need da money..."

"Whoa, whoa, whoa," said Wil, laughing. "You're not in trouble, Miss Agata; I just don't remember meeting you. Listen, I'll be here for a few more minutes. You go get your pin, and then come back and talk to me. I promise, I'm not going to send you home."

In a flash, Aggie exited the White Ballroom, with no intention whatsoever to return. She was going to have to hide somewhere no one would ever look, after which she would have exactly one chance to find and make contact with either Richard or Lottie before she was caught.

Wil watched her leave, wondering how he could've spooked this older woman so badly. At first glance, she didn't seem the type to be easily intimidated. He hoped he'd be able to put her mind at ease once she came back.

He fielded a few more questions from the staff and then dismissed them to their present duties. He thought he'd stay a bit longer to wait for Agata to return, and to talk with some of the staff as they were leaving the ballroom. One of the waitresses came up to him.

Judy: Hello Wil, we met a few weeks ago, when you came to meet the people who'd be working tonight, but I don't expect you'd remember my name.

Wil: Hi. It's Judy, right? I'll admit that I'm not the greatest with last names when there's a large number, but I never forget a face. I remember you were sitting on the left-hand side of the room, in the third row. Let's see...4th chair from the right?

Judy: Oh my word! Yes! How in the world did you remember that? That's amazing!

Wil: I've always been able to scan a room and later remember the dumbest little things. (*Laughing*) Not that where you were sitting was dumb; I didn't mean that.

Judy: Oh, honey, don't you worry. I didn't take it that way.

Wil: Wow, I'd better get some tact going here before the night begins or I'll have all my parents' guests offended before the first course is served. Like with that woman before. Agata? Do you know her or know why she got so freaked out?

Judy: Actually, that's why I came up to you. I met her on my way in to work this afternoon. She's a sweet, sweet lady, but times have been really tough for her, and she really needs this job tonight to help make ends meet. You probably haven't met her because she told me she was a last minute staff add-on by your mother.

Wil: Really?

Judy: Aggie said that she's friends with your mom's personal maid, Bessie, and that when Bessie heard your mom talking about how she was worried there wouldn't be enough cleaning staff for tonight, Bessie told your mom about Aggie. Well, your mom, so kind as I've heard her to be, hired her right on the spot, just from Bessie's recommendation!

Wil: That sounds like my mom.

Judy: And so Aggie's real nervous about tonight because if she doesn't do well, she's worried Bessie will get in trouble with your mother.

Wil: Got it. Thanks, Judy, for all of that info. If you see Agata, will you send her on to me? I'd like to try to put her mind at ease.

Judy: Yes, sir.

Wil was now even more puzzled about Agata than he was before. Yes, it was true, the scenario sounded exactly like something his mom would do. She spent her life looking for people she could help. The only problems were: one, his mom had specifically requested to have no part in any of the staffing for the evening, and two, his mom's never had a maid named Bessie.

THIRTEEN

AFTER DARTING OUT OF the White Ballroom, Aggie was not sure where she'd be able to hide for almost three hours until the DuLondes made their opening statements to the guests. She knew the bathrooms were not the option they were before, as 200 guests would be arriving and would certainly notice if one of the doors was locked for that long. She thought about trying to keep inconspicuous in the kitchen because there would be so much activity going on in all the different areas. But then again, even if she would be able to blend in, there was still the issue of the missing doubloon. Certainly, someone would spot she didn't have one, especially since Wil had singled her out at the staff meeting.

Then she had the idea of going outside to her car and laying down on the back seats until it was time to find a DuLonde. She needed to find herself a window to get her bearings and figure out the best way to her car. She stepped into a room that had soft yellow walls lined in white molding, and it contained 3 small pianos and a golden harp in the corner.

Aggie was thankful for the large marble fireplace that jutted out right next to one of the windows. It provided a little crevice of a corner that she could stand in while she scanned the view outside. Because she was on the second level of the mansion, she was at a vantage point to see quite a bit of the outside lawn. She spotted a strip of a parking lot, but she could not tell if it was the one that held her Chevy. What she did notice, however, were four of the young Confederate Soldiers, part of Wil's security team, walking around the lot. They appeared to be scoping out all the cars, even looking inside the windows of some. Where they already on the hunt to find her?

She pressed herself deeper into her corner, hoping she could make herself unseen to any passersby. She was at a complete loss what to do next. *Choooh*, she thought. *Dis place got over 4 dozen rooms in it, dere's gotta be at least one that an old Cajun can hide out in til it's time to find da DuLondes.* She held her breath and listened for any voices or movement outside the room. Once she was sure the hallway was vacant, she left the Music Room in search of a hiding place.

She came to the grand Entrance Hall of Nottoway, and once again had to resist every fiber of her being that wanted to wonder at all the details of this castle Harold and she had always planned to visit. But as she hurried through, she knew there just wasn't time to gawk at the beautiful architecture, or at the antique tables and statues she was passing, or the high white ceilings flaunting their fancy chandeliers. Aggie did take notice, however, of a stairway descending to the lower level of the mansion, and without another thought, she decided to take her chances down the stairs. This would put her on the same level she originally entered with Judy; perhaps she'd be able to find the staff locker room, where they'd left their purses. By now, Aggie was more than willing to squeeze herself into an unused locker for 3 hours, if it meant not being caught and arrested for trespassing.

It was dark and uninviting on the bottom floor, evidently not an area where any festivities were planned for the evening. She heard some kitchen activity happening to her distant left, probably the overflow of catering for the dinner, so Aggie thought it best to move in the opposite direction. She happened by what looked like a small lounge and bar, also dimly lit and vacant for the night. She ventured deeper into the basement of this cavernous mansion, and finally came to a room that served as a small museum for the site.

Aggie sensed this was her spot. It was quiet in the museum, and it was a room set apart. If she kept the door slightly open and listened very carefully, she was sure she'd be able to hear if anyone was approaching. Also, because the only lights in the room were the small ceiling spotlights that shone down on certain exhibits, it was dark and shadowy. She'd easily be able to hide in a corner if someone looked in. Aggie felt this was her best chance to stay out of sight.

She found an old wooden box and moved it to the location in the room that she'd be able to both hear and see most advantageously. And then once again, she sat down to take in some deep breaths. Closing her eyes, she tried to calm herself in the dark solitude of this museum. She encouraged herself that she'd come this far successfully; she couldn't give up now. Only one more thing to accomplish: contact with either Richard or Lottie DuLonde.

Aggie opened her eyes and began to read a large wooden sign in front of her. She happened to have placed her box in front of a display that shared the history of Nottoway and how it was built. A man named John Hampton Randolph, a hugely wealthy plantation owner had decided to build Nottoway in 1855. He hired the then-famous architect Henry Howard to design the mansion, and it took four years to complete the intricately detailed and enormously expensive project.

Aggie read through the list of impressive features for which the home was renowned, including the fact that where she was sitting used to be a bowling alley for the Randolph's eleven children. In addition, the house was finished not only with gas lighting throughout, but also with flushing toilets and running hot and cold water in the bathrooms; all unheard of at that time. *How dis man have so much money?* she thought. *All dat must have cost a fortune!*

She scanned through more of the information until she came to some stats that helped answer her question. At the height of his success, Mr. Randolph owned over 1000 acres of land between two plantations and held over 500 slaves to run his businesses. In fact, the very bricks that made up the 14-inch thick walls of this mansion were handmade and baked by his own slaves. In order to handle that large of a work force, the slave quarters contained a bathhouse, a hospital, and a meeting house used for daycare during the week and church services on Sundays. Mr. Randolph housed the slaves in 42 cabins, whitewashed and set off the ground in case of flooding, with a vegetable plot behind each structure. The cabins had two rooms with a family living in each room.

"Chooooh!" whispered Aggie. "What was dat like? To work all day on a mansion like dis and den go home to a cabin where da whole family lived in one room? Lawd, have mercy. How could we ever have let dis kinda ting to happen in our country? How did dose white folks look into the eyeballs of dose black people and not see them as human beings? How did they make it fine to treat dem all like dey were animals?"

Her disgust at this racial and social injustice make her think of Leona. She knew there was no way Leona would ever step foot on a plantation, just for the sheer fact of how they were built. To her, places like these were icons of human oppression. Thoughts of Leona reminded her of her promise to Leona, and she slipped her phone out of her pocket to call her. Leona answered on the first ring.

"What's taken you so long to call me? I've been waiting! What's happening? Did you get to them yet?"

"Not yet," Aggie answered, trying her best to sound like she was calm. "I've gotten in da party just fine, and I'm just waiting for da DuLondes to come down to greet everyone."

"Where are you right now?"

"Never mind dat. Now listen, Leona, if I don't call you by tomorrow morning, you have to promise me you'll get dat laptop from my car."

"What do you mean, 'if I don't call you'? What's goin' on? What kinda mess've you gotten yourself into?"

"*Non, non, non,* dere is nothin to worry bout."

"Girl, you need me and Dave to come over there? Because we will. We'll hop in the car right now and snatch you right on out of there."

"Dat's not what I'm sayin," Aggie stressed. "All I mean is just in case..."

Aggie heard a creak outside the door, and she held her breath.

"Aggie?...Auntie Aggie, are you still there?"

"I gotta go," Aggie whispered. "Just get dat laptop to da right people who'll help us, you hear me?"

"I promise, I'll do whatever it takes."

"I'll call you later."

Aggie quickly hung up and listened for a few moments, but couldn't hear anything over the sound of her heart pounding in her head. She worried that if someone did look in the room and couldn't see her, surely she'd be discovered anyway, as they'd be able to hear the beating of her heart.

No other sounds. No other people. False alarm.

Aggie let out a deep sigh as the tingles of adrenaline coursed through her body. She picked up her wooden box, moved it back to its original location, and then walked deeper into the museum. There was a very small theatre room used to show a documentary about the estate, and it was pitch black inside. Whether this room was the optimum place for her to see and hear, it certainly was the best place to keep her form hidden from any onlookers. She checked her watch. 5:00pm. Two more hours.

FOURTEEN

THE OLDER CAJUN WOMAN seemed to have disappeared. Wil had waited in the White Ballroom for nearly twenty minutes for her to return, but she never came back. And while this woman appeared to be the last person in the world who'd pose a threat, he just could not take any chances. He wrote down her name, along with the contact information of a friend of his dad's who worked for the Secret Service, and gave it to Tyler, the head of his security team. Wil asked him to phone the agent, as many times as needed, until he was able to speak to him personally. Once contact was made, he was to ask the man to acquire any information he could on Agata Prejean.

Now, two hours later, he and his Confederate posse were surveying the growing crowd of guests at Nottoway. Five of the young men had been given descriptions of Agata, and were searching the entire premises to find her and bring her to Wil. At present, no one had been successful in their pursuits. The rest of his team were now watchfully roaming as they expertly dodged the dozens and dozens of large Southern Belle hoop dresses that were now filling the rooms, hallways and balconies. As Wil was performing a habitual scan of the crowd, his mom snuck up beside him.

Lottie: Doesn't this party just take the cake? I love seein all these costumes in this grand mansion. It's like we've truly been taken back in time.

Wil: Hey, Mom, you look amazing! I mean, I've never seen the movie, but you do look just like the pictures I've seen.

Lottie: How have I raised you, Wil DuLonde, and you've never seen *Gone With the Wind?* Did I completely fail you as a mother?

Wil: (*laughing*) Uhh...mom, it's a chick flick. Don't you remember? Whenever you'd pull out that DVD, it was my cue to go shoot some hoops.

Lottie: For the last time, sugar, it's not just a chick flick. It's about the Civil War, and it has fightin and killin, not to mention, all of our dear Atlanta burnin to the ground at the hand of those Yankees. And it has great heroes in it, like Rhett Butler; he's a real man's man.

Rich: (*entering the room*) Who's a real man's man? Is your mother talking about me again?

Wil: (*noticing his dad's Rhett Butler costume*) Well, that all depends upon which one of you is asking: you or Rhett Butler. And, she's trying to convince me that *Gone With the Wind* is not a chick flick.

Rich: Ha! Don't try to win that battle with her, son. Just do what I've done all these years; watch the movie with her and act like you're not sleeping.

Lottie: (*to Wil*) Oh, don't let him fool you, sugar. He loves it just as much as I do.

Rich: See? I've got her convinced.

Lottie: Richard! You cry every time Bonnie Bell falls off her horse and—

Rich: Let's not ruin the ending for him, Lottie. God know's he going to marry someone just like you who is obsessed with it and makes him watch it every year. Let's at least give him the chance to be surprised. (*whispering to Wil*) And I've never cried during that damn movie.

Lottie: I heard that. (*to Wil*) And yes he has. Every time.

Wil: (*laughing*) OK, you guys. Dad, you make a great Rhett Butler. You both look awesome; clearly the best costumes of the night. Anyway, I have an off-the-subject question for you guys. Does the name "Agata Prejean" mean anything to either of you?

Rich: No, not that I can think of. Should I know that name?

Wil: Probably not. I'm sure it's nothing. She was just a lady I met earlier tonight at the staff meeting. I wanted to know if either of you knew her.

Rich: Never met her. So, right now it's 6:45. What time are we supposed to greet everyone?

Wil: At 7:15, right here in the White Ballroom, and then again out on the balcony for everyone else.

Just then, Tyler entered the back of the ballroom and made eye contact with Wil. From the nod of his head, Wil understood that to mean Tyler had gotten the info on Agata Prejean.

Wil: I gotta go and take care of something. I hope you guys are happy with how things are going so far.

Lottie: Oh, Wil, it's beyond my expectation! Thank you so much for all you've done.

Rich: Me, too, Wil. We owe you a huge favor for pulling this off so magnificently.

Wil: Dad, it's me who'll forever owe you for all you've done for me these last months. Now go and enjoy yourselves! I gotta go back there and talk to Tyler.

Wil quickly strode across the room, anxious to see what Tyler had found out about the woman. Tyler handed him an iPad.

Wil: Did you read the info? Anything come up on her?

Tyler: Actually, no; the files just came to my inbox. Since I was right here, I thought I'd bring them to you.

Wil: Thanks. Let's walk over to somewhere it's quiet. We can go to my dad's room upstairs.

They flew up the velvet carpeted staircase and Wil led them to the door of the Nottoway Master Suite. He unlocked the door, strode in and sat down at the antique rosewood table. Wil began swiping through the files of information on his iPad. Meanwhile, Tyler took a minute to look around the large suite that consisted of a main bedroom, a sitting room, and a large modern bathroom.

Tyler: Dang! Can you imagine if this was your everyday kind of life? Oh wait...yes, you can. You grew up in the Garden District.

Wil: Dude, my house is nothing like this. We only have 12-foot ceilings; these are all 15.

Tyler: (*sarcastically*) Riiiiight, OK. Yeah. That's totally different.

Wil: Plus the square footage of this place is probably 15 of my parents' house.

Tyler: Still. That's way more than I can say. I grew up with just me and my mom in a New York ghetto, and I'm pretty sure our ceilings barely cleared 7 feet.

Wil: Whatever. That don't mean a thing. None of that money—my parents' money, I should say—could've saved my life over in Iraq. Hell, I wouldn't even be here right now if you hadn't been there to haul my ass outta that mess and put me on that truck.

Tyler: (*joking, as he walked to check out the sitting room*) Speaking of which, I've been meaning to talk to you about that...maybe some kind of monetary compensation from your dad for bringing his only son back to life?

Wil: Hey, I'm already working on it.

Tyler: (*surprised, he popped back in the main bedroom*) No way, dude! I was just messin with you. Don't you dare say anything to your dad about that. You'd've done the same for me; that's just what we do.

Wil: Chill out! I've just talked to him about helping you with your computer start up.

Tyler: I don't know what to say, Wil.

Wil: No worries, we can't talk about it now, anyway; we've got to get back to the party. Besides, this info on Prejean doesn't tell me a damned thing. She's pretty clean. She was married to a guy named Harold, who died back in the mid-90s, she worked most her life for some folks in Lafayette. Their names were Bacchus, and they also died in the 90s from a car wreck. They left behind one daughter, named Macy, who later married a guy named...*his voice trailed off as he began swiping to new info on the iPad.*

Tyler: What?

Wil: (*Under his breath*) No way!

Tyler: What?!
Wil: Well, well, well. It looks like this ol' gal isn't that clean after all. Prejean worked for a couple whose daughter eventually married Jack DuLonde, my dad's brother.
Tyler: Your dad has a brother?
Wil: A twin.
Tyler: He's got a twin?!
Wil: Yeah, that's the uncle I told you about. We think he's the reason Dad's been getting those death threats. I mean, my dad would never say it, but he sounds like a real douche-bag, into drug trafficking and all that goes with it. Dad thinks Jack owes some cartel a ton of money, and they think they'll be able to score the cash from my dad.
Tyler: And this old gal works for Jack's wife?
Wil: Well, I don't know about that. All this says is that she worked for his wife's parents until they died. But after working for them for almost 30 years, she had to have had some kind of relationship with the daughter and with Jack.

Wil shot up from his chair and pulled the small radio out of his pocket. He used it to communicate with the security team.

"Listen up, guys," Wil ordered. "I need all of you to meet with me asap at the Fountain Courtyard. Whatever you're doing right now, drop it, and be at the fountain in exactly two minutes. Out." (*to Tyler*) "Come on, let's go. I don't know what this ol' gal is up to, but I'll tell you one thing: I'm gonna find out."

With razor-sharp focus, the two young men quickly made their way to meet the others outside the mansion at the Fountain Courtyard.

FIFTEEN

AGGIE CHECKED HER WATCH. 7:10. Her stomach was a churning mess, and her adrenaline was firing so freely, she began to feel a bit light-headed. "Girl, you gotta get yourself together," she orderd. "Dis ain't no time to lose it, Agata Prejean. You gone go up dere and get to one of da DuLondes, and dat's just gone be da way it's gone be."

She took a long deep breath and stood up to try and loosen her body before making her way back upstairs to the White Ballroom. "Hal? You watchin all dis? Can you please go to St. Peter right dis very minute and ask him to send me down some extra angels to carry me through all dis? Lawd, have mercy!"

She exited the museum and glided down the hallway until she found the stairs she had descended three hours earlier. As she hurried upwards, she could hear the conversation sounds of the large party growing louder and louder. Aggie prayed under her breath that somehow her *Bon Dieu* would part the waters of this crowd for her to make it to her promised land.

When she topped the stairs, the view stopped her in her tracks. It was the same Entrance Hall she'd walked through when she found the staircase, but now it was filled wall-to-wall with guests dressed in the most beautiful and elaborate costumes Aggie had ever seen. The women were rustling around in their Southern belle dresses, yards and yards of fabrics in every color, accompanied by men dressed in regal Civil-war era suits. She felt as if she was seeing a vision from the past, and wondered if this was really what a mid-1800s ball would've looked like.

Aggie knew she couldn't tarry, however, and she scanned the room to gain perspective. At the moment, there was only one young man dressed as a Confederate soldier in the room, and he was talking to one of the guests. She checked her watch. 7:18. Right now, Richard and Lottie DuLonde were addressing the folks in the White Ballroom, and afterwards, they'd make their way through this Grand Hall to the front balcony.

Aggie spotted a server's tray half-filled with hors d'oeuvres on a nearby table. This was her ticket! She sped over to the table and picked up that tray like it was her best friend. Balancing it on her left hand, she perched the tray up in front of her left collar lapel, precisely the location where the gold doubloon was supposed to be. She began milling amongst the guests, trying to stay closely behind the largest groups possible, all the while side-stepping any of Wil's regime.

A large hand landed on her shoulder. Aggie jumped in fright, and in doing so, her silver plated tray tumbled downward, clanking loudly on the hardwood floor. Much of the crowd turned toward the noise as hors d'oeuvres spilled all around her feet. Aggie ducked down as quickly as possible, hoping the young man in the Confederate soldier costume hadn't seen her face.

"I'm so very sorry, ma'am," a man's voice said. "I was just going to ask you for an hors d'oeuvre. Please, let me help you with this."

"No, no, no!" urged Aggie, keeping her face bowed down towards the floor. "I'll get it all cleaned up, sir. You just stay up dere and keep enjoyin yourself. It won't take me but a minute, sir. See? I'm already almost done."

She scurried as fast as she could to pick up each piece of food and to wipe up the floor, the whole time praying under her breath that none of the staff or security would come over and try to help.

Aggie knew she was now going to have to make an exit. Since all the folks surrounding her had seen her tray drop, she couldn't very well stand up like nothing had happened and try to serve more of those hors d'oeuvres. In order to remain in her crouched position, she pretended some of the snacks had spilled farther away so she could scoot herself to the outskirts of the crowd, hopefully completely unnoticed.

To her left, she heard the familiar clinking of kitchen and serving activity. Holding her tray in the position to hide her missing doubloon, she darted into that room. It was filled with over a dozen servers, all dressed in white, busily emptying and refilling their trays of pre-dinner treats. She had to get out of there before any of the other servants saw her. She turned on her heel and disappeared back into the massive Entrance Hall. Scrutinizing the crowd to locate any security, she found four of them, but they were all close to the front of the hall near the enormous 11-foot main balcony doors. She could tell by the quieting of the crowd it was almost time for Richard DuLonde to welcome this section of the party.

As the assembly began to face the direction of the mansion's main entrance, Aggie wove her way to the very back of the crowd. She found a trio of tall male guests and hid behind them. Once standing in place, she could feel her knees trembling from anxiety.

The entire room went silent, and Mr. DuLonde began to greet his guests. Aggie couldn't quite make out the details of his face from her vantage point, but she knew it must be him. Both of the DuLondes were dressed in beautiful costumes, Richard as Rhett Butler and Miss Lottie as Scarlett O'Hara. Aggie smiled at how stunning both of them looked and reassured herself that folks as fine as this would certainly help a good Cajun woman like herself.

Aggie noticed all eyes in the room were focused on the DuLondes, except for the six Confederate soldiers who were facing the crowd. Their eyes were scanning to and fro to examine the guests' faces, no doubt, trying to find hers. The thought made Aggie shudder as she once again crouched over to keep from being seen. Her watch read 7:22. Judy, the woman whom Aggie had met in the parking lot, had told her that dinner was going to begin at 7:30 in a formal dining room located on the grounds, outside the main mansion. Aggie knew it was now or never. She would not be able to keep herself hidden any longer, and certainly wouldn't be able to sneak over to wherever dinner was being served.

As she heard Richard DuLonde giving directions to the crowd about their short walk to the dining room, the "Randolph Ballroom" as he called it, Aggie gathered her courage. She really wanted to exit as fast as she could in the opposite direction, but instead, she thought of Elle and Skye, and her girl, Macy. Nothing mattered more to her than them, and she was the only one who could get them away from that Jack.

She took one last long look at Miss Lottie's dress, Scarlett's flowing light green BBQ dress, and then checked the room to see if she saw any other green dresses. Knowing she would be ducking down on her way to Miss Lottie, she wanted to make sure she found her way to the correct hoop skirt. Aggie noticed only two other dresses of the same color, but they were sewn of dark evergreen velvet. She glanced back at the exact location of Miss Lottie, submerged herself in the crowd, and began threading her way through every opening in the crowd that might lead her to Mrs. DuLonde.

It was difficult for Aggie to keep track of how much distance she'd covered, as she felt lost in the moving sea of guests. However, she didn't dare stand up to look, for every step towards Miss Lottie was also a step toward Wil and his security team. Just then, she spotted the light green dress! In a matter of five or ten steps, Aggie would be able to approach the woman. She held her breath and pushed her way towards the soft, flowing green material. Aggie stretched out her hand and grabbed hold of one of the hoops in the dress.

"Oh!" said a startled Lottie, as she felt herself being pulled to a stop. She turned, expecting to see her dress caught on something, but instead found an older woman on her knees staring up at her.

As their eyes met, Aggie lost all of her words. She was breathing heavy, not from exertion but from fear, and her face revealed her despair.

"Please excuse me," said Lottie, concerned. "Ma'am, did you fall? Are you OK? Give me your hand, and I'll help you up."

Lottie reached out her hand, and although Aggie took it, she didn't use it to stand. Instead, she gripped onto Lottie's hand with both of hers and pleaded, "Miss Lottie, please. I need your help. My girls need your help. Please, you and Mr. DuLonde da only ones who can save 'em. I can't do it by myself, Miss Lottie. Please..."

"I'm sorry, I don't understand what you're talking about. Who are you?"

"I know you don't know me, but please, hear me. I know yo family, and dey need yo help! Please, Miss Lottie, you da only one who can help 'em!"

Before anyone could say another word, Aggie felt two strong arms swiftly lift her to her feet. Two Confederates were on either side of her, and Wil had now positioned himself between Aggie and his mother.

Facing Aggie, he said quietly, "It's over, ma'am."

Then to his friends, he said, "Matt, can you and C.J. escort Miss Prejean to the Iris Cottages? I have a room waiting there for her and I'll be right behind you."

"Wait a minute, Wil," said Lottie quietly. "What are you goin to do with this woman? Obviously she needs help of some kind. And how do you know what her name is?"

The guests were distracted as they were being directed toward dinner in the Randolph Ballroom, but the DuLondes spoke in hushed tones as to not draw attention.

"Mom, I said I'd take care of this. You don't need to worry about it, just go on and enjoy the rest of the evening. The party has barely started, and Dad's going to want you with him."

"But Wil-"

"Mom," Wil said firmly. "I've got this." He nodded at the guys to escort Aggie out.

"Wait, Matthew," Lottie insisted. "Don't you take another step."

Matt looked confused as to whom he should obey. But Miss Lottie had always been a second mom to him, so he chose to stay put.

"What's going on over here?" Richard asked.

"Dad, this woman here is hooked up with Jack."

"What?" Richard was surprised.

"For all we know, she's the one who's been sending those emails."

"What emails?" Lottie asked.

"It's nothing, honey," Richard said.

"What emails?" Lottie would not be refused.

"Someone has been sending some nasty messages," Richard said under his breath. "We think they're linked to Jack, that he's gotten himself in some sort of mess."

"Is *that* why there's been so much security?" she asked, looking at both Richard and Wil.

Wil referred to his dad, and Richard nodded.

"Listen to me," Lottie said firmly. "This woman is not a threat, I'm sure of it. Now I'm not goin to go over to the Randolph until I've at least talked to her. Please. Just give me a moment with her to find out what's goin on." She could tell Richard was softening. "You and Matt go to dinner and start without me, and Wil can stay with me while I talk to her. I promise, this will not take long."

Wil was disapproving, but Richard nodded his acceptance to Wil. And as Lottie walked ahead with her arm around Aggie, Richard whispered in his son's ear, "Keep your mom safe."

Wil strode to catch up and walk ahead of the women the short distance to the Iris Cottages, and listened as the women began to introduce themselves. When they arrived at the cottage, Wil opened the door for them and said, "Mom, I'll be right out here if you need me."

Lottie smiled and shook her head at what she knew was him being overprotective. The cottage room had a crisp feel with soft, light green walls and two wooden beds with curved white antique headboards and all-white bedding. The floor was a dark espresso hardwood, a nice contrast to the pastel colors of the rest of the room. In the corner of the cottage was a small dark wood kitchen table with simple plantation-style chairs.

Lottie suggested they sit on the couch and managed to sit down at, adjusting the hoops on her dress so she could get as close to Aggie as possible. Reaching toward her, Lottie took hold of both the woman's hands, she looked with great compassion into her eyes and said, "Please, honey, don't be afraid to tell me why you've come tonight. I want to help you with whatever it is that you need."

A dam of emotion broke in Aggie, as she crumbled forward and began to sob. Lottie scooted next to her, put her arms around her, and held her tightly as her back shook with her cries. Even with Aggie's story still unsaid, Lottie could feel the depth of this woman's grief, and her eyes also began to well with tears. She could sense this was a holy moment. Right now they were strangers, but Lottie knew that by the end of this night, their souls would have become knitted together.

SIXTEEN

ELLE WAS SNATCHED OUT OF SLEEP BY her dad stumbling around the hotel room, cursing as he stubbed his toe on something. Bright light poured in as he flung open the curtains. As soon as she stirred, he growled at her.

"Get up! You need to shower and fix yourself up. We're going out today, and I'm gonna take you to see some of the judges for the show on Friday. I want to give you an edge over the other girls, make sure you bring home a big prize. And wear your new dress. They need to be able to recognize you that night." Before Elle could respond, he left the room, still muttering under his breath.

As Elle shook off her grogginess, she began to notice the strong odor of the room. Stale cigarette smoke and a sour, vinegary alcohol smell. It was the same smell that often clung to her father like an invisible coat, but in this small space, it was especially nauseating. She got out of bed and tried to open the old window that looked like it had been painted shut. After quite a bit of effort, she was able to force the old window to open an inch; it wasn't as far as she wished, but it was enough to breathe in some fresh air. She only allowed herself a few moments at the window, however, because she had no idea how long she had to get cleaned up. And she certainly didn't want to face the wrath of her father if she wasn't ready on time.

Elle stepped into the very small shower and looked around for shampoo. The only container she could find was empty, so she decided to skip washing her hair. Her mom had washed it right before they left, so she thought it would be fine. It was an awful shower because the water pressure and temperature kept changing. One minute the stream was strong and hot and the next it was weak and freezing cold. She washed her body as quickly as she could and hopped out.

Elle rolled her eyes when she realized there were no dry towels. The only two the room had her dad had left as wet, crumpled wads in the corner, and she was not about to use one of those. Hoping her dad had left something dry for her, she looked until she found a washcloth on the edge of the sink. She dried herself as best she could and then put on her new pink dress.

The back of the room's front door held a long mirror, and Elle smiled at her reflection. Her soft, curly red hair fell past her shoulders, and the deep pink of the dress made her cheeks appear flushed. She wished her mom was here to see her. Everything about this trip would've been made right if only her mom would've come with them.

Elle heard Jack's key opening the hotel door, and she stood up straight so she could gain her dad's approval for her appearance. The door swung open, Jack threw a brown bag of food on the bed, stormed into the bathroom, and slammed the door shut. He didn't so much as glance at Elle. Dejected, she sat down on the bed and opened the bag of breakfast. Its contents for her were the exact same as they had been for the last few days: one bottle of milk, one bottle of water, one hard roll with butter and honey for breakfast, and one slice of spinach pie for lunch.

She chose the milk first and just as she started pulling off the bottle's tab, Jack burst out of the bathroom. "Are you stupid? Why're you wearing that new dress to eat in? You're going to get food all over it!"

"But you said to get ready and to put on this dress," Elle answered.

"I paid a lot of money for that dress and if you mess it up, little missy, there's gonna be hell to pay."

Elle wasn't sure what to do. Should she keep the dress on, like he asked her to do in the first place, or take if off until she was done eating? She wasn't sure what the right answer was, and she was afraid to make the wrong choice. She sat on the edge of the bed, looking down at her feet.

"Elle!" She nearly jumped out of her skin at his loud command. "Just eat your food, and *don't* get yourself dirty. We're leaving in a few minutes."

Elle covered her lap with a pillow and ever so carefully, and quickly, drank her milk and ate her roll.

ELLE FOUND IT DIFFICULT to keep up with her father as they briskly walked through the streets that to Elle looked more like alleyways. It was quite chilly, and Jack had only allowed her to wear a small, white button-up sweater because he didn't want a coat to cover up the new dress. In addition, he'd bought her a pair of faux-leather, pink ballet flats that were so stiff, they rubbed on the tops of her heels as she walked. Even before they'd met the first judge, her feet were already forming large blisters.

Jack entered the lobby of a small hotel, and began looking around for somebody. Elle saw the man who had been acting as his interpreter since they'd been here, and she nudged her dad to ask if that was who he was looking for. Obviously it was, because Jack ordered Elle to sit down while he crossed over to meet him. They talked briefly, and then Jack motioned for Elle to join them. Just before she'd reached her father and the interpreter man, they both turned to walk ahead of her down a hallway, Elle assumed to one of the hotel rooms.

Although this hotel was quite small, Elle wished they were staying in this one instead of the older, stinky one with the tiny shower. This place smelled much cleaner, and the carpet looked like it was newer. The trio stopped at a door with the number 145 on it. The interpreter knocked on the door. At first, the door was only cracked open, and the person inside spoke in deep whispers to the interpreter. After several exchanges, the door opened wide, and Jack motioned for Elle to walk in front of him into the room.

Inside, there were two men, a large man, who had been the one who opened the door, and a lean man wearing a suit and sitting in an armchair by the window. Elle looked up at the large man as she passed by and noticed his skin was very tan and leathery. She also thought he was the hairiest man she'd ever seen. On his head, he had thick black and gray bushy hair, and his giant arms were coated with the same bushiness. He was wearing a yellow polo shirt, stretched smooth over the massiveness of his chest, and with all three buttons undone, she could see a mound of chest hair spilling out the top. He looked like he could crush a car with his bare hands if he needed to.

The skinny man in the corner had a large glass bowl of purple and green olives placed next to him, and he was continuously popping one after another into his mouth, after which, he'd wash them down with a gulp from an over-sized glass of dark red wine. As he lifted his glass to his lips, Elle noticed his fingernails were perfectly manicured, and in her opinion, too long for a guy. He snapped a finger and motioned to have Elle step closer to him. Elle looked at her dad, who responded by giving her a stern push toward the man.

Elle went to him and stood in front of his chair. She felt awkward as he scrutinized her from head to toe, and then flicked his hand in a circle indicating he wanted her to turn around. She obeyed. After a few seconds, she could feel the man was touching her hair. He ran his fingers through it, taking his time to play with her curls. The light sensation of her hair moving across the back of her neck caused Elle to shudder, and she could hear the man behind her laugh. He tugged on her shoulder to make her face him again. Once their eyes met, he leaned forward until she could feel his hot breath on her face. Nervous, she looked down at her feet, badly wanting to back away. A few long moments passed, and the man finally reclined back in his seat.

He waved his hand again, communicating he was done with her, and Elle quickly walked to stand beside her dad. He went back to his olives and wine, and the apelike man escorted them out to the hallway. Jack, Elle and the interpreter walked back to the hotel lobby in silence.

As they exited the hotel, Jack asked his friend, "How do you think that went?"

"I've never seen him touch a girl's hair like that, so that's good. You want him on your side because he'll be the richest man at the deal," he said in his thick, Greek accent.

"It's that red hair she got from my mother-in-law," Jack said, and then added snidely, "Ha! I guess she's worth something after all. Let's go meet the next one."

Elle wondered who Jack meant with that unkind remark. *Mom is worth something after all, or I'm worth something after all?* she thought. *Or is he talking about my mom's mom?* Either way, Elle thought it was a mean thing to say, and her feelings were hurt. *Certainly, he must be talking about Mom's mom because he wouldn't say that about Mom, or me, right?* She chose to believe Jack would only say that about someone he'd never met, as Macy's mom had already died by the time her parents had gotten together.

"Speed it up, Elle!" yelled Jack.

Elle realized she was several paces behind the two men. She started to run but her heels burned so badly from the new shoes, she almost fell down. She decided she'd rather get her feet dirty than to keep wearing those awful slippers.

"I don't want these new shoes to get scuffed," she called to Jack as she stopped to take them off. "I'll put them back on as soon as we get to the next place." Shoes in hand, Elle ran to catch up with the men, and she found it much easier to keep up. She did stay focused on the cement, though, to make sure she didn't step on a piece of glass or any other sharp object that might be scattered on the roads.

Elle wondered how many judges they would be meeting, because her feet were going to be a mess if she had to walk like this all morning and afternoon. The beauty contest was only a couple days away, and if she had terrible blisters, she'd never be able to walk properly on the stage. But she was too afraid to talk about it to Jack. She knew he'd just get mad at her and tell her to suck it up. Elle hoped the hotel they were staying at had band-aids.

SEVENTEEN

GALEN WOKE UP IN PAIN. His body was completely contorted in the wooden chair, and his neck was throbbing from the position. He opened his eyes and for a moment was unsure where he was, or how he got there. This unfamiliarity caused him to shoot out of his chair like a rocket and looked wildly around the brothel room. As soon as he saw the girl, the entire night came back to him, and he tried to quiet his breathing. She had finally gone to sleep and he didn't want to wake her.

As his gaze fixed on the young girl, he slowly stepped back until he could feel the cement wall against his back. He was feeling light-headed and needed the support, but he could not take his eyes off this beautiful girl. As she slept, her face looked so pure and innocent, and he wished he could touch her somehow to let her know that everything was going to be okay.

But everything was not going to be okay.

And Galen had no idea how he was going to do anything to help her.

He looked out the window to check for the time, then instinctively pulled his cell phone out. 6:45. What time would that woman come back to fetch him? Certainly no later than 7? How do these girls keep this up all night long? He felt like he'd been there for days.

The night had progressed painfully slowly. Even though Galen had tried to communicate to the girl that he was not going to try and have sex with her, she watched him like a hawk for hours. And every time he tried to speak to her, she'd become so distressed that he vowed to remain quiet and only attempt to use his motions to communicate. He attempted to act like she wasn't there, leaning back in the terribly uncomfortable chair like it was a sofa, but the entire time, he could feel her eyes boring into the back of his head.

Forever, it seemed, went by before Galen was able to hear the slow steady breathing that only could come from sleep. He had ever so carefully adjusted himself in his chair so he could crane his neck around to verify that the girl had finally succumbed to sleep. And now, as he watched her, she was in the exact same position as she was hours ago. *She must be passed out from exhaustion,* he thought. *I wonder when the last time was that she was able to sleep when it was actually dark outside?*

Then he noticed her starting to shake. What was happening? He was sure she was asleep but her arms began to fight off an invisible predator, and then she curled up and began to weep. Her cries were not mixed with the fear from last night, but rather, they sounded like the cries of a small, helpless child. Galen could not keep himself from going to her and trying to comfort her. He knelt down on the concrete next to her bed and put his arm protectively around her, whispering, "Shhh."

He was shocked that the girl reciprocated his embrace. She melted into him, giving him the courage to hold her with both of his arms. For several moments, he rocked her gently while she cried softly. And then he said, "I promise I will help you."

The sound of his voice made the girl explode out of his arms and scamper herself into the far corner of her bed, gathering her sheet frantically to cover herself. Sheer bewilderment and terror masked her face, and in her glare was a piercing look of anger and hatred.

"I'm sorry! I'm so sorry!" Galen said, but she did not understand his words.

What just happened? Galen thought, as he backed away and held up his hands in surrender. *I thought I was getting through to her. Was I hugging her while she was still asleep?*

The sound of the doorknob rattling snapped them both out of their confusion, and Galen quickly called, "Just one minute!"

He shot up, threw off his shirt and tossed it on the chair. He turned from the girl, quickly unzipped his pants, and waited for the door to open before he acted like he was pulling his jeans on.

"Your time is up," declared the madame.

Galen turned to grab his shirt and snuck a glance at the girl while he pulled it over his head. The look of utter surprise on her face almost made Galen smile as he realized how crazy this must appear to her. How could he tell her that he is only trying to help her?

"The girl was great," Galen told the madame flatly. "She was great the whole night."

"Really?" The madame seemed very surprised. She walked over to the girl and when she lifted her hand to pat her head, the girl winced in fear. The madame giggle-snorted, "She's one of our newer girls, so she's still a bit squeamish. I'm happy to hear she did good for you."

Galen pulled out some cash from his jean pocket. "Here's some extra for you to make sure she rests today. I put her through a lot tonight." He tried to laugh, but he was not very good at playing the part of a buyer.

The woman escorted him out, turning only to lock the girl's door with the padlocks.

AS GALEN STEPPED OUT OF THE STRIP CLUB, the cool, crisp morning air met his face. It wasn't until then that he realized how dank the air had been inside the brothel. While there had been a small window in the girl's room, the closed door hindered any cross-breeze. He wondered if she was ever allowed to leave the confines of that tiny space and walk about in the fresh open air?

Galen's brother and friends from the night before were not there to greet him, and for this, he was thankful. He felt such a mass of emotions. Combine that with the exhaustion of an entire night faking sleep in an uncomfortable chair, and he honestly didn't know how he would've responded if he saw them. What he did know was, it wouldn't have been good.

Although he was carrying enough money to hail a taxi to drive him home, he chose to walk. At least he'd walk for the time being, or until he could sort through the events of the previous night. Where was he to go from here? What was he going to do? He knew he couldn't simply walk away from that brothel, wipe the memory of the girl from his mind, and go on with life as he had before. As if nothing inside him had changed.

Because everything inside him had changed.

At the end of the block, he slowed his stride to wait for an opening in traffic to cross the street. No sooner had he stopped when a young woman called out to him. She was standing a few steps behind him, under the awning of a stone building.

"You look like you could use some comfort," she said. "I'm sure I could take care of you this morning."

Galen ignored her. Without looking, he knew she was a prostitute, and he'd had enough of her kind in the last 12 hours.

"Come on, honey. What better way is there to start off your day? I promise, I'll make it worth your while, baby."

Irritated, he turned to confront her. And for the first time, he saw—really saw—the Thessaloniki red-light district. He had forgotten about his blindfold the night before and how he had only experienced these streets through his other senses. But even if this had not been the case, the light of day exposed the brothels in a starkness that could've never been seen in the dark of night.

In his imagination, Galen had thought the area would look like the kind of places he'd seen in the movies, like Amsterdam, or even like Las Vegas. He expected more lights and neon signs. But here, the brothels just looked like rows of plain, ordinary apartment buildings. And the street he was on almost seemed like the edge of it all, with several railroad tracks and warehouses on the other side. That was when he remembered he had heard the occasional distant sound of train whistles throughout the night.

He noticed all the white light bulbs that were attached to many of the buildings. He knew those lights were to communicate which ones were brothels, and which were open for business. As he scanned the horizon, he couldn't find one building with a light that was not illuminated. It disgusted him that places like this keep their doors open 24 hours a day, 7 days a week.

As far back as he could remember, Galen had held the entire class of women who chose this way of life in contempt. Prostitution was a legal profession in Greece, and he had harshly judged them for picking this as their career of choice. There were so many other noble and worthy employments to be had, and yet these women decided to embrace this kind of degrading lifestyle.

So far removed from any woman whom Galen encountered in his normal sphere of relationships, these women were easy for him to categorize into one definitive subculture; 'sub' being the operative word. Certainly, they deserved whatever consequences their profession offered, he had thought. They were the ones who showed up to do the work day after day. They were the ones who chose to dance on a pole, on a lap, or on anything else they needed to in order to pick up the highest cash tips. And at any time, they could have chosen to walk away from this grime and find a more respectable life.

But now, after spending the night in that hole-in-the-wall jail cell, he had been humbled. His frame of reference had been altered, and he could no longer keep the same degree of separation between himself and these women. He had been eyeball to eyeball with one of them, and clearly, she had not chosen this life. The look of pain and terror in her eyes was his proof; that young girl was a victim, quite possibly a slave.

How many of these other people started out like her? He could no longer assume that all these girls volunteered for their position. These were surprising thoughts for Galen. Who would ever choose this as a lifestyle? Wouldn't a woman, if she had any other option, pick anything other than the life of a prostitute? But then, if this is true, how did they get here? Why are they here, and better yet, why don't they just walk away from it? Why do they keep doing it? Not all of them are locked up like the girl he met last night.

"What's takin' you so long, honey?" the woman asked. Her voice brought Galen's focus back to her, and with a keener awareness, he noticed the hardness of the woman's features. At first glance, she appeared youngish, but a longer look revealed her ragged and worn out features, and in a few decades, she'd probably look just like that old wench at the brothel. A newfound compassion caused him to soften his response.

"No thank you, ma'am. I hope you have a good day." As he began to cross the street, he heard her call back, "You don't know what you're missing, baby!" Galen pretended not to hear, and kept walking forward.

How long would it be until that young girl in the brothel looked like this woman here on the street? The knot in his stomach tightened to the point of nausea.

"Never," he said. "She will never become that. Not if I can help it."

On his way out of the brothel, he had mentioned to the older garish woman how the girl had obeyed him well and that he wanted to come back again. She seemed surprised, and she joked with him about how much "work" it had taken to finally get the girl to submit.

At this, he burned with hatred for this small woman, wanting to lay his own hand of strength and authority all over her pasty, heavily made-up face. But not wanting to ruin his charade, he managed a smile. Then through gritted teeth, he warned her to not beat her anymore, at least not until he was done paying her visits. He made the wench swear to feed her and let her rest. Only then did he promise to come back that evening.

Galen laughed out loud. "What in the hell do I think I'm going to be able to do for this girl?" He was totally unaware he was now talking out loud to himself as he strode down the sidewalks. "My money will only pay for so many nights. And then what? Am I going to just stop showing up? Or, am I going to try to see if I can take her out of that room? Even if I did somehow get her out of there, what would I do with her? It's not like I could take her home with me! What would my mother say? No people I know would take a girl like that in their homes. So, where would she go? How would she live? For chrissake, I don't even know what country the girl is from!"

His frustration brought his pace to a run. Running was always the best escape for Galen, and even though he was not dressed for a workout, his body quickly shifted into his natural jogging rhythm. For the next hour, he was able to lose his thoughts inside the pace of his run.

HOURS LATER, Galen was walking down the street where he lived. He was hoping he would be able to sneak into the back door of his house unnoticed by any of his family. But he had no such luck. Nikkos was waiting for him.

Nikkos: My god! You look like hell!

Galen didn't look at him. He kept walking toward the house.

Nikkos: Seriously, brother. Your girl must've really worked you hard.
Galen: I don't want to talk about it.
Nikkos: Why not? I want to hear all about it! I was starting to get worried that something had happened to you because it's taken you so long to get home. But from the looks of you, obviously, she went strong all night and morning long!
Galen: Stop it, Nikkos. I said I didn't want to talk about it.
Nikkos: Why not? You should be thanking me! So tell me, did that old wench make you pay double for the morning, or did she throw that in for good measure? Because, if she gave you the morning too, man, what a deal. Maybe I'll have to go back there for myself.

That did it. In a flash, Galen had his brother pinned at the neck against a tree. Nikkos, completely caught off-guard by the physical strength of his younger brother, lost his breath.

Galen: Now you listen to me: if I ever find out you went back to that brothel, I will personally rip your balls off. Do you understand me?
Nikkos: What the hell is wrong with you?
Galen: And I don't want you talking about last night. To me, or to anyone else, for that matter.
Nikkos: Why not? It's a monumental occasion.
Galen: (*tightening his grip on Nikkos' neck*) I said what I said. Do you understand? I'm warning you, Nikkos, just leave it be.
Nikkos: OK, OK...I get it.
Galen: (*leaning into Nikkos' face*) I want you to give me your word you will never go back to that brothel.
Nikkos: Why? What happened last night to make you so crazy?

Galen shoved his arm even deeper into Nikkos' neck. Unable to speak, Nikkos managed to lift his hand up in surrender. Galen released his brother and turned toward the house.

"Never speak of it again," he hissed as he walked away.

Nikkos sat on the ground, leaning against the tree and trying to regain his breath. He'd never seen his brother come undone like this.

Galen was the one who always kept a level head, never allowing his emotions to get the better of him. Nikkos couldn't imagine what had happened inside that brothel to cause this change, but at least for the time being, he wasn't about to ask.

EIGHTEEN

"WHAT TIME IS IT?" Richard's voice whispered through the darkness. Lottie looked up from the glow of her computer. After a short and fitful attempt at sleep, she was tired, but her mind would not let her rest.

"Honey, what time is it?" he asked again. "Come back to bed."

"I'm so sorry to keep you up, baby. I'll go into the sittin room."

As Lottie was gathering her laptop, Richard swiped his phone to check the time.

"Lottie, it's 4 a.m. Did you get any sleep at all?" He was now sitting up and switching on the reading lamp beside the hotel bed.

"Don't get up. There's not need for you to get up yet. I'm goin to be just fine; I'm just takin care of some things before we meet with Aggie this mornin."

"Come here, babe. At least for a few minutes so we can talk."

Lottie reluctantly returned to bed. She knew the warmth of the comforters and the arms of her husband would try to lure her into a place of peace, but after all the information she'd just been bombarded with in the last several hours, she didn't want to feel peace. She wanted to be angry. And mournful. And revengeful.

She placed her laptop and phone within arm's reach on the nightstand before climbing back into the 18th century mahogany poster bed. The DuLonde's had rented the entire Nottoway Mansion sleeping quarters for family and friends, but of course, they were staying in the Master Suite, where the first owners used to sleep almost 200 years ago. The moment Lottie snuggled in next to her husband, her defenses melted away, and she began to cry. Richard knew to not try to "fix it." He simply held her and gently stroked her hair.

"I don't know how I'm goin to face her today," Lottie said after several minutes. "Richard, I cannot fathom how that woman is goin to handle this. When I left her last night, the look on her face was so full of hope; she looked at me with so much confidence that I was goin to be able to help her. But now that I know what's really goin on, how am I gonna tell her that this is way beyond my reach?"

Richard waited a moment to respond. He was still groggy, and he didn't want to say something that would make her leave his embrace. Besides, he was still a bit in the dark about all that had transpired last night. Lottie had left the party, right before dinner, to talk with Aggie, but only was absent about 45 minutes. Then she came back to lead the benefit ball with perfect poise. He could sense there was something bothering her, but she hid it so well behind her Southern charm, that he had no idea of the magnitude of that Cajun woman's problems until after the ball, when they were getting ready for bed. Lottie told him about Jack, and how his wife, Macy, a very close relation to Aggie, had recently died, and how Macy had pleaded with Aggie to make sure her daughters were taken care of. But the conversation was not detailed enough for him to understand why his wife was now so completely undone. And the mention of his twin brother's name always cast a heavy shadow on his heart.

As children, the two boys were inseparable and the best of friends. It wasn't until their late teens that their paths began to split as Richard grew more responsible and focused, and Jack became everything opposite. Always conniving and looking for a fast buck, Jack was out for himself, willing to do whatever he needed to make his fortune. For many years, Richard tried to bend Jack's direction, to convince him to build a more disciplined life, but his efforts were ineffective.

Shortly after high school, Jack disappeared out of Richard's life. Once, early in Richard and Lottie's marriage, a cop had shown up on their front porch, trying to gain information on Jack's whereabouts. Another time, Richard caught wind of a marriage between Jack and a girl with a more-than-modest inheritance. But after these incidences over 15 years ago, Jack seemed to have completely fallen off the grid, and Richard often wondered if his brother was still alive. Then the threatening emails began to surface, demanding the repayment of a very large sum, or else there would be harmful measures taken. Jack was definitely alive, and obviously, as slippery as ever.

"Tell me more about what's going on, honey," he said. "What's happened between last night and now that has made you so upset?"

Lottie didn't answer him, so after a few moments, Richard tried to coerce her to talk.

"It's just too much...I don't even want to hear myself say the words!" Lottie exclaimed as her sobs released again.

"Ok....Ok...," she muttered as she wiped her eyes and regained her composure. "Here it is. Last night Tyler took a laptop Aggie had brought with her. It belongs to Jack, and Macy told her everything Jack was doing was on that computer. Well, you know Tyler; it took him about twenty minutes to hack into all of Jack's emails and look through his documents. I don't know how anybody could possibly be this evil, but honey, your brother right now is taking his youngest daughter to Greece to sell her."

"What?!" Richard couldn't comprehend her words.

"He is taking her to *sell* her to a..." Lottie had to turn away to attempt to not break down into tears again. "Her name is Elle and she's only *ten years old!* He's taking her to sell her to a brothel owner!" By now Lottie was shaking from emotion. "She's ten and he's selling her to someone who is going to pay a lot of money to have sex with her! A ten year old! I don't know if she'll be one of those child brides...or a sex slave...or...I don't even know what."

Every fiber of Richard's being wanted to jump up out of the bed. Somehow maybe if he moved around he would get away from the words his wife had just spoken to him. Adrenaline began shooting off inside of his gut and he needed to spring into action. But his wife needed him more at this moment, so he suppressed the instinct to fight and tried to keep his breathing controlled.

Moments passed before either of them uttered another word. Only the sounds of Lottie's cries and sniffles filled the room.

Finally, Richard broke the silence. "When?"

"What do you mean?" Lottie asked.

"When is Jack planning to do this?" With every word Richard spoke, his level of rage mounted. "Did Tyler get that information? Is it done, or is there still time to stop him?"

"Tyler has been working all night in Wil's room. The last text I got from him is that the selling has not happened yet. I think he even used the word 'auction'? But that can't be it, I just can't believe that can be it. But I've been on the computer doing research, because this kind of thing couldn't even be happening in this day and age, right? But the information I just read was awful!" Lottie sat up and reached for her computer. "I mean, I've been hearing about human trafficking, it's not like I didn't know stuff like this existed, but look at this website, Richard, look at this!"

She opened a website and began scrolling through the many pages of statistics about human trafficking, each fact worse than the one before: $150 billion industry worldwide, $99 billion generated from the U.S.; an estimated 21 million victims worldwide, 5.5 million being children; an estimated 100,000 children trapped in the sex trade in America alone. Richard could no longer refrain, and he jumped out of bed, ready to fight. Grabbing his phone, he dialed Wil who answered on the first ring.

"Come over here now, please," Richard commanded. "And bring Tyler and that laptop."

He threw his phone onto the bed. "Damn that brother of mine! How could he have done something like this?!"

"What can we do to help them? What can we possibly do?" Lottie was desperate.

"Listen to me, Lottie," Richard resolved, "I will do everything I can to get that girl back. I will leverage any resource, or any relationship. This is not going to happen! Jack is not going to get away with this, and when I get my hands on him..."

"You're going to have to stand in line," Wil said soberly as he entered their suite with his key. Tyler was right behind him. Richard could tell by the looks of them that neither his son, nor Tyler, had slept at all.

"Both of us have been going through these emails," Wil was referring to Jack's laptop, "and we've gotten a pretty clear idea of where he is and what he's planning to do."

"Show me," Richard said.

The three men sat down at the nearby table, and Tyler began from the beginning of the email chain. The emails had begun a few months ago, and each one in the thread gave more information about Jack's scheme.

For the first time in hours, Lottie was able to take a deep breath, knowing her men would find a way to stop the horrors of Jack's scheme. "I'll make sure y'all have plenty of coffee and a big breakfast," she said. And she realized she was now looking at these three very capable and well-resourced men with the same look Aggie had towards her last night: one of hope.

NINETEEN

THE CARDS ZIPPED THROUGH AGGIE'S FINGERS as she expertly shuffled the deck. Skye and Aggie sat across the table from one another as the two went head-to-head in a Canasta championship round. It was summer, and Elle was napping in a hammock on the back covered porch. With quick flicks of her wrist, Aggie dealt the cards so swiftly, you barely saw them in flight as each one sailed across the table to its rightful owner and in a perfect pile.

Aggie: Now why you tink you gotta get yourself one a dem birds for a pet?

Skye: How can you deal and talk at the same time? I can never make it work. If I talk, then I deal the wrong number. If I count in my head, then I can't talk. How do you do that?

Aggie: *Mon Sha,* MawMaw's been dealin cards since before I could walk. It's just da way it was in my family. My Papa loved to play cards.

Skye: I wish I could've met him, your daddy.

Aggie: He was a great man. He with le *Bon Dieu* now, probably up dere beatin the Holy Trinity at Caribbean Stud Poker! Ain't nobody ever beat da man at dat. Now, Skye-girl, answer me dis question: why you tink you gotta get yourself one a dem white birds?

Skye: I don't know. I've always wanted a Snowy Egret. They're white and beautiful, and their songs are so pretty.

Aggie: It ain't enough to see dem out in da trees? To hear 'em singin to God every mornin? Why you want to go and put one in a cage?

Skye: So it can be mine. I want to have one for a pet. Haven't you ever wanted to have a pet?

Aggie: Well, sure. I had all kinda pets when I was a girl, but only da one's dat are supposed to be pets. Dogs, cats. God made dose animals to be pets. But a bird? A bird's not supposed to be a pet, *Sha*. Sure, I know folks who've kept birds as pets, locked 'em up in a cage just so dey can look at 'em, but I could never do it. Just cuz folks do someting, it don't make it right.

Skye: Why? What would be wrong having a bird as a pet?

Aggie: Skye-girl, bird's are supposed to be free to fly throughout da whole entire sky, dat's how *le Bon Dieu* made 'em. You take away dere flight, you take away dere very life. It's just not right. Besides, a bird's not all dat pretty just sittin in a cage. *Chooh*, but when dey're up in da sky with dey're wings outstretched, glidin above da trees; now dat's beauty at it's best. Ain't nothin like it.

Skye: I guess...

Just then Aggie and Skye heard a muffled scream from the back porch. Like lightening, Aggie jumped up from the table to check on Elle, but when we got there, she saw a man struggling with her and carrying her away! Panicked, Aggie tried to run to the catch the man, but her legs felt as if they were filled with sand, and she couldn't get to Elle fast enough.

Coming from the house, Aggie heard Skye scream, "MawMaw Aggie!" and she knew Skye was in trouble, too. Her heart raced as she got back on the porch but now the door to the kitchen was locked! She could hear struggling and fighting going on, but Aggie could not get to Skye either. Not knowing what else to do, Aggie frantically knocked on the door over and over, as she felt her world closing in on her.

Aggie's eyes popped open as she heard the sound of a door knocking. She was in a cold sweat and her heart felt like a caged animal trying to escape her chest. Rubbing her hands over face to try and get her bearings, she could not make out why someone would be knocking on her bedroom door. After a few deep breaths which helped calm her down enough to focus her eyes, everything came back to her. Nottoway. The DuLondes. Last night's ball. Her meeting with Lottie.

"Aggie, dear?" a voice came through the cottage front door. "It's me, Lottie. Can I come in for a moment?"

"Oui, oui!" Aggie called back. "Just a moment, give me just a moment."

Aggie, still dressed in her white uniform from the night before, got up and answered the door. Lottie was standing on the porch with a small tray of coffee and food, along with three large shopping bags looped around her forearms.

"Lawd have mercy, *Sha*. Come in here, and let me help you with dose tings."

Aggie took the silver tray from Lottie and carried it over to the small wooden table in the sitting area by the windows. Lottie set the shopping bags down on the bed that Aggie had slept in, and then took off the scarf she had around her neck.

"Good morning, Miss Aggie. Can you believe this cold spell we've been havin? It's so strange! Why, I almost cried the other mornin when I woke up and saw snow on the ground. I'd *just* planted some spring flowers, and now I don't think they're goin to make it. It's crazy. Did you sleep well? I hope you were able to sleep after all the fuss last night. Was your bed comfortable?"

"*Oui, oui,* Miss Lottie. Don't worry about a ting; everyting was just right. But I sure would love to have some of dis coffee, can I pour you a cup?"

"Please, Miss Aggie, just call me Lottie, or Charlotte, whichever you prefer. And, yes, I've already had some coffee, but you feel free to serve yourself. I know I've already said this but I have to again: I am so very sorry about how Wil treated you last night—"

"*Mais, non, non, non,*" Aggie interrupted. "Wil is a good young man. He was just lookin out for his mama. Besides, he was very respectful to dis ol' Cajun woman."

"Thank you for those words," Lottie smiled. "Miss Aggie, we've obviously got some things to talk about." She took Aggie's hand and led her to sit on the side of the bed. Then she sat next to her and looked solemnly into her eyes.

"Honey, I'm not goin to beat around the bush with you; we've got a lot to accomplish today. After you told me your story last night, Wil and one of his army buddies, Tyler, took that laptop from your car. Ty specializes in computer hackin and all that kind of stuff I'll never understand, and they were up the entire night gettin information about Jack...and what he's gotten Elle into."

Aggie noticed Lottie's chin was starting to quiver, and she stopped talking in order to regain her composure. She cleared her throat and began talking again, this time slower and more deliberately.

"I've gotta warn you, Miss Aggie, the details Wil and Tyler have uncovered are not goin to be easy for you to hear. But I want you to know, and I give you my solemn word about this, we all are goin to do everything in our power to get both your girls back to the U.S.

"You don't know this yet, but my Wil was a tremendous asset to our government when he served in the Special Forces. He's just like his daddy, with a work ethic like no other, and he rose up in the ranks very quickly. The only reason Wil is home now is because several months ago, he was severely injured in a terrible Al Qaeda attack. He almost died."

"Oh, Miss Lottie," Aggie said. "I'm so sorry. Dat must've been awful for you and Mr. DuLonde."

"Yes; it was a very stressful time for all of us, to say the least. But the reason I'm tellin you this is because I want you to know that if anyone can come up with a strategy to get Elle, it's Wil. He's an expert in this sort of thing. In addition, my husband and my daddy have connections with top government officials, and when it comes to family, they'll have no problem usin their influence to get done whatever they need done. Miss Aggie, are you alright with that?"

Aggie nodded her head.

"Good." Lottie said as she looked at her watch. "Right now, it's almost a quarter past seven. What we'd like to do is for you to come and join us up in our suite so we can talk about...well, all that's goin on. We'd like to start right at 8:00, do you think you can be ready by then?"

Aggie smiled, a little sheepishly, and glanced down at her white uniform. "*Mais oui*, I don't have much to do to get ready."

Lottie's eyebrows sprang up. "Oh, I almost forgot! I knew you hadn't expected to stay overnight, so I took the liberty to buy you a couple things, I hope you don't mind. Everything is in those three bags."

"*Chooooh!* Miss Lottie, you didn't have to do dat—"

"Remember, it's *just* Lottie, and it was nothing."

Curious, Aggie asked, "How did you know what size to buy?"

Lottie laughed and said, "Oh, honey, it's a god-given gift of mine. I just got a knack for it; with one look up and down, I can tell you the size of any woman, her garments, her undergarment, *and* her shoe size, give or take a 1/2 size. Besides, all these things are from Chico's, and their active wear is nice and stretchy, so it's easy to size. I hope you like everything I got, or I should say, that my assistant got. She was up at the crack of dawn making her friend, who's the manager at the Baton Rouge Chico's, open her store so we could get these for you before you woke up."

Aggie wasn't sure how to accept such a generous gift. She said softly, "I don't know what to say, Miss Lottie."

"Please trust me, Miss Aggie, after all you've been through, it's the very, very least I could do. Now you gotta get yourself freshened up before our meeting at 8. Neither Richard nor Wil know how to act if someone's late to one of their meetins. That tray over there has fresh coffee and water, along with a full breakfast. We'll only have fruit and snacks at the meetin, so please have your fill before you come. I'll see you then."

Lottie leaned over to give Aggie a hug. "You're not alone, Aggie; we're in this together now." Then she waved and exited the room.

Aggie sat down on the bed and breathed. She found it peculiar that she could feel such heavy dread and yet also sense the lightness of hope simultaneously. But there was no time to analyze; she could not be late for the meeting.

TWENTY

AGGIE POURED HERSELF A CUP OF COFFEE and sat down to try and comprehend the good fortune that was coming her way. "*Bon Dieu*, I don't know how to tank you for settin up dis meetin with da DuLondes. *Merci, merci, merci*. Dis is all beyond what I ever could've asked. I gotta believe you have dis ting in da palm of your hand and you gone help us get Elle back safe and Skye home from her school."

She took a long drink of coffee and thought of Lottie's words, 'Miss Aggie, the details are goin to be hard for you to hear.'

Lawd have mercy, I hope I have da strenth to bear it all. I cannot stand to tink dat little Elle might be brought to harm. And I swear, I'll kill dat Jack if he's to blame for it all.

She shuddered at the truth of that thought. Never before had she felt an honest desire to take away a human life; it went against everything she'd ever confessed to believe. But if Jack truly had brought evil upon her Elle, Aggie would not think twice about breaking the 6th Commandment.

Aggie finished her coffee and breakfast, washed up, and then emptied out the Chico's bags. Aggie was shocked at how many items Lottie had purchased for her. There were three active wear suits, one black, one purple, and one gray. All the pants were the same style but each corresponding jacket was designed differently. Six matching shirts, three short-sleeved and three long. Three beautifully patterned scarves. A very nice black leather purse paired with a pair of black leather clogs that fit Aggie's feet perfectly. And just as Lottie had said, everything, including the undergarments were sized correctly.

"*Choooh!* Hal, you're not gone recognize your Aggie in dese clothes. Dat woman went and spent over a tousand dollars on dis ol Cajun like it was nuttin'! And every single one of dese garments is exactly what I'd pick for myself. Ha! Only it'd all be from Lafayette at da Acadia Mall T.J. Maxx...and it probably wouldn't be Chico's. I gotta call Leona and tell her about dis!"

Aggie grabbed her cell phone, and noticed there were five texts from Leona sent late last night, each progressively more urgent for Aggie to respond. "Oh, I'm gone be in trouble," she said as she pressed 'send.' There was barely one ring before Leona answered.

"Oh thank God! Why didn't you text me back last night? Where are you? Are you in jail?!"

Aggie couldn't help but laugh, "Leona, calm yourself. I'm so sorry I didn't text you back; I must've been asleep already. No, I'm not in jail; I'm the furthest from jail I could be!"

"What happened? Tell me, tell me!"

"Well, at first I wasn't sure how I was gone get to Lottie, but I don't have da time to go through all dat...I'll fill you in when I get home. But dat Lottie, she's an angel sent from God in heaven. She listened to everythin, and she promised to help me get little Ellie back, and get Skye-girl back from her school in London. She even had her assistant go and buy me about a tousand dollars of clothes at Chico's 'cause she knew I didn't bring clothes with me last night."

"Why did she buy you so many? Those rich folks don't know how to keep it simple. You're only there for a day!"

"Lottie is just dat generous. *Choooh,* I could go on a cruise with all she got me."

"Oh, honey, I can't believe it! Do they know where Jack is? Have they talked to him? Is Elle alright?"

"Girl, I need you to get on your knees and pray. She came dis mornin and told me dat her boys found out some information dat sounds pretty awful. I'm supposed to meet with dem all to hear about it in just a few minutes. I feel sick to my stomach."

"Auntie, you get ready for your meetin...I'll be here prayin for you. Call me as soon as you know anything."

"I will, *Sha*. Love you, and tank you for da prayers."

"Love you, too, Auntie."

Aggie sighed as she disconnected, saying a few prayers of her own. Then she selected the black outfit with the light blue shirt, and as she dressed, she tried to think of the last time in her life, if there ever was one, when each item on her body was brand new. She couldn't think of one and wondered if this was an every day occurrence for Lottie DuLonde. Checking the clock, Aggie realized she only had 10 minutes to make it to the meeting on time. She grabbed a scarf to wrap around her shoulders and left the cottage.

As she stood on the porch, Aggie took a moment to take in the magnificent view of the white Nottoway Mansion. She'd always read Nottoway was the largest antebellum mansion in the entire South, and from her vantage point, she believed it to also be the most beautiful. The only mar, and it was an enormous one, was the fact this historic treasure was built on the back of Southern slavery. The chilly morning air caused Aggie to tighten her scarf-turned-shawl around her shoulders, and she walked briskly around the Iris Pond toward the enormous historic home.

Aggie had forgotten to ask Lottie where to enter the mansion, so she decided her best bet would be to go through the huge front doors. Because Nottoway now functioned as a full-service bed and breakfast, at the very least, there ought to be a receptionist at a front desk. The door was unlocked, and sure enough, Aggie was greeted by a young woman dressed in a sharp suit.

"Good morning, you must be Mrs. Prejean," she said. "It's so nice to meet you. I'm Rebecca, Mrs. DuLonde's personal assistant. I'm here to show you to the DuLondes' suite."

"Rebecca, are you da one who got up so early to go and buy all dese clothes?"

"Oh yes! Don't you worry about that, Mrs.Prejean, I live for that kind of stuff! Plus, the manager of that Chico's is my mom's bestie; they went to high school together. She lets us in after hours—or before hours, in this case—all the time."

"Well, tank you very much, *Sha*."

"Are you Cajun?" Rebecca asked.

"To da bone," Aggie proudly replied.

"Oh, that's so cool! My finance's granddaddy, Mr. Floyd; he's a

Cajun, too. He lives in Lafayette and absolutely lives for Mardi Gras every year, so you know he was in heaven for the last several days."

"Honeychile, did you know I'm from Lafayette?"

"Are you serious? I cannot wait to tell Greyson, that's my fiance's name. Where do you live?"

"North Lafayette, on Bellot Street."

"Did you get out to any of the parades this past weekend? Lafayette gets almost as insane as New Orleans during Mardi Gras weekend!"

"When my husband, Hal, was alive, we never missed a parade, not even one. But dis year, I wasn't able to get out dere."

"Oh, you sure missed a good one! Greyson's granddaddy is a member of two or three krewes, and is one of the only people to ever have been named King of Lafayette's Mardi Gras Parade *twice*."

"Go to bed, *Sha!*" exclaimed Aggie. "Mardi Gras King *twice?* Dat's unheard of."

"I know, and Mr. Floyd is not shy to tell you all about it, too. He is the oldest living float rider in Lafayette, and he *loves* to throw on the floats during the parades: beads, doubloons, coins, candy, whatever. Mr. Floyd claims that he can pick a target over 30ft away, throw the Mardi Gras beads, and hit his bull's eye every single time." She stopped walking. "Oh, look! We're already at their room, and I've talked the entire way. I'm so sorry, Mrs. Prejean. (*whispering*) I kinda do that a lot. So anyway, this is the master suite, and it's where Mr. and Mrs. DuLonde stayed last night; it's the actual bedroom of the people who lived here back in the Civil War days. Isn't that so cool? And all the furniture is the original! If you look closely, the posts of the bed are totally hollow, supposedly where the Randolph's would hide away treasures during the war."

The door of the bedroom opened, revealing Lottie.

"I thought I heard your voice out here, Rebecca," said Lottie.

"I'm sorry, Mrs. DuLonde, you know me, I got to talking to this nice lady—"

"I know, Rebecca, bless your heart. You do love your words, don't you, sugar?" Lottie said. She looked to Aggie. "I'm so glad you're here, Miss Aggie; we've got some nice warm coffee and fresh beignets waitin for you. Thank you so much, Rebecca, I'll text you if I need you for anything else."

"Yes, ma'am. Nice meeting you, Mrs. Prejean," said Rebecca as she left the room.

"Please come on in, Miss Aggie, and make yourself at home." Lottie led Aggie into the Master Suite.

The room was a beautiful room with slate blue painted walls fully trimmed in white. The high ceilings were dressed with dazzling white plasterwork and had an elegant crystal chandelier hanging down the center. All the furniture was a rich rosewood, including an oblong table set to serve five that seemed too big to have been part of the normal bedroom set-up. Aggie assumed it had been moved in the suite just for this meeting.

"You look beautiful in your new outfit, Miss Aggie. Do you like them?"

"Oh, Miss Lottie, you bought me too much! Dis ol' woman don't need dat many clothes."

"Please listen to me, Aggie. God has blessed my family with more money than we could ever need...what good is it if I can't do things like this? Please accept it all as a personal gift from me, and as my thanks for you takin the courage to come all this way and open up your life to Richard and me. Please."

"Tank you, Miss Lottie."

Lottie gestured to an armchair for Aggie to have a seat. "Rich, Wil and Tyler are in the sittin room workin on your laptop," Lottie said as she sat across from Aggie, instinctively crossing her legs at the ankles and placing her hands formally in her lap. She would've seemed completely composed were it not for her thumbs that kept nervously crossing over each other. "Tyler is Wil's SOF buddy, and he's the one I told you about who can do just about anything with a computer."

"What's SOF?" Aggie asked. She could sense the tension in the room, and felt her heart beating more rapidly than usual.

"Oh, SOF. That means Special Operations Forces. Tyler served with Wil during his last deployment in Iraq, and in fact was responsible for saving Wil's life. He's a Yankee, but we love him."

She tried to squeeze out a laugh, but only managed an awkward chuckle. After a moment of thick silence, Lottie stood and called to the men, announcing Aggie's presence. Wil emerged from the connecting room and reached out to take Aggie's hand.

"Good morning, Miss Aggie. I'm so sorry, if we got off on the wrong foot last night. I'm glad you came here and that my mom got to spend so much time with you..." Wil's voice trailed off because he could tell Aggie wasn't listening to a word he was saying. She was too distracted looking up at something past his face, and she now had an expression of shock, like she was facing a ghost.

Wil turned to see what she could possibly be staring at, but he only saw his dad standing behind him. Lottie was the first to figure it out. "Miss Aggie," she said, "Does Richard still look *that* much like Jack?"

Aggie seemed in a trance as she stood to greet him. "Sorry...I'm so sorry," she whispered, her eyes still hanging on Richard's face. "It's not right to stare, but I just cannot stop. Mr. DuLonde...you're da spittin image of dat Jack. Da black hair, da blue eyes, da mouth..." She stopped for a moment trying to absorb the likeness. "I mean, I saw da pictures on da computer, but I had no idea dat eyeball to eyeball you'd look so much like dat man."

"Miss Aggie," said Richard gently, "I cannot tell you how grateful I am you came to find both Lottie and me." He slowly stepped toward her and reached out both his hands to take hers. His voice cracked with emotion as he said, "I don't know how I can possibly apologize for the pain my brother has caused you and your family. I knew Jack had gone down a terrible road, but not until last night did I know the depths of his wicked life. And how many people he's hurt."

Aggie's eyes, still gaping, filled with tears. Aware of his towering height, he bent down a bit towards her and said, "I promise you, Miss Aggie, I'm nothing like Jack, and I will do everything in my power, I'll use all my influences, I'll pay any amount of money, I'll do anything I need to, to get your girls back home. Lottie, Wil and I are committed to you, Miss Aggie, and we won't give up until we've got them back home."

Beginning to weep, she almost lost her balance, but Richard was right there to catch her. His long arms swallowed her up, and for a moment he comforted Aggie. Lottie slid over to take Aggie from his arms and lead her to her seat at the table, speaking loving encouragement the whole time.

Once Aggie was seated, Lottie picked up the coffee server from the center of the table and filled Aggie's cup. She then turned to the others.

"We've got so much to discuss, how about we get started?" Lottie said. "But first, let's take a few moments to enjoy some coffee and beignets before they get cold. That'll give us a bit of time to get better acquainted with each other."

As they approached the table, Lottie had a specific agenda for their seating. Richard sat at the head, Lottie to his left and Aggie had been seated to his right. She asked Wil to sit next to herself and for Tyler to sit next to Aggie. Once seated, the two Nottoway waiters began pouring coffee and serving the piping hot beignets.

TWENTY-ONE

FOR TWENTY MINUTES, the five sat at the oblong table, chatting and giving further introductions. How Hal and Aggie had met, how Richard and Lottie had met, what schools Wil had attended, Tyler and Wil's time serving together in the Special Forces. And then, as if some unseen, unheard alarm had sounded, the conversation reached a lull and an uncomfortable silence blanketed the room. The only sound was the tapping from Tyler on Jack's laptop. For the last few minutes of the conversation at the table, he had been distracted, appearing to have a renewed sense of urgency to his probing.

Aggie saw Richard nod towards Lottie, an obvious cue that it was time to delve into the information they'd found about Jack. Lottie asked the waiters to clear the dishes from the table and to leave behind fresh carafes of coffee and water. The last server placed a new basket of hot beignets next to the drinks before checking with Lottie to see if there would be anything else they needed. Lottie excused the waiter and watched as he exited their room. She waited until he was completely gone to speak.

"Miss Aggie," said Lottie slowly as she picked at the corner of the cloth napkin she'd just neatly folded, "we need to fill you in on what the boys have found out about Jack and Elle. I know I told you this earlier in your cottage, but please let me reiterate. The facts you are about to hear are unthinkable. But even as you listen, please keep in mind that you are in the best possible hands."

Aggie nodded her head and felt a corset of anxiety tightening her chest.

"Wil," said Lottie. "Can you please tell us, startin from the beginnin, everythin you and Tyler got from that laptop?"

"Yes, ma'am," he said. He looked diagonally across the table at Aggie. "Miss Aggie, last night when I was asking you questions about Jack, you told me that he had recently gotten into the business of buying and selling horses."

"Dat's right. Dat's when tings began to turn around for dem with money. It was how Macy and Jack were able to send Skye to dat school in Europe."

"Right." Wil pressed his lips together, taking a moment to find the right words. "Miss Aggie, The first thing you need to know is that Jack has never been in the business of buying and selling horses. He might have used words to make you believe that he was, but the truth is, that was all code to cover what he was really doing."

"What was dat *peeshwank* really doin? Ain't nuttin gonna surprise dis old Cajun woman."

"What he was really into was the buying and selling of girls."

"Well now, dat night I found Macy, she was tryin to tell me somethin 'bout how he was doin dat. But I don't tink I really understand what all dat means."

"Maybe you've heard a term being thrown around on the news these last few years? What Jack was really doing is called human trafficking, sex trafficking in this case, and it goes on all over the world. Probably has been going on from the beginning of time. Basically, what happens is, a girl is sold to someone, and that someone uses her to make money by forcing her into prostitution, pornography, and the like. You don't have to think too hard to imagine the horrors these girls face.We're uncertain how he got involved in this, or who even were the victims of his crimes, but we do know the names and contact numbers of the people he's been working with. And we know that he is selling the victims to brothel owners in Greece."

"Lawd have mercy," Aggie whispered as she leaned back into her seat. "Dat Jack got da devil in him to do such a ting...even if it was to try and send Skye to dat school. Macy would never've gone along with someting like dis, if she knew. *Mais,* Skye don't need to be dere if *dat's* how it's bein paid!"

"Wil," Tyler said.

Wil motioned to Tyler as if to say that he should wait to give input. "Miss Aggie," Wil continuted, "What we do know is that the next victim in this is Elle. He's taken her to Greece to sell her."

"Wil," Tyler said a bit more firmly, but Wil gave him back a subtle shake of his head.

"I'm sorry, but you have dat all wrong," Aggie insisted, "Jack took Elle to London to visit her sister at her new school."

"Wil, you *need* to look at this," Tyler said sharply. "Right now." And Tyler slid the laptop over in front of Wil. He quickly got up from his seat to flip through the information he'd just discovered.

Aggie felt it impossible to take a deep breath as all the focus at the table was toward Wil and Tyler. She tried to take a drink of her water, but even her sip of water felt like she was swallowing sand.

Wil's face went white and his eyes looked shocked. Lottie had only seen this expression a few times in Wil's life, and these occasions were only the grimmest of circumstances. She wondered if Tyler had just uncovered the fact that it was too late to help Elle.

"What made you look for this?" asked Wil.

"Well, as we were sitting here, and Aggie was talking about the girls, something just didn't seem to add up to me," Tyler said. "There was one email that I'd flagged last night to go deeper into, and so I followed the hunch, and, well...there it all was."

"What is it, son?" Richard asked.

Wil looked up at his dad with bewilderment. "Dad, she looks just like Madison," he whispered. To this, Richard got up and stood next to Tyler. Tyler spoke into his ears, but too softly for Lottie or Aggie to hear.

"What? Please tell us," Lottie urged.

As Tyler slid the computer over to show Richard what he'd found, Wil quickly reined in his emotion and looked across the table at Aggie.

"Miss Aggie, there is no way to say this to you other than just to say it. Skye is not at an art school in London. Last night we found emails that allowed us to know Jack had been dealing in trafficking for some time, but we didn't know who the girl, or girls, were that he sold. But just now as we were talking, Tyler found an older email account of Jack's that shows us that six months ago, he didn't take Skye to London to go a school....he took Skye to Greece and sold her. She was his first victim."

Lottie gasped as her eyes filled with tears. She reached across the table and took Aggie's hand in hers. There was a long moment where no one could find any words big enough to respond to such a harsh and painful truth.

Aggie removed her hand from Lottie's and said politely, "I'm sorry, but dat's just not true. And Wil, dat's an awful ting to say. I know Jack's bad, I mean, I've seen him do some pretty awful tings, but dis? I just can't believe dat he'd sell his own flesh and blood, his own little girl, like dat."

Wil looked has his mom to see if there was anything she could say to help.

"Aggie, listen—" Lottie whispered, barely keeping herself together.

"No!" Aggie insisted. "*You* listen. You wrong! Dat bastard did *not* sell my Skye! Besides, Macy would get emails all da time from Skye tellin her how happy she was in dat school. *Choooh*, I even got a few emails from her; I saw 'em with my own two eyes. You wrong! You all are *wrong!*"

Tyler interjected slowly, "Miss Aggie, you *did* get emails from Skye, but Skye didn't send them; Jack did. They were generated from this laptop. He had made a fake email account and he was the one who actually wrote and sent those email letters. Miss Aggie, if you'd like, I can pull them up on right now and show them to you."

Aggie didn't answer; she was too dumbfounded. She simply sat in her chair, eyes focused on the table, head wagging back and forth. After a few moments, she spoke.

Aggie: (*under her breath*) I'm gone kill dat Jack.

Lottie: Excuse me, Miss Aggie?

Aggie: (*louder*) I said, I'm gone kill dat Jack!

Wil: I promise you, Miss Aggie, Jack will pay for what he's done. I'll see to that.

Aggie: So what you're tellin me is dat Skye has been workin in a brothel all dis time? What a *petite fille* like her gonna do in a place like dat? Cook and feed da hookers? Clean da rooms? What?

Lottie: I don't know. We're not going to know exactly what she's been doin until we rescue her, right Wil? We can hope for the best, but truthfully, she's been gone for over 6 months now, so we're also going to have to prepare ourselves for the worst.

Aggie: What you mean by dat?

Lottie: (*slowly*) From the research I was doing last night about human trafficking, the girls are not being sold to work in the brothels as servants. They are sold to be sex slaves. It's very possible, Miss Aggie, in fact most likely, that they've been forcin Skye to...*her voice trailed off, unable to say the words.*

Aggie just sat there continuing to shake her head.

Aggie: No. (*pause*) No. (*pause*) *Main non*, why Jack take Elle, den? Can you tell me dat? He took Elle to go and visit Skye, so she can't be in one a dose brothels. If Skye has already been sold, den why'd he spend all dat money to take Elle on da trip with him?

Rich: Miss Aggie, my brother has been lying to you all. This is what Wil has been trying to tell you this morning. He's not taking little Elle over to Greece with him to visit Skye. He's taking her there so that he can sell her too.

Aggie: (*exploding*) What?! What's wrong with you people? Ya'll *motier foux* (half crazy), sayin sometin like dat! She's just ten... Who's gone buy a tiny ten year old?! What you gonna do with a girl dat young? Dis crazy! Ya'll crazy! None o' dis is true. Miss Lottie, why you bring me here to listen to all dis? I thought you were a nice woman, actin like you care bout me, buyin me all dese fancy clothes, but dis whole ting is just to torment me! Why ya'll tryin to do dis to me? Lawd, Lawd, Lawd! I got da *Mal au Couer* (I need to vomit)!

Aggie looked frantically around the room looking for a toilet. She ran to the bathroom and slammed the door.

The rest sat at the table in silence for several moments. Lottie, with tears streaming down her face, looked over at her husband. She could see he also was struggling not to break down.

"I cannot fathom how difficult this all must be for that woman," he said, choking back tears. "She's finding out, all in a matter of a couple days, that everyone she's held dear has been taken from her. And worse, that those two young girls are being terribly abused in the worst way possible."

After a few more minutes passed, Lottie said, "It sounds like she's gotten quiet in there. I'll go and see if there is anything I can do to help her." She poured a glass of water for Aggie, walked over to the bathroom, and tapped lightly on the door. "Miss Aggie?" Lottie could hear the woman crying. "Miss Aggie, I've brought some nice cool water for you, may I come in for a bit?"

Lottie waited, but Aggie did not answer. Lottie made the executive choice to go in anyway, and she slowly opened the door. "Miss Aggie?" she barely whispered as she entered.

Aggie was sitting on a closed toilet, elbows in her lap, and head buried in her hands. She didn't look up when Lottie came in, but she did acknowledge her by softly saying, "I'm so sorry, Miss Lottie, I don't usually raise my voice to folks like dat."

"Don't you even think about apologizin to me, Miss Aggie," Lottie said as she came and sat at her feet. "I cannot imagine what it must be like to be hearin this kind of information. If my babygirl was here, I think I'd just die on the spot to know she was trapped in a world like that."

"What you mean, 'if my babygirl was here?' You and Mr. DuLonde got a daughter, too? I thought you only had Wil."

Lottie sighed and dropped her eyes from Aggie's. "We did have a daughter, a precious girl named Madison Jayne. After Richard and I had Wil, we tried and tried to have another baby but we couldn't seem to make it work. After several years of tryin, I finally fell pregnant with a little girl. But when she was 12 she was diagnosed with cancer. She went through treatments and eventually the cancer went into remission, and we were all overjoyed. But then a year later, it came back with a vengeance and within only a few months, she was gone. Exactly three years ago. She's the reason Richard and I throw this benefit ball every year. If little Madison was alive, she'd be turnin 16 this year; just a little older than your Skye."

"Ooh, honeychile, dat's so sad. I'm sorry you had to go through dat. Dey's nuttin like losin a baby...nuttin else dat can cut dat deep."

"Sometimes I think Wil took it the hardest. He was always her big brother and protector. When the cancer came back, he had just gotten stationed overseas and he was only able to get back just hours before she died. I know that haunts him and he thinks if he'd've been here, he could've saved her somehow. Ever since Madison was born, Wil was always tryin to save her from everythin."

"Harold and I tried and tried to have kids, too. For years. But nuttin ever took; I just couldn't hold any dem babies in past da first ten weeks. But Macy was my girl, 'specially after her own folks died, and dose girls of hers are my grandkids. Dey not my flesh and blood, but dey's still my girls."

"Yes, I can see that." Lottie reached up and laid her hand on Aggie's knee. "Sometimes the truest family is not blood-born, Miss Aggie, it's heart-born."

"Dat's true, Miss Lottie. You know dat's true."

"Listen, honey, I do want you to hear a glimmer of light about everything. Elle has not been sold yet; the auction that Jack—"

"Auction?!"

"Yes, I'm sorry. That's how they sell the girls sometimes; in an auction. And that event is not until this Friday afternoon, so there is still time to keep her safe. Tyler found many of the details on Jack's laptop, and from readin all his emails, they have a pretty good idea about where in Greece they are and who it is they're lookin for. It's a city called Thessaloniki, and apparently, there is a huge market for girls there."

Aggie took a long drink of water. "Is dat why Jack went all da way over dere?" she asked.

"Wil thinks Greece was just where Jack happened to know someone. The emails show he has a friend who knows exactly how to connect him with the right people there. Also, I think I need to tell you that after this trip with Elle, Jack was probably never comin back here again. He mentioned in one email that after he got all his money from...well, from takin Elle over there, he wasn't comin back to the States."

"He was just gonna leave Macy for dead, wasn't he? After he done used all da money her folks left her, he was just gonna leave her for dead. He's da devil's chile for sure, dat Jack."

"But listen, Aggie, Wil's formulating a plan. Because of the info Jack left in his emails, he's almost 100% sure he'll be able to get to Elle before she disappears. I'm sure it was an oversight for Jack to have left that laptop behind, but still, I'm very surprised at how much detailed information the boys were able to find. Jack didn't delete any of his emails, and many of them are very incriminating; not just about the things he's doing with the girls, but other illegal activities as well."

"Mais, dat *peeshwank* ne'er been da brightest bulb in da bunch. What about my Skye-girl?"

Lottie exhaled a long breath. "I don't have the answers to that, but I'm sure that's goin to be a little more complicated. We're going to have to see what kind of strategy Wil and Tyler can work out. That might be a little like tryin to find a needle in a haystack. But even if he doesn't find her while he's there, we won't lose hope...we'll not give up tryin until we do."

"How's dat?" Aggie said exasperated. "Even if he does find da girls, how in da world we gone get dem back, all da way from Greece?"

Lottie just smiled at her. "Look at me, Aggie. This is what Wil does. In all his years with the SOF, he has strategized dozens of top secret rescue missions in much more dangerous places than Greece. If anyone can do it, it's Wil. We're all goin to be leavin this afternoon on the company jet, and we'll arrive in Greece on Wednesday afternoon. That'll give Wil over 48 hours to put his plan to action."

"Who dat leavin tonight?"

"You, me, Wil and Tyler. Once we're in Greece, you and I will check into a hotel, and basically just wait out those two days before we meet back up with Wil. Richard is only allowing me to go under the terms that we stay close to the hotel the entire time. He's afraid if Jack sees us, things might get dangerous. So Tyler will be with us for our protection, and then Wil will do his thing."

"Wait a minute. I can't go with you, Miss Lottie, I don't have a passport. I ain't never been out da United States!"

"You have to go with us, Miss Aggie. You're the only one those girls know, and they're goin to be in such a state...Honey, you have to be in there when Wil brings them to us; I'm sure you can see that. Elle and Skye are goin to need you from here on out. Don't worry about the passport; that's just a minor detail, and my husband is already workin on it. Jack's not the only one who has connections, and Richard's are far more powerful and influential, not to mention on the right side of the law. Trust me, you'll have a passport and a visa by the time we leave. Tyler will be stayin with us the entire time, just in case we need him, and Richard will remain in the States takin care of things here."

"My head's spinnin with all dis."

"You'll have time on the flight to digest it all, but right now, we're on quite a tight time frame. I've arranged for a driver to take you back to your house in Lafayette to pack for the trip. You need to take the time in the car to make a list of any essentials you need to take: medications, vitamins, personal items, and the like. We'll be back by Saturday evening, so you don't need to pack too much, and that girl you met before who showed you to this room, Rebecca; she has a new suitcase for you to use. Also, last night when we talked, you said that the girls would often stay with you, am I rememberin that correctly?"

"*Mais oui*. Dey stay with MawMaw Aggie for weeks on end."

"So then, I'm assuming you have some of their clothes at your house?" Aggie nodded. "Perfect. Please make sure to grab a few outfits for both Skye and Elle. We're just not certain what kind of state they'll be in when we get them, and we'll want to make sure they are as comfortable as possible. Can you do that, too?"

"How you tink of all dese details? I'd never tink about doin dat."

"Oh, honey, I don't know. I just do, that's all."

"Miss Lottie, how'll I ever tank you for all dis? For all dat Mr. DuLonde and Wil are gone do?"

"Aggie, dear, we're family now, and that means from this moment on, we're all in this thing together. Do you understand that? We're family. We'll see this thing through to the end, and then Richard and I are gonna help you give both Skye and Elle the kind of life Macy always dreamed she could."

Aggie took a deep breath and mustered a hint of a smile to Lottie.

"Miss Lottie, I'm so sorry I called you crazy."

"Ha!" said Lottie as she stood to help Aggie stand. "I promise you, honey, I've been called worse."

The two women embraced each other for several breaths.

"We're in this together," whispered Lottie.

"We in dis together," Aggie whispered back.

TWENTY-TWO

"NOW LISTEN VERY CAREFULLY, Rebecca," Lottie instructed her personal assistant. "You need to take care of anything Ms. Prejean might need. Is the driver here, yet?"

"Yes, ma'am, and I've already had all of Mrs. Prejean's belongings loaded and packed into the car. He's all ready to drive her to Lafayette."

"Good. I want you to call Ms. Prejean every hour, on the hour, to check in and to see if she's thought of items she needs for you to pick up and bring to the airport. Also, make sure you are closely in touch with the driver. Did they send us Thomas today?"

"Yes, ma'am, and I have his personal cell number in my phone."

"Wonderful." Then Lottie looked at Aggie. "You're goin to like Thomas. He's one of the best drivers we've got. He likes to chat, but, honey, if you need yourself some quiet time, he's more than happy to give it to you. All you need to do is speak up."

Back to Rebecca, Lottie said, "Did you make sure the car had plenty of food and drinks for Ms. Prejean?"

"Yes, ma'am. Fully stocked."

"Excellent. Miss Aggie, the weather in Greece this time of year is chillier than what we Southerners are used to—oh, whatam I talkin about?—it's been downright freezin here the last week or so! If you pack all the clothes I had Rebecca pick up for you this mornin, along with a nice, warm overcoat, I think you'll be just fine.

"Now, it's just about 9 o'clock right now. You should get to your home by 10:30. Do you think you'll need more than an hour to pack up everything for you and the girls?"

"Dat should be just fine," Aggie said.

"Great. Rebecca, you need to make sure to tell Thomas that he must have the car packed and ready to leave Ms. Prejean's home no later than 11:30. Our flight leaves New Orleans at 3:05, and it's going to take about 2 1/2 hours to drive from Lafayette to the airport. Tell him to park in his usual spot at the airport and to escort Ms. Prejean through the terminal, all the way to our jet. Do you have any questions?"

"No, ma'am," Rebecca answered. "I'll text you if anything comes up."

"Good girl." Lottie stepped close to Aggie and put her hand on her shoulder. "Listen, honey, please do not hesitate to call me or Rebecca if you need anything in the next few hours. Otherwise, I'll be at the airport waiting for you."

Lottie could see an overwhelmed look on Aggie's face. She moved her hand from Aggie's shoulder to her cheek. "You look at me, Miss Aggie. We're gonna get your girls back. In just a few days, you're gonna be snugglin' with your grandchildren, one on each side."

Aggie nodded, tears filling her eyes. "Tank you, Miss Lottie."

Lottie gave Aggie a hug, whispered her love for her, and then escorted her toward the door. "You've got to get on the road, honey. Rebecca will take you to the car."

Lottie led the two women out of the room and closed the door softly behind them. Her hand still up on the door frame, she sighed heavily before leaning her head forward to rest against the wooden frame. Only when she was certain Rebecca and Aggie were out of earshot did she allow herself to fully release her emotions.

The instant Richard saw his wife's shoulders shaking from her sobs, he arose from the table and was right behind her. His strong arms encircled her, and she clutched onto his arm as he pulled her back against his chest. For moments, they stood embracing, Lottie weeping, Richard softly stroking her hair.

"I just have no words," she whispered in between sobs. "No words to describe how I'm feeling right now. So sad, and scared, and angry."

"I know, baby," Richard whispered back. "Me, too."

"How could someone do such a wicked thing? To his own flesh and blood? Honey, those girls are just *babies!* It's unthinkable what kind of a person could do something like this."

Having no answers, Richard simply held her tighter and kissed the top of her head.

Both Wil and Tyler were still at the table. Tyler, sensing the family needed privacy, quietly motioned to Wil that he was going to go back into the sitting room to work more on Jack's laptop. Wil nodded, and Tyler exited, silently closing the door behind him.

"Baby, let's go sit down." Richard led Lottie over to the antique loveseat and sat her down next to him. She brought her knees into her chest and melted into him.

Wil grabbed a box of tissues, came over to his parents, and sat down in the rosewood armchair opposite the loveseat. He passed a few tissues to his dad, who slipped them to Lottie. The three sat quietly for several minutes. Finally, Lottie sat up and broke the silence.

"There," she said as she carefully wiped her eyes with the corner of the tissue. "I'm all done with that. Well, for now, at least. We don't have time for me to sit here and cry the day away while those girls are over there needin to be rescued. What needs to be done?"

Richard laughed at the sudden composure of his wife.

"What?" she asked him. "What are you laughin at, Mr. DuLonde?"

"You," he said as he caressed her cheek. "You're a 'Steel Magnolia' through and through."

Lottie smiled up at her husband. "I just can't help it. It's how my mama raised me. She'd always say, 'There's no time for blubberin when there's work to be done!' Now, what time is check out today?"

"We've actually reserved all these rooms until tomorrow, remember?" Richard answered. "So we can take our time and leave whenever we're ready."

"I'm actually going to check out in just a few minutes," said Wil. "I've got to be in Baton Rouge by 10am to meet with some folks who'll be able to give me some insight into the business of sex trafficking."

"Who are you meeting with?" Richard asked.

"Well, interestingly enough, when Tyler and I were Googling about human trafficking, we came across an organization located right near here that works to fight against this. Trafficking Hope. They even have a home that specializes in caring for girls who've been rescued out of sex trafficking."

"Trafficking Hope. Why does that sound familiar to me?" asked Lottie.

"You know all those billboards that are always up along I-10 that are about trafficking? These are the people who put those up."

"Yes, I do remember seein those. There was one up on the way to my spa," she said. "Wow. I'm ashamed to admit it now, but I probably saw that thing a few dozen times, and never really thought about what it meant."

"Well, this is them. They're pretty involved with what's happening here in Louisiana, and most importantly for us at this moment, they are linked with another organization in Greece that specializes in helping rescue girls from the brothels there, called the A21 Campaign. I left an urgent message late last night, or should I say early this morning, on their hotline. I gotta tell you, I'm pretty impressed at how quickly they responded. I got a call from a gal first thing this morning and she set up a meeting with me and some of their folks today at 10.

"I'm hoping they'll be able to help me get a better idea of this whole network, as well as give me the contact info for who I need to talk to at the A21 org in Thessaloniki. We're only going to have 48 hours to complete our mission once we get there; I need to connect with as many sources as possible, extract as much info as I can, between now and when we touch down in Greece."

"OK, now, forgive me for askin this, maybe I'm just bein a mama, but I'm sorry, I just need to ask it. Why are we not using our FBI, or our embassy there, or even the Greek police force to find the girls?" Lottie asked. "I mean, for all you know, Wil, you might be steppin into a hornet's nest."

"Mom—" Wil was irritated.

"Well, I'm just sayin. You have no idea the kind of danger you're puttin yourself into."

"For chrissake, Mom, what do you think I've been doin for the last 8 years in the SOF? Playin desert Lazer Tag with a bunch of my buddies?"

"Listen, Son," Richard said sternly. "Don't talk to your mother like that."

"Well, seriously, Dad. I've been face to face with some of the most dangerous Al Qaeda there is and lived to talk about it. Do you honestly think I won't be able to handle a few brothel owners in Greece?"

"First of all, Wil," Richard said, "you don't need to remind us of your resume. Let's not forget I personally nursed you back from the grave from your last mission. And second, let's not downplay the situation here. You're *not* just dealing with a few rinky-dink whorehouses. You know just as well as I do from all the info we've gathered these last several hours, that this trafficking deal is a very sophisticated operation. So you can't be naive to the reality of what you're signing up for."

"Yes, sir," Wil said quietly. "I wasn't trying to downplay anything; I'm fully aware what I'm getting into. And, I'm sorry, Mom. I shouldn't have raised my voice at you."

"We love you, Wil; you're our only son," Lottie said. "It's not that I don't think you're capable; I know you are more than. But I'm also a mama, so naturally, regardless of how experienced or skilled you might be in this sort of thing, I'm still goin to be worried sick about my son's safety."

"Alright. I get it, Mom. Listen to me." And Wil's expression changed to one of great compassion. "One thing I've been thinking all night is, what if this was Madison? Right now I'd give anything to have just one more day with her. So what if she disappeared, and we found out this had happened to her? Do you think that I'd care for even a half of a millisecond about what might happen to me if it was in my power to save her from those bastards?

"Dad, I understand the risk. So do you. And yes, Mom, it's probably going to be dangerous. I may even be risking my life. But how could I live with myself if I passed on this opportunity to help these two girls, who happen to be my own cousins, when I know in my heart I can do this?

"We don't have the time to get our FBI involved. Elle is going to be sold *this* Friday, and by the time we'd talk to our guys here, and they'd get the people mobilized on a mission, it will be too late. Elle will have been sold, and long gone. The American Embassy in Greece isn't going to be able to do anything for us, either, with this kind of time frame. And as far as the Greek police go, Aeton says we just don't have the time to know which of those cops are on the up and up. There's so much corruption in the system, some of the police over there are just as involved as the traffickers."

"Who's Aeton?" asked Richard.

"That's the guy I told you about, my SOF friend in Greece."

"Oh, right, right, right. Got it."

"Wait a minute," said Lottie. "Can you fill me in on who Aeton is?"

"Aeton was in the Greek military, a member of their ETA, which essentially is equivalent to our SOF. These guys are the real deal, total machines. Several years ago, a dozen SOFs were sent to Athens to help train some of their ETA forces. Aeton was one of the Greek leaders that I was assigned to, and we became good friends. He left the service last year, and has since gotten married and had a kid. But he's still pretty involved with training the younger guys over there. Anyway, he's going to meet me in Thessaloniki as soon as we land. Really, there'd be no way I'd be able to do this without him. He'll serve as my interpreter, definitely get me into places I'd never be able to find myself, *and* he'll provide the weapons we might need, the stuff I'd never get past airport security."

"Well, now, that's the best piece of news I've heard yet," said Lottie. "I was hopin you'd be packin plenty of heat to take care of those horrible people. You have my permission to shoot every single one of them in the—well, where it would hurt the most."

Wil chuckled a bit. "We'll do whatever we need to do to get the girls. But nothing more. I don't want to cause too much of a commotion so our exit can stay as clean as possible."

"I'm really glad Aeton will be there to help. You make sure you let him know he will be very well compensated for his trouble," said Richard.

"To tell you the truth, Dad," said Wil, smiling. "I kinda already promised him that."

"Good job," Lottie said. "You think just like your father."

Checking his watch, Wil said. "I've really got to head out if I'm going to make it to my 10 o'clock." He called over in the direction of the sitting room. "Hey, Tyler! We've got to get to our meeting."

"Oh dear!" said Lottie, standing up to face Tyler as he emerged from the side room. "I almost forgot you were in there! How rude of us to be banterin, leavin you cooped up in that sittin room."

"Mrs. DuLonde, you don't need to apologize," said Tyler, Jack's laptop in hand. "I knew you guys needed your time to work things out.

And as far as what we'll be doing in Greece, don't you worry about a thing, ma'am. Thanks to Jack's loose-lipped emails about where and when the auction will take place, at least half of this mission will be very straight-forward."

"Yes, and thank you for saying that," Lottie said. "After all this is over, I want to make sure and meet your mama. She raised herself a mighty fine young man."

"She'd love to meet you, too, Mrs. DuLonde."

"Come on, Tyler, we've gotta go," said Wil, halfway out the hotel room door. "Mom, if we don't see you back at the house getting packed up, then we'll meet you at the airport."

Richard and Lottie watched as the two young men hurried off. Lottie looked down at her husband, still sitting on the loveseat.

"Richard, are you sure we're goin about this the right way?" she asked.

He pulled her down on his lap and hugged her. "I don't know, babe," he said. "I hope so. I don't know if we have any other options. One thing is certain, though, and that is this: we've got to try our best to undo the harm that brother of mine has caused. We've got to get Elle, and by the grace of God, find out where Skye has been all this time. "

TWENTY-THREE

SKYE STOOD AT THE WINDOW, looking through the bars at the street below. It had been many, many days since she'd been awake in the afternoon and had the chance to look out at her surroundings. Not that she cared to get out of her bed, even if she was awake. She hated this place and her life here more deeply than she ever thought possible. And she wished she could just die. And she resented that guy who let her sleep all night long so that now she couldn't sleep and so she was being tortured by every moment that counted her toward another night of being violated over and over and over.

Who was he, and why did he spend the entire night here, just to sit? Who pays to just sit and do nothing?

As she stood watching, a bird came and sat on a tree close to her barred window. Birds always made her think of MawMaw Aggie. It sang a beautiful song and Skye wished she could touch it.

How can it be that such an awful place as this would be allowed to hear a song as pretty as that bird is singing? If MawMaw Aggie was right about there being a god, how could he let that happen? How could he give something so good to people who do such terrible, horrible things? No one here deserved such a gift. They're only worthy of ugliness and darkness. And most definitely maggots in all their food. She almost smiled at the thought of the old witch eating maggots.

Skye was sure MawMaw would have some kind of answer to defend her "Bon Dieu." She always had good words to say about him and to explain why he did what he did. Even during the summers, when the girls would stay at Aggie's house, she would tell them the same bedtime story almost every single night. Both Skye and Elle used to snuggle into their pillows and drink in each word. Skye had heard it so many times, she knew it by rote.

"A long time ago, *le Bon Dieu* created da universe. He made da moon and da stars, da land and da sea, and all da many, many tings dat live in da world. He was very happy, but only for a short while. Den, he became very sad. He had nobody to share all his treasures with.

"He wanted someone to dance with at a *fais do-do*, someone to deal the cards for a round of boure', someone to share *His joie de vivre*. He was very, very lonely. And so, you tink you know what *le Bon Dieu* did? Da's right! He made Cajuns! *Laissez les bons temps rouler!* Let the good times roll!

"And for a long time, he was very happy. Da earth was den full of many people. But den, once again *le Bon Dieu* became very, very sad. Someting was wrong. Someting was missing! He had an *envie*, a deep craving, in da bottom of his heart. He looked across da earth to and fro, and fro and to. *Mias oui*, indeed someting was missing. He could find it nowhere.

"What was *le Bon Dieu* lookin for? He was lookin for da one ting dat was missin from da earth. A beautiful girl with eyes da color of da blue, blue sky and with hair as black as night. He was missin a very special girl who was brave and smart, who loved to dream big dreams, and a girl who always worked hard to take care of others. And so, you tink you know what he did?

"*Bon Dieu* made *la petite fille*, a little girl, and he named her Skye because he gave her eyes as clear da blue sky. Now he was finally happy, and he grinned ever'day from ear to ear from da moment she opened her eyes to da minute her head hit her pillow at night. Den he would wait and wait and wait and wait all night long until she opened her eyes da next morning."

And then, MawMaw would smother her neck with kisses, sending her into peals of laughter.

As Skye stood at the barred window remembering this story, her gut began to churn with anger. From where she was right now, living in this horrid cage, every one of Aggie's words rang totally untrue! How could Aggie have fed her such a bucket of lies? And how could Skye ever have been so foolish as to believe a story as ridiculous as this?

In sudden outrage, Skye grabbed the bars, and with every ounce of strength she possessed, she shook them. But the iron rods were securely fastened, so Skye was the only thing that moved as she violently wrestled with them. She fought with her enemy until all her energy was spent, and she finally slunk to the cement floor. Crumpled in a ball under the window, Skye allowed herself to cry deeper than she had since she'd been locked up in this prison.

In her heart, she cried out for something in the universe to be good, to notice her captivity, and to show her some mercy. But as she scanned the tiny room, her feelings confirmed what she knew to be true. No one here was good, not even herself now that she had become so defiled. No one cared about her captivity. And no one was going to show mercy. She only had herself, and it was time she took her life in her own hands and figured out a way to end it.

Skye barely finished that thought and the lock on her door began to jiggle. The witch was here. Why is she coming in here this early? Did the woman find out that she really didn't have sex with the guy from last night? Would she get beaten for something that wasn't even her fault? The thought of a beating didn't threaten Skye anymore; in fact, maybe if the beating was bad enough, she would be able to escape this hell forever.

As the door opened, Skye stood up to meet her assailant. It was the madame and her servant woman, Dula. For maybe the first time the old hag didn't wear an evil frown; she was smiling at her. Dula was her same dreary self, however, eyes to the ground and never making any eye contact. Skye wondered what that servant woman looked like under that curtain of hair that always enshrouded her face. Dula was carrying a purse and a little bag. The madame motioned for Skye to sit down on the bed, the entire time chattering on to Skye, even though the girl couldn't understand a word she said.

She slapped Dula on the arm and motioned her to approach Skye. Dula spun on her heel and gave Skye a doughnut-like roll. Skye held it for a moment, not sure what to do with it. Was she asking Skye to hold it for her? Skye was confused about how to act until the madame motioned to her and said in English, "You. For to eat."

The witch giggle-snorted at Skye as she hesitantly took a tiny bite out of the doughnut as if it was a foreign object. Then the woman stuffed her own pastry entirely into her mouth, chewing and talking in Greek, with bits of half-chewed pieces flying every which way. She shook off her hands and poked at Dula again. Trained to understand the madame's every whim, she took a pretty pink satin dress out of the purse. It was more like a slip than a dress, with thin ribbons for straps and lace along the hem. The madame motioned for Skye to put it on.

The only piece of clothing Skye had was the blue camisole she was wearing. Everything else had been taken away from her the night she was brought here. And when the cami was dirty, she had to lay naked in her bed until Dula brought it back, cleaned. Why was she giving her something else to wear? What was she going to make her do now?

Skye stood up, slipped off the blue camisole and exchanged it for the pink one. It fit her body much nicer, and Skye liked that it was longer. The blue one stopped at her hips; this one covered her to her mid-thigh. The woman clapped in approval and scurried out of the room, leaving the door open. Dula shuffled quickly behind her.

Alone, Skye stared at the open door. The witch had never left the door unlocked and open unless it was time for her shift. Skye could feel the familiar feeling of nausea begin to engulf her. Maybe because she got to sleep last night she was going to have to make up for it now by working a day shift? Maybe that's why the woman gave her something new to wear while she cleaned the blue camisole.

Skye sat down on her bed, resolving that somehow soon, she would find a way to bring this all to a fatal end. She leaned herself against the wall, waiting for the witch to return with a new client, but when she did, she was only accompanied again by Dula. Carrying a food tray, Dula walked over to Skye and handed it to her. She was surprised that this tray had twice as much food as normal. The madame motioned to the girl to eat all of the food and then to lay down and sleep. She came close to the girl, patted her on the head, and then the pair quickly left the room.

Skye could not fathom what had come over the woman, or why she was acting so nice to her. What could all of this mean? First, there was the night with a guy who didn't even try to touch her, and now a complete change in how the witch was treating her. She had even included dessert in her lunch!

But before she could ponder too long, she heard the old woman lock the padlocks outside her door. Skye took a deep sigh of relief, realizing this sound to mean she would not have to work a day shift. So for the time being, she could have solitude, and at that moment, it was really all Skye cared about.

Skye ate everything on her tray, and marveled at the feeling of being full. She could not remember the last time she was not hungry. The feeling made her drowsy, and she fell back on her pillow and fell deeply asleep.

⚜

GALEN STOOD OUTSIDE the bank contemplating as he ran his fingers through his thick hair, a nervous gesture of his that his mom was always trying to get him to stop doing. He was searching his mind for any excuse, even just one, that would convince him not to do what he was about to do. Was he just being impulsive and emotional? Maybe he was just exhausted and if he waited for a few days he would see the flaws in his plan. He would realize it was ridiculous. And the impact of the prior night would eventually fade away, hopefully along with the pit of dread in his gut.

But then he thought of the ramifications for the girl if he didn't get involved. How many men would be coming into her room, in only a few hours, and begin raping her? For hours on end, the men would pass each other in the hallway, one going in, one going out, and put that girl through god-only-knows what. The thought made Galen want to vomit.

The injustice of the situation burned inside of Galen. He knew he'd never be able to live with a choice of inaction; at least not now after all he had seen. He'd never find the way to erase the look of fear and hatred the girl had on her face, an expression all too mature for such a young girl to convey. In addition, now every time he looked at his sister, Dimitra, he'd think of the girl and wonder what might've happened to her and if she was ever able to escape from that dungeon. He couldn't just walk away. Now, after being with her for an entire night, Galen felt responsible. He didn't really understand what that meant, or how this situation would end up playing out, but what he *did* know was he couldn't do nothing.

He walked into the bank and looked for someone to help him, someone whom he was absolutely certain didn't know anyone in his family. He couldn't afford for casual gossip to ruin his plan. Galen had told his family he'd taken a short-term, mid-night job to be able to raise the money he needed to buy his first car. This allowed him the latitude to stay out all night, for as many nights as he needed, without his father asking any questions. If somehow his parents heard he'd been in his bank *withdrawing* a large sum, there would be an avalanche of interrogations, and too many questions Galen had no idea how to answer. After picking a teller he'd never seen before, he walked up and filled out the slips needed to withdraw 750 euros. This would be enough for three nights with the girl. Hopefully he would have figured out a plan by then.

As the woman counted out the money, Galen could feel his stomach begin to churn. In so many ways, this money represented freedom for him. He was the second-born son, and being so, he understood he'd need to be the one accountable for making his dreams for the future come to pass. Nikkos, the first-born, would naturally be offered the option to take over the family furniture business, so his destiny was a no-brainer. Maybe that was why he lived his life in such a cavalier way? All he had to do was show up, not wreck anything, and he'd have all the money he needed to make a fine living.

While Galen had never regretted that the universe chose him as the number two son, he did come to realize, at a very young age, that the secondary title also came with a curse. He'd be on his own to finance any vision that involved straying from his family's path. This included college abroad, any entrepreneurial endeavors he might attempt, and all that went with those choices. As a result, Galen had lived a focused and purposeful life; studying to make the highest grades, working every job he could get his hands on, and saving as much money as possible. Every decision he made was with an awareness of his future goals in mind. Until today.

Withdrawing such a sum was completely out of character for the conservative, calculated Galen. He looked at the money he was now holding in his hand, knowing it was a precious commodity, every penny a testimony of determination and hard work. To throw it away on an impetuous moment of pity was something Galen knew he'd regret forever. But for reasons he could not yet articulate, he simply couldn't help himself. She was worth it.

His mind went back to the vision of her as he had watched her sleep. She had seemed so delicate as she lay there, and the longer he had watched her sleeping, the stronger his passion had grown to protect her. To help her. To get her out of there. Never again would a man touch her, mistreat her or make her degrade herself at his command. Galen felt his cheeks flush with emotion for this nameless girl as he once again scoured his mind for a reasonable plan of escape.

The plan had to be flawless, and not without extreme luck from the gods. He rehearsed in his mind the different ways in which he could sneak her past the old woman, but he wasn't sure how he'd make it past those guards in the foyer. And then he thought of what might happen to the girl if his attempt to rescue her failed. She'd probably be beaten senseless, and he certainly would never be able to see her again. Those concerns were very sobering for Galen.

He neatly folded the sum of bills into his wallet, and exited the bank to hail a cab to go back home and plan his strategy for the night.

TWENTY-FOUR

"WIL, DON'T YOU THINK you should try to sleep a little bit before we land in Greece?" Lottie asked her son. "If you start now, you'll still have two hours before we touch down."

Not looking up from his iPad, Wil said, "I'll sleep on the flight back."

"Wil, that's days from now—"

Still engrossed in his computer, "Once the girls are safe, and we're all on our way home, I'll sleep."

"Wil—"

Finally meeting her eyes, he answered, "Please stop being 'mom' right now. I've got a mission to accomplish, and you've gotta know, this is how I roll." And he went back to his iPad, swiping from page to page and organizing his rescue plan.

Lottie stood still for a moment, wanting to say more, but instead she chose to edit herself and return to her seat. Tyler, who was sitting opposite Wil, excused himself to get something to drink. He stopped by Lottie's seat and asked if he could get her a snack or a beverage. Keeping her gaze outside the airplane window, she said, "Not right now, Tyler. Thank you very much."

Tyler walked to the serving station and opened the small fridge, helping himself to a Coke and a single serving tray of fruit and cheese. He took his snack back to the seat across from Lottie, and sat down.

"Miss Charlotte, this jet is like nothing I've ever seen," Tyler said. "Do you always travel in planes like these?"

"Oh, sugar, not *always*," she answered. And then she chuckled, "My daddy's jet is even larger than this one."

Tyler laughed. "What in the world was it like growing up around so much money? Before today, I've only seen the view from a seat in coach."

"I don't know, honey. I can't really say what it's been like because I've never known anything other," she said. "But I will tell you this: it's times like these that I thank the good Lord in heaven that he's chosen to bless us." Her face became quite serious. "Tyler, I can't stop thinkin about what would've happened had Miss Aggie not come to find us. And then when we eventually did hear about the girls—once it was too late—how would we have felt that we had it in our power to help them, but were never given the chance? It makes me sick to my stomach just thinkin about it."

"Well, to be honest, ma'am, from my perspective of growin up in the inner-city projects, I've seen plenty of folks who have the money and are given the chance, and still don't do a single thing to help someone else in need."

Lottie looked at Tyler for a moment. She smiled and said, "That's very true, Tyler. And I'm ashamed to say that I'm sure my own family, as well as Richard and me, have seen those needs time and time again but chose to look the other way."

"Please, Miss Charlotte," Tyler quickly replied. "You have to know that I wasn't referring that toward you guys at all. You're some of the most generous people I've ever met."

"Thank you, honey, but you've just known us for a few years. I'd be lyin if I said we've always acted the way we do today. In fact, when I look back, it's quite clear that Richard and I took very good care of ourselves, and of Wil and Madison, before we ever thought about helpin any of the folks around us. Why, it wasn't until we all experienced Katrina that Richard and I opened up our eyes to the people who needed help, and who were right under our noses. I mean, it's not like we were ignorant of them; we knew the needs were there, but...I don't know...we were too busy buildin our own deal. And even after the hurricane, while it might be true that we've given large amounts of money to help people, all of that was still only out of our abundance. It's not like any of that givin caused us worry about where our next meal was comin from.

"No...It's not until you meet someone like Miss Aggie that you come face to face with true generosity. I bet that woman has spent her whole life givin and servin and helpin people, even when it was her last roll of quarters. And no doubt, she'll keep on givin 'til her last dyin breath. That's just the kind of woman she is. And what makes her even more special is that she does the things she does, just because it's the right thing to do. It's not for any type of public recognition; you can tell she couldn't care less about anything like that. She'll just keep lovin on the folks around her, and in the end, at least in the big scheme of things, hardly anyone will ever know her name."

The two sat for a few minutes thinking about what had just been said. Tyler broke the silence. "Speaking of Miss Aggie, I haven't seen her for the last several hours. Where is she?"

"She's asleep in the cabin bedroom."

"What?" Tyler asked. "This jet has a *bedroom?*"

"Didn't Wil show you around before we took off?"

"Hell no! Oh, pardon me, Miss Charlotte; I mean, heck no." Lottie waved her hand at him as if to say, 'Don't worry about it.'

Tyler continued, "Ma'am, you've seen him today; he's in ranger mode. Giving a tour of the aircraft is the last thing on his mind."

"Yes. Well, you see that door over there? That's a small cabin with a nice bed in it. After we ate, I urged Miss Aggie to go in there and sleep. The woman is simply exhausted, so much so, she isn't even aware how much. I'm glad she agreed, because it's goin on six solid hours that she's been in there sleepin. I'm sorry that boy of mine forgot his manners and didn't give you a chance to take a look around the jet."

Tyler laughed at her comment. "I hate to break the news to you, Miss Charlotte, but your son's never been one to play host or to mind his manners when there's something important to be done."

"Well now, thank you Tyler," she said, as she winked at him. "Now I'll go to my grave knowin I completely failed as a good Southern mama."

"Wow, I'm just putting my foot in my mouth every time I'm opening it, aren't I?"

"I'm just teasin you, sugar. Wil's just like his father; when there's a job at hand, he's all work and no play."

"And that's exactly why you don't need to worry about whether or not the guy gets any rest. I've operated with a lot of soldiers, and Wil's the best there is. I've seen him go 5 days straight on basically no sleep at all and still stay the sharpest man on the team. He's a beast when it comes to things like this."

"Thank you, Tyler," said Lottie, managing a smile. "Even so, it's impossible for me to stop worryin. Especially after his last mission."

"Nothing about that day could've been prevented, ma'am. Those bastards came out of nowhere. I'm sure this won't be anything like that, not to mention that Wil has done an amazing amount of work in these last 24 hours to ensure that it won't be."

"I've barely gotten him to say two words about what his plan is once we touch down. Can you tell me anything? Anything at all? Like, how did your meetin go with the Trafficking Hope people in Baton Rouge? Did you get the information you needed? Were they able to help you get connected with that organization in Greece? Once we get there, do you know who you're lookin for? Where you're going? How you're gonna get find Skye?—"

"Whoa, whoa, whoa," said Tyler, chuckling at her barrage of questions. "Slow down a minute, Miss Charlotte."

"I'm sorry, sugar. But my son hasn't told me a thing!"

"O.K. I'll do my best to let you in on what I know. You realize, I'll be staying with you and Miss Aggie, right? So Wil hasn't given me all the details of what he's planning, but here's what I've gathered so far: I was at the meeting with the team from Trafficking Hope. They were very knowledgeable about the entire issue, even about how much this kind of thing is going on right now in Louisiana. You'll be shocked to hear some of the stories they told us about little girls being trafficked right in New Orleans, but I won't go into any of that right now. I know Wil is planning on sharing all that with you once we get back to the States. He wants to connect you with the Trafficking Hope team because he said the work they are doing is right up your alley.

"Anyway, they hooked us up with the right people in Greece who could help us. One of their main guys was able to shed light on how the sex industry is structured in Thessaloniki, and how to approach the people involved. We gave him the addresses we got from Jack's emails, and he told us the area Jack is targeting is primarily a part of the red light district that mostly services the Greeks.

"This was really good to know, because Wil probably would've just gone in there and tried to gather intelligence, not realizing that the fact he was American would deter anyone from talking to him. A lot of the brothels there turn away foreigners, and if you don't speak Greek, they usher you right on out. Now in the areas that are newer and more urban, this isn't the case, but where we think Elle is being sold, it is. That's where Wil's Greek military friend, Aeton, will be absolutely key. Honestly, I don't know what we'd've done without that contact. He's going to be our ticket in to those brothels."

"If that is true, then how did Jack get on the inside of their circle?" asked Lottie.

"We don't know for sure. His contact must either be Greek, or has some very good friends who are. We're not going to know for sure until we get Jack."

"And once we get him, he's gonna rot to death in a snake infested jail cell, right?"

"Let's hope so," said Tyler. "Now...Once we touch down, I'll be taking you and Miss Aggie to the Electra Hotel, but Wil's gonna hit the ground running. Aeton'll get Wil from the airport, and it's possible that we won't see him again until this entire mission is over. I'll be in touch with him via cell, and maybe even meeting him if he needs something, but you need to know that until he's got the girls in hand, you might not be seeing him."

Lottie sighed deeply. "Thank you for tellin me that. That's good information for me to have, for sure. Do you know *exactly* how he plans to rescue the girls? How is he gonna get Elle out of that auction? And how in the world is he goin to find Skye?"

"Miss Charlotte, a mission like this isn't that cut and dried. It'll be very organic, even from hour to hour, because while we have a great foundation of intelligence, there still are many variables at work. But no one thinks better on his feet than Wil. He's a genius. And if Aeton is as good as Wil has said, then you've got a dream team going in after those girls."

Just then, Tyler noticed Wil. He looked at Lottie and then nodded his head in the direction of Wil. She glanced over her shoulder at Wil's seat. She smiled when she saw that he'd set his iPad down on the table in front of him and reclined his chair. He was sleeping.

"Well, it looks like he obeyed you after all," Tyler said in a low voice.

"Yes, but you'd better not tell him that," she answered. And as Tyler stood up to return to his seat, she added, "And don't you dare wake him up!"

TWENTY-FIVE

SOMETHING WAS NOT RIGHT about the beauty contest. At first, Elle assumed that since this pageant was being held in a foreign country, they just did things differently here. But after the past two days of walking all over the city to meet the judges, as well as overhearing Jack's remarks along the way, Elle was beginning to dread having to take part in the event.

First of all, there were more judges for this pageant than Elle had ever seen. The American beauty pageants that she'd watched on television usually had only four or five judges, but this one had at least ten. And that was only the number of judges they were able to meet. Jack told Elle that on the day of the contest, there would be many more judges, probably another dozen or so. That seemed like way too many for something like this. Especially since all the girls had to do was stand on the stage, walk down and back on a little runway, and smile. Apparently none of the contestants needed to talk, to change clothes, to perform a talent, or anything else that was normally done; all they had to do was stand there. Why in the world did there need to be so many judges?

In addition, Elle didn't like any of the judges they had met. It seemed odd to her that almost all of them were men, most of whom spoke in a foreign language and looked at her in an unusual way. Every single one of them made her feel squeamish and uncomfortable. Only one of them was a woman, and she looked like the last person on earth who should be judging a beauty pageant. She was short and stocky, she wore way too much make-up, and her clothes were so tight, Elle could make out every bulge, dimple and pantyline. She had hobbled over on her high, pointy heels to look closely at Elle's face, and when she did, Elle could see that her gross red lipstick had smeared all over her front teeth. And she kept patting Elle on the top of her head like she was a puppy, while she talked in an awful sing-songy way. Even Jack appeared to not like her for some reason, but he had to be nice to her because she happened to own the venue where the contest was taking place.

It was early in the morning on the second day of judge-meeting when Elle, her father, and the interpreter had arrived at this woman's performance space. It was weird to Elle because as they had entered the front doors, they passed by a dozen men who were being ushered out. The men looked like they were drunk and acted quite surprised to see the daylight. Elle wondered what they'd been doing in the warehouse-turned-theatre all night.

The interpreter talked briefly with the big man who guarded the entrance, and after a few sentences, they were given admittance. As they walked in, Elle heard the interpreter tell Jack that this place only closed down one hour every morning in order to be cleaned, so they didn't have much time to meet the owner before it re-opened.

The entire structure was one spacious main room, lit with strips of fluorescent lights mounted high up on the ceiling. Below those house lights, Elle could see a black grid of stage lights, now turned off, and all of them looked to be focused on the stage areas. She wondered why, even with all the strips of lights illuminated, it still looked so dim in the room, but then she noticed everything was painted black. The walls, the cement floor, the ceiling, and even all the tables and chairs were black. In addition, there were no windows anywhere to be seen. *No wonder those men who were being pushed outside were blinded by the sun,* Elle thought.

The only other person who was present in the room was an older, hunched-back man who was mopping the floor. The older man dropped his mop, shuffling off to get something. The sounds of the mop's handle hitting the concrete echoed through the space.

"He's going to get the old hag," the interpreter said. "She'll show your girl what she's supposed to do on Friday afternoon. She owns this joint, you know, and then another one a couple blocks over that is much larger than this one. This is just a show club, but the other place she runs is a full-service deal. It has everything a guy would want, a huge club, lots of side rooms, and a ton of girls upstairs for whatever you'd like to do."

Elle wondered what the interpreter meant by that.

"Yeah, yeah, yeah. I've met the gal before, remember? This is where I came the last time I was here," Jack answered.

The interpreter thought for a second. "That's right," he said. "And wasn't she the one who actually bought your—"

Jack interrupted with a loud clearing of his throat.

"Yeah, but let's not talk about that right now." He looked over at Elle to see if she'd been listening.

"Got it," the interpreter said, obviously understanding something Elle did not.

The hunched-back man returned and hollered something back to the interpreter, after which he picked up his mop and resumed swishing it across the floor. Shortly thereafter, the short, stocky woman came tottering in, her heels clicking on the concrete. She seemed happy to see them, as she over-projected her words to them. Even close up, she felt it necessary to talk in what MawMaw Aggie would've called her "outside voice."

For several minutes, Jack, the interpreter, and the old woman talked. Elle wished she understood whatever language the old woman spoke because while her father only talked in low tones, this woman was loud and clear. Perhaps she could've offered Elle some clarity about what exactly this beauty pageant was.

Jack came back over to where Elle was standing and told her that the old woman was going to take her up on the stage and give her instructions about what she was supposed to do during the contest. He was very firm with Elle, warning her that she had better comply and do whatever the old woman asked of her. He reminded her that not only was this woman one of the judges, but also she owned this place, so Elle needed to do her best to impress her. The intensity of his direction scared her. The last time he'd said this was days ago when they'd gone to visit that awful doctor. Elle prayed that the ugly woman would not ask her to do anything she didn't want to do or touch her the way that doctor had.

But everything turned out alright. The woman communicated with Elle through the interpreter, sing-songing the entire time, and the only thing she did was take Elle up on the stage and show her where she was to stand and walk. The stage was shaped like a "U", with long narrow, curved runways extending from the large center part. She instructed Elle that on the night of the pageant, Elle was to wait until her number was called, go and stand at the top of the "U" for a few seconds, then walk up and down each of the runways, right first, then left. She then needed to stand again in the center until she was motioned to leave.

In the middle of the black stage wall, there was a door that served as an entrance and exit to the performing space. The woman told her that there was a room behind that door where Elle would wait with the other contestants until it was her turn to go.

And that was it. The lipstick-smeared old woman patted her on the head, said a few more words to the men, waved her fat, wobbly arm with motions that it was time for them to leave, and then had hobbled off in the same direction from which she came.

Now, as Elle sat alone in the hotel room, once again brooding over the details of their stay, from the time they'd arrived until this moment, she felt a foreboding in her heart that had not been there before. She knew she couldn't deny the fact anymore that something was very wrong. But what exactly that 'something' was, she didn't know.

The one thing she was certain of, if she was truly honest with herself, was that since they'd left Louisiana, she hadn't felt safe. Her dad was turning out to be someone she did not like at all, definitely not someone she could trust. And the people they'd met hadn't made her feel good on the inside either. Sure, many of them had been complimentary, but not in a way that made Elle feel comfortable. Again, she didn't know why, she just knew they seemed sneaky somehow, or like they all knew a secret that she didn't...and they weren't about to let her in on it.

The only thought that brought relief was the image of seeing Skye again, and that was going to happen in just a few more days. She couldn't wait to jump into her arms and hug her. She imagined she'd probably cry like a baby and embarrass Skye in front of her school friends, if they were there, but Elle didn't care. Just thinking about it now made Elle want to cry. But instead, she chose to comfort herself with the thoughts of being with her big sister again. They'd talk about all the wonderful things Skye had been up to at her new school, they'd go see all the fun places she and her friends hung out, and they'd laugh and have fun just like they used to.

All Elle had to do was make it through the next couple days. And then she'd be with Skye, and everything would be OK.

TWENTY-SIX

SKYE AWOKE TO THE SOUND of knocking. *It must be time to get up for school,* she thought as she sensed the light through her closed eyelids. *What day is it? Do I have school today? I can't remember going yesterday, so I'm sure it must be a school day. Did I do my homework? Man, I still feel so tired, I wonder if Mom'll let me stay home from school today.*

Then she felt someone gently shaking her shoulder to wake up, and she heard a woman's voice, in broken English, say, "Time for you to get ready." She recognized it as Dula's voice.

She shot up in bed and opened her eyes. Reality. The brothel. Her room. Hell.

More than anything else in the world, Skye wanted to slip back into the freedom of her unconscious imagination. But she also knew the bitter price the witch would make her pay if she didn't obey Dula. She shook off her grogginess, sat up, and looked around the room, trying to figure out what time it was. Dula had set down another tray and was already making her way back outside her room.

Skye felt completely confused, both mentally and physically. Never had the madame allowed her to have so much food. And from the looks of the light from outside, this was much earlier than usual to get ready for the awful night ahead. Skye fell back onto her bed and looked at how the light came through the barred window and cast a shadow across her wall. This shadow-grid had become a clock for Skye, her only way to mark the passage of time.

Each morning, she'd desperately watch for the shadows of the bars to appear and project themselves on her ceiling because this signified a near-end to her shift. An eternity would pass as she followed the shadow-clock's painstakingly slow movement to the middle of the ceiling. But once there, Skye would begin to feel relief knowing at any moment, it would be time for the witch to knock on the door, make the last man leave, and then lock the outside padlock.

The next marker was when the shadow passed by the corner where the ceiling and wall met, and climbed halfway down the wall. On some days, this was when the witch would come back with a tray of food for the day and check the room for cleaning needs. On the days she didn't arrive at this time, then Skye knew she would have to wait for food until the grid slid down the entire wall and crept to the center of the concrete floor. In Skye's depressed state, she hadn't cared to figure out if there was a pattern to the times and days so she never knew what to expect from afternoon to afternoon. But on this day, Skye was startled by the witch's early entrance this morning, and again by Dula just now.

And why had Dula brought another tray of food? Skye examined it and saw that it was just a small roll and a cup of something.

Skye picked up the small cup and felt its warmth. She peeled off the lid, and smelled the wonderful aroma of chocolate. Had the witch actually gotten her a hot cocoa? Skye's head was spinning, not able to comprehend the kind gesture or the motive behind it. She knew this woman was pure evil, so it was impossible the witch was doing any of this out of the kindness of her heart. Skye was sure she didn't even have one of those. It scared her to think about what the madame was going to make her do now.

She had no answers. But she did have a hot drink in her hand, and when she took her first sip, it was like heaven in a cup. It tasted almost as good as the homemade hot cocoas MawMaw Aggie used to make for them, and the girl's sensory recall transported her back into the security of MawMaw Aggie's beautiful sage and butter-yellow painted kitchen.

"*Choooh*! Dat Starbucks ain't got nuttin' on dis ol' Cajun woman," MawMaw would say as she carried the tray to the round wooden table. "Starbucks wish dey knew Aggie's secret to da perfect hot cocoa! And dose tings dey try to pass off as pralines are a disgrace! Dose wouldn't melt in da mouth of a fire-spittin dragon. *Mais non, non, non!* But Aggie's pralines, now, dat's a whole 'notha story, ain't it, *Sha?*" And she'd set down the tray of cocoa and homemade pralines. Skye and Elle would wiggle in their seats waiting for MawMaw to give them the cue to dive in.

Skye closed her eyes and reveled in the sweet memory of Aggie, trying to recall every detail of her house. Perhaps if she concentrated hard enough, she'd somehow be transported back in time, before any of this nightmare began. She could feel the warm drink hitting the bottom of her empty stomach, just like those early mornings at MawMaw's. She visualized the smooth wooden kitchen cabinets, painted butter-yellow, and their metal knobs molded like daisies. And the light green walls. And the window above the sink with the yellow and sage striped curtains. And the bright green ceramic frog that always sat to the left of the sink, his mouth wide open to serve as a holder for Aggie's S.O.S. pads.

The ache in Skye's heart for MawMaw Aggie grew unbearable, too much for her to contain. She let out a deep groan as she hurled the cup across the room, hot chocolate exploding in the corner where the young man had sat in the chair all night. Surprised at the volume of her outburst, she snapped back into survival mode, fearing the mess would anger the witch, perhaps enough to invoke a beating.

The witch would never forgive her for destroying something she paid for, and who knows what she'd make Skye do to pay her back? It was only a matter of time before someone came back in her room, so she darted around to clean up the evidence of her explosion of anger. Skye remembered the small pile of tattered rags underneath the nightstand, and quickly started mopping up the floor and ceiling. Unfortunately, some of the liquid had run under the chair and into the corner, so she scooted it over to clean every last bit.

As she was down on all fours, examining the concrete for anything she missed, her eye caught a glimmer coming from the opposite corner of the room. *What is that?* she wondered, and she crawled over to see the source of the sparkle.

She reached out to grab the item and the moment she touched it, she knew what it was. Wholly astonished, she sat frozen to the concrete staring at the small broken bracelet gathered in the palm of her hand.

Several moments passed as the motionless girl's eyes stayed fixed on the silver treasure, all the while dropping steady tears on the charms as if to wash away the dust. It was the charm bracelet MawMaw had specially designed for Skye's thirteenth birthday.

The dainty bracelet consisted of sterling silver links and three handcrafted charms. The center charm was an ornately wired, round birdcage. The charm to the left was a sterling silver heart, engraved with: *To My Skye-girl*, and the charm to the right was a small bird with her wings open in flight.

> "You see dat birdcage? It's beautiful, but it's empty, just as a birdcage should be," Aggie had said. "And dis petite bird? Dat's your pet egret you've always wanted to catch, *Sha*. She's flyin free, never ever to be put inside any kinda cage. Dat's you, Skye. You're a beautiful bird dat *le Bon Dieu* put on dis earth to fly da open sky with your dreams. You can't never let yourself be caught in any cage, you hear me? You're a bird, *Sha*. And you're gonna soar up as high as your dreams can take you. And dis heart? Why, dat's MawMaw's heart dat'll always be with you no matter where dose dreams take you. No matter how high, no matter how far, Aggie's love'll always be with you, *Sha*." Aggie had latched the bracelet on Skye's wrist and hugged her long and tight. Skye had whispered her vow to never, ever take the bracelet off.

Over and over, Skye replayed this scene with Aggie, as she scooted to her bed. She had no idea how the bracelet ended up hidden in the corner under a covering of dust. All of her personal belongings had been stripped from her that first and very violent nights in the brothel. And while many of the details of those long 72 hours were too horrific to remember, she did recall trying to fight off her attackers in the beginning. She fought until they beat her fight out of her. Perhaps in the brutality of it all, the bracelet had been ripped away and forgotten.

Many links had been torn off, so there was no way to put it on her wrist. But then again, now that Skye had this in her possession again, she wouldn't have worn it anyway for fear the witch would notice and steal it away forever. No, she would be very vigilant to keep this precious memento safely hidden from any person who came into her room from now on.

Clutching the silver charms to her heart, Skye curled up in her bed, heart aching, and she wept. She knew she was supposed to be getting ready, but she didn't care. Let the madame come and beat her. Let her kill her. She simply didn't care. She just wanted to be free.

TWENTY-SEVEN

BEFORE THE PLANE HAD COME to a full stop, Wil was already grabbing his duffel bag, gearing up to race as fast as he could through security. And the moment the stairs were in place outside the aircraft's exit, he was ready to go. He said a quick good-bye to Miss Aggie, bent down to kiss his mom on her head and tell her not to worry, and gave a final fist bump to Tyler.

"I'll be in touch," he called over his shoulder as he left the plane, already calling Aeton on his cell. "Dude, you here yet?"

Aeton: Almost. I'm going to stay in my car because I don't want to take any chances toting guns through the airport.

Wil: Ha! That's right. We gotta remember we're civilians now.

Aeton: When you've gone through customs, go to baggage claim, and find the bridge marked "Beta." When you walk outside, I'll be in the beat-up black VW.

Wil: Cool. See you then. I'll text you when I'm almost there.

Aeton: Out.

As Wil stood in line at Customs, he thumbed through the pages of information he planned to review with Aeton once he got in the car. He'd already faxed everything to him, but he wanted to confirm that Aeton had taken the time to thoroughly digest the details. The information about Elle was cut and dry, at least as far as the time and location of the auction. At the auction on Friday, the sale of the girls would begin, and because Elle was so young, Jack's contact had written she'd most certainly be early in the bidding. Since the youngest girls sell at the highest prices, the people who ran the auction wouldn't want the buyers to hold on to their cash, waiting until the end for the big ticket items to come out. The man had written that if Jack was lucky enough to have the youngest girl, which was very likely since Elle had just turned 10, then she'd probably win the highest bid of the entire event.

Upon reading these transcripts again, Wil wondered if he'd truly possess the restraint not to physically rip Jack to shreds for putting Elle in this type of situation. Let's just hope I don't actually see that bastard face to face, he thought.

It was Wil's turn at Customs. He slid the papers into his bag and walked up to the agent's station. Wil passed through without a hitch, and as he left the Customs area, he thought of how different things might've been had he not had a contact who already lived in Greece. *Thank god for Aeton. I'd really be taking my chances trying to get my weapons through airport security. I'm sure my dad would've figured something out, but that'd just taken more time, and we barely have enough of that as it is.*

He sent a text to Aeton and then checked his watch. Wednesday, 19:30. Only two days to rescue Elle. But it's not Elle he was worried about. He'd already got that information. Skye on the other hand, he had absolutely no idea how he was going to find her in this short of a time frame.

Wil realized he was almost running, but he didn't care; it helped him burn off some adrenaline. He located the bridge marked "Beta" and exited the airport. He looked around for a black VW, and heard a car horn to his far right. Aeton was standing next to the parked car, waving. Wil had forgotten how tall Aeton was, and how much they looked alike. With Aeton's dark hair and green eyes, they could pass as brothers. He ran over to the car, and the two men greeted each other with a man-hug.

Wil: Dude! When you said look for the beat-up VW, you weren't kidding. Ha! We're going to look like circus freaks folding ourselves in and out of this tiny car.

Aeton: I know. But I had to borrow my brother's car because we just bought a new minivan, and the part of town we're going tonight isn't the safest. My wife will beat me if someone broke into it.

Wil: You bought a minivan? Serious?

Aeton: Hey, we got a baby now. We have to look the part.

Wil: (*as both were getting in the car*) Oh that's right, man, I'm sorry; I can't believe I forgot about the baby for a sec. You got pics?

Aeton: Of course. Just pick up my cell, and you can have a slideshow.

Wil: (*looking through the pictures*) Wow. She's a cutie. She must look like your wife.

Aeton: (*laughing*) Thanks.

Wil: (*pulling the papers of information back out of his bag*) I hope you don't mind if we dive right in. Were you able to make sense out of all these pages I faxed earlier? And do you know exactly where we need to go tonight? I tried to Google Earth the street names mentioned in Jack's emails, but the images that came up seemed either really out of date, or not the right ones.

Aeton: Two things about where we're going: #1, it doesn't look like what you Americans might think a brothel district would look like. It's not Las Vegas. Thessaloniki does have places like that, but the area Jack's in is the older part of the red-light district. It looks more like a cross between a residential area and an industrial area. I had to read through those email copies twice, because I have to say, it's strange to me that your uncle would choose this place to make a deal. I'd think there'd be more money in the other parts of the city.

Wil: Yeah, well, that douche-bag doesn't seem to be all that smart. From what we gathered, it appears this just happened to be where Jack's contact knew the right people in the biz.

Aeton: And that is very much how things work here; it's all about relationship and who you know, which brings me to #2: you're going to have to let me do all the talking... even if some of them can speak English. When I was down there last night poking around, I realized that the brothels and strip club owners are used to dealing with Greeks only.

Wil: Yeah...that's what one of our contacts told me. What's that all about?

Aeton: It's just how things are here. Now, the gals walking the streets, I think they'll go with any guy, depending upon what their pimps have told them to do. But the actual establishments are fairly closed to foreigners. However, if I play it that you're my friend who I'm trying to show a good Greek time, I'm pretty sure we'll be fine, but you'll have to let me lead.

Wil: As far as anyone will know, I'm a mute. So you checked it out last night?

Aeton: Yes. I walked around talking to some of the other customers down there who seemed to know what they were doing. Then, I went into a few clubs and sat at the bar, asking the bartenders where the best places were to find young girls. I got several leads.

Wil: Awesome. What about the auction? Were you able to get us into it, or are we gonna have to pull a Rambo?

Aeton: (*laughing*) Let's only use that as a last resort, ranger. We have a meeting in the late morning with a woman who owns the joint where the girls will be sold. Apparently this old lady is a major player in the whole brothel scene; she controls a lot of people, and almost everyone I talked to seemed to hate her, and fear her.

Wil: You're a rockstar! How'd you get all the way to the top so soon?

Aeton: You said money's not an issue, right?

Wil: Absolutely.

Aeton: That's how I did it. I promised we'd bring big money, but only if she'd meet with us.

Wil: Who were you talking to?

Aeton: One of her body guards. I got the right name from a bartender down the street. The guard wouldn't let me speak directly to her, but he called her on his cell while I was standing right there.

Wil: So, how much do we need for tomorrow?

Aeton: Six figures. Cash.

Wil: No problem. I'll text my dad and have him wire a quarter to a bank by our hotel.

Aeton: Make sure you have it in hand by our meeting tomorrow, or we might as will skip it. She's going to want to see for herself.

There's no way we can build trust with her in such a short amount of time, but if we have enough cash right there, I'm pretty sure she'll let us into the auction.

Wil: (*As he was composing the text on his phone*) Do you think 250'll be enough?

Aeton: At least for our meeting, yes; as long as it's in euros. We'll have to watch for her response, try and read if she's impressed or not.

Wil: Done.

The two men rode in silence for a while as Wil finished his text. It burned Wil up on the inside to give such a large amount of money to anyone who would take part in this disgusting and corrupt industry. He'd much rather storm in there and kill the whole lot than hand over one red cent to that old woman, or any of the other brothel owners, for that matter. And Wil hadn't hesitated to let his dad know how he felt, too. Before Wil had boarded the plane for Greece, he'd gone around and around with Richard about how much money he should allow himself to lose.

"Wil, it's *just* money," his dad had said. "Who cares how much it takes to get Skye and Elle back? I'd rather lose my whole fortune and have them home safe, than to keep the money and lose those girls!"

"Dad, I'm not saying we should jeopardize their safety," Wil argued. "I'm just saying we shouldn't let those bastards get any more money than they've already made off all the poor girls they've got locked up."

"You're missing the point, Wil. I don't care about the money, and I don't even care who ends up with it...as long as we end up with the girls."

"I don't understand how you can stand to see those people get rewarded for committing some of the worst crimes possible?!"

"I'm not going to argue about it anymore, son," Richard said. "I want your word that you'll give them whatever amount they ask. Let's not make this situation harder on ourselves than it already is. What is the money for, if not to use it for something like this?"

Wil finally conceded. "Alright, alright. You win. Besides, it's your money; you can give it to whomever you wish."

As Wil now watched his phone, waiting for a text back from his dad, he shook his head, still feeling the sting of that argument. His idea of justice was to make a wrong thing right, and part of that was making the bad people pay for their actions...not reward them with riches. But he'd given his word, and that was that. Moreover, he knew he needed to focus himself on the moment at hand. He wondered if, after Aeton had spent the prior night scoping out the red-light district, his friend had come up with a feasible strategy for locating Skye.

"So, Aeton," Wil said. "What do you think is going to be the best way to locate Skye? Do you think we just need to go from brothel to brothel?"

Aeton didn't respond right away, and Wil wondered if he'd heard the question. There was a traffic light ahead that had just turned red and Aeton was slowing down the car. But once it had fully stopped, Aeton looked over at Wil. From the serious look on his face, Wil could see the question was heard; he simply wasn't sure how to answer it.

Looking back at the traffic light ahead of them, Aeton exhaled heavily. "Wil," he said. "You've got to know that she could be anywhere by now. One of the bartenders I talked to last night was bragging about how often the girls are rotated in and out. Depending upon what kind of brothel she's in, she could've even been sold again and moved out of the city, maybe even the country."

"Yeah, I know," Wil said. "The woman at Trafficking Hope told me the same thing, but we at least have to try our damnedest to find her. I can't go back to Miss Aggie, and tell her Skye's lost without honestly being able to tell her we did our best."

"I'm up for whatever you need," Aeton said.

Wil: When I was talking with our contact here, he said that when you go into the brothels, they can show you upfront what girls they have. He said some places will line them up and have them walk past the guys in the lobby, and others will have a small book with pictures to choose from. Is that true?

Aeton: He'd know more than me. I've never been in one, other than last night.

Wil: If you don't have another plan, then, I suggest we systematically go from place to place and see if we can find her. What do you think?

Aeton: Let's do it. *Aeton slowed his driving.* We're here.

Wil: Really? This is it?
Aeton: I told you, it wouldn't be what you'd expect. Keep an eye out for a parking spot.

Wil was surprised to see the streets lined bumper to bumper with cars. They had to drive up and down several streets before they were fortunate and found an opening on the side of the road, just large enough for Aeton to squeeze his VW into. This spot seemed close to the main action, and they only got it because a car had just left the spot.

The streets were filled with men of all ages, of all walks of life. And littered throughout the edges were girls trying to connect with one of the men. In just the time it took for Wil to get himself out of the VW, he saw two girls, who had been leaning in to the windows of nearby cars, just hop in them and be driven away.

"I cannot imagine the kind of life all these girls live," said Wil sadly.

"I know," Aeton answered. "Come on, let's get to it. We've got a ton of ground to cover."

TWENTY-EIGHT

GALEN HAD TO SWALLOW HIS PRIDE when he first got into the cab and read off his destination. The cab-driver, clearly familiar with the area, had started to snicker and tease Galen about what kind of girl he'd be having tonight. Trying to ignore his jests, he simply sat back, asked the man to drive, and pretended to rifle through the orange backpack he'd brought with him. He hated that someone thought he was going to engage in such filth, even if it was only a guy he'd probably never meet again. The driver had taken the hint, and hadn't said another word.

What in the world am I trying to prove? Galen thought. *Where is all of this going to take me? It's not like I have an endless supply of money...even if I drain my entire savings on this girl, then what? If somehow I'm able to get her out of there, where will she go? She can't even speak any Greek! And when eventually my parents find out my money is gone, what in the hell am I going to tell them? "Oh, yeah. I used to have all that money, but I spent it all on a prostitute. But don't worry, Pop! I never had sex with her; I just sat there all night and talked with her."* Galen had to chuckle at how ridiculous that sounded.

Tonight he was determined to get the girl to talk to him. He only had a limited amount of money to pay for her, and he was feeling the pressure of time. He also couldn't risk the madame catching on to his plan. There's no telling what that evil woman would do to him if she found out. People who sell people for a living are capable of anything.

He needed to get the girl to talk, and it had to be tonight.

Galen hadn't worked out exactly how he was going to get her out of there, or what he was going to do with her once he did, but at the very least, he needed to get some information from her. Maybe once he knew a bit about her story, the exact strategy would fall into place. His thoughts went around and around, analyzing every angle of the situation he had put himself in, until the cab began to slow down, and he knew he had reached the brothel. As he paid the fare, he avoided eye contact with the driver to spare himself from the man's cheesy grin, and quickly hopped out of the car.

As he stood on the road outside the strip club, he noticed how much more activity was going on than when he'd left the place earlier this morning. Every corner had several girls standing around, talking to the men as they passed by. Some of the women were leaning into cars; Galen assumed they were trying to make a deal. He stood and watched one of the girls as she obviously sweet-talked the man into choosing her, because the car door opened, she disappeared inside, and they drove off.

How does that woman know that guy isn't going to do something terrible to her, maybe even kill her? She has no idea what kind of person she just left with! Galen was dumbfounded as the reality of the profession, along with its potential dangers, began to sink in. Then he noticed one of the prostitutes had spotted him, and was walking his way. Before she had a chance to approach him, he turned and entered the strip club foyer.

Two large men greeted him and made him pay the entrance fee required to go deeper into the club. Once inside, Galen was now able to see for the first time, the club in full swing. Last night he'd been blindfolded, so he'd only heard the sound of the music and smelled the sour alcohol coming off all the men. Tonight, he could see the room was large and dark, with most of its illumination coming from the flashing lights on the stages, of which there were three: a large center one and two smaller off-shoots. Several young girls were dancing throughout these stages, some on poles, some on higher platforms, and some bending over to tease the dozens of men who lined the edges. Then throughout the room, girls, in various phases of nakedness, roamed about with trays, a few more were sexually poised on small tables, while others could be seen writhing up against the men standing against the walls. Galen didn't even want to know what was happening in the far corners that were too dark to see into.

He closed his eyes to try and recall which direction Nikkos had gone to find the upstairs brothel. He'd been so tired and emotional when he left early that morning, he'd forgotten to take note of his exit. If his memory served him correctly, they had walked into the crowd and then around to the right. Galen opened his eyes, acted like he knew exactly what he was doing, and weaved his way through the crowd and over to the right. Once on the edges of the bar, he saw a dimly lit hallway with a red painted spiral staircase at the end. This was the right way.

His heart began to pound in his chest as he circled up the red iron staircase. Anxious adrenaline coursed through his veins, and he felt his face, armpits and hands begin to sweat. Everything inside him wanted to turn back and forget the entire plan, but he couldn't seem to turn himself around. His legs were resolute to make it to the top of the stairs. He had to see the girl again.

The little fat woman he'd met that morning appeared to be waiting for him, because as soon as he emerged to the second floor, she was right there to welcome him, lipstick-smeared teeth and all.

"Ooooh, Love!" she sang to him. "I've been waiting for you, and so has your girl!" And she giggled wickedly at him. "I've made sure she's nice and fresh for you. I even dressed her extra pretty for your entire night; you're still paying for the entire night, right?"

Galen wanted to smack the woman's grin right off her face, but he knew he had to play along with her. "Yes," he said. "And are you sure you did that? Because I'm not going to be paying the full price for her if you've had her working all day, too. I like my girls to be awake and ready to please while I'm with them." Galen gritted his teeth in disgust at his own loathsome words.

The old hag squinted her eyes and looked at him sideways. "But last night, your friend said this was your first time."

Galen had forgotten Nikkos had told her this. He tried to laugh it off. "Ha! Oh yes," he said. "That. That was just my brother trying to make you feel sorry for me and maybe even get a bargain from you. No, last night was *definitely* not my first time." Galen stopped for a second to see if the woman was believing his story. She seemed to.

Running his fingers through his hair, he continued, "It was my first time here, though, and I'm looking for somewhere new to go. I'm tired of the spoiled whores I'd been having at my old place. I want something younger *and* fresher. So you better not be trying to pull a fast one on me, giving me the stale leftovers from the day."

The woman quickly answered, "Oh no, no, no. Your girl has been resting all day, just like you asked. Will it just be you tonight? I thought you said you would be bringing some others with you."

Wanting to distract her, Galen pulled out the large wad of money he had just withdrawn from his bank account. "Don't you worry," he said while counting out the bills. "I've got lots of friends who I can bring, but first, I want to make sure I can trust you. My guys are like me; they'll want to buy all-night shifts; we like to train our girls to do what we like, if you know what I mean."

"Yes, yes, I do, Love," giggle-snorted the old woman.

"But, before my friends dole out tons of cash like this, I need to make sure you're going to make good on your promise to have fresh girls."

"Oh, I will, Love!" she promised. "For you and your boys, I will!"

"Well, let's just see how this week goes. If you follow through, then by the weekend, you'll be a very happy woman. I'll bring a dozen others with me."

"I will, I will. Don't you even doubt it, Love."

"Great. Then let's get started. Where is she?"

The woman picked up her large ring of keys. "Oh, she's in the very same room as last night. I don't like to move the girls around from room to room once I buy them."

Galen felt his stomach churn at her words. Had he heard her right? Had she said 'once I *buy* them'? He realized he was stepping into dangerous ground by asking, but he needed to know. "What do you mean, 'buy them?'"

For a split second, the woman seemed shaken, but almost as quickly as the worry appeared on her face, she masked it with a lipstick-smeared, toothy smile. She turned the tables on Galen by asking suspiciously, "What is the backpack for? Are you trying something kinky, because if you are, there's an extra charge for that."

"No," said Galen, "I just have someplace to be in the morning, so I brought my stuff with me."

Just then three men entered the room, and the madame was quickly distracted from Galen and his backpack. She clapped her hands and a thin, middle-aged woman shuffled in.

"Dula, take this boy back to number 10," the madame said handing her the big ring of keys. And then she quickly snatched them back. "I forgot I've already unlocked the door. Just take him down and make sure she's ready for him."

Without looking up, Dula started shuffling down the dark hallway. Galen took a deep breath and followed her. His his stomach was fluttering, and he wondered why he was so nervous to see the girl again.

THE WITCH HAD ONCE AGAIN left the door slightly ajar. Skye studied the two inch opening, desperately wishing she could walk through it and break free. It would take about three steps for Skye to leave her jail cell, but in her heart, she knew it might as well be three million. She'd only be caught, thrown back inside, and whipped or beaten for her audacity to escape.

And today, her imprisonment seemed worse than ever. Because of the great amount of sleep she'd had last night and even today, she felt a stronger clarity of mind than she'd felt in a long time. As the impending doom of the night's shift was racing toward her, she knew she wouldn't be able to count on her fatigue to give her the gift of delirium to make it through the horrors she was about to experience. She felt on the verge of vomiting at the thought of the many men she'd have to service tonight, with their sour odors and their hideous hands.

The thought was unbearable. She looked around her room to see what her choices would be if she could finally muster up enough courage for suicide. There were no sharp objects at her disposal, and the witch surely never brought anything like that in with her meals. So unless she could figure out a way to make a knife, cutting herself was not an option.

There was a lamp plugged into the wall. Maybe she could break the bulb and try to cut herself? Or maybe she could try and electrocute herself? But the thought of that option made Skye shudder, and she doubted she would ever have the guts to actually do something like that.

She glanced down at her bed and wondered if the sheets could be fashioned into a noose. She looked up at the ceiling to see if there was any kind of hook or bar that could support her weight. But the ceiling was smooth, and had nothing at all that would work. She then noticed the bars on the window. Those would definitely be strong enough, if they were high enough.

Skye walked over to the window to get a closer look. At the tops and bottoms of the bars, there was about one inch of each bar that jutted out horizontally before the metal curved to its vertical length. She felt the top of the bar to find out how slippery it was. Because the bars were so old and rusted, they felt very rough and prickly. She was pretty convinced there was enough texture for the sheet to stay in place.

Skye was surprised at herself; how resolute and calm she was as she stood there, planning out her own death. She looked down at her charm bracelet that she still clutched in her hand. She replayed Aggie's words in her mind once again:

> "You see dat birdcage? It's beautiful, but it's empty, just as a birdcage should be," Aggie had said. "And dis petite bird? Dat's your pet egret you've always wanted to catch, *Sha*. She's flyin free, never ever to be put inside any kinda cage. Dat's you, Skye-girl. You are a beautiful bird dat *le Bon Dieu* put on dis earth to fly da open sky with your dreams. You can never let yo'self be caught in any cage, you hear me? You're a bird, *Sha*. And you're gonna soar up as high as your dreams can take you."

While deep down she knew MawMaw never meant for her to interpret the bracelet like this, she felt killing herself would be the only way she'd ever be able to experience the freedom of that little silver bird. And isn't that what MawMaw would want for her anyway? She'd said it herself: Skye was never meant to be put inside any kind of cage.

Skye promised herself that tomorrow would be the day.

The door creaked open and she hurriedly slipped her bracelet under her pillow. She didn't bother to look up when the man came in, nor when she could tell that Dula was trying to get her attention. It didn't matter who it was; in fact, Skye generally tried to avoid eye contact with every visitor so she'd never have those wretched faces burned in her memory. She heard Dula leave the room and close the door. Then she waited for the man to speak, or to come over to her bed.

The first one of the evening was always the worst because he broke the hours of solitude she'd have during the day, her only relief from the horrors she'd face each night. She closed her eyes as she sensed the person in her room was moving about, and she felt she could implode with the dreadful anticipation of her attackers touch. The seconds seemed like hours as she sat on her bed waiting. And as her heartbeat ticked past the moments, still nothing was happening. The man had not approached her yet. Finally, unable to take the suspense, she focused her eyes and wildly looked around the room.

She gasped in surprise. It was the young man who had just left her room that morning. What was he doing here? Why was he back? Has he come to get what he didn't get last night? Questions swirled in Skye's head as she stared at the man.

He seemed nervous and uncertain, standing awkwardly with his hands in his pockets and his mouth open, as if he wanted to say something but didn't have the words. Then he did the same thing as he'd done the night before, motioning that he didn't want anything from her.

Skye was dumbfounded. She could not understand what was happening, why the witch was being so nice, why the guy was back in her room, or why he was paying money to just sit in that chair all night. She didn't know what to do, or how to act, or even how to feel about all that was happening. She wanted to believe this guy was not here to violate her, but after what she'd experienced during the last months, Skye had come to believe there was no one left in the world, except MawMaw Aggie, her mom and her sister, who was not out to hurt her. She sunk into her pillow and began to cry softly as she thought of her family.

TWENTY-NINE

ELLE WAS SO DESPERATE to see someone she knew besides her dad, she felt as if her soul was moaning within her. She'd grown despondent over the last day and a half, unable to eat any of the food Jack brought to the hotel room. All she did was lie on her bed and try to sleep. She wasn't interested in reading, watching television, or talking; she simply tried to sleep the days away until she would see Skye.

And Jack didn't even seem to notice, or if he did, he certainly didn't show the least bit of concern. He only thought about himself, what he wanted to do, and where he wanted to go. Now, as Elle lie in her bed glaring over at the sleeping man who was supposed to be caring for her and spending time with her, she could only feel contempt.

He could not care less for her, and she wished she had the courage to totally mess up the pageant, just to get back at him. But Elle wouldn't dare. She'd never done anything so rebellious, and he might even make her go straight home without ever seeing her sister. While she couldn't wait to be home with her mom and MawMaw Aggie, she certainly didn't want to risk losing the chance to be with Skye.

A soft buzzing sound came from the small table separating hers and Jack's beds. It was his cell phone receiving a message of some sort. Elle wondered if maybe it was a text from her mom? She sat up in bed so that when Jack checked his phone, he'd see she was awake. But Jack didn't budge. He was asleep deeply enough that he hadn't even heard the vibration go off.

Elle could see the small message light pulsing on the side of Jack's phone. She was dying to know if the text was from her mom. For several minutes, she debated whether or not she should check it. Normally, Jack never let anyone else touch his cell, but Elle tried to justify this instance as being a special circumstance. What if it was an emergency? What if her mom needed something that Jack should know about, this very minute? Surely, he would understand why Elle took it upon herself to look.

Her rationalizations convinced her, and very quietly, she scooted to the edge of her bed, listening to make sure Jack was sound asleep. Holding her breath, she reached over to grab his phone and to slowly bring it back to her bed. She hid under the covers so the display light wouldn't shine too brightly.

As she touched the screen to illuminate it, Elle's heart sank. It wasn't a text from her mom; it was from a person called "stableboyz." Because of the name, she assumed, it was probably one of the guys Jack sold horses with. She touched the screen again to turn it off, but instead, she accidentally opened the text. It read: "talked w 1 of the buyers for the deal. he's real interested in ur mare. got a fetish for ginger hair. he's ready 2 pay big money. its lookin good 4 u!!"

Elle wondered what those words meant. She didn't know her dad was selling any horses while they were here on vacation. And then it occurred to her: she had her father's cellphone in the palm of her hand. She should try and call her mom!

Elle lost her breath for a second; she'd give anything to talk with her mom. Looking back at Jack, she could tell he was completely zonked out. There was no way he'd hear her, and he wouldn't even know she'd done anything until he got the bill in the mail. She was so excited, she could hardly restrain from giggling.

Attempting to be completely silent, Elle slid out of her bed and tip-toed to the bathroom. She closed the door, and sat down with her back against it. She didn't risk turning the bathroom light on, so she had to manage the call in the dark. It wasn't until she was scrolling down Jack's contacts, that she could see how shaky her hands were from nervousness. She found Macy's name and pressed 'send'.

As she listened to the phone ringing on the other end, her insides began to whirl and her mind dizzy from excitement. After three rings, she heard her mom answer the phone, but before Macy had a chance to speak, Elle gushed.

"Oh Mama! Mama! I'm so glad you answered! I miss you so much, and wish you were here. We still haven't gotten to see Skye yet, and I miss you so much!"

"Hold on a minute, honey," an unfamiliar woman's voice said. "Who is this?"

Surprised to hear a voice other than Macy's, Elle wasn't sure what to say. She lifted the phone from her ear to make sure she'd pressed the correct contact. The screen said "Macy," but this person was definitely not her.

"Ummm..." said Elle. "I'm calling for Macy DuLonde. Can I talk to her please?"

"Listen, honey, can you tell me who you are?" the person asked.

"I'm Elle, her daughter. Can you please get my mama?"

There was a moment of delay before the woman said, "Elle, is this your daddy's phone?" Elle was afraid to answer. "Honey, is this your daddy's phone?" she asked again. "Can you please let me speak to your daddy?"

It was Elle's turn to pause as she tried to think of how to answer that question without telling the lady she'd snuck her father's phone in the middle of the night while he was sleeping.

"Can you please just get my mama?" Elle asked. "I really want to talk with her."

"Honey, your mama is...well...she can't talk right now; can you—"

"Why? What's the matter with her? Who is this?" Elle was getting more anxious by the second.

"Honey, this is Miss Lillie at the Maringouin Police Station." The woman was speaking very gently. "I really need to talk with your father, sweetie; we've been tryin to call him every day for almost a week now."

"Why?! What's happened to Mama? Is she alright?" Elle had completely forgotten to keep her voice down as she felt a panicky feeling rise within her. "Please, is Mama OK? Is she OK?"

Elle's body skimmed across the bathroom tiles as the door behind her aggressively swung open.

"Who in the hell are you talking to?!" Jack yelled in a raspy voice. He flipped on the light, and both of them squinted their eyes to adjust. "Is that my cell, you little brat?"

"Daddy, I'm so sorry! It's just that I was missing Mama so much, and I thought it would be OK if I called her for just a second. I was only going to talk with her for one tiny second, and you can totally take the money in my piggy bank to pay for it. But Mama didn't answer! The police station did!"

"Give me that phone," he whispered. And when Elle handed him the cell, he covered the speaker and added, "And get your ass back in bed before I beat it black and blue." He shoved her out of the bathroom, then slammed and locked the door.

Elle's concern for her mother overshadowed her fear of getting spanked, and she stood close to the door to overhear what was being said. Her dad's voice changed to a civil tone as he continued the call:

"Yes, this is Jack DuLonde.....Yes, I believe I have gotten your messages, but I'm out of the country, so the reception is very bad. The voice mails were breaking up and I couldn't make them out.....Can you tell me why you have my wife's cell phone?.....Why can't you just tell me over the phone?.....Yes, I understand that, but like I said, I'm out of the country at the moment, so I'd appreciate it if you just told me right now.....What?.....I'm sorry, but could you say that again?.....When did this happen?....."

Elle heard Jack unlocking the bathroom door, so she shot herself like a bullet into her bed. He came over to his suitcase and began looking for something. She could hear the sound of Miss Lillie's voice on the other end, but it was impossible to make out what her words were.

"Ummm..." Jack said. "I'm sure you can understand that I don't know what to say right now..... I'm sorry, I can't hear you..... What? Can you repeat that? You're breaking up....Hello?.....Hello, are you still there? There's only silence coming from your end..."

Elle wondered why Jack was saying that because she could plainly hear the sound of the woman's voice; maybe she couldn't decipher what Miss Lillie was saying, but Elle could certainly hear there wasn't silence.

"Hello?....I'm sorry, I think I've lost you.....Hello?" And with that, Jack not only ended the call, but he also turned off his phone altogether. He stopped ruffling through his bag and sat down on his bed.

Jack was dazed and his eyes darted around the room as if searching for an answer to something. He got up to walk back into the bathroom and muttered under his breath, "Macy, your timing was always horrible." And he slammed the door behind him.

Elle lay terrified in her bed, feeling like her world was crumbling apart.

THIRTY

WIL AND AETON HAD BEEN searching for several hours. And for the last square mile or so, Aeton had been urging Wil to stop so they could take a break and buy something to eat. Finally, after the worst attempt of the night had failed, Wil relented and agreed to put their search on hold for a bit. They found a bar that served food, and went to the furthest table in the corner. Neither had words to describe what they'd just experienced. Solemnly, they ordered beer and sandwiches from the server, reclined back in their chairs, and silently waited for their drinks.

At the beginning of their search, when it was just early evening, their strategy had been to meticulously walk down each street, going from brothel to brothel, strip club to strip club, and carefully check off every street and every building they found to be a hub to buy sex. Each location had a white lightbulb illuminated over an open door. But in order to hide the inner entrance from the passerby, there was always a curtain hung over the inside of the doorway, or just a little further down the entry's hallway.

Once the pair would venture inside, Aeton would tell the owner a story about how he was trying to show his pal a good time and that he wanted to see the youngest girls they had. As their contact had informed them, sometimes the owner would hand them a menu with pictures of the girls, sometimes there would be pornographic photos of their options posted on the wall, or sometimes the owner would have the available girls file out and stand in a line.

In most cases, the young women would stand with their eyes cast downward, and Wil's heart broke for how depressed each one appeared. But even worse was when the young girls would parade themselves into the foyer and try to pose sexually, playing the role of seductress. All the while, in their expressions, was a quiet desperation to be doing anything other than vying to win the attention of a 'John'.

Wil's stomach burned with anger and disgust. Girls this age should be in school, not living and working in a place like this. How many of these girls are being forced to be here? He couldn't believe that even one of them chose this lifestyle.

Three hours into their searching, Aeton had an idea to try a new approach. This time, they'd spent more time in each location, attempting to build relationships with both the owners and the 'Johns', and when they felt it was safe, they'd even show a picture of Skye to the patron and ask if she looked familiar.

Just before midnight, they'd gotten excited because a bartender in one of the clubs claimed to have recognized the young girl. He was a frequent visitor of a small brothel several blocks from where he worked, and he thought the picture looked like one of the prostitutes there. Wil and Aeton had darted out of the club, almost sprinting their way towards the brothel the man had described.

When they arrived, they were taken into a tiny foyer, as the owner bartered with Aeton over fees. Wil was disgusted at how filthy the place was, and when he craned his neck to see past the owner, it was clear the girls' rooms were even dirtier. None of the rooms had doors, just curtains on rods, and each cubicle was only big enough to hold a mattress on the floor and something that resembled a roll of paper towels. And by the wads of paper in the corners, it looked like there weren't even trash cans in them, either. While Wil was eager to find Skye, he hoped she had not spent the last several months living in this horrific place.

In the end, after Aeton described what he wanted to buy, the owner called over his shoulder at one of the girls. When she emerged from her 'room,' Wil's heart skipped a beat when he saw her black hair curling at her shoulders. But when she come close and lifted her face, she was definitely not Skye. And Wil was happy for it because the girl's face had been beaten recently. In addition, she looked only twelve or thirteen years old as she stood there in a skimpy slip that clung to her barely formed breasts.

At the sight of her, rage enveloped Wil and he wasn't sure he could restrain himself from beating this brothel owner into the ground. He turned on his heel and briskly walked out, Aeton right behind him. Wil was so amped up, Aeton had to almost jog to keep up with him, and this was when Wil finally agreed to stop the search for an hour or so.

It wasn't until Wil had finished his first beer before he could manage a conversation with Aeton. "After we eat, what's our next strategy?" he asked.

Aeton took a few moments before he responded, "Brother, I don't know."

"Let me see the map," Wil said.

Aeton pressed out the small map of streets that they'd been working from. From the markings on the streets, Wil assessed that they'd only hit a quarter of the brothel district.

"We've got to pick up the pace," Wil said. "Let's power through and make sure to get at least 75% of this map covered tonight. I say we go back to our first strategy and go place to place asking to see the girls. I get why it's beneficial to try and build relationship, but we don't have the luxury of that much time."

"Agreed," answered Aeton.

The server arrived with their dinners, and both men ate in silence.

AGGIE LOOKED OUT OVER THE CITY and breathed in the crisp cool air. Because she'd slept most of the flight over to Greece, she was unable to sleep now. Not wanting to wake Lottie, she took a blanket and her bible and went outside on the balcony. There was a small light out there, and she'd be able to read by it if she moved her chair directly underneath it.

"Hal, I ache for you tonight," she whispered heavenward. "I need you here with me to walk through dese next days. Dere's so much to take care of. We gotta get dese girls back, and den I gotta tell 'em about

Macy, and den we all gotta go back and lay dere mama to rest. And den we gotta figure out a way for dem girls to stay with me and not dat *peeshwank* Jack. I know dat Miss Lottie says she's going to help me, but how do I know dat for sure? I just met dese folks and how do I know I can trust 'em to help me take care of all dis? And on top of all dat, my phone won't let me call Leona here in Greece! I'm lucky to get a text through."

Aggie knew there was no way for Hal to speak back to her, but she always listened, just in case. And she felt the pang of disappointment when his voice didn't somehow break through the divide between heaven and earth. She decided to go to a higher level. "Dear Lawd, I need you to speak to me. Dis's too much for me. I know you promised me dat you're faithful and dat you'll not allow me to be tempted more dan I can stand. But just how strong do you tink your Aggie is? What do you think I'm made of? All of dis happenin to Macy, then to Skye, and now to Ellie? I know you're supposed to be perfect, but I tink in dis case you're wrong! Dis is too much for me to handle, and you're wrong!"

Shaking her head, Aggie tried to hold back her tears. She was tired of crying. Instead, she closed her eyes and tried to listen for any sign, any voice that would lead her through this wilderness.

As she rested her head back against the tall back of her chair, the base of the chair creaked in a familiar way. The sound transported her imagination back to an old, very small farm house. She was only seven years old, and she was sitting on her own MawMaw's lap. Rocking on a rickety wooden rocking chair, her MawMaw said, "Dose dat wait on da Lawd will renew dere strength. Dey'll rise up in da sky like eagles, and dey'll run and never grow weary; dey'll walk and never lose dere strength."

Aggie was surprised that she had forgotten this precious memory of her MawMaw. She'd heard her MawMaw repeat this verse almost every time she was with her, and eventually, Aggie would say it with her.

No woman who had ever lived on the planet was stronger than her MawMaw. Not only did she have to work her fingers to the bone all her life just to help feed her family, but she'd also experienced the pain of losing two children. One at the age of five from scarlet fever, and her only son at the age of 30 from a senseless, brutal lynching. Her son was a hard worker and never rose a fuss anywhere, and the whites around him didn't appreciate that his business was beginning to succeed. So they killed him mercilessly.

MawMaw was the angel who deposited the seeds into Aggie's young heart that would eventually harvest into a deep and trusting relationship with the Lord. And on this night in Greece, Aggie sensed it was MawMaw right now who was watering those seeds once again to strengthen her heart for battle.

"Thank you, MawMaw," Aggie whispered, as she allowed the verse from the Book of Isaiah to rotate over and over in her mind. "I will wait on you, Lawd, and I know you gone renew my strength. And I pray for Wil right now, dat you raise him up like an eagle so he is not weary. And for my blessed Skye-girl. Give her strength to hold on until we find her."

Aggie began to feel a peace settling into her soul, and she drank it in like an ice-cold lemonade on a hot summer day.

THIRTY-ONE

GALEN'S HEART BROKE to hear the girl crying. He wasn't sure why his presence made her start to cry so mournfully. He hadn't done anything to her but attempt to be kind and gain her trust. And he knew that if much more time went by, one or both of them would fall asleep. He could feel his head swimming from the fatigue of not sleeping last night, and the girl looked like she could sleep for days on end and still not have enough.

It was time to put his plan into action. Earlier, he'd come up with a strategy to get her relaxed enough to talk to him, and the best way he knew to do this was through food. Not to mention, the girl appeared way too skinny; he thought she'd probably not had a good meal since she'd been there.

Earlier that afternoon, Galen had asked his mum to cook a bunch of extra food for him to eat while he was working his so-called "night-shift" job. And to really get her to do it right, he told her one of his workmates was a German who'd been mouthing off about his disappointment with Greek cuisine. Galen knew those comments would spur his mum to cook her best dishes, because nobody could make Greek food as good as she did; everyone in town knew that. And anyone who didn't, his mum would be on a mission to convince them of this undeniable truth. Galen was sure if he could just get this girl to eat some food with him, she'd realize he was not there to harm her, maybe even start to trust him.

True to form, his mum packed an ample amount of *spanakopites, moussaka,* and *koulouria*, her melt-in-your-mouth butter cookies. She timed it out so the food would be coming fresh out of the oven right at the time Galen had to leave, and she put the food in individual plastic boxes, servings for both Galen and his German workmate. And in an effort to keep the meal warm for as long as possible, she enveloped them in copious amounts of aluminum foil.

Galen then wrapped the packaged meal in a small fleece blanket and put the whole thing in his orange backpack. He thought it best to try and keep the food's smell contained so that once he'd entered the brothel, the old woman didn't get suspicious, or ask why he was bringing in so much food.

He also decided to pack a small, folded map of the entirety of Europe. He hoped that even if he could simply get the girl to point to the country from which she came, he'd be able to start formulating a way to get her back home to her family. Did she have any family to speak of, and if so, have they been searching for her this entire time?

He thought now was as good a time as ever to talk to her.

"Listen," he said in a low voice. "I know you don't understand what I'm saying right now, but I'm going to talk to you anyway. We've got to find a way to get you out of this place. I'm not going to be able to keep coming and staying here all night long. So you've got to help me out and tell me where you're from."

The girl looked at him while he was talking, and she didn't seem to be getting afraid at his words, so Galen took that as a good sign. Granted, the look on her face wasn't the most inviting, but at least she wasn't curled up in a ball, frightened. He wondered what she'd do if he approached her.

But when he stood up and faced her, he saw her jump a bit and push herself slowly against the wall. He definitely did not have her trust yet. Maybe once he gave her the food, she'd realize he was on her side? He picked up his backpack and started to unpack it.

"I brought you some food. You look like you could use a good meal." Galen felt silly talking to a girl who couldn't understand a word he said, but he thought that if he spoke with a gentle tone, she'd feel more comfortable to try and communicate back. "I had my mum make us some food; it's really good Greek food. Nobody cooks better than my mum, and I know you'll like it. You've probably not had anything good to eat in this place."

He took the container of the *spanakopites* over to the girl and tried to hand it to her. She just squinted her eyes at him, obviously perplexed, and wouldn't reach out to receive his gift. Galen sighed in frustration.

"OK, I get it. You probably never had a guy come in here and offer you a home-cooked meal. Maybe if you see me eat it, you'll know it's safe. This right here is *spanakopites*, and you'll love them. They're little puffy pastries with spinach and feta." He set down the container, along with a fork and napkin, on the edge of her bed. Then we went back to get the rest.

"This is *moussaka*. And this little bag has my mum's famous *koulouria*. It's her own secret recipe, and these cookies will melt in your mouth." And with that, he popped one in his mouth and said, "mmmmmm," hoping that his response would give her the impetus to try one.

No luck. The girl just sat there looking at the food, showing no desire to eat any of it.

"Well, I'm hungry," said a disappointed Galen, "so I'm going to eat before it gets colder than it already is." And he sat down in his chair and started to eat his food. He could sense her eyes on him, which caused him to feel hyper-aware of himself, so he shifted his posture so that his profile was to her. Many uncomfortable minutes passed as Galen ate his meal, all the while strategizing what to do next.

SKYE WAS UTTERLY CONFUSED. Who was this guy and why was he bringing her food? Why would he do something like that? Did he feel guilty about what he was about to make her do, and so he's giving me some kind of peace offering first? She decided she was not going to take anything from him, no matter how good it smelled. All that would do is make him think he'd done her a favor and that now she'd owe him one.

She tried to distract herself away from the man, and she turned away from him. But with every passing moment, the awkwardness in the room only grew thicker.

The guy must've decided to stop eating because now he was rustling through his orange backpack. She couldn't help herself, and she glanced out of the corner of her eye to see what he was looking for. He pulled out a little brochure and began to unfold it. Skye realized it was actually a map of some kind. As soon as he had it open, he walked over to her.

She was sure he was going to finally make his move. Skye sat frozen on her bed and turned her head away. Empowered by the confidence that this was going to be her last night in the brothel, she began contemplating whether or not she should fight him off.

She closed her eyes, took a deep breath, and waited for the guy to touch her. She heard the sound of him moving the food containers onto the floor, no doubt to make room for himself next to her. But instead of feeling the bed sink with his weight, she heard the crinkling of the map as he smoothed it out on the mattress.

He began talking to her, gesturing to the map. Skye's eyes opened wide, not knowing how she was supposed to react. His expression was clear that he wanted her to respond, but she had no idea what he had said or what she should say in return. He spoke again, this time more agitated, pointing again to the map. Skye looked down and realized he'd brought with him a map of Europe. What did he want her to do with that map?

The guy stood up and began to pace the room, ruffling his fingers through his hair. He was visibly upset about something, and Skye was becoming more and more nervous about the situation.

He halted and turned directly to her. He spoke again, this time slower and more pronounced, or so it seemed to Skye. It didn't matter, though, because she still had no way of knowing what the guy was saying. He made a slight grunt of frustration, which made Skye jump a bit, but even so, he didn't let up. He strode to her bed, got on his knees, and leaned into her so that his nose was almost touching hers. Very intensely this time, he spoke again, in a gentle raspy whisper, but right in her face. His dark brown eyes stared deeply into hers, enveloping her, and she felt as if she were drowning in them. When he stopped talking, he remained close to her face, unwilling to break his gaze until she gave him whatever it was he wanted.

Not since she'd been here had she been face to face like this with anyone. She'd never allowed herself to make eye contact with a single one of those men. But now, she found her eyes glued to his, unable to break away from his passionate gaze. She felt entranced by him, and somewhere inside her heart that she thought had been beaten to death, she sensed a warmth and a great desire to trust him. Perhaps feeling more naked and vulnerable than ever before, an electricity surged through her being. She began shaking from his confrontation, feeling helplessly cornered.

Desperate for him to back off, her face trembled and her eyes filled with tears as she whispered, "What do you want from me?"

At her words, his eyes popped open and he stared at her in amazement as he gasped and sat back on his knees. A long moment passed, still with their eyes locked. Only their breaths could be heard above the deep bass rhythm vibrating from the club below.

Finally, Galen smiled and broke his stare. "Of course!" he said to himself. "How could I have been so stupid?!" And when he looked back at her, he realized she didn't understand what he was saying, so he whispered in English, "Are you American?"

Now it was Skye's turn to gasp as she heard the language of her home spoken to her, by someone other than the witch, for the first time in months. Her hands went up to her face, and overwhelmed with emotion, she began to cry.

"Please, you tell me, are you American?" he whispered again.

With her face still buried in her hands, all Skye could do was nod her head and weep. She then pulled her knees up to her chest, wrapped her arms around her legs and bowed her body into a ball.

She could hear the young man folding the map, then standing himself up. He walked over to his backpack and put the map away. He then came back to her and knelt on the floor next to the bed.

"My name is Galen," he said in a very thick accent. "Sorry, my English is not so good, but enough for to talk. I promise I not harm you. I want for to get you out of this terrible, terrible place."

With those words, Skye melted to her side on the mattress, uncontrollably weeping. She buried her face in her pillow to try and muffle her loud groans of emotional release.

"It's OK," Galen said softly, and put his hand on her back. "You cry. I wait here until you ready to talk." She allowed him to embrace her as her tears flowed freely.

Just then, Galen thought he heard something just outside the bedroom door. He glanced over to Skye to see if she'd heard it, too, but she made no indication she had. Unwilling to leave the girl who finally was allowing him to hold her, he only craned his neck to try and hear anything through the closed door.

THIRTY-TWO

WIL WAS DAZED as he walked into the Electra Hotel. After 10 hours straight of walking the streets of Thessaloniki, going from brothel to brothel, strip club to strip club, looking for any sign of Skye, Wil felt weary and defeated. He and Aeton had not so much as found the tiniest thread that might lead them to Skye's whereabouts. The magnitude of what they were attempting to accomplish in such a short amount of time was beginning to sink in, and Wil wondered if he was out of his league.

He walked all the way to one of the elevators before it dawned on him that he hadn't been inside this hotel. He was sharing a room with Tyler, who'd already checked in, but Wil had yet to get a key. Shaking his head at his absentmindedness, he turned to go back to the front desk.

It was 05:45, and Wil couldn't wait to take a shower. Not so much because he was dirty; he looked pristine right now compared to how gross he'd get during some of his military operations. It was more that he wanted to wash his mind from all the filth he'd seen over the last several hours. During his years in the service, he'd never chosen to join any of his fellow soldiers when on occasion they'd go looking to hook up with girls in seedy bars or strip joints. So, tonight was Wil's first experience "hooker-hopping" as one of his buddies used to call it. He remembered how he used to roll his eyes at his friend when he'd use that phrase; but now, the thought of those words made him want to retch.

Many of the girls he met tonight appeared well under eighteen years of age, and all of them had a similar hollow look in their eyes. Even in the pornographic photos the brothel owners would show Aeton and Wil, behind the makeup and sexual poses, their "bedroom" eyes looked vacant. In several brothels, the owners would line up the girls before the men in the lobby, so each man could make his selection. Wil had felt himself ready to come undone. His impulse was to bash in the head out of every single man in the place and to rescue all the girls to safety. And knowing he and Aeton had the ability to quickly accomplish these beatings only intensified his temptation to fight.

It was a huge concern for Wil that he was finding it difficult to keep his emotions in check. This was completely out of character for him, and he hated the unsteadiness he was feeling. Wil had always been lauded by both commanding and fellow officers of his ability to maintain his unwavering focus, no matter what the situation. Nothing ever shook Wil. But tonight had.

This sobered Wil, and he knew he had to get himself under control before his late morning meeting with the woman running the auction. She was supposed to be a sharp one, with a reputation of being able to sniff trouble a mile a way. He had to make sure he was on point during this meeting. So even though Wil normally never took breaks, he knew he needed one now.

He showed the receptionist his ID, and she handed him his key. Room 320. He thanked her and started again in the direction of the elevators.

He rode the elevator up to the third floor, found his room, and entered as quietly as possible. He didn't want to wake Tyler, and more importantly, he didn't feel like talking about the night he'd just had. As soon as the door cracked open, Wil let out a sigh of disappointment. The room light was on.

Tyler was sitting outside on the balcony, drinking a cup of coffee. At the sound of Wil's entrance, he quickly came to meet him. But Tyler was an extremely perceptive man, and the moment they locked eyes, it was as if they had an entire conversation. Tyler gave him a casual head-nod greeting and said matter-of-factly, "Your bag is over there. What time do you need to head out again?"

"Right now it's 05:50? I need to meet Aeton at 09:30, he's picking me up outside."

"Great. I was just about ready to go down, get more breakfast, and walk around a bit, so you can have the room to yourself. Just fyi, your mom and Miss Aggie's suite is right next to ours, and our rooms basically share a balcony. So only go out there when you're ready to chat."

Wil chuckled. "Got it. Thanks."

As he knelt down to put on his shoes, Tyler said, "I'll text you around 09:00 to see if you need me to bring you back some food." Tyler grabbed his wallet and room key and strode to the door.

Just as he'd opened it, Wil said, "Thanks, dude. I appreciate it."

"No prob, man." And he was gone.

Wil flopped himself down on his bed, set his watch for 08:30, and closed his eyes. A deep sleep was indeed waiting for him, but the mental journey to get there was not fun. As he drifted off, his mind turned into a cruel slideshow, fast-forwarding through all the hundreds of girls' faces he'd looked into throughout the last hours. Each girl's expression was more fearful than the one before, her eyes pleading with him to rescue her out of her torture. He wrestled with these images for quite a while until finally his fatigue took over and he fell asleep.

WIL SPRANG UP IN HIS BED, his adrenaline already pumping. He felt sweat rolling down his chest and was sure he'd just had a nightmare, but he chose not to recall its details. Instead, he gathered his mind to focus on his whereabouts. Hotel. Greece. Skye. Elle. Meeting with Aeton.

He spun around to grab his watch, and just as he did, his 08:30 alarm sounded. He smiled at himself, knowing even with all that had happened in the last few days, his internal stopwatch was still spot on. This little sign of acuteness gave Wil the confidence he needed, that his ability to handle this mission was up to par.

He jumped out of bed, feeling as if his 2 1/2 hour nap had actually been a full night's sleep. As he showered, he went through a mental check list: dress, coffee, eat, meet with Mom, get the money Dad wired, meet Aeton outside the lobby at 09:30, coffee again, meet auction lady, continue search for Skye.

As he dressed, he felt his stomach burning with hunger, and he wondered if Tyler had any leftovers out on the balcony that he could scrounge. He walked out and found some cold, rubbery toast and a half pot of coffee. He stuffed the bread into his mouth and for a moment forgot to chew when he looked up and saw the view before him. The sight of the bright aqua Mediterranean Sea was stunning.

"It's beautiful, isn't it?" he heard someone say behind him. He'd forgotten Tyler's words about his mom's suite being next door. But Wil was glad to hear her comforting voice.

"It really is," answered Wil without turning around. "How come we never took a family vacation to Greece? This place is incredible."

"I don't know. But after this is all over, maybe we'll come back someday and take a cruise. (*She paused for a moment*) I wasn't expecting to see you until the Friday afternoon pick up. Is everything OK?"

"Oh, yeah," said Wil as he stuffed another piece of bread in his mouth. "I needed to pick up the cash Dad wired, so I figured I might as well grab a shower while I'm at it."

"I just got back from pickin up the money. And not to make you look cliche' or anything, but I wasn't sure how one carried around that much cash. So, I also bought a briefcase for you to carry it in." She disappeared inside her suite for a moment, and returned with a brown briefcase. She handed it to Wil.

"Thanks so much, Mom. This is great. Yeah, who carries a quarter of cash anymore? Unless you're a criminal or something. Anyway, Aeton and I decided we shouldn't carry it all in one place. He's picking up some cash belts for each of us to wear on our bodies, and also, I'll keep part of it in my leather laptop bag."

"Yes, of course," she said. "That makes total sense."

After a long pause, she said, "Do you mind if I ask you about last night?"

"No," Wil said, checking his watch. 08:52. "But unfortunately, I haven't much to tell you." He stretched his neck so he could glance into his mom's room to see if he Aggie was nearby. "Where's Miss Aggie?" he asked quietly.

"Right now, she's downstairs in the restaurant."

Wil looked directly into Lottie's eyes and said carefully, "Mom, I'm not gonna lie to you. Chances are very slim that we're going to find Skye. I wish I could tell you differently, but..." his voice trailed off for a moment. "Aeton and I went from place to place last night; I can't tell you how many girls we saw, never imagined there could be so many brothels in such a small radius. I mean, when I was in that meeting with Trafficking Hope, they told me what it was going to be like here, but I don't know, I guess I didn't believe them, or thought they were exaggerating...I don't know what I thought. But after last night, I finally got a scope of what we're *really* dealing with, and it's a way bigger machine than I'd realized, with many different levels, at that. Plus, these people are constantly moving the girls around, from brothel to brothel, even city to city.

"As far as Elle is concerned, we've got a specific time and address; as a matter of fact, in a few minutes, we're even meeting with the gal who's running the whole auction tomorrow afternoon. But to find Skye..." Wil just shook his head. "I think we need to prepare Miss Aggie about what she should and should not expect from this trip."

Lottie sat down in the balcony chair and looked out at the sea.

Wil could see her eyes filling with tears. "Honey, you can only do what you can do. That's all we're askin. Let's focus on gettin Elle, and we'll do our best to locate Skye; but if we can't, well, we'll just have to come up with another plan of attack. As far as Miss Aggie is concerned, I'll talk with her today, when the time is right. We both are wantin to keep our minds occupied while we're waitin, so we're goin sight-seein to the White Tower and several of the Thessaloniki churches. I'm sure the right moment will come for me to tell her."

"Whoa. Wait a minute. You guys are going out? I'm not sure that's going to be safe. I think you should stay right here in the hotel. What if Jack would happen to see you?"

"Honey, what are the chances of us runnin into Jack?! That's crazy."

"Nope," Wil said, shaking his head. "Dad would not like it."

"Alright..." Lottie's mind was turning trying to find a way to convince him. "What if Tyler goes out before us and scopes out the place? I promise the only place we'll go is the White Tower. There and back. Done. Seriously, we all know Jack is not here to sightsee." Lottie could tell Wil's silence meant he was considering it. "It's goin to be torture to be cooped up in this hotel all day long."

"Alright, but I'm going to talk to Tyler to make sure he checks everything out with a fine-tooth comb." Wil's phone went off; it was a text from Tyler. "Listen, I need to go downstairs and grab some food. I'll be in touch throughout the day with updates."

"Sure, sure. You go, honey," she said. Before she could add anything else, Wil was gone.

THIRTY-THREE

JACK HAD STAYED CLOSE to the hotel the entire morning. This long in his presence made Elle very uncomfortable, especially since the incident last night with his cell phone. But he hadn't said a word to her about it, and Elle wasn't about to bring it up. Certainly, he hadn't forgotten, and Elle was concerned if she talked of it, she'd only bring punishment upon herself.

Plus, her dad was acting strange. All day he'd been very fidgety and nervous. He was smoking almost nonstop, in addition to carrying on several text conversations on his phone. A few times he needed to make or answer a call, and without fail, he'd leave the room to talk. Elle knew not to assume his exits were a courtesy towards her; she'd come to realize this past week that Jack never did anything as a courtesy towards anyone but himself. Most likely, he was hiding yet another part of himself from her.

She wondered how long Jack had been so detached from the family, not to mention, so deceptive. Had he been like this her whole life? She tried to remember back as far as she could to find even the faintest warm memory of her father. She replayed past birthdays and holidays and searched these mental pictures for images of a nice Jack. Was there a recollection of a daddy-daughter hug, a meaningful talk, or a bedtime story?

Nothing. Elle was shocked to discover that she couldn't think of one time where her father had initiated loving contact or communication. In fact, now that she had replayed these memories, she realized that *all* of them involving a hug or a fun conversation, she had been the one who had approached him. Her dad had never initiated the contact. And it was painful to accept that, in truth, he also had never really welcomed her affection; he'd simply tolerated it.

Had he been this way to Skye, too; or was his nastiness only directed toward her? Elle decided she'd surely talk to Skye about this when they were together. While she didn't wish for Skye to have also been the brunt of Jack's disapproval, Elle also would be crushed to find out her father's aversion was only for her. Either way, she wanted to know the truth. No longer was she afraid to voice her feelings about Jack's rejection to her sister, or her mother. In fact, Elle promised herself that as soon as she returned home, she would also share with Macy all of her new discoveries about Jack. Maybe MawMaw was right, and they all should get away from Jack and move in with her.

And if Elle was going to be brutally honest with herself, she would admit that her mom had been on a very scary downward slide. It wouldn't just be safer to move in with MawMaw; it was becoming a necessity. Her mom seemed out of control, and Elle did not know what to do to help her come back to being the mom she used to know. Elle knew she was using drugs again, even making the stuff in the kitchen in front of her. Her mother's body had become so thin, and the color of her skin did not look right.

For the past several months without Skye in the house, Elle couldn't count how many meals she had to fix for herself. In addition, there were instances when she would have to search for some money in her mom's wallet, or room, or drawers so she could walk to the corner store and buy some groceries for breakfast and dinner. Elle had started to become the caretaker of her mother, and she had been growing very weary of it. It had been weeks since Macy had invited MawMaw over, and Elle missed her greatly. She knew that if MawMaw would so much as take one glance at Macy, she'd whip things into shape for everyone.

The image of home reminded Elle of her cell phone conversation with Miss Lillie the night before. She wondered for the millionth time why the Maringouin Police Department had her mom's cell. She couldn't come up with any good reason, and that made her feel sick to her stomach. To try and believe the best, she worked diligently to convince herself that probably her mom had simply lost it at Bobbens Supermarket, or even had just dropped it while getting gas at the Jr. Food Mart. Both of those places were close to the police station, and someone could've found it and walked it right over there to turn it in.

However, Miss Lillie's voice seemed more concerned than just a lost-and-found item, and the memory of her tone worried Elle. She was certain Miss Lillie had given Jack all the details when he grabbed the phone away, and she ached to ask him about everything the woman had told him. But she couldn't muster up the courage.

Elle's only solace was that finally, she could stop counting days and begin to count the hours until she'd be with Skye. It was Thursday, the pageant was tomorrow, and by that evening, she'd finally be with Skye! *And if I do happen to win big prizes, like Daddy says I will, then maybe he'll at least be happy enough to tell me what Miss Lillie said. Or, maybe even let me call our home phone number to talk to Mama?*

Elle glanced over at Jack as he flipped from station to station on the TV. She sighed. *Fat chance that anything I do could ever make Daddy happy.*

She prayed tomorrow would come quickly.

DULA HATED THE AUCTIONS. Her normal schedule of cleaning the rooms, delivering food, and washing the laundry permitted her to exist through each day without having much interaction with anyone else. But when there was an auction, her schedule was upside down, there was triple the work, and worse, the madame made her work with the girls who were going to be sold. This was torture for the middle-aged woman who tried to avoid communicating at all costs. People were a source of pain for her; to use her, to beat her, to rape her, or to berate her. Auction time forced her to break her usual vow of silence.

The girls that just needed to be told what to do once they were onstage at the auction were easy, as most of them had been through the process before. But there were two types of girls Dula dreaded working with: the new girls, most of whom didn't speak Greek and were terrified, and the throw-away girls, who were either past their prime or had done something to get themselves beaten. When the madame had called Dula this morning to the Black Cell, Dula was weary to see this girl was both a new girl *and* a throw-away.

The Black Cell was a large concrete room with absolutely no windows. It's where the Madame brought the new girls on their first night, and where they were beaten, drugged, and raped until they were broken in. Only when the girl had forever lost her spirit and desire to fight back did the men stop their violence against her. Some girls were broken in a night; some girls took as many as three nights. All were beaten and bloodied by the end of the process, and it was Dula's job to heal them and put them back together.

When Dula arrived at the Black Cell, the Madame was standing over the throw-away, who appeared to be in her mid-teens. Her hands and mouth had been covered with electrical tape, and her back was bloody from several lacerations. It was not unusual for the madame to whip a girl if she didn't obey her orders exactly. Dula had her own scars to prove it.

Bending over, the madame ripped off the tape from the girl's hands and mouth, causing her to moan in pain. "Take this trash to your room and make her ready to sell," she ordered as she balled up the gray tape and put it in her pocket. "Make sure she wears something to hide the marks."

Dula wished she had enough courage to roll her eyes at the domineering woman. Of course she knew to hide the marks. She always had to hide the marks. But instead, Dula simply kept her head downcast and shuffled toward the crumpled girl. As she tried to support the throw-away to standing, she noticed her exotic-looking black hair. Dula wondered if she was from France or Spain with that shiny black hair. *No matter,* she thought. *I will never know anyway.*

Dula and the girl slowly shuffled through the maze of hallways within the brothel until they at last reached Dula's room. This was Dula's sanctuary, and she only shared it when she had less than 48 hours to heal a girl's wounds. Those instances required around-the-clock ointments and poultices, in which Dula was an expert.

She escorted the girl to her bed, helped her to lay on her side, and then turned to grab a pair of scissors. When Dula spun back around with scissors in hand, the throw-away's eyes filled with terror and her body started trembling. It was too much work to attempt to communicate that because of the wounds on her back, it would be easier to just cut off her camisole. Dula simply went to work ignoring the girl's cries, knowing that in a moment, the girl would figure out that her intentions were not for torture.

After removing the bloody camisole and assessing the cuts, Dula was pleased to see it wasn't as bad as she'd seen before. Knowing the madame possessed not one ounce of compassion, she assumed the whipping was lessened because the auction was only a short time away. Damaged goods never sell well.

She left the naked girl on the bed and shuffled toward the favorite luxury of her sanctuary: a bathtub. None of the girl's cells had anything more than a toilet and a small sink. But Dula's captivity was graced with an old, stained bathtub, and it was her prized possession. She began to fill the tub with warm water, adding healing spices and ointments to the bath. She knew once the girl soaked in this medicinal bath, the pain from her wounds would be greatly reduced. Then, Dula would give the throw-away a special tea to make her sleep deeply. Not only would this enable the healing to accelerate, but it would also give Dula the privacy she treasured so deeply.

THIRTY-FOUR

WIL WAS STANDING OUTSIDE when Aeton pulled up to the entrance of the Electra Hotel. He ran over to the VW and knocked on the passenger window. Aeton stretched across the seat to unroll it.

"Hey, man," Wil said. "Did you get any sleep?"

"Only a bit." Aeton answered. "Honestly, I was too disturbed by what we saw last night."

"Me too, Bro. I wanna kill those bastards. You can just park the car here for a sec while we go in and figure out how to situate all the cash," Wil said. "Do you have the belts?"

"I've got them. Are you sure it's OK to park here?"

"Yeah, as long as it's only for a few minutes. I already checked with the front desk."

Aeton grabbed a small duffle bag from the back seat of the car and got out. As they entered the lobby, Aeton asked, "How did your dad get all that cash to you in such a short amount of time?"

"Who knows? It's my dad; he always can pull off stuff like that."

Aeton held up the bag that had the cash belts inside. "Where do you want to go to put these on?"

"You know what? I was thinking we could just use the bathroom down here, but now I'm thinking we'd better be safe and use my room," said Wil. "The stairs are right here; it'll be much faster to take these than wait for the elevator."

The young men bounded up the three flights of stairs to Wil's hotel room. Once inside, Wil flopped the briefcase down on the bed and opened it. The sight of its contents stopped Aeton in his tracks. "Look at all that money!" Aeton whispered. He reached out to touch the piles of euros. "I've never seen that much cash in my life!"

"Yeah, it is kind of weird to see it all in one place like that," Wil said matter-of-factly. And then he noticed Aeton, who seemed in a trance as he was unable to take his eyes off the money.

"Bro," Wil said sharply. "What's wrong with you? Seriously, it's just money. Are you going to be OK, because we've got to keep our heads in the game."

Still staring at the money, Aeton said, "I'm sorry...it's just...I've never seen that much cash before."

"Look at me, Aeton," Wil directed. He waited until Aeton made eye contact. "It's just money. Think of your new baby girl, and what you would do if any of those people got a hold of her. You wouldn't think twice to pay this much money to get her back."

He shook his head and said. "You're right. I'm sorry. I just have never seen that much, let alone been in the same room with it. I mean, I can literally *feel* the power coming off of it."

"Aeton." Wil was annoyed.

Embarrassed, Aeton looked downward. "Right. You're right. I'm sorry."

"So, you're good?" Wil asked, not fully convinced. "You sure you're not gonna go all *Gollum* on me?"

Aeton tried to laugh. "Yeah, man. I'm good."

"OK," said Wil, "Cause all I'm saying is, if I hear you start calling that money '*my precious*,' I swear, I'll kick your ass."

Aeton put his hand on Wil's shoulder, and looked him squarely in the eyes. "I'm over it. I promise, you can totally trust me."

Wil took a moment to assess his friend. "Alright. I believe you. Just keep your baby girl's face in the forefront of your mind if you feel yourself starting to slip."

The men got to work separating the money, filling the pockets of the cash belts, and strapping them on their bodies. A portion of the money went across their chests, and another portion was belted around their thighs. The remainder went into a small, black leather laptop bag.

They checked themselves in a full-length mirror to make certain the money was hidden under their clothes. As they were leaving Wil's hotel room, Aeton's cell phone rang. Wil could hear a bit of confusion in Aeton's responses, but since he was speaking Greek, Wil didn't understand what was being said. They ran down the stairs to the lobby, and exited the hotel.

Aeton ended his call and said, "Well, there's been a slight change of plans."

Wil: What do you mean?

Aeton: Remember that bodyguard guy I told you about?

Wil: The one who's our 'in' with the gal holding the auction tomorrow?

Aeton: Yes. That was him on the phone. We're still meeting with the old woman, but the location has changed at the last minute.

Wil: Why?

Aeton: He wouldn't say anything except that she wanted us to meet her at one of her other strip clubs.

Wil: Hmm. Do you think we should be suspicious?

Aeton: Hell yes! I think we need to be suspicious of everything we're doing. These people sell people for a living. Who knows what else they're capable of?

Wil: Well, as long as we're not going to some old abandoned warehouse, I think we'll be OK. At least she didn't cancel completely.

Aeton: No, it's definitely not in a remote area, he gave me the address, and described the outside of the club.

Wil: You got your gun right?

Aeton: Gunsss, brother, as in more than one.

Wil: Yeah, me too. Just in case, we better make sure they're easily accessible.

Aeton: Roger that, as you Americans say.

Wil: Roger that.

THE WHITE TOWER WAS an astonishing experience for Aggie. Throughout her life, she'd never been much of a traveler, and certainly had never been a tourist outside the United States. Now, to be visiting what many considered to be one of the most beautiful regions in the world, Aggie could hardly believe her eyes. As she stood outside on the terrace, the White Tower's highest rooftop, it wasn't enough for her to simply see the panoramic view; she wanted to take it in with all her senses.

For moments, she'd close her eyes and smell the saltiness of the Aegean Sea, and then she'd focus on the sounds of the birds, and the fresh breeze running across her face. And when she'd reopen her eyes, she'd once again be taken aback at how incredibly gorgeous the scene was before her.

It was a very clear day, so she was able to see the entire city, as well as miles across the sea. The water was bluer than anything she'd ever witnessed, and the sky over Thessaloniki appeared to be several times larger than the one over Lafayette.

Lottie walked up close to Aggie and said, "It's just magnificent, isn't it?"

"*Chooh,* Miss Lottie, I ain't never seen anyting like dis. I wish Hal was here to see it."

"Did you and Hal travel much?"

"*Mais, non,* not all dat much. Dere was a time we used to drive all over da South to tailgate at LSU Tiger games. Ha! Dose were some a da funnest times we had together. Hal had *beaucoup* football brothers like dat. And once, for our 20th anniversary, we drove all da way to see Niagara Falls. But I've never seen anything like dis. I'm sure dat's not how it was for you and Mr. DuLonde."

Lottie softly laughed. "Yes, Richard and I have seen quite a bit of the world. We've been very fortunate, Miss Aggie. I will promise you this; once we get the girls home, and all this is behind us, we'd love for ya'll to travel with us whenever and wherever you like."

Aggie paused for a minute and then said, "I'm sorry, Miss Lottie, I don't know what to say. Both you and Mr. DuLonde have already been so kind."

"Well, now," Lottie said as she slipped her arm through the crook of Aggie's arm. "Don't give us so much credit. It'll be purely selfish on our part! Now that we're family, we're goin to want to get to know ya'll much better and spend lots and lots of time with you and the girls."

The new friends walked side by side for a few moments, making their way to the other side of the terrace. They chuckled at each other when they noticed how they were being shadowed closely by Tyler. Once they were looking out in the other direction, Aggie stepped away from Lottie and gazed at the sights. This new vantage point allowed them to see directly into the heart of the city. Aggie grew solemn.

"*J'ai gros couer*," Aggie whispered.

"What, sugar?"

"Oh. Dat's Cajun for: I feel like cryin," Aggie said softly as she gazed at Thessaloniki. "How can someting so beautiful be a place where dere's so much evil? *Le Bon Dieu* shouldn't let the two live side by side like dat." She took in a deep breath. "Somewhere out dere is my Elle and my Skye-girl. I can't wait to squeeze em and take em home."

"Miss Aggie..." Lottie waited to go on until Aggie made eye contact with her. "I don't think I've told you yet that Wil made it back to the hotel for a short time this mornin, and I had a chance to talk with him about what he'd seen last night."

"Does he know where Skye is yet?" Aggie asked.

"That's just it," Lottie said carefully. "Last night, Wil and his friend searched high and low throughout dozens and dozens of places. They must've seen hundreds of girls. Not only that, they also learned from some of the men that were there about how often the girls are rotated around...in the city, and even into other countries." She paused to determine if Aggie was catching on to what she was trying to communicate. Aggie seemed unmoved.

"What I'm wanting to say to you, honey," Lottie went on, "is that even though it's only been several months since she's been here, Skye could be anywhere by now. Anywhere. Some of those brothels move the girls in and out weekly. So, Miss Aggie, what I think you need to understand is that it is highly, *highly* unlikely that the boys are goin to find Skye in this visit."

Aggie's expression still didn't waver. In fact, the corners of her mouth turned upwards into a small confident smile, and as she looked back into the city, she said resolutely, "Dey gone find her."

"Of course, honey. Of course we'll find her. We will look high and low, and we'll never stop lookin until she's home safe. But on this particular visit...Miss Aggie, it's most likely not goin to happen."

Aggie stood firm. "Dey gone find her, Miss Lottie, and dat's just gone be da way it's gone be."

"Aggie, listen—"

"*Non, non*, you need to listen to me, *Sha*," Aggie spoke with great love. "I understand what you're tryin to tell me, and I thank you for it. But here's what you don't know, and dat's dat God is on my side. Dat may sound foolish to you, but I know da Good Lawd didn't bring me dis far to leave me now. I just know dat I know, dat's da truth. He made da way for me to get to you, and he'll make da way for Wil to find my Skye. I don't care how it looks right now, Miss Lottie, but I *know* he gone do it."

By Lottie's expression, Aggie could tell she didn't believe her.

"I'm tellin you, he gone do it. You just watch. I don't wanna hear another word about it, Miss Lottie. *He gone do it,* just you watch."

Lottie sighed. "Alright, Miss Aggie. Not another word."

THIRTY-FIVE

"ARE YOU SURE this is the right place?" asked Wil as he scanned the front of the strip club that looked more like a prison. It was made of gray concrete, and some of the upper windows had bars on them. And it certainly didn't have the obvious neon signage that the New Orleans clubs had all along Bourbon Street.

"There's only one way to find out," Aeton said.

"We didn't come here last night when we were looking for Skye, did we?"

"We went to so many freakin places, Wil, I couldn't begin to remember them all. But look over there down by all the warehouses; do you see those railroad tracks? I don't remember coming near those...so my best guess would be that we did not make it here last night."

"It's hard to believe that after going all night hopping from brothel to brothel, there still are so many we have left to check. Although, as far as this place is concerned, it's probably a good thing. If the woman we're meeting was in this club last night, there's a very good chance she'd recognize us today."

"Yes," said Aeton. "You ready? I'm sure this is the street the guy gave me."

"Let's go."

"Remember, let me do *all* the talking."

"As far as she'll know, I'm a mute."

Aeton led the way as he opened the large black doors to the club.

Directly inside was a small foyer inhabited by two brutish men. Behind them were two more doors that swung open into what Wil could only assume was the main hall of the strip club. Aeton stepped up and spoke to the men, and as their focus was on Aeton, Wil took the momentary opportunity to size them up.

They looked alike, almost like brothers, having the same build of about 6'5" and each weighing in over 300 lbs. One had his head completely shaved, and the other wore a buzz cut. The bald one had a cloudy eye, and by the way he looked around, Wil was sure he was partially, if not fully, blind in that eye. They kept their weapons strapped on opposite sides of their back, which caused Will to make a mental note that the bald guy was left-handed. Both of them wore pointy, metal-tipped cowboy boots.

Aeton was speaking to the man with the buzz cut, who must've been the leader of the pair, because the bald guy simply stood there, hands behind his back, chest jutted out. Wil thought he was obviously trying to look dominating, and he wished he could prove who was really the alpha dog by throwing the guy down on the floor and making him beg for his life.

After a few minutes, the main guy gave them entrance. When he lifted his hand to push open the strip club doors, Wil saw it was covered with terrible burn scars. But by no means was the brute trying to conceal his deformities because his fingers were littered with gold nugget rings. Even so, Wil assessed that if need be, he and Aeton would be able to take them out.

The lead guy escorted Aeton and Wil into the club and the other followed behind them. *This is so freakin surreal,* thought Wil. *What in the hell am I doing walking in between these two mutants with a quarter of a mil in euros strapped to my body? Oh god, this better work.*

Once again, Wil focused his energy on scoping out the place, and from a quick scan, he spotted four alternative exits, in case of emergency, as well as several items lying about that could be used as weapons. The room was empty, save the stages, the tables and chairs, and the various alcohol stations. He heard someone approaching from the far right, an inconsistent rhythm of clicks from a pair of stilettos. From the way the two bodyguards stood at attention when they also heard the sounds, Wil assumed it was the woman who owned this joint.

The short, fat woman in high heels seemed to defy gravity as she quickly hobbled, yet at the same time, glided over to the group of men. She spoke in a sing-songy way to her guards, and when she got close to them, she patted them condescendingly on their chests. However, the moment she addressed Aeton, she instantly turned suspicious and cunning. Wil observed their interactions, making sure to remain completely poker-faced.

Aeton and the woman spoke for several minutes; but all the while, she kept looking over at Wil. She seemed to be bothered by him, so much so, she abruptly stopped talking to Aeton in order to hobble over to him. Wil upheld a neutral and unthreatened posture as she scrutinized him up and down. Squinting her eyes, she stared at his face, as if she was trying to decide if she'd seen him before. She looked into his eyes and spoke directly to him.

Wil didn't understand a word she said, but he was not about to be the one to break eye contact; he simply waited for Aeton to interpret.

"She thinks you look familiar, and she's asking if you've ever met," Aeton said.

Wil shook his head 'no.' The woman paused for a moment, poring over his features, and then spoke something else in Greek.

Aeton said, "She's asking again if you're absolutely sure you've never met." Wil could tell she was trying to ascertain if he was lying, so he continued to look the old woman straight in her eyes, and once again, he shook his head. For what seemed like a full minute, she continued to examine Wil head to toe.

Then, as abruptly as she'd stopped talking to Aeton, she began chattering again, motioning for them to come and sit at a table. The three sat as Aeton and the woman continued negotiating, and the guards remained standing beside the table.

Aeton turned to Wil. "She wants to see the money."

Wil set the black leather laptop case on the table and unzipped it to show its contents. She pulled out a stack of euros and thumbed through it. Then both Aeton and Wil lifted their shirts to reveal their money belts. Aeton appeared to be informing her how much cash was being carried in each location, and how it all added up to $250,000. He pointed to his thigh and pulled his pant leg tight over the money belt so she could see it was full of cash, and then did the same to Wil's leg.

The old woman stood up, took a stack of the euros and tried to put it in her pocket. She appeared confused as to why the bills wouldn't fit. She reached her other hand around and stuck it in the pocket, and when she felt what was in there, she rolled her eyes and giggle-snorted. She dug out a ball of wadded-up gaff tape. Tossing it aside, she made a comment to the body guards, who in turn laughed with her.

Now able to stuff the stack of cash in her pocket, she made one final comment to Aeton and then hobbled away on her stilettos, returning from the hallway from whence she came.

"Let's go," Aeton whispered to Wil.

The two men stood up and headed straight for the club doors without so much as nodding to the body guards. Once they had exited the strip club, Aeton said, "We're in."

THE SQUEAK FROM THE COT alerted Dula her three hours of solitude were over and the naked girl was waking up from her sleep. Earlier, Dula had made the girl lie on her belly so she could apply an ointment to her back, and now that the paste had dried it was itchy. The girl was trying to reach back and scratch her sores! Dula sprang up and smacked the girl's hands away, saying, "No!" Dula could not risk her opening the cuts that were already scabbing over. She pressed the girls hands down on the mattress and shook her head "no" to the girl, then she rushed over to her herbal pharmacy.

Keeping a watch on the girl, Dula began mixing a fresh ointment. It was a special mixture of chamomile, calendula, and witch hazel that her grandmother used to use on Dula years ago after her own father would beat her. The smell of the ointment always made her think of the only person who ever showed kindness toward her. But her grandmother had died when Dula was only 9 years old, and from then on, her already hellish childhood only grew darker.

Dula doused a large sponge with warm water and carried both the sponge and the salve over to the girl. First, she used the sponge to moisten the paste that had dried on her back, and in gentle circular motions, she washed the skin clean. After carefully inspecting the cuts, she began to apply a second round of her healing paste. Dula was happy to see how quickly they were scabbing over, and she knew the madame would be very happy with the result.

After the aromatic ointment was fully applied, Dula helped the girl sit up. She held up a sheet so the girl could cover her front while she sat on the cot. Then, Dula presented the girl with a tray of food. Thinking the throw-away must not have eaten in at least a day, she expected the girl to dive into the lunch. Most girls did in her circumstance. But this one did something no one had ever done before. After looking at the food, which Dula knew full well was much better than what she was used to eating, the girl handed the tray back to Dula. At first, Dula thought she was rejecting it, but then she realized the girl was offering it to Dula to take her helping first before she ate herself!

In her surprise, Dula broke her rule of non-engagement and made eye contact with this very strange young woman. Her eyes did not emulate the usual deadened stare of these girls; she looked deeply into Dula's gaze and was trying to communicate something that Dula could swear were good intentions. Once again, the girl motioned for Dula to eat, clearly offering her the first helping. The older woman's face flushed with a forgotten emotion she could not name, and she became embarrassed, quickly looking down and allowing her hair to once again cover her face. She shook her head "no" and gestured for the girl to eat the food.

Dula crossed to the corner of the room while the girl began devouring the tray of olives, cheese, meat cubes, and bread. Sitting in her only chair, she felt confused about what to do next and how to keep unconnected from the girl, now that eye contact had been made. And she felt guilty for ever thinking this girl was a throw-away.

THIRTY-SIX

HER NAME WAS SKYE.

Galen couldn't have been happier that he finally knew her name, and even better than that, she was an American! No doubt her government would work quickly to get her back home, once he was able to get her out of that terrible place and take her to the proper authorities. He smiled at the thought, as his taxi drove him to what he knew would be his last visit at the brothel. After the prior two nights, and so much of his money, he finally was going to be able to help her escape. His heart raced just picturing her running away from the brothel.

It will all be worth it, Galen thought. *All the risk, all the money I spent, and whatever backlash I get from my parents because of it. Every bit of it will be worth knowing she is safe. And that she will be from now on.*

The night before had not been easy. He understood why she would be so hesitant to trust anyone, but as the hours went by, he had started to worry that the morning would come before he'd convinced her to let him help her. It took much time and many gently spoken words for Skye to begin to open up. In fact, it wasn't until he began to explain his plan for her escape that she finally shared her story with him.

She had told him she didn't know exactly how long she'd been in the brothel, but her guess was less than one year, maybe as little as six months. She was from America, a state called Louisiana, and her father had brought her here and sold her. Her face had turned to hate as she mentioned her father. He'd told everyone that he was taking her to London to attend a special, advanced high school, but when they arrived in Greece, he'd made her take part in a beauty pageant. Only it wasn't a pageant at all; it was a place where people came to buy girls. After giving this information, Skye had closed back up, refusing to disclose anything else. But Galen could fill in the rest of the details on his own.

He'd told her she didn't need to talk anymore, and he offered her the food again. "Please eat," he'd urged her. "You need strength for tomorrow."

At last, she received the food, and when she had bit into the spanakopites, her face had lit up, almost to a smile. After her first taste, Skye didn't need any more encouragement to eat every last bit of the food Galen's mum had made. While she ate, he shared with her his plan for her escape.

He would bring his backpack again, only this time, it would be filled with an extra set of clothes, a pair of his sister's jeans, and a shirt that would be exactly the same as the one he'd be wearing. Once he got to her room, they'd wait a couple hours before they put the plan into action. Skye would put on the clothes, stuff her hair into his cap, take the orange backpack, and once they were sure the madame was not watching, she'd pose as him as she left the brothel.

He very clearly had described her exit, drawing out on a piece of paper exactly where she needed to go. She'd have to keep her head down, and walk quickly down the hallway, descend the red spiral staircase, pass through the strip club below and go out the door. Galen had taken Skye to her barred window and pointed out to her a large hedge of bushes by the sidewalk, a few short blocks up. He knew he needed to pick a hideout that could clearly be seen from Skye's window so that there would be no question about the exact location. Once she'd made it outside, she was to turn left, walk up two blocks, and crawl inside the bushes to wait until he met her.

Galen would watch from her window to make sure she made it to the hedge safely. Then, he would wait another hour or so to leave himself. He told Skye he'd once again stay until he was sure the old woman was working with another customer, and dart out then. He'd quickly run to the bushes, let her know he was there, and hail a cab. As soon as the cab stopped, Skye would come out of her hiding place, and they'd both ride safely to his house. Finally, once they were at Galen's home, she'd be able to telephone whomever she needed, and they'd begin the process of getting her home to America.

The look on Skye's face when he'd gotten to the end of his plan and had said "then you'll be on your way home to Louisiana," was indescribable. She looked almost angelic to Galen, as this was the first time he'd seen her face illuminated with such hope. Her expression faded quickly, however, as her own fear and doubts crept in.

Galen did his best to squelch her doubts. He'd taken her hands softly in his and whispered to her, "No fear. I help you get out. I promise to god." She'd nodded her head, and Galen could sense she really wanted to believe in him.

And he could relate with her, because he was working hard to believe in himself, too. He could feel his own uncertainties about what he was about to do. He was terrified at the thought of what would happen—to them both—if his plan did not work. What if the owner caught Skye as she tried to leave disguised? Or for some reason came back in the room to find only Galen? Or, what if Skye was not emotionally stable enough to handle the full exit? Would they beat her? Kill her? Kill him?

"Isn't this the place?" the taxi driver said loudly.

Galen hadn't even realized the car had stopped, or that the cabbie had been talking to him. He looked out the window and felt his stomach churn at the sight of the club. Part of him wished he'd never seen this place, never encountered this underworld, and never began to care so deeply for the young girl trapped inside.

"This is it," said Galen, as he paid the man his fare. He grabbed his backpack and stretched his legs out of the cab. "At least tonight'll be my last time ever to set foot inside a place like this."

He walked into the front doors and was surprised to see two different guards at the entrance. Because they didn't recognize him, they made him pay the fee before they allowed him to enter into the club. *It must be those other guys' day off,* he thought. *How lucky for us. These new guys totally won't notice that I'll be leaving this place twice tonight.*

And he interpreted it as a good sign that all would go well.

Galen looked at his watch and realized he was a bit earlier than usual, so he stood in the back of the club for a few moments. He didn't want to appear overly anxious to the old hag upstairs. Earlier that morning when he'd left, the woman had once again begun to grill him about when he'd be bringing his friends. Her comments were sharp and suspicious. He did his best to convince her that in just two nights, he would be accompanied by his entire lot of friends. He told her they'd all planned to stay for two nights straight, coming and going as much as they pleased, and with lots of money to waste. At his promises, she'd given him a strange look, and Galen couldn't read from it whether she was buying his lies or not.

He paced back and forth in the back of the crowd until finally, he couldn't wait anymore. He felt he might explode out of his skin if he stayed down here another minute. He darted through the room and as he climbed the red spiral staircase, he could feel heat rising in his face and neck. He stopped for a moment and took some deep breaths to try and slow down his heart rate.

As soon as he reached the top, the old woman was waiting for him. She smiled broadly at him and said, "Hello, Love! I see you just cannot get enough of my girl in there." Galen gave his best effort to smile back at her. "Really, Love," she continued. "I have much better girls than the one you seem so in love with. How about you add a little variety in your night and pick one of my other girls?"

Galen felt taunted by her. "Not tonight," he said. "Maybe tomorrow night, once I'm with all my friends, we'll be able to share notes with each other and change things up."

"I thought as much," she said. "You have your money?"

It wasn't until Galen reached out his hand to pass the money over to the woman that he realized how nervous he was. His hand was trembling as he placed the bills in her hand. He hoped she didn't notice, but she was far too keen to let it slip by.

"Ooooh!" she giggle-snorted. "Are you still nervous to see your little piece in there? Look at you shaking like a leaf!"

"No, I'm not nervous," he snapped. "I've just had too much coffee today. Too many cups always makes my hands shake like that."

"Hmm," she said. "Follow me, Love."

Galen walked behind the short hobbling woman, wondering if on this particular night she was making the choice to walk extra slow down the narrow hallway, or if it simply felt that way. Galen couldn't wait for this night to be over.

The woman fumbled with her keys as she fingered through them to find the correct one for Skye's door.

"It's that one," Galen blurted out, pointing to the correct key.

The madame burst into laughter. "Ooooh! You're nervous *and* impatient tonight! Well, let's see if we can calm those nerves for you." And she unlocked Skye's door. She stood at the entrance as the door swung open, and as she gestured for him to go inside, she gave him a strange smirk.

Galen ignored her condescension and passed by her. Once inside, his eyes darted around the room. From the bed to the chair in the corner, to the sink, and back to the bed. The room was empty. Skye was gone.

He whirled around and demanded, "Where is she?"

The woman spoke back in her singsongy way, "I told you, you should've picked someone new tonight."

Galen's head felt like it was on fire. "Where is she?! What did you do with her, you old bitch?"

"Are you trying to threaten me, Love?" she seethed. "Trust me, I'm not a woman you're going to want to threaten." She narrowed her eyes at him. "Are you so stupid to think I couldn't see what was happening between you and that precious little whore of yours? Well, my Love, tonight you're going to wish you'd never laid eyes on her."

She moved into the room, leaving the door gaping open. But the space was instantly filled with the two large door guards, the ones who usually greeted Galen every night at the entrance. Apparently, it wasn't their night off, after all.

"What did you do with her??!!!" Galen yelled at the woman.

"She's dead," the madame said matter-of-factly, and then sent him a chilling stare. "And if I ever see you again, I will not only do the same to you, but also to your family." She turned on her heel and walked toward the door. Then she added to her two henchmen, "Don't kill him. I don't want to have to cover up the death of a Greek, but make sure to throw him out far away from here."

Panicking, Galen charged for the door. "Skye!" he yelled at the top of his lungs. "Skye!" And the men plowed into him like bags of cement. He felt a fist burrow deep into his gut and another slam into the side of his jaw. He could taste his own blood filling his mouth as another blow hit his ribs. He lost his breath and fell to the ground, his head forcefully hitting the concrete floor.

The men let up for just a moment as Galen opened his eyes and realized he was right next to Skye's bed. He looked under the cot to see if there was anything at all he could use to defend himself with. The only object he saw was a tiny silver chain. He reached out to grab it and realized it was a girl's charm bracelet.

He tried to stand up, but he only got to his hands and knees before the two men launched their second round of attacks. As they ruthlessly continued kicking him in the sides of his stomach and legs, Galen slipped out of consciousness.

THIRTY-SEVEN

AGGIE WAS DETERMINED TO FIND herself a church. As she descended the elevator towards the hotel lobby, she knew it was a long shot, but she had to get herself onto holy ground before her mind exploded. She didn't even care if it was a cathedral or even Catholic, just as long as there was a cross hanging somewhere. Certainly there would be a Greek Orthodox church open somewhere.

The elevator opened, and Aggie approached the concierge. He was a short man, only one or two inches taller than Aggie, and he wore a thick black mustache.

"Please, sir," Aggie said to him. "Could you tell me if dere's a church open anywhere around here?"

The concierge looked up from his newspaper and gave her a strange look. "A church? Ma'am, it's past 6 o'clock, and all the city tours would have ended by now."

"*Non, non, non.* I'm not lookin for a tour. I'm lookin for a place to sit and pray."

"I'm sorry, madam, I don't understand." He said as he gave her a confused look. "Like I said, all the churches in the city would be closed by now for visitors. They'll re-open in the morning."

Aggie was not one to give up. "Sir, are dere any God-fearin folk on your staff? Anyone here dat goes to church? Can I talk with one a dem folks?"

The man seemed indignant at her request, and he smoothed down his mustache with his right hand before he answered her.

"Ma'am, I'm sorry I cannot help you. I am certain all the churches are closed for the evening." And he returned to his newspaper.

Aggie stood stubbornly at his desk for a moment, hoping her presence would redirect his attention. But he continued to ignore her, and acted like he was engrossed in his paper. She turned with a huff and walked over to one of the large leather chairs that was sprinkled throughout the lobby. She sat down to try and strategize a new plan. "Dis girl ain't givin up dat easy, Mr. Man-with-da-black-caterpillar-mustache," she mumbled under her breath. "Dere's gotta be a way for dis God-honorin ol' woman to find herself a church."

She wondered what would happen if she simply went outside the hotel, hailed a cab, and asked the driver to take her to a church. "Surely he'd know if dere's a Catholic church in dis city."

Aggie checked her purse to make sure she had plenty of euros in her wallet, and decided to risk trusting a foreign cabbie. As she walked past the concierge and out the front doors, she quietly prayed, "Bon Dieu, I'm trustin in you to go before me and lead me to da right taxi."

The winter evening had brought with it a chilly breeze, and Aggie pulled her scarf around her neck. She spotted a taxi waiting on the street, and approached the passenger door.

"Excuse me, do you speak English?" she asked.

"As sure as shootin!" the young man said.

Aggie almost fell backward from surprise. "Are you American?" she asked.

"Why, yes ma'am! I'm a thoroughbred Texan, and proud of it," he said with a broad smile.

Aggie quickly opened the car door and scooted into the back seat before anyone else could claim this cab.

"*Choooh,* you da *last* ting I expected to find here in a Greek taxi cab," Aggie said. "Why you so far from home, *Sha*?"

"Well, ma'am, I decided to take a year off and backpack through Europe, but after only a month here, I found myself totally smitten with the prettiest gal I've ever seen. So I got myself a job to support myself while I'm tryin to win over her parents, which ain't gonna be very easy. Where are you from?"

"I'm a Louisiana Cajun, to da bone, and my name's Miss Aggie," she said as she reached over the front seat to shake his hand.

"Nice to meet you, Miss Aggie. Where can I take you tonight?"

"I'm lookin to find me a Catholic Church. Not one dat's old and on da tourist route, but one dat's actually still workin and havin mass. Are dere Catholics here in Greece?"

"I'm not sure, ma'am, I've never had anyone ask me. But let me check my map." He typed "catholic church" into his GPS and waited for a result to come up. After several seconds, he said, "Yes, ma'am! There's an Immaculate Conception of Holy Mary on Fragon Street, just a little over a kilometer from here. You want me to take you there?"

Resisting the urge to stand up and hug the young man, Aggie wiggled a bit in her seat as she said, "*Oui, oui!* Take me dere as fast as you can, *Sha!*" And as the taxi pulled out into traffic, Aggie hoped the Catholic churches here in Greece were open to the public, like they were back in Lafayette.

In just under five minutes, the car stopped, and the young man announced, "This is it, Miss Aggie. When you get outta the car, just go down that little walkway, and you'll see it."

Aggie paid the fare, and added several euros for a tip.

"Thank you kindly, Miss Aggie. Now when you leave, you'll need to come back here to hail another cab. All you need to say is 'the Electra Hotel' and they'll know exactly how to get you back to your room."

"Tank you so much, *Sha!*" Aggie said as she crossed the street and headed in the direction the cabbie had sent her. She breathed a sigh of relief at the site of the small cathedral and its dark wooden entry doors, and she hastened inside.

Tugging on the wooded doors, she was surprised they were unlocked. Aggie spoke her thanks to her *Bon Dieu* and reverently entered the church. She dipped her right middle finger into the small dish of holy water, genuflected, and made the sign of the cross.

When she looked up and saw the two lines of dark, wooden pews separated by an aisle of red carpet, she felt a tangible wave of relief and peace. "Hal, you see dis?" she whispered. "Dis look like da Cathedral your mama used to go to. It's got da red carpet, da dark pews, and da giant statue of da Virgin Mother smack dab in da middle of da altar... just like your mama's church did."

She looked around, and besides herself, she found the place was vacant. “Nobody here but me and da Lawd,” she said as she walked to the front of the sanctuary. “Dat’s OK, cuz dat’s all I need.” And she knelt down in one of the front pews to bow her head and begin to pray.

“Lawd,” she whispered, “I come before you now, head bowed and body bent. You know why I’m here, so I’m not gone beat ‘round da bush. You gotta show us where my Skye-girl is, and dat’s just gone be da way it’s gone be. She your Skye-girl, too, Lawd, and you love her even more dan I do, so I know you ain’t gone sit by and let her be in dis place no more. *Chooooh*, I’ll pray all night, if dat’s what it takes, but you gotta show yo’self strong.” Aggie’s voice began to crack with emotion. “Dey say it’s impossible for us to find her, but I know it ain’t impossible for you, Lawd. Nothin is impossible for you, my God! Now you know I ain’t never come beggin like dis to you, Lawd, but tonight, I’m on my knees and I’m beggin you! Please, oh please, my God who can do all tings, who knows all tings, and who works everyting out for good for dose who love you and are called accordin to your purpose...You can see *exactly* where she is, so don’t you keep her hidden no longer! You gotta show Wil how to get her out dis place! Please, Lawd......please.....”

Aggie bent forward and rested her forehead onto her folded hands. She couldn’t hold her fear and anxiety back any longer, and she began to cry, her quiet moans echoing through the hollow archways of the sanctuary.

THIRTY-EIGHT

IT WAS ONLY THREE HOURS into their second night's search for Skye, and already both Wil and Aeton were feeling drained from the sights and sounds. Fortunately however, from the looks of their marked-up map, they didn't have too many more brothels to cover. As they drove to their next destination, Wil scoured the chart of streets to find any strays that might have been skipped.

"I'm not sure what to do next after we hit these few streets," Wil said. "From the looks of this, we've X-ed out every single location where brothels have been registered. The only place we haven't gone is the area we went to today to meet the auction lady."

"And we can't go back there," Aeton said firmly. "We can't risk her seeing us unless you're ready to actually go through with it and be a real customer."

Wil was offended. "Dude, I can't believe you'd even suggest that."

"Chill. I'm *not* suggesting it," Aeton retorted. "All I'm saying is we can't risk it if we're just looking. We can't play both buyer and savior in that woman's domain."

"Ok, then what do you suggest after we case these last few blocks?"

The needed concentration to parallel park superseded Aeton's ability to answer his question. Not being able to get the car in on his first try, his frustration leaked out in his words, "I can't believe people can jam into these tight spots. And look! There are more people out here on the streets buying sex than last night! Don't they have jobs? Who does this on a week night?" Only on the third attempt was Aeton able to park the car properly along the street.

Once the car was turned off, Aeton used the dome light to search the map. After several moments, he said, "Because prostitution is legal here, all the brothels have to be listed as businesses, and those are the ones I've marked here. But I'm thinking there has to be a ton of brothels that are underground, and run by either Albanian mafia or local syndicates who consider themselves above the law. And these places might be filled with girls who are trafficked. In fact, they probably are *mostly* filled with girls who are trafficked since they turn the biggest profit. Once we've exhausted these streets, I think that's where we need to go next."

"Great thinking, A. How do you think that'll play out?"

"Well, my guess is that those spots are absolutely by referral only. They gotta know their clientele isn't going to turn them in. We'd have to walk *very* carefully in those circles. The danger ratio will be much much higher...I don't know..."

Wil knew his Greek friend did not have the same risk tolerance that he did when he was single and serving as a marine. With a new wife and a new baby, his priorities had shifted. Wil also knew that while Aeton was always up to help a friend out, much of the reason he was giving such committed time and energy was because of the large stipend Richard was paying him. A higher threshold of danger, and Aeton might opt out.

"Let's just focus on these streets," said Wil, "and if we don't find anything about Skye, *then* we'll decide what to do next."

The men climbed out of the VW and began walking toward their first destination. About two blocks down, Wil almost tripped on what appeared to be a bum sleeping in the middle of the sidewalk. He was crumpled in a ball, and it seemed odd to Wil that this would be the place a homeless person would pick to take a nap. It was totally random, not to mention, right in the middle of the sidewalk.

He thought he should try to move the poor guy out of the pathway of people, but Wil wasn't sure what state he was in, or how he'd respond if he was awakened. He leaned down to get a closer look at him, but his face was covered up by his orange backpack.

"Come on, man," said Aeton, several steps down the sidewalk. "What's the hold up?"

Wil hesitated for a moment, but then ran to catch up with Aeton, and they briskly strode further down the street.

"Did you see that guy back there?" Wil asked. "He was lying right in the middle of the sidewalk...totally passed out! I'm surprised nobody's stepped on him."

"Probably just a drunk. He wouldn't feel it anyway."

After about a dozen or so more strides, Wil stopped.

"What?" asked Aeton.

"I don't know," he said as he turned back toward the direction of the car. Wil started walking back.

"What?" called Aeton, "Did you forget something?"

"I'm sorry, this'll just take a second," Wil called over his shoulder as he quickly walked back to the bum.

When Wil reached the guy, he noticed the guy's cell phone on the sidewalk that looked like it had been in his hand just moments ago. Curious, Wil leaned down and picked up the orange backpack to assess the situation. He shot up and yelled back to Aeton, "This is no bum! Get over here now!"

The young man's face was bloody and swollen, and even from the light of the streetlamp, Wil could see the color of his skin was not good. Dropping to his knees, Wil carefully moved the teenager to his back. He was not breathing.

"Aeton, I need you to call an ambulance right now," Wil ordered as he checked the boy's abdomen for any gaping wounds. "He's pretty beaten up, but there aren't any punctures or cuts. I'm starting CPR."

Wil could hear Aeton talking to the local emergency hotline while he began pumping the boy's chest. After 30 chest compressions, Wil gave him two breaths, and then began the rotation again. 30 compressions. 2 breaths. 30 compressions. 2 breaths.

The boy coughed up some blood, and Wil helped tilt him to the side to allow the fluids to exit safely. He tore off his hoodie and used it to clean up the blood and was relieved to see the boy beginning to breathe on his own. They were labored breaths, but he was doing them independently.

"An ambulance is on its way," Aeton said.

The young man groaned and said something inaudible.

"Tell him help is on its way and try to get him to talk," Wil said to Aeton.

In Greek, Aeton said, "We've got help coming. Can you talk? Who did this to you?"

The boy just shook his head and tried to breathe.

Then he managed, "I was...too late...They killed her. "

"Who? What are you talking about?" Aeton asked.

"The girl...Skye...She's dead," and it sounded like he was crying.

Wil looked up at Aeton. "What did he just say?"

"What did you say her name was?" Aeton asked.

Through labored cries, the boy choked out, "Skye. Her name was Skye."

"Did he just say Skye?!" Wil gasped.

And the boy opened his eyes and said in English, "Are...you American? Did you come for her, too?" His head went back against the pavement, and as he closed his eyes again, tears fell. "I tried...but....too late...they killed her." And he lost consciousness again.

Wil noticed something fall out of the boy's hand, and when he picked it up, he could not believe his eyes. It was a broken silver bracelet with three charms. An open birdcage, a dainty silver bird in flight, and a heart with the engraved script: *My Skye Girl*

"Oh my god," Wil whispered. "Miss Aggie."

"Get away from him!" a voice yelled frantically in Greek. "What have you done to him?!! Get away from him, or I swear I'll kill you!" And a young man ran up to Aeton and Wil and tried to push them away from the boy.

"Wait a minute!" said Aeton. "We're trying to save him. We found him like this, and he wasn't breathing. My American friend here might've just saved his life!"

"Oh my god, oh my god!" Nikkos exclaimed sorrowfully when he saw Galen. "What did they do to you?!" And then in English, he said to Wil, "I'm sorry...Thank you. How bad is he?"

"I'm not sure, but we have an ambulance coming," Wil answered. "Who are you?"

"I'm Nikkos, his older brother. This is all my fault. I told him not to go back there, but it's still all my fault. Listen, we don't have time to wait for an ambulance; that could take too long. My car is right over there! I didn't even park. Please help me get him in the car."

"How did you know to come here?" asked Wil.

"He called me on his cell, and he was able to tell me where he was, but then he just stopped talking. I thought he was dead! I drove as fast as I could to get here. My car is right there! Please help me!"

"Slow down, Nikkos," Wil said calmly. "Take a breath for a second. My friend and I will help you...as long as you let us call you later and check up on him."

"Of course!" Nikkos said. "Please help me right now."

Nikkos ran ahead, opened the back of the SUV, and quickly pushed all the seats down. Galen groaned as Wil picked him up as gently as possible, and Aeton walked alongside to help support some of his dead weight.

"Here," said Nikkos directing them to the back of the car, "Put him here in the back. This will help him lay down."

"Listen to me," said Aeton while they laid Galen in the the vehicle, "Take him to Saint Loukas Hospital on Panorama. Do you know where that is?" Nikkos nodded. "My sister-in-law works there, and I'll call ahead to make sure they know you are coming." But Aeton wasn't convinced Nikkos was listening clearly. "Nikkos, I need you to look into my eyes. Are you sure you're ok to drive him?"

Nikkos took a deep breath and was able to set his hysteria aside for a moment. He looked back at Aeton and said, "St. Loukas on Panorama. I know where it is, and I will be ok to drive him. I promise."

"Give me your cell phone," Aeton said. When Nikkos handed it to him, Aeton entered his cell phone number and called himself. "That's my cell number, and I'm going to be calling you throughout the night to check up on him. Also, we're going to need to talk to him in a day or so when he's able."

"Why?" asked Nikkos, suddenly protective.

"Don't worry about that now," Aeton said. "Just know that we are with you, and we want to find out who did this to him."

"Ok," Nikkos said, relieved. "I don't know how to thank you." And he got in his car.

Aeton and Wil stood dumbfounded in the middle of the road, watching as he drove away. It wasn't until a horn from a waiting car blared that the men were pulled back into their present surroundings and walked back onto the sidewalk. Wil sat down on the edge of the street and looked down at the broken charm bracelet in his hand.

"How am I going to tell Miss Aggie?" Wil said quietly to no one in particular.

Aeton sensed Wil needed a moment, and said, "Dude, the car is only a couple blocks down. Just sit there for a minute. I'll go get it and pull it up."

Aeton waited a few seconds for Wil to acknowledge him, but he just sat there staring at the bracelet.

"Wil? Did you hear me?"

Wil nodded, and Aeton took that as his cue.

Alone, Wil tried to sift through the barrage of emotions swirling inside his heart: Disbelief to think Skye was actually dead. Certainly he could not have failed so entirely on this mission to find her in time? Guilt and shame to face Miss Aggie and tell her that he was not able to help her after all, and that Skye was gone forever. Self doubt in his ability to ever get things right. He didn't get it right with Skye, just like he didn't get it right with Madison. What makes him think he's going to get it right tomorrow with Elle? Rage. Sheer rage at merciless Time that steals the moments away, making it impossible to save the ones you love the most.

Rage won the emotional struggle, and from the very core of his being, Wil let out a loud resonate bellow up to the heavens. And then he dropped his head into his hands and wept deeper than he'd allowed himself to weep since his little sister's funeral.

THIRTY-NINE

WIL STOOD OUTSIDE AGGIE'S HOTEL DOOR for several minutes trying to think of the right words to say. He leaned up against the wall and looked down at Skye's broken bracelet and wondered about the day Miss Aggie must've given this to her. Was it a birthday? A Christmas present? Why did Miss Aggie chose these particular charms? And he knew the bird must've been something very special to them both, because he remembered with what care he would always take to pick out gifts for Madison. His gifts for his little sister had to be perfect, and something that was unique between them. Her favorite gift from him was a gold locket necklace, and for a joke he'd engraved 'BBF' on the inside for 'best brother forever.' He'd always say to her, "I'm your best brother; remember to treat me right!" and Madison would say back, "You're my only brother; but I'll treat you right anyway." She always wore it, and even had it on the day she died.

Wil's eyes filled with tears when he thought about how careful his mom had been to remove the necklace, and a few days after the funeral, she'd given it back to him. Wrapped in a gorgeous velvet box, Lottie had put a picture of both of them inside the locket. That box was now Wil's prized possession. This bracelet will now be Aggie's most prized possession.

I can't stand out here forever, Wil thought. *There's no other way to do it than to just do it.*

He took a deep breath and softly knocked on the door.

Inside, Lottie and Aggie had been playing cards to pass the time.

"I wonder who could be at the door?" Lottie asked as she walked toward the door. And she said softly to the visitor, "Tyler, is that you?"

"No, Mom; it's me," Wil answered from the other side.

"Oh!" said Lottie as she opened the door. "We weren't expectin you to..." her words trailed off the moment she saw the look on his face. "Wil. What happened?"

Wil put his hand on his mom's shoulder, but his eyes were on Aggie.

Lottie shot a worried glance to her and said, "What is it, son?"

Wil's eyes were razored on Aggie as he slowly walked toward her. All his years of training to control his emotions seemed to slip farther away with every step closer to her. He knelt down next to where she was sitting, as tears filled his eyes. When he opened his mouth to speak, he could only muster a whisper, "Miss Aggie..."

Aggie reached out and put her hand on his unshaven cheek and said softly, "What is it, chile? What do you want to say to me?"

"Miss Aggie," he tried again. With his head lowered, he said, "I'm so sorry. I didn't get to her in time."

"What do you mean?" Aggie asked.

"Skye. I didn't get to her in time. Please...please forgive me for not getting to her in time." And he put his hand in Aggie's and released the bracelet in the palm of her hand.

Stunned, Aggie lifted up the bracelet to her lips. "No!" she whispered. Shaking her head and closing her eyes, she repeated, "No! Not my Skye-girl."

Lottie stepped closer to the pair and gently interjected, "Wil, what do you mean? What does this mean?"

Without looking her in the eyes, he answered, "Tonight we found out that she's been..." Wil wasn't ready to say those words, so he took a deep breath and began from the beginning. "Tonight, as we were searching for her, we met up with a young man who knew her. He was actually trying to help her escape from her brothel, and when the people who had her figured out his plan, they beat him almost to death. We found him on the side of the road in pretty bad shape. As we were helping him, he gave me Skye's bracelet and that's when he told me." Wil looked back into Aggie's eyes and pleaded with her, "I'm so sorry, Miss Aggie, I don't know how to tell you how sorry I am that I didn't get to her in time."

"Wil," Lottie asked, "what did the boy tell you?"

Wil could tell by the look in Aggie's eyes that she already knew what he was going to say. But she needed him to say the words.

With tears streaming down his cheeks, he breathed, "They killed her."

Lottie's gasp could be heard as the words penetrated Aggie's heart.

"Noooo!" moaned Aggie, "Not my Skye-girl!" Her emotion grew to anger. "NO! Not my Skye-girl!!" And she bolted up and out onto the balcony, slamming the slider behind her.

Wil could see Aggie starting to pace the length of the balcony, and he couldn't bear to see her pain. He put his head into his hands, and felt his mom's arms drape around his back. They both began to cry. With every breath, Wil could not stop saying he was sorry.

HOURS LATER, AGGIE STILL SAT on the balcony. Wil had left their room and Lottie had brought out a thick blanket for Aggie. "I'll be inside, and if you need anything, please promise me you'll wake me up if by some chance I've fallen asleep," Lottie had said. Lottie made Aggie promise, but they both knew Aggie would not ask, and certainly wouldn't wake her up.

Still holding on to the bracelet, Aggie had no more tears to cry. She rested her head back on her chair and allowed herself to vividly remember the day she gave this gift to Skye. How Skye loved it. How she'd hugged her MawMaw and promised to never take it off. She could even remember how Skye had smelled that day.

"I had dat made just for you, Skye-girl," Aggie had told Skye, "And dat bird? Dat's you, *Sha*. You were born to soar da skies just like dat beautiful bird. Don't you ever let anyone put you inside no cage." The irony of those words embittered Aggie, and she allowed her wrath to be kindled toward her God.

"Lawd God, you gotta help yo girl, Aggie," she seethed. "Where are you in dis?! Where are you, can you tell me that? Or are you just gone sit up dere on your big fancy throne and keep your mouth shut?! ANSWER ME!" And her volume made her shiver a bit. Half of her knew she should never speak to God in this way, and half of her didn't have the energy to care one bit.

"Where were you in Macy's dyin? Where were you in Skye bein taken? Where were you?? Cuz dis ain't what you promised me! You said you'd never leave me or forsake me. You said you'd bless me and my household. Well, you must be lyin', cuz dat ain't what you've been doin!

"And not to mention, *I've been stickin up for you* around dese folks! I've been sayin how dey just need to watch how you gone do impossible tings and bring my girls back! You makin me look like an ol' Cajun fool!!" Aggie started shaking her finger at God. "I don't understand what you doin, here. You've always come through for yo Aggie...where are you now??? Look, I know Macy made some bad choices dat backfired on her, but Skye...*she just a girl!* She just a little girl with big dreams and she ain't never done nothin to deserve any of dis! So, why? Why you let dis happen??

"*Choooh!* I don't know why I'm wastin my breath tryin to get any answers from you. You just gone sit up dere in your heaven and not answer me anyway."

Disillusioned, Aggie turned her chair away from her imaginary subject, as if she was turning her back on him. She pulled her blanket tightly around her shoulders, and exhausted, closed her eyes. It wasn't long before she drifted off into sleep.

GALEN OPENED HIS EYES to a nurse hovering close to his face. Startled, he jumped to scoot back, only to find his attempt futile; he was lying in a bed. He whirled his head around in panic, attempting to figure out where he was, but it felt like his body weighed a thousand pounds, and his head even more.

"Shh, shh, shh!" said the nurse. "You're fine, Galen, you're fine. Just lie back and relax. You've had a bit of an accident, and you're in the Saint Loukas hospital, and you're going to be just fine."

"Brother, I'm here," said Nikkos.

At the sound of his older brother's voice, Galen relaxed his head and closed his eyes. "What happened to me, Nikkos?" Galen whispered.

"That story has yet to be told, brother; and I'm almost afraid to ask you any questions. Mum and Pop just left to get some food, though, so we've only got a little bit of time until they get back." Then Nikkos said to the nurse, "We're going to be fine here, miss. I'll call you if we need anything."

As the nurse was leaving, Galen asked his brother, "How long have I been in here?"

"Several hours now. It's almost morning. You almost got the life beaten out of you, remember? And then you called me to pick you up down in the red-light district. What in the hell were you doing there anyway?"

Galen's throat felt like sandpaper. "Is there any water? Can I have a drink of something?"

Nikkos grabbed a cup of water that was sitting on the table next to Galen's bed and held it up to his lips. Galen took a long, steady drink.

"Thanks, Nikkos." He stopped to take a few breaths and then asked, "What kind of drugs am I on; I feel like I've been buried in sand."

"They got you on some pretty heavy stuff, because otherwise, you'd be screaming from the pain. I thank the universe you called me when you did, brother, because if you hadn't you could've died out there. Luckily there were a couple guys who found you before I got there and helped get you breathing again."

"What? Am I really that bad off?"

"You have a pretty serious concussion, but that's not the worst of it. Whoever beat you up did a great job on your ribs. You've got a few broken ones, and one of them punctured your lung. And then just as I got you here, you started going into shock seizures...which completely freaked me out. I thought you were going to die right there. The doctors say you're going to be fine, though; but you will be in this place for three or four more days."

Galen tried to remember what had happened to him, but the last thing he could recall was going to Skye's room and finding her gone. Then the old woman had brought in her two thugs, and that was it. He had no recollection of anything from the point the bodyguards started beating him until just a few minutes ago when he woke up in this hospital.

The two brothers sat in silence for awhile.

Finally, Nikkos said, "Look, brother, I've just got to ask you what you were doing there. You've been so weird ever since I took you to get laid for your birthday, and honestly, I thought you hated me for it. But then, you call me from there to come and pick you up, and your backpack is filled with all sorts of interesting things...a pair of girl's jeans, including a pair of underpants, a shirt that is exactly the same one that you were wearing, a pair of girl's running shoes. What's this all about?"

Galen was too weak to deal with the interrogation of his brother.

"Alright, Nikkos," Galen said slowly. "Here it is, and if you laugh or make fun of me, I swear I'll never talk to you again." He stopped to wait for Nikkos' response.

"I promise I won't laugh," Nikkos said, and he scooted to the edge of his seat.

"The night you took me to that brothel, I met a girl named Skye. I didn't know her name at first, but she finally told it to me last night. Nikkos, the girl you paid for that night on my birthday? Did you know that she was only as old as our sister, Dimitra? And I never had sex with her, by the way, there's no way I could do that...especially after seeing that look on her face." He stopped to take some breaths. "She was kept in an awful room that had padlocks on the outside of it to keep her in. She was not there by choice. I tried to talk with her, to help her, but she wasn't Greek. And when I left that morning, I just couldn't walk away and pretend it never happened."

"Good god, Galen...what did you get yourself into?"

"For the next couple nights, I went back there and bought her shift—just like you did—so that she wouldn't have to have sex with all those men. My plan was to have her tell me where she was from so I could help her escape."

"How in the hell did you pay for all that?!"

"I used my savings." Galen ignored his brother's gasp and went on, "So we had a plan, I had it all figured out, and last night I went there for the last time...only when I got there, that bitch who owns the place had somehow found out. Skye was gone. She told me she killed her. And... well...you can see what they did to me."

Again, he stopped talking for a bit to take some breaths. His chin was trembling, and he gave up trying to cover his pain. As he closed his eyes to catch his breath, tears ran down the sides of his face.

"Go ahead, Nikkos," he whispered. "Make fun of me if you want."

Nikkos was at a loss for words. He leaned over and kissed Galen on top of his head. And then he said. "I could never laugh at you for doing something like that, little brother. My only hope is that one day I'll be half the man that you are."

FORTY

WIL SAT BY HIMSELF AT A TABLE, looking out the window. It was 04:00, and today was the day of the auction. Thankful that he was able to manage to rest for a few hours, he now was hoping his coffee would clear his head. He was feeling the pressure to be at the top of his game for today's mission. But more troubling than the pressure were the ghostlike voices in his head shouting self-doubt into his every thought and plan for the day. He leaned back, closed his eyes, and replayed the game plan from the top.

Sensing someone's gaze, Wil looked over his shoulder and spotted Miss Aggie. He could tell by her eyes that she'd been looking specifically for him. He sighed. He wasn't sure a conversation with her at this moment was going to do anything but feed his doubts. But she'd tracked him down, and here she came.

"Good morning, Wil," said Aggie.

When he looked up to greet her back, he was surprised to see her countenance. He was expecting to be confronted with more sorrow and more questions about Skye, but Aggie instead had a look of something quite the opposite. Wil was confused.

"Good morning, Miss Aggie," he said a bit sheepishly. "I hope you were able to get some sleep last night. I don't know what I can say to—"

"*Non, non, non.* Listen to me, *Sha,*" Aggie said gently as she sat herself down next to him. "I know it's early, but I came here lookin for you. I got somethin to tell you."

Wil shook his head and opened his mouth to say something, but Aggie put her hand up. "No, chile, just listen." And she looked deeply into his eyes before continuing. "Last night was just awful hearin what you had to say about my Skye-girl...just awful. And I sat out on dat balcony havin it out with my God." She smiled and chuckled a bit, "I was madder dan a *seekahsah*—oh, dat's a wasp—and you should've heard some o' da words I was shoutin at *Le Bon Dieu*...I'm surprised He didn't strike me down with a big bolt o' lightning!

"*Chooooh*, I thought I was gonna die inside, and I was up for hours tryin to make sense outta all dis. But dere were just no answers." She shook her head and then leaned forward. "But den da strangest ting happened...When I woke up on dat balcony dis mornin, my heart was filled with da most precious peace. I can't explain it, dere's just no way to explain it, but I can't deny dat it's right here. It's like I'm totally surrounded by da deepest peace.

"I know it's da Lawd, Wil. Da only other time I'd felt a peace dis deep in my heart was a few days after Hal died. It was da Lawd lettin' me know dat everythin was gonna be ok. And even though it was such a hard time in my life, He was right. Everythin *did* turn out ok. And dat's when I knew I needed to come find you."

Wil was confused on a few levels. One, how it could be possible Aggie could be feeling this way after knowing what she knew? And two, what did any of this have to do with him? He certainly wasn't feeling the sense of peace Miss Aggie was describing.

"I don't know what any of dis means," she went on. "But I know dat my God has dis whole ting under his control. And we just have to trust him, Wil."

This request was too much for Wil to consider. How could she choose to trust a god who allows young girls to be tortured like Skye was? And what about kids like his sister who are ravaged with disease? Where was her god with Madison? He couldn't hide his doubt from this woman, but before he could say anything she reached out and kindly held his hand. Her touch was so soothing, he lost his words.

"Look at me, Wil," and she waited until their eyes met. "You're a good man. None of dis is your fault. Do you hear me? *None* of dis is your fault. Not what happened to Skye, not what's happenin to Ellie, and most of all, not what happened to your precious little sister."

Wil tried his best to fight off Aggie's words about Madison. How could she say so adamantly that he was not to blame? She wasn't even there. But unexplainably, her words of love were sharper than his inner-armor, and they somehow pierced through and accessed the wound of guilt he'd been harboring in his heart.

"We need to put last night behind us," Aggie declared. "*Chooooh*, we don't even know if dat boy knew for sure what he was talkin about. But today is all about gettin my Ellie, and you are da man to do it. You've got everythin it takes to make today a success, and I owe my life to you, *Sha*. Dere will never be anythin I can ever do to pay you back all dat you've done for me in just dese few short days."

Wil felt himself absorbing this woman's hope and courage like a sponge. And there was a strange and new sense of lightness in his heart. Perhaps there was something to this impossible peace that Miss Aggie was trying to convince him of?

Fixing his eyes back at her, he said, "I'm not sure you just did."

"What?" she asked.

"Pay me back."

Aggie smiled broadly at this brave young man and charged, "Let's go get my Ellie."

ELLE HAD NO IDEA WHERE her dad could be this early in the morning. Normally at six o'clock, or at least since they'd been in Greece, Jack would be passed out in his hotel bed from a night of doing who-knows-what. But Elle didn't want to spend too much time thinking about her dad because that would only dampen her mood. Nothing was going to wreck this day, because today, she was finally going to get to see Skye.

Unable to contain her excitement, the young girl shoved off her blankets and started jumping on her bed. She didn't care that it was so early or that people might be trying to sleep in the room next door. She had to let out her pent up energy somehow, and since her dad wasn't anywhere to be found, she allowed herself to bounce as high as she could.

After several minutes, she collapsed onto her bed, heart racing and blood pumping. She giggled as she rolled back and forth on the mattress, saying in a high-pitched voice, "Today's the day to see sissy! Today's the day to see sissy!"

She closed her eyes and began to imagine her sister's face when she saw her. And what kind of marvelous things would they do? Elle, of course, had never been to London, and she'd heard there were real life castles and places to go to see crowns filled with diamonds and rubies. And there was a queen who still lived there; maybe they would see her? And there were those red soldiers with the huge poofy black hats that guarded a palace. They definitely needed to go and see those guys. But even if they did nothing at all, Elle couldn't wait to be with her big sister.

Now, the only obstacle between her and Skye was that weird beauty pageant. And Elle had decided, no matter how her dad had treated her since they'd been here, she was still going to do her best for him. She figured, the happier he was with her performance, the happier he'd be to take Elle to Skye's school as soon as the contest was over. In fact, she was going to be the ideal angel today, obeying his every command, and even doing things before he had to tell her. This thought prompted her to start getting ready for the one o'clock pageant.

She hopped out of bed and ran to the closet. Pulling out her new pink dress, she carefully smoothed it across her bed, hand-pressing any wrinkles. She stepped back to admire it and imagined how pretty she was going to look today; especially if, after she washed her red hair, she took the extra time to dry her curls into perfect ringlets.

Elle hummed to herself as she skipped into the bathroom and turned on the water for the shower. *I cannot wait to see Skye,* she thought happily. *This is going to be a great day, and there is absolutely nothing that could possibly ruin it!*

⚜

DULA FELT A TINGE OF SADNESS knowing it was time for her visitor to leave. Today was the auction, and the madame would be coming soon to inspect her merchandise. The girl had just finished eating her breakfast and was getting up to use the toilet in the corner. Dula could tell by the way the girl moved that the pain from her beating was very slight. As the girl passed a large mirror hanging on the wall, she was startled from her reflection.

Had she not seen that mirror before? Dula thought. *She jumped like she thought someone was coming for her.* And then Dula remembered that the cells for the girls only had small, smoky mirrors, and most of those were cracked. This was probably the first time she'd seen herself in a clear mirror since she's been here.

The girl stared long at her naked body, as if she was looking at someone other than herself. She walked slowly to the mirror and touched the reflection of her face, and Dula could see the girl's sorrow as she looked at her gaunt face. Tears welled up in the girl's eyes. And then she turned a bit to see the damage the madame had done to her back. Dozens of thin cuts striped her back in haphazard diagonal patterns. Now her tears began to flow freely as gazed at the proof that her innocence was gone forever. These scars would never let her forget that. Relating all too well to the pain, Dula's eyes stung with her own tears.

The girl turned to look at the Dula, and their eyes locked in a soulful conversation. For a moment, the girl seemed comforted that her caretaker would share her heartache.

Both of the women jumped from the sound of the door springing open. Embarrassed by her nakedness, the girl ran back to her bed and covered herself with her sheet. The madame giggle-snorted at her obvious intimidation over the girl.

"How does she look?" snapped the madame to Dula. "Is she ready for auction? Bring her to me."

Dula hated this woman intensely and wished she had the courage to do something about it. But there was no use. Head downward, she shuffled over to the girl and coaxed her out of her bed to standing. The madame motioned for the girl to turn around, and she examined Dula's work.

"Very good!" the madame said, and patted Dula on the head. "I have a nice long slip that will cover all the marks. Nobody will know the difference." And handing Dula a long, emerald green slip, she barked, "Put it on her."

Dula gently helped the girl slide the silky fabric over her body.

"Perfect," the madame was pleased. But then she became serious and leaned into Dula's face. "Make sure to go over what she is to do in the auction, and if she does not do well, I'm going to blame you. She is to be in place backstage by 12:30, and sit her in the very back. Make sure she doesn't talk to anyone until she goes onstage and I can be rid of her forever. I never should've wasted money on her in the first place."

The madame left them, but not until she marched over to the girl, viciously grabbed her hair and forced her ear close to her mouth. Dula couldn't hear the words the madame was hissing, but she knew they were evil threats. Shoving the girl away from her, the madame hobbled proudly out of the room, and slammed the door behind her.

The sound of the door's bang made the girl leap like a scared cat. She scurried over to the bed, melted onto the mattress and began crying. Before Dula could stop herself, she went protectively over to the young woman and tried to hold her. Her offering of comfort was awkward, as she had not done something like this before, but the girl did not seem to mind. Rather, she sunk into Dula's arms and cried so woefully, Dula was swept along with the current of emotion.

After several minutes, the girl looked deeply into Dula's eyes and whispered in her native language words Dula knew. They were priceless words of thanks, and Dula wondered how this one girl could've possibly penetrated through the miles and miles of thorny brush that had been protecting her heart for what seemed an eternity.

FORTY-ONE

WIL PACED HIS HOTEL ROOM waiting for Aeton to arrive for their final meeting, the morning of the auction. Everyone besides Aeton was present: Tyler, Lottie, and Aggie. The time was 10:35, five minutes past their original start time, and Wil hated when meetings began late.

"Chill, dude," Tyler said. "I'm sure he'll be here any second."

Annoyed, Wil didn't acknowledge Tyler. Instead, he opened the hotel room door and looked up and down the hallway to see if maybe Aeton was approaching.

"I'm going to try him again," Wil said, but as he picked up his cell to call, it rang.

"Where the hell are you?" Wil answered. "Everyone else is here waiting for you." He swung the door back open and stepped out into the hallway to talk with Aeton. Even so, the others could hear Wil's muffled voice as he spoke aggressively into his phone.

Tyler sat down on the bed and smiled at Lottie and Aggie, who were sitting side by side on the hotel loveseat that was positioned against the wall between the bed and the sliding glass balcony doors.

"He always gets like this at crunch time," he said. "He doesn't settle for anything less than perfection."

"He's just like his father," said Lottie, trying to smile. She wanted to say something to lighten the mood, but her mind was blank. Too much had transpired in the last 12 hours. As usual, she sat properly with her hands folded in her lap, but also as usual when she was upset, her thumbs were at work nervously crossing over each other. Aggie slid her hand over to cover Lottie's hands, and whispered, "Ever'ting's gone be alright, *Sha*."

Lottie's only response was to nod her head and then turn to look out at the gorgeous view of the sea. Separating the love seat and two leather club chairs was an oblong coffee table, and lying open on it were three street maps of Thessaloniki. The maps were marked up with a red sharpie, as Wil had drawn the route lines from their hotel to the auction site, and from the auction site to the airport. Earlier this morning, Tyler had once again practiced the drive in order to ensure he had memorized each route perfectly.

Bursting back into the room, Wil said, "Aeton's still ten minutes away. There was an accident, and he's stuck in traffic."

"Wil, we have plenty of time before we have to start," said Tyler. "And really, there's not much for us to talk about, anyway. It's cut and dry for me and the ladies, because all we have to do is wait in the SUV. Plus, I already know the route, I even drove it again early this morning while you were sleeping. We can just chill for a few minutes until he gets here."

"Nope. I'm not waiting for him." And Wil crossed the room to sit in one of the club chairs. He handed one of the maps to Tyler, one to Lottie, and he kept the last one laid out on the coffee table.

"OK," Wil said. "It's about 10:38, and the auction starts at one. Aeton and I will be leaving around 11:30 to grab some food and then head over to the auction site, which is right here." He pointed to the red square he'd drawn on the map. "You guys need to be checked out of the hotel and parked in place no later than 12:45. When we met with that lady who is running the auction, she told Aeton the buying and selling will happen in two segments, each part taking anywhere between 15-30 minutes, depending upon how many girls are in each one.

"We think that Elle will be in the first group, and if that's so, then we'll be able to cash out during the break between the two auction segments. So, in actuality, if the auction starts on time and all goes well, we could be leaving the location as early as 1:30. I'll send Tyler a text as soon as we are ready to exit. Ideally, you'll leave your parking spot, pull the SUV as close to the entrance as possible, and we'll load up directly from the site."

"How you gone get Elle to go with you?" asked Aggie. "She's gonna be scared stiff if you just lift her up and take her out."

"We have no other choice, Miss Aggie," Wil said.

"But what are da folks gone do if dey see you carryin a screamin young girl over yo shoulders? What if dey try to stop you?"

"That's a good question, Miss Aggie, and we did think of that," Wil said, "but on the other hand, if these people make their fortune by doing this kind of thing, I can't imagine it'll be the first time a young girl has resisted being taken away by someone she didn't know. I hate to say it, but I don't think the people there are going to care if Elle goes kicking and screaming. To them, that's just an every day part of the business."

"Lawd, have mercy," Aggie whispered.

"And as soon as she gets to the car," Lottie said, "she'll see you, Aggie. And you'll be able to get her calm in no time."

A moment passed while the team was processing the information. Then, Tyler cleared his throat and said, "So I hate to be the wet blanket, but we haven't talked much about alternative outcomes. What if something goes wrong? What if you can't text us? Or someone outbids you? What's our plan B?"

"We haven't talked about it because there is no plan B," answered Wil. "Plan A is to get Elle, and as far as I'm concerned, failure is not an option. Done deal. That's why it's so important for you to park close enough to the venue that you have a good view of the front. From the moment you park, dude, you've got to keep a razor-sharp focus on that entrance; especially if the time keeps going by and you haven't heard from me.

"But make no mistake: no matter what it takes, I'm not leaving that place without Elle, and I mean, no matter what it takes. So you can assume that if I come running like a bat outta hell with a little red-haired girl on my shoulders, you best get ready to haul ass once we get in the car."

"You got it," said Tyler.

"Good," Wil said and stood up from his chair. As he walked toward the door, he turned and asked, "And then we'll all head straight to the airport. Any other questions?"

"Nope," said Tyler.

"Mom?"

Lottie shook her head.

"Miss Aggie?" Wil could tell by the look on her face she had something to say. He could see her fingers rubbing the charms of Skye's broken bracelet. He asked again, "Miss Aggie?"

"Wil," she said slowly, "Dis may not be da right time to ask dis, but I'm afraid I won't get another chance. You just said we're gonna head straight to da airport after we get Elle. But, what about Skye? Aren't we gone do somethin about her before we leave?"

At that question, Wil sighed and dropped his head. A few moments of silence passed between them.

"I don't know how to answer that, Miss Aggie," Wil said softly.

Aggie's lips were trembling, but her voice was steady. "Don't we at least need to talk to some authority? I don't want to leave da country without doin sometin to know for sure what happened."

"I give you my word," Wil said solemnly, "We will find out who did this to her. Once that boy, Galen, is able to take visitors, we will get all the information from him. I promise you, we'll have justice. I know this will be difficult for you, but right now we need to keep our focus on Elle. Let's get her back first, and then we'll strategize the next plan."

Aggie nodded in agreement.

Wil's cell phone rang.

"That's gonna be Aeton, I bet he's down at the entrance." Wil said quietly. He answered his phone and said, "Hold up, Aeton." Then he looked up at the others in the room. "Is there anything else we need to cover before I leave?"

When no one spoke up, Wil said, "OK. I'll see you all in just a few hours, with Elle in hand. Let's roll." He grabbed his black leather laptop bag that was still filled with cash, patted Tyler on the back, and exited the room.

ELLE WANTED TO SKIP down the sidewalk, she felt so much excitement about the day. But Jack had already yelled at her twice for skipping ahead of him. They had just gotten out of the taxi, and were walking to the building where the beauty pageant was going to be held. Elle felt like a shaken can of pop.

"Are you sure they're not going to want me to perform anything, Daddy? Most pageants have a talent portion. I'll totally do it, if that'll make me win." Elle was chattering a-mile-a-minute. "I could sing a song; me and Skye used to sing together all the time, and I know lots of songs. I don't even need a piano to play; I could sing without music."

"You won't need to sing," Jack replied.

"I'm just saying, I could if you need me to. Don't think that I can't do it, if the judges ask for something at the last minute. Because I can. I'll totally do whatever you want me to do so I can win this pageant for you."

"You won't need to do anything but just stand there," he said as he stopped walking. "This is the place. Listen to me: I don't want you to say anything to anyone once we get inside here. You stand next to me until that woman takes you back into the waiting room. Don't talk to any of the adults, and when you are backstage waiting to go out, I don't want you to talk to any of the other girls who are back there, you hear me? Not even one of them."

"Why not? It will be boring back there to just sit—"

"I said what I said, Elle," he scolded harshly. "The other girls back there are not your friends. They're going to be wanting to win this thing too, so they might say bad stuff to scare you, or to try and make you not want to compete."

"Oh." Elle hadn't thought of that.

"So you keep your eyes to the ground, and your lips zipped, you hear me?"

"Yes, Daddy."

"Good. Now let's go inside."

Jack opened the big black doors, and they were greeted by two enormous men. Elle knew she was small for her age, but she still wondered if these men were giants of some kind. They were huge, and the top of her head didn't even come up to their hips! She couldn't help but stare.

Her dad whispered something to one of them, while Elle kept gazing at the other man, who was bald. She noticed he had one eye that looked very cloudy, just like her neighbor friend's cat did when it had gotten cataracts. She felt her dad tugging her out of the lobby and into the larger room, and she remained mesmerized by the giants until she was fully inside the theatre and the lobby doors had closed. She began to look around, but her dad hissed at her, "Stop it! I told you to keep your head down and your mouth shut!"

Elle tried her best to obey, but her curiosity kept getting the best of her. Whenever she'd think her dad was not looking, she'd glance up through the corners of her eyes to get a snapshot of her surroundings.

It was very dark in the room, much darker than it had been on the day they'd met up with the owner, when she'd shown Elle how to walk on the stage. Knowing she might get a slap if she looked up at the warehouse ceiling, Elle just assumed that all those fluorescent lights must've been turned off, leaving only the stage lights turned on.

She heard a familiar voice, and knew instantly that it was the interpreter who had been showing Jack around since they'd arrived. He and her dad talked in hushed tones, so she wasn't able to make out too much. She closed her eyes to focus in on their words, but it was no use; however, she did notice that all the voices in the room sounded like they were men's. That was not at all what Elle would've anticipated. Back home, pageants like these were usually judged by women.

There was one woman's voice that stuck out above the rest, a shrill, sing-songy sound, and it continued to grow louder as she approached Jack and Elle. The girl knew it was the lady who owned the theatre. Continuing to talk in her 'outside voice,' she briefly spoke with the interpreter, patted Elle on the head, and then clicked away from them to greet someone else.

"What did she say," asked Jack.

"She said it was good we were here so early, because you could walk around with her to let people get a good look at her before the deal," said the interpreter.

"Yeah, I'm not so sure I want to do that," Jack said. "It's pretty dark in here, and I can't make out the faces of people until I'm right up on them."

"Who cares? No one's going to know you, plus your chances to get a good—"

Jack cut him off, and pulled him away. The only words Elle heard before the two men were out of earshot was Jack telling him about a weird phone call he got from the police. Elle wondered if her dad was talking about the call from the Marigouin police, who had her mom's cell phone? Or if he was referring to something else?

FORTY-TWO

"I CAN'T BELIEVE we're getting here so late," Wil said as he ran down the sidewalk. "And that the only parking place was a half mile away."

"For the last time, man, I'm sorry," Aeton said. "There was nothing I could do about that accident. Plus, it's only 12:45. We're going to get there in just a couple minutes, still almost 15 minutes before it starts."

"I realize that, but I wanted to be there by 12:30. We have no idea how long it will take for us to check in, or whatever we have to do, to get our auction number."

"We're going to be fine," Aeton said, trying to keep up. "You need to slow down. Don't you think it's going to look weird for us to walk in there sweaty and out of breath? I don't think we should look that over-anxious."

"You're right," said Wil, and the pair walked two more blocks at a regular gait until they approached the warehouse. Stopping, Wil said, "OK. Anything we need to review?"

"Nope," said Aeton. "We've been over it, and we're good."

"We're not leaving here without the girl," Wil said.

"Got it."

"No matter what."

"Got it."

"No, man, look at me," Wil said. "Even if for some crazy reason something happens to me. You've got to promise me that you'll follow through and get her out of here. Nothing is more important than the success of this mission."

"Wil, you have my word," Aeton said solemnly. "Getting her safely to the car will be my top priority."

"Good. Thanks for being my wingman on this," Wil said. "There's no way I could've done this without you."

"It's what we do," Aeton said matter-of-factly. "And you'd've done the same for me."

"Anytime. You ready?"

"As I'll ever be."

"Me too. Let's go in."

Aeton opened the door to find the two large body guards from the day before manning the entrance. He and the main guard exchanged a few sentences before they were given admittance.

"It's pretty cut and dry," Aeton whispered to Wil. "The bidding happens with just our hands. And the guy was careful to add that we could only pay in cash, and if we tried to screw them, we'd find ourselves at the bottom of the sea."

"That's an original threat," Wil whispered back, sarcastically.

"Yeah, well, they're not paid for their creativity."

Wil scanned the room. It was quite dark, as the only illumination originated from the stage lights, and those were at half-power. The stage was a "U" shape, and small round tables with four seats each were gathered inside the legs of the runway. Because the auction was about to start, most of the people had already taken their seats. With a quick calculation, Wil assessed there were 45-48 people, and from the look of the backs of their heads, almost all were male. In addition to the men sitting, the room was lined with a few dozen standing men, all large and obviously employed as body guards. From their apparent disunity, Wil assumed they were not all employed by the old woman who ran the place, but rather, had come individually with each bidder.

"I guess we forgot to bring our bouncer," whispered Aeton.

"What are you talking about? I thought you were it," Wil said.

"Riiight. Where do you want to sit? There's a table closer to the front, or one right in the back."

"Back, definitely. Let's remain as anonymous as possible."

As they quietly sat at the small table, Aeton whispered, "Trust me.

After you drop a quarter of a mil in the auction, the last thing we're going to be is anonymous."

THIS WAS NOT AT ALL what Elle was expecting. Sitting in the room behind the stage, she had no idea what to think about this beauty contest, or about the actual contestants. First of all, this backstage room was very cramped with people, and there were only a few chairs on which to sit. A musty smell clung to the air, reminding Elle of the time MawMaw Aggie's basement had flooded. And the feeling inside the room was not good; Elle didn't know exactly how to describe it, she just knew it wasn't good...even a bit scary.

Because she was one of the shortest girls in the room, she couldn't see every girl, but the contestants she did see were not happy to be there at all. In fact, there were a few girls who had been forcibly pushed into the room, and when they didn't obey the person who'd brought them, they got slapped in the face. And Elle thought it was odd that she was the only girl without a chaperone. Some of contestants were one-on-one with a chaperone, and some were five or six to their chaperone; either way, it looked to Elle like she was the only one without someone watching over her.

Elle also wondered why the other girls were dressed like they were. Many had on little dresses that looked more like the slips her mom wore underneath her clothes; and some of the slips were so short, Elle could see their lacy underpants. A few of the older girls had on what looked like a bra or a girdle, and underpants. And not one of the girls looked as young as she was. Scanning the room again, she began to feel very out-of-place, certainly far too little to be a contestant in this beauty pageant.

As each moment passed, she was becoming more and more nervous, and she wished there was someone for her to talk to. Elle didn't care anymore that she'd promised her dad not to speak to anyone; she felt if she could connect with just one person, it would keep her from getting sick. The only problem was, she couldn't hear anyone using English.

She started to slowly push her way around the room, hoping to find a friend to play with. Even if the girl didn't speak her language, maybe they could draw on something, or sit and play hand clapping games. No one seemed interested in her, though. The moment she'd get a girl to make eye contact with her, that girl's chaperone would either come and stand between them, or move the girl away from Elle. Maybe her dad was right. Maybe these girls were so focused on winning, they wouldn't be nice to her anyway.

Elle spotted a girl with long black hair sitting by herself in the far corner of the room. She was wearing a long, emerald green slip, and she didn't seem have anyone watching over her. Elle couldn't tell how old the girl was because she was sitting on the floor facing the wall. She started to go towards her to see if she would be interested in playing, but she was stopped by sudden movement in the front of the room.

Everything got quiet as someone in the front was ringing a bell. When Elle turned to look, it was the sing-songy lady standing on a chair talking to everyone. Elle couldn't understand her language, but it seemed like she was giving everyone instructions. As she was talking, the old woman saw Elle standing nearer to the back of the room. She stopped speaking, pointed directly at her, and waved emphatically for Elle to come back up to the front.

Elle was surprised how quickly the other people in the room were to obey the old woman's every command. Seeing her point to Elle, the crowd automatically parted, making a slight aisle for Elle to easily get back to the front of the room.

As Elle approached the sing-songy lady, the woman gave her a big lipstick-smeared smile, and said, "You stay up here. You number three for to go out on stage."

Elle's heart skipped a beat. The pageant was starting, and she was number three to go out! On one hand, she was ecstatic that she was close to the beginning, so that she could get this stupid contest over with. On the other hand, knowing that in just a couple minutes she was going to step out into the unknown made her want to throw up. She took some deep breaths and tried to calm her nerves.

THE LIGHTS BEGAN TO DIM, indicating the start of the auction, and a single spot stayed on an area just right of center stage, where the old woman was standing. Speaking into a microphone, she began to give the rules for the auction. Aeton interpreted for Wil:

"There will be 35 girls in the auction today, and they'll be sold in two parts. The first eight girls are prime, as they are brand new and doctor certified as virgins. They'll come out one by one, and the woman will start the bidding. After they are sold, there will be a short break, during which the bidders who won any of the first eight must pay and take their girl. The next section of bidding will start on the remaining 27 girls. They will be sold in order, according to their age, youngest to oldest.

"To bid," Aeton continued, "you need to raise your hand and be acknowledged by the old woman. Once she does so, your bid is binding, and you can't retract it. If you win a bid, and you try to take it back, her guards won't let you leave until you've paid."

The woman was still talking as Aeton said, "And now she's just talking about once we get our merchandise, we need to leave quickly so that she can re-open for business."

"This is freakin surreal," said Wil.

"I know," said Aeton. "I can't believe how normal these people are acting, like we're all here just to buy a pair of shoes."

"Shh," said Wil. "It's starting."

The house lights went out, and the stage lights brightened to full strength. Some music with a dance beat started playing and the first girl emerged from the center stage door. Wearing a short, black satin slip and high black heels, she appeared disoriented and confused as she squinted her eyes and craned her neck to see the audience. However, the moment she stepped forward, a spotlight hit her, blinding her, and causing her steps to falter.

Wil's stomach churned at the sight of this young girl. Because of the bright make-up on her face, he couldn't predict an accurate age, but as she wobbled her way down one length of the runway, he knew she was young enough to have never worn heels this high. And, she obviously had no clue why she was here or of her impending fate. When the girl passed by groups of men, Wil noticed they began whispering to each other, probably creating strategy for their bidding.

Once the girl had returned to the center of the stage, the old woman motioned first for her to stand still, and then for the sound guy to turn down the music. Flashing a grotesque smile at the crowd, the woman raised her voice and began the bidding. Wil sat dumbfounded as the men went at it, hands lifting all over the place, and the old woman taunting them with higher and higher bid amounts. Wil and Aeton glanced at each other, nonverbally sharing the shock of what they were witnessing.

The bidding quickly soared to 70,000 euros, and then more than half the hands stopped participating. The woman was able to tease the last few bidders upwards, until finally, the girl closed at 95,000.

Wil observed the process. Just after the bidding ended, the man who had won the girl stood up just a bit from his chair to make himself known to the old woman, and her two guards. The young girl was told to return to the backstage room by using the same center stage door from which she'd entered.

Dear god, thought Wil. *I have got to keep my head on straight. I seriously want to kill every goddamned person in this room! I hope Aeton was right, and that Elle is at the beginning of the line of girls. I'm not sure how long I'm going to be able to sit and watch this.*

FORTY-THREE

ELLE'S STOMACH WAS FLIP-FLOPPING inside of her. The second girl had gone out a few minutes ago, and with each passing moment, Elle knew her turn was inching closer. Every part of her wanted to run away, and if there had been someplace for her to go, she quite possibly would've given in to the temptation. But there was nowhere to go except out on that stage, and her head was whirring with nervousness.

Elle tried to breathe deeply, but her chest wouldn't stretch open enough. Then she realized it was because she was hugging herself so tightly. Forcing herself to drop her arms, she took some breaths, only to subconsciously fold her arms right back up.

The stage door opened into the room and the girl who'd gone before her exited the stage. Elle would have given anything for that girl to know English so she could've asked her what it was like, and she tried to read the girl's face for the information. But the girl looked just as scared and confused as Elle felt, which only intensified Elle's urge to throw up.

The contestant before her had left the stage door open, and Elle stood staring at it, frozen with fear. She imagined it to be a mouth of a gigantic lion, and if she stepped into it, surely she'd be eaten alive.

A woman behind her pushed her on her back, harshly whispering undecipherable words. When Elle turned to face her, the woman was speaking a foreign language, waving her arms for Elle to get out onstage.

Elle knew she had no choice. Her legs tingled with anxiety, and as she stepped up the stairs to make her entrance, her knees were vibrating and weak. She breathed in one last deep breath and stepped through the door.

The second she emerged onto the stage, a white spotlight blinded her eyes. The bright light was all she could see, and it disoriented her to the point she completely forgot what she was supposed to do. She felt panic rise in her chest, fully aware she had been instructed to do something once she got out here, but just what that something was, she could not remember. And so she stood inside the belly of that lion, paralyzed.

WIL WAS STUNNED WHEN ELLE APPEARED. Miss Aggie had told him she looked small for her age, even shown him pictures, but until he saw this young girl walk out, he hadn't imagined how little she actually was. Maybe it was the maturity of this situation that magnified her youth, or the vile humanity surrounding her that made her appear so pure and chaste. At first, all Wil could do was sit in his chair and stare at the child forced on parade.

And he wasn't alone.

The crowd had grown eerily silent, enthralled by this 10-year-old girl, as she fidgeted nervously onstage. The spotlight shone on her beautiful, long red ringlets, while her clean, un-made-up face glowed white. Unlike the two girls that had walked before her, Elle had just barely entered puberty, and she looked almost doll-like in her pink satin dress.

However, the crowd's silence was only momentary, because when the old woman raised her hand to start the bidding, the room erupted with energy and sound. Every hand waved wildly, vying for the auctioneers' attention. Men were shouting, as the testosterone levels spiked into overdrive.

Wil felt an anger burn within his chest like never before, as these wolves frothed at the mouth and fought to win the prize of this child. *This is humanity at its worst,* thought Wil. *And I don't think I would have believed that people could stoop so low, if I wasn't sitting here watching it.*

He felt Aeton punch his arm.

"Dude, aren't you going to bid?" he asked urgently.

Keeping his eyes glued on Elle, Wil answered, "Not until we get closer to the end."

By now, Elle's eyes had adjusted to the spotlight, and she appeared fully confused by the action of the crowd. Wil noticed she was scanning the people, searching for someone. It took a couple of times going over the people, but then he saw Elle's eyes fix on someone in the audience, and the connection seemed to make her relax. Wil followed her eyes to find out who was on the other end of her stare.

It was Jack. Wil's eyes widened at this man who was a mirror image of his own father.

Or was he? Wil's righteous father would never have had the expression on his face that Jack did right now. It was one of greed and smugness as he smiled and watched the sale of his own flesh and blood. The worst kind of sale, at that. This was an auction that would turn this precious, innocent child into a sex slave.

With hatred flaring, Wil used this emotion to sharpen his senses and focus his mind to the mission at hand. But not before he made a vow to himself that once he'd gotten Elle safely out of here, he'd hunt this man down and make him pay for his sins.

"Where's the bid?" Wil asked Aeton.

"175, and it's still rising rapidly. We're going all the way, right?"

"Absolutely. I had my dad wire an extra 50, so if we take away what that woman grabbed the other day when we met her, we can go as high as 290."

"Good, because I think we're going to need it."

Bidders were in a frenzy as the woman continued to raise the stakes. Realizing her command over the room, she took her time as she calmly sing-songed the bid amounts higher and higher. 190...

200...210...225.

It wasn't until she hit 230,000 that a threshold was reached, and over half the room dropped out. 235...240... Several more gave up on the bidding. 245...

"OK," said Wil. "Get in there. Take your time, and go all the way. I don't want Jack to see me, so this is all you." Wil slouched a bit in his chair, and once again focused on Elle.

The woman called again for 245, and there seemed to be no takers...245...The energetic bidding had come to a close, and a silence blanketed the room.

Aeton lifted his hand, which made the woman giggle-snort with glee, and she quickly began to raise the bids again. Only one other man was still in it with Aeton, and he was bidding with a confident air.

250...255...260...265...

Aeton was starting to get nervous.

ELLE HAD FINALLY LOCATED her daddy's face in the crowd, and his expression filled her with relief. He was smiling, and apparently very proud of how she was doing. This reassurance calmed her mind, and she remembered she was supposed to have been walking up and down the runways. She wondered if she should start that now, or stay put?

She wished she could understand what was being said, and why the judges kept raising their hands to the fat lady. Or, why at first everyone was waving, and why now only a couple were. Were they voting or something? The format for this beauty pageant reminded Elle of the time she went with MawMaw Aggie to what she called an estate sale. The people there had numbers on little white ping-pong paddles, and they'd lift them up to try and buy the things they wanted.

Elle could see clearly now into the audience, and only two of the judges were still voting. One was a guy in the back of the room, too far away for her to see his face, and the other was a weird man she'd met a few days ago when her dad had made her hike all over the city to meet these judges. He was the creepy one who was eating huge green olives and who kept touching her hair. She shuddered at the thought of him.

Back and forth the two men waved, and Elle wished she could just leave the stage. There was nothing left for her to do, and she felt completely awkward standing here as the audience stared at her.

The room grew very quiet, and Elle noticed that the crowd was no longer looking at her. All eyes were now on the creepy man. Even the old lady was focused on him, seemingly waiting for a response from him. And the man did not look happy.

Elle wasn't sure what was happening, so she glanced over at her dad. He was still smiling, even broader than before, so she was relieved to know the lag in the voting was not because she'd done anything wrong.

The fat woman sing-songed a few more sentences to the man. His only response was to wave his hand and shake his head. She waited for a few seconds to speak again, while the tension in the room thickened.

The creepy man stretched up in his seat and craned his neck to try and see the other judge in the back who had been voting with him. Then Elle saw him swivel the opposite way to make eye-contact with a different person, who was standing to the side. Elle strained to see who it was, and recognized it was the enormous, hairy man who had greeted them in the hotel room the day Jack had introduced her to the creepy man.

The pair communicated nonverbally across the room, and after a few exchanges, the huge man shook his head 'no.' When the creepy man turned forward again, Elle noticed quite an angry expression on his face.

The fat woman must not have noticed his annoyance because she sing-songed again to him, which only served to make him even more irate. He emphatically shook his head, and in an outburst of emotion, he swiped his hand across his table, causing his glass to shatter on the floor. Elle nearly jumped out of her skin at the sound, and was surprised that the fat lady's reaction was only to burst into laughter.

The fat lady motioned to the judge in the back, causing the other judges in the room to shout a few comments at him as well. Then she turned to Elle and motioned for her to exit. Elle glanced over at her dad to make sure she should obey, and only after he nodded at her, did she turn and leave the floor.

As she returned to the backstage room, she thought, *Thank god that's over with; it was the weirdest beauty pageant I've ever seen. And why were they all yelling at the fat lady like that while I was out there? Well, at least I know that my dad looked happy about how everything went. Now all I have to do is wait back here for him to come and get me. Then we can get out of here!*

FORTY-FOUR

THE ONLY SOUND INSIDE THE VAN was the movement of their bodies as they shifted in their seats, anxiously awaiting the text from Wil. Both Lottie and Aggie were sitting in the back of the minivan, and Tyler was in the driver's seat. It had been over a half hour since they'd found their parking place, just one block from the auction venue, and in that span of time, not one word had been spoken.

All the luggage had been stored behind the third row seats, except several items Aggie had kept behind for when Elle had made it safely inside the van: a complete change of clothes, including socks and shoes, and her beloved white stuffed animal, Mr. Monkey. Aggie's hands rested on these items, gently clasping Skye's broken charm bracelet.

For the last several minutes, Aggie's eyes had been closed as she whispered inaudible prayers for her *Bon Dieu* to help Wil succeed in his mission. All the while, Lottie monitored the auction warehouse for any sign of Wil.

Tyler's phone chimed, notifying him of a text. At the sound, Aggie let out a verbal gasp, as she felt her stomach jump up into her throat. Lottie hopped out of her seat and leaned in toward Tyler.

"What is it?" Lottie asked. "What's happened?"

"Just a minute, ma'am," Tyler said as he touched the screen of his phone. He quickly read the text and replied, "They got her."

Both Aggie and Lottie let out sighs of relief.

"Dey got her in dey hands?" Aggie asked. "So, are dey on dere way out da place?"

"Oh wait," said Tyler, correcting himself. "I'm sorry. They got her in the auction, but they haven't made contact with her yet. Wil says there's going to be a break in about ten minutes; they'll pay for her then, and get the hell out. But all is going as planned."

"Tank da Lawd, tank da Lawd, tank da Lawd!" sang Aggie as she picked up Elle's shirt, laid it on her lap and started to press it flat with her hands. "Not too long now, li'l Ellie, and you be sittin right here in MawMaw Aggie's lap."

"Now we just have to believe those boys will get her out safe and sound," said Lottie as she settled back into her seat and refocused her eyes toward the auction venue.

"Da Lawd's gone do it," said Aggie with a smile.

IT WASN'T UNTIL ELLE EXITED the stage and the next girl walked out that Wil and Aeton felt the freedom to talk. With the music playing and the crowd focused on the next item up for bid, the young men assumed it was safe to scoot the backs of their chairs closer and communicate about what had just transpired.

"I was getting worried there for a minute," said Aeton. "If that guy in the front had raised the bid by just a few more thousand, we would've had to make a run for it."

"Yeah," answered Wil, still slouched in his chair. "And that probably would've been bloody. Did you see Jack up there?"

Aeton nodded. "And he saw me too. I can't wrap my mind around how satisfied with himself he looked as the bidding kept growing. And once the old lady up there pointed at me as the winner, that douchebag had the audacity to nod at me like he was giving me his approval! I wanted to grab him by his balls and beat the living crap out of him."

"Don't even get me started. It kills me he's finally getting his hands on my dad's money. He's gonna walk away with two hundred eighty-five thousand euros of it, for selling his own daughter. That's over four hundred and twenty thousand US dollars! I want to kill him."

"And if you give me the signal, I'll take care of that for you."

"No way. That pleasure will be all mine, in due time. Only, death is too easy of a sentence for him; I want him to rot his life away in a skanky prison cell...with a very large, gay cellmate."

The girl onstage had finished her walk on the runway, and the woman was about to start the bidding. Wil and Aeton sat back in their chairs, both anxious for the first phase of this auction to be done, so they could pick up Elle and make their way back to the car.

Wil watched as the bids rose for this innocent child, just 13 years old. She stood in the center of the stage chewing on the nail of her thumb. The girl looked every bit as confused as Elle, and the two girls before her. It was clear that none of them know the truth about why they were here. How many millions of dollars would be exchanged in order to purchase these girls?

The bidding closed and she was purchased for just under 85 thousand euros to a tall Slavic man wearing an extremely expensive three piece suit.

The old woman waved her offstage, and the fifth girl came out. She looked Slavic, and was a bit older than the others; Wil estimated around 15 years old. She sold for 45 thousand euros, and was followed by two more girls of similar appearance. They both sold for just under 40 thousand euros.

The eighth and last girl in the first phase of the auction was Asian, and like Elle, she set the room ablaze with a bidding frenzy. The old woman upfront had stressed this girl was not only the sole Asian in the sale, but she also was the men's last chance of the day to buy themselves a certified virgin.

Wil felt his gut churning with anger as these savages shouted out their bids, fighting to 'one up' the other. In the end, she sold for 225 thousand euros to the same man who had almost won Elle. And then the sing-songy lady announced the end to the first phase of the auction.

Aeton translated to Wil the woman's next words of instruction:

Those who had purchased any of the first eight girls were to meet her two enormous body guards at a small table, located against the wall on the right side of the warehouse. Once the money was exchanged for the girls, they were to remove their merchandise from the room before returning to their seats for the second half of the auction. Because this first portion of the auction had taken longer than expected, the second round would begin in only a few minutes.

"Let's put all the money in the leather bag," said Wil. "That way, you can go over there to pay, and I can hang back and watch your back. I don't want Jack to see me; I have no idea if he's been keeping up on my family, and we can't risk him recognizing me."

"Got it," said Aeton. "As soon as I get Elle in my hands, we'll move out."

"I'll send Tyler the text right now so he can get the car ready," said Wil. "Let's get 'er done."

Before standing up, the men emptied their cash belts into the black leather bag, making sure they filled it with an accurate count of 285 thousand euros.

FORTY-FIVE

JACK MET ELLE AT THE FRONT of the stage with a smile on his face. As soon as Elle saw her father, she ran to him.

"Did I do OK?" she asked. "Daddy, did I win? That was the weirdest beauty pageant I've ever seen! But did I do OK?"

"You did great," Jack replied.

"Did I win, then? Are you happy? Can we go see Skye now?"

"We can go, in just a minute," he said. "There's only one more thing I have to take care of before we go see Skye."

"Yea!" she said, jumping toward her dad so she could hug him."I cannot wait to see sissy!"

"Calm down, girl!" Jack barked. "You're making a scene. Now listen to me. We're going to go over there, so we can get your prizes, and when we do, I think they're going to want to take you somewhere for pictures before we leave. There'll probably be one or two of the judges who'll ask you to go with them, and I want you to do it without saying a word."

"Where will he take me?" asked Elle.

"Just somewhere to take pictures, because you won 1st place."

"I did? I won 1st place?!" she shrieked, hugging her father once again.

"Stop it!" hissed Jack, as he held firmly onto both of Elle's shoulders in order to calm her down.

"Are you sure I won?" asked Elle, confused why her dad wasn't more excited. “What about all those other girls backstage? They haven’t even been voted on yet.”

“Don’t worry about them; they’re in a different contest. You want to see Skye, don’t you?” Jack asked. Elle nodded emphatically. “OK, then,” Jack continued, “you only have to do these very last photos, and you’ll be on your way. You go with whoever takes you, and then he’ll bring you right back to me, and we’ll go visit Skye.”

“OK, Daddy,” Elle said. “Whatever you say.”

She took her dad’s hand as they walked through the many judges toward a table against one of the walls. The fat, sing-songy lady was standing behind the table, and in between two huge men. Several people had lined up in front of the table, and all the girls who’d been contestants with Elle were grouped to the side of it.

“You need to go stand there with the other girls,” said Jack.

“Daddy, why is that girl crying so hard?” she asked, pointing at one of the young girls. “She was in the back screaming, and the fat, old lady actually hit her to make her stop!”

“Uhhh...she’s probably just sad she didn’t win.”

Elle felt bad, if what her daddy had said was true. As she took her place in the group of girls, she wished she knew how to speak the other girl’s language so she could maybe help her feel better.

Wil was just fifteen feet from his Uncle Jack, and he had to use enormous discipline to not confront him. He loathed this man, who appeared identical to his father, but who acted in every way repulsively opposite from him. Wil’s heart beat firmly in his chest as he forced himself to keep his distance from Jack.

Aeton was fifth in line, and Wil observed the transactions going on so he could mentally calculate an exact exit time. The old woman was dealing with the money exchange. She talked to her two body guards as she received and counted the money, stashed it for the time being in an open safe, and made notes on a pad of paper. Once the client had fully paid, the woman would allow him to take his girl and exit the building. Since all the cash was going into the same place, Wil assumed the sellers would settle with the fat woman at the end of the auction.

After three people had gone through the process of check-out, the woman spoke a few words to her body guards and left them to finish the transactions. She quickly hobbled over to the stage and made an announcement on the microphone. Her words invoked the rest of the audience to once again take their seats. The second phase of the auction was about to begin.

Wil watched Elle as she stood quietly, unwittingly waiting for her buyer to steal her away. Next to the other seven girls, who were easily four to five inches taller than her, Elle looked so little. No wonder her bidding shot up so high, so quickly; she was the only one here who could fully satisfy the perversion of a pedophile. Wil was overcome with gratitude that Miss Aggie had searched out his family, and that they all were able to rescue Elle from the hands of such a wicked fate.

Aeton was up to the table. It was only a few more minutes, and they would all be out of the warehouse.

The music from the stage began, signifying the reopening of the auction. Wil glanced over and saw a girl walking on the stage, but he quickly returned his focus to Elle, Aeton, and the money exchange.

The main bodyguard was counting the money, as Jack stood close by with an eagle-eye on his every move. Once the guard was satisfied with Aeton's amount, he nodded at Jack, who in turn, took Elle by the hand and walked her over to Aeton. Wil couldn't believe how smoothly this was transpiring, and he twisted his head away from Jack to avoid an encounter.

Jack whispered a few words to Elle and pointed to Aeton. Elle nodded to show she understood, she approached Aeton, and took his hand. Completely stone-faced, Aeton made eye contact with Wil, and then turned with Elle in hand to lead her out of the warehouse. Wil was a few steps ahead of them, and as he moved toward the warehouse entrance, he pressed send on a text to Tyler that read: "Get ready. We're walking out now."

As Wil, Aeton and Elle walked calmly towards the exit, the music on the stage stopped playing, indicating the start of the bidding on the first girl of the auction's second phase.

Wil sensed Aeton and Elle, who'd been behind him, had stopped moving. Wil spun around to assess the situation, and found Elle frozen in her tracks, her eyes glued to the stage. Wil followed her gaze to see the old woman's hand in the air, about to signal the first bid, and standing next to her was a girl who was wearing a long emerald green slip, and her long black hair was slightly covering one side of her face. But even so, Wil could not deny that this girl looked identical to the picture he and Aeton had been using...

"Skyyyyyyyye!" yelled Elle. "Skyyyyyyye!!"

The girl onstage, who had been staring vacantly at the floor, snapped into focus. Her eyes madly scanned the room to find the source of the voice.

"Dear god," Wil gasped to Aeton. "That's Skye!"

"Skyyyyee!" Elle screamed again. "It's me, Elle!" She had released herself from Aeton's hand, and was now sprinting toward the stage.

Aeton was just as shocked as Wil. "What's the plan?" he asked.

"You get Elle to the car!" Wil commanded. "That's your number one goal. I'll get Skye."

Skye was stunned. Was she hallucinating, or had she actually heard her sister's voice? She ran to the front of the stage and knelt down to see below the bright spotlight beams.

"Elle?" Skye called. "Elle! Is that really you? How did you get here??!!"

Elle was trying to maneuver her way through the tightly packed tables and chairs. She called up to her sister, "Skye! I didn't know you were in the beauty contest too! Does Daddy know you're here?"

Wil took a second to evaluate the room. Aeton was just a few feet from Elle, but Jack was moving quickly toward her as well. The old woman had stepped forward and was grabbing Skye around her waist, attempting to pull her back to her auction position. Wil knew he needed to scatter everyone's attention.

Without thinking it through, he ran over to the table with the two body guards, where they had just purchased Elle. Determined to disable them, Wil jumped over their table, and plowed into the guard whom he knew was blind in one eye. He jabbed that guard deeply into his good eye, blinding him, at least temporarily. The large man dropped to his knees in pain, and Wil kicked him squarely in his temple, causing him to fall unconscious.

The other guard attacked Wil from behind, pounding his back with extreme force. Knocked into a ball, Wil was able to reach down and slip out the knife he had strapped to his ankle. He lunged it at the brute, and from the warm liquid he now felt on his hand, he knew he'd succeeded in making contact. With the full weight of the man collapsing on top of him, they both hit the concrete fast, and Wil had to wrestle himself free from underneath the enormous body. Unsure where he'd stabbed the man or how long the wound would keep him down, Wil knew he needed to move quickly to cause a distraction big enough to disrupt the entire room.

He darted to the open safe and began whipping out pile after pile of euros, flinging them all up into the air. Creating a massive whirlwind of bills, he shouted, "Money! Euros! Take your euros!"

The room exploded into action with sounds of tables and chairs scooting across the cement floor, and men yelling at each other. Wil could hear the sing-songy lady screaming into the microphone for people to remain calm and to go back to their seats.

Wil needed to make it to the front of the room to save Skye, but now he was hindered by the crowd of men, including Jack, who were dashing in his direction to get their hands on the whirling money. As fast as he could, he began to weave his way through the thick mob of treasure-hunters.

Aeton was only several feet away from Elle when he came face to face with the man who had bid against him in the auction. He was a slender man, in a sleek suit, and he pressed his chest against Aeton's.

"Did you really think I'd let you buy my little red-headed prize away from me?" he said in Greek.

Aeton was shocked this slight man would dare threaten him, as he was clearly physically dominant. Aeton laughed at his threat, but as he lifted his hand to knock the man away, he felt himself being picked up from behind, as if he weighed nothing at all, and thrown several feet to his left. Aeton's body was airborne for a full two seconds before it crashed on top of a table. He slid off the top of it with such velocity that he became entangled inside two wrought iron chairs as he continued to slide across the concrete floor.

Elle had reached her sister who was crouching down at the edge of the stage. Her words began spilling out to her beloved sister, who appeared completely surprised to see her.

"Oh Skye! I can't believe you're here! I've been waiting so long to see you, and I've missed you tons and tons. Did you know I was coming to visit? Is this where your school is? I have so much to talk to you about. You look so different from that last—"

Skye cut her off. "Elle, stop talking. What are you doing here? Who brought you here?"

"Daddy did! He brought me—"

"Oh my god, oh my god," Skye said as she tried to jump down off the stage. "Listen to me, Elle. You've got to get out of here. No matter how you do it, you've got to get out of here! Do not trust Dad, whatever you do, do not trust anything he tells you!!"

The witch decided to give up screaming into the microphone and trying to maintain order, and she advanced toward Skye. Seeing the girl was trying to get down off the stage, the witch latched onto Skye's long hair to keep her up on the platform.

"Let go of her!" Elle shrieked at the old woman. "Skyyye!"

"You get backstage, you little slut!" the witch hissed to Skye.

Skye was fighting to regain her balance, but the witch's grip on her hair was too strong.

"RUN, Ellie! Get OUT OF HERE!" Skye yelled.

"But Skyyye!" Elle screamed.

"NO!" ordered Skye. "RUN, ELLE! GOOOO!"

Elle had no clue where she was going to go, but from the look on her sister's face, she knew she needed to obey. She spun around with every intention of making her way to the outside doors, but she only took a few steps until she felt someone grab her. It was the creepy man, who had voted so strongly for her.

"You will come with me," he spoke English into her ear. "I take care of you from now on."

His voice sent a chill up and down Elle's spine, and she began to sense the gravity of danger she was in. She began to kick and scream as loudly as she could. The man's hand aggressively clasped over her mouth as he said, "You not fight. You fight, I beat you." The terror in Elle overrode his warning, and she bit down as hard as she could on his perfectly manicured hand. He tried to pull his hand back, but Elle was in shock. She just kept clamping down on it. Not until she tasted his blood in her mouth did she realize what she was doing, and opened her jaw.

The man threw her to the ground as he yelled words at her she didn't understand, and then shot verbal orders to his enormous, hairy bodyguard. Elle noticed that he'd just used his brute strength to throw the man she'd been walking with over some tables. But now, his focus was directed upon her and she was his next victim. Knowing she'd have absolutely no chance freeing herself from the clutches of that ape, she stayed on her hands and knees and began scrambling under the tables and chairs toward the back exit.

"Something's not right," said Tyler. "It's taking too long for them to get out of there."

"How do you know?" asked Lottie.

"Wil's last text said they were about to walk out, and that was minutes ago," Tyler replied. "Something's happening in there."

"Oh Lawd, Lawd," whispered Aggie. "*Mon Dieu*, reach yo hand in dere and make da way for my girl!"

"What should we do?" asked Lottie. "Should we do anything?"

"No. Wil's orders were to stay put."

"But we can't just sit here..." said Lottie.

"We have no choice," answered Tyler. "Keep a sharp lookout, but get ready to fly, if need be."

Wil scanned the room for Aeton and Elle. Neither could be found. Had Aeton really gotten her out of there so quickly? He took a few steps to find Skye, but then noticed an empty chair scooting slowly across the floor. Elle was hiding under it, crawling her way toward the door.

In an instant, Wil threw the chair aside and grabbed hold of Elle. She began screaming at the top of her lungs, "Skyyye! Help me Skyyye!!!"

Wil heard the subtle sound of a gun with a silencer going off. He had to get her out of here now. Ducking his body over hers to protect her, Wil wrapped his arms tightly around Elle, picked up her light frame, and ran towards the exit. He didn't hear another gun shot, but seconds later, he did feel the burn of a bullet's contact as it pierced his left calf.

His adrenaline covered the pain as he ran through the double exit doors and was blinded by the bright sunlight. He shook his head violently to make his eyes adjust as quickly as possible. He heard a car horn to his left, and he began to run toward it. Eyes clear, Wil saw the blue minivan and waved an arm for them to come.

Elle felt one of the man's arms release its grip, and she used the opportunity to try to kick and wriggle free. Losing his balance, the man stumbled, allowing Elle to push herself away from him. She fell to the sidewalk. As soon as her feet hit the ground, she took off sprinting as fast as she could away from her captor. Elle had no idea where to go; all she knew is she had to find someplace to hide.

The car pulled up beside Wil.

"Do you see her? Go get her!" Wil ordered.

"Aren't you gonna get in?" yelled Tyler.

"No, I've gotta go back in there and get Skye!"

Aggie let out a scream of shock.

"What?!" exclaimed Lottie.

"Skye's in there, too! Tyler, GO! Get Elle before she gets away or something happens to her, and then make sure you come back around here to get me and Skye! We'll be coming back out in a few minutes."

When Wil stood up, he felt the pain of the bullet in his calf, but it only took a few steps for him to focus past it. He had to get back in there and rescue Skye.

Tyler floored the gas to catch up with Elle.

"Just get close 'nough for me to talk with her," Aggie said.

"Yes," said Lottie. "If you pull ahead of her, Tyler, you could even stop the van, and Miss Aggie could get out. I'm sure once Elle sees her, she'll get in the car."

"Good plan," said Tyler.

The van drove past Elle and stopped about a half a block ahead of her. Lottie swung open the side panel door, and helped Aggie jump down.

Aggie walked to the middle of the sidewalk and faced the oncoming Elle. The moment Elle saw Aggie, she stopped running.

"MawMaw?" she gasped, out of breath. "Is that really you?"

"It's yo MawMaw Aggie, chile, in da flesh. I come all dis way just to hug yo neck. Dat's how much I missed my sweet Ellie."

Elle ran toward Aggie and fell into her arms. They both began to cry.

"I was so scared! MawMaw, I don't even know how to tell you about it...I was so scared!"

"I know, honeychile, I know. But Aggie's here now. You safe, *Sha.*

You safe." Aggie, still crying with joy, sat back on her heels and rocked her girl.

Elle shot up. "Skye!" she said. "MawMaw, Skye is in there, and there was this big fat woman who was pulling her by the hair! She's a mean, mean lady, who I saw hit some of the other girls in the beauty pageant. We've got to get her outta there!"

"I know, *Sha.*" Aggie worked hard to keep her voice calm. "And we are gonna get her out. You know dat man who just brought you out? Dat's Wil, and he's a good boy. All dem others in dere, dey evil, but da one who carried you out, why, he was bringin you to MawMaw. And now, he gone go get Skye."

"Who is he?"

"He's a guardian angel sent from heaven, but we'll get into all dat later, Ellie. Right now, let's get back in da car so we can go get Skye, and den we all can go home. I even brought Mr. Monkey with me for you to play with."

Elle hugged Aggie tightly, and then they both got up and climbed into the van.

FORTY-SIX

SKYE HAD TO SAVE ELLE! As the witch was pulling her toward the backstage room, Skye could hear Elle's screams. She scratched at the witch's hands to try and get herself free, but it didn't work. However, her attempts did create a momentary lag in the tugging, just enough for Skye to look out over the chaotic crowd and see Elle being carried out the door. Her mind screamed with the urgency to protect her sister from what had been done to her.

The witch had forced her to wear high heels for this event, and because Skye was normally shut up in her room, she wasn't used to steadying herself on them. As a result, the old woman held the advantage as she jerked the young girl off the stage. However, just as the witch was about to push Skye through the backstage door, Skye heard the sound of glass shattering. She felt herself suddenly released, and the force by which she was fighting with now worked against her as she plummeted forward into the stage floor. What had happened?

Skye reeled back to face her assailant to find her crumpled in the doorframe leading backstage. Standing over the madame was a trembling Dula, with the remains of a wine bottle in her clenched fist. Through a tearstained face and with a raspy voice, Dula said, "Go! Go NOW!"

Skye popped up, and kicked the witch one last time, wishing the old hag would've been conscious to feel the blow. She smiled at Dula, the woman who had so tenderly healed her wounds, and then headed for the main exits, hoping to catch up with the people who stole Elle.

Meanwhile, Wil, who'd just left Elle in the care of Aggie, now was running to the warehouse entrance to pull open the doors. But they wouldn't budge. Someone had locked the doors.

"Damn it!" he said as he yanked as hard as he could to move them. He drew his gun and shot at the locks, but the doors remained bolted tight. The old woman and her crew must've locked everybody inside the warehouse to make sure none of the money escaped. He stepped back to scan the premises, to find an alternate way into the building.

There were no windows on the face of the warehouse, so he knew he had to start circling the massive structure. Running full speed to the right, he turned away from the main road and inspected the building's side wall. Nothing. No windows, no fire escape, no exits.

He continued to the rear, and found a loading dock. He climbed up the short brick wall to a single door that stood next to the dock. He tugged on the handle, not surprised to find it locked. But that was nothing a few bullets from his gun couldn't fix. He pulled out his gun and fired strategically at the spots where he believed the locks were located.

He leaned in to try the door, and when he aggressively jerked on what remained of the handle, the door swung open so freely, he almost fell over. The room in which he entered was pitch black, but the light from the open door provided enough illumination to see. There were huge set pieces and wooden crates haphazardly stored throughout the room, and from the dust and cobwebs everywhere, along with the thick carpet of dirt on the concrete floor, Wil could tell no one had been in here for a long, long time. He quickly began darting through the maze of storage to find a way back into the main warehouse space so he could rescue Skye.

Skye was unable to see a clear pathway to the exit doors; too many people were yelling and fighting with each other, clogging her way. Deciding her fastest route would be around the crowd, she sprinted to the left.

She'd barely gotten speed when a man came out of nowhere, and she smacked right into him. When she looked up, she was shocked to find herself face to face with Jack.

An avalanche of emotion swept over her as she staggered back, eyes wide open, staring at her father.

"Hello, Skye," said Jack, and he opened his arms to her. "I'm so, so glad I've finally found you. You don't know how desperate both your mother and me have been to get you home."

Skye stood still, mouth agape.

"I know what it must've looked like, Skye, all those months ago when I first brought you here," he said. "But I promise you, honey, I had no idea what kind of place this was."

"Where's Elle?" Skye managed to say.

"Thank god, she's made it out safely, Skye," said Jack, "and I want you to know that I'm here to take you away from all of this. In fact, that's exactly why I'm here...to take you home."

Skye's mind was buzzing. Was this real? Was her father actually saying these words to her? Jack extended his hand towards her. "Come on, Skye," he said urgently. "We've got to get out of here, before anyone finds us out.

"Come on, girl, let me protect you and get you outta this hellhole. Let me take you some place where you'll be safe."

"Where's Elle?" Skye asked again. "Why did you bring her here?"

"We both came here to get you, Skye, and now we've got to get out of here...Now! Come on, I'll explain all of it to you later."

Skye couldn't think. His words made no sense to her, but more than anything in the world, she wanted someone to protect her and to take her to a place where she'd be safe.

Wil felt as if something was magically leading him through the darkness, down hallways, and around corners, because in just a matter of a few minutes, he'd found his way back inside the large auction room. He emerged through a door on the side wall of the warehouse interior, just opposite where he and Aeton had paid for Elle. The stage was to his far left, and the exit door to his far right. And the entirety of the room was in utter chaos.

Wil sprinted toward the center of the room, and found Aeton trying to stand up.

"Bro, what happened to you?" asked Wil.

"It doesn't matter; I got thrown. Where's Elle?"

"I got her out, and I'm back to get Skye."

Wil noticed Aeton's left arm was not moving. "What's up with your arm?"

"My shoulder's dislocated. Don't worry about it; I'm fine." Aeton growled through gritted teeth as he snapped his shoulder back into socket. "Let's go get Skye."

Jack was becoming impatient with Skye. He shook his outstretched hand, gesturing for her to grab hold of it. "Come on, Skye, take my hand. If you want to escape, now is the time!"

Skye knew what she needed to do, and she reached out to take her father's hand. He smiled at her, and he pulled her close to him.

"Good choice, Skye," her dad said.

With tears in her eyes, she looked up into his face and said, "I will never, ever go anywhere with you again." And with that, she unleashed her hatred upon this man who was supposed to be her father, supposed to love her, supposed to protect her. She kneed him as hard as she could in his groin, crying as she watched him double over in pain. Rage filled her chest, and when he fell to his knees, she kicked him again and again and again. Everything in her wanted to kill him.

"There she is," said Wil, pointing. "There's Skye."

"Oh my god, she's pummeling Jack!" said Aeton.

"Good girl," said Wil. "But look over there. A couple of the old woman's thugs are coming to get her, can you see that?"

"Let's go!" said Aeton.

Aeton darted over to Skye, and with one arm, pulled her off Jack. She was sobbing as she flailed about, trying with all her might to break free from Aeton's grasp and to get back to beating her father.

Wil grabbed hold of Jack's shirt and slammed him onto the ground. "I'm comin back for you, Uncle Jack."

Wil sprang up, took hold of Skye and said in her ear, "Listen to me, Skye, we've got to get you out of here. My name is Wil, and you don't know me, but I promise you, I'm not here to hurt you. Aggie Prejean sent us; and she's waiting outside in a car for you. We've already rescued

Elle, now all we need is you. Please, I'm begging you to trust me."

"MawMaw Aggie is here?" she asked.

"Yes, Skye," Wil answered softly. "Aggie is just outside that door." He directed her focus to the large exit doors. "Your MawMaw Aggie has clothes for you and everything else. Please, please, let me take you out of here."

Skye melted into his arms and began sobbing uncontrollably.

Wil hoisted her up and said to Aeton, "Let's go!"

Seeing the witch's thugs closing in on them, they ran as fast as they could toward the entrance. They went through the doors to the small lobby, but found the doors to the outside were still locked tight with a horizontal steel bolt. And the bolt was stuck.

"Aeton, you've got to hold those lobby doors closed while I work with this bolt!" Wil carefully set Skye on the ground and said, "Don't worry, Skye, this'll just take a minute."

He tugged as hard as he could on the bolt, jiggling it back and forth to free the exits.

Aeton had discovered the top vertical bolts for the lobby doors and had fastened them, but the bodyguards were fiercely pounding on them, threatening to rush in.

"Wil, you've got to hurry. These little locks aren't going to be able to keep them out much longer!"

"I've almost got it, man," yelled Wil, "Hold them back!"

With one last yank, Wil burst open the front doors, gathered Skye in his arms and ran outside. As the trio dashed out, Wil heard a car horn to his right, and he sprinted toward it.

The two body guards were shouting behind them, and Wil instinctively knew they were about to fire their weapons. He saw the minivan had stopped about thirty feet from where he was, panel door open wide.

"Skye, you're going to have to run to that blue minivan. Both Elle and Aggie are in there waiting for you!" As he set her down, he felt a familiar heat pierce his back. It was another bullet.

"GO! GO! GO!" he yelled to Skye as he spun around to return fire on his predators. Aeton had already taken one of the men out, and as Wil fell to the ground, he made a clean shot into the forehead of the second guard.

In the van, Lottie's face was filled with horror as she saw her son collapse to the ground.

"Wil!" she screamed. "WIL!"

She lurched toward the open door, but Tyler spun around, grabbed her arm and yanked her back into her seat.

"No, Miss Charlotte!" he said. "You can't go out there. Look over there! There's more guys with guns coming outta the warehouse.

"But—"

"No!" he shouted sternly. "They'll kill you!"

Four men, guns cocked, had emerged from the building. Once they saw Skye running to the van, they opened fire. A bullet could be heard hitting the back of the vehicle.

"Get Skye in the van!" Wil shouted to Tyler, "And then get the hell outta here! NOW!!"

Aeton and Wil began firing back at them.

Skye ran to the van that had already begun to move, and leaped into the open door. Aggie's arms were outstretched wide towards her, and Skye fell into her lap. As the van started to accelerate, she sank into the softness and safety of her wonderful, loving Aggie, and started to weep.

"Oh my Skye-girl, you safe," whispered Aggie as she stroked her hair and began to cry with her. "You safe, my girl, you safe. *Le Bon Dieu* brought you back to me, and you safe. Aggie's gone watch over you from now on, and nothin's ever gone hurt you again, *Sha*." Aggie bent over her and kissed her cheek. "I promise you, nobody's ever gone hurt you again."

As they sped away, Lottie helplessly watched through a blur of tears as the image of Wil lying on the pavement grew smaller and smaller. With each inch of distance, she could feel her heart ripping deeper, not knowing if she would ever see her only son alive again. And by now, dozens of people were spilling out of the warehouse's open doors, the sounds of approaching police sirens causing them all to run in every direction. Lottie looked back at Aggie joyfully hugging her girls. While it was a beautiful image, Lottie couldn't help but wonder how profoundly that image had just cost her.

Elle snuggled into the side of her MawMaw and sister.

"Oh Elle!" whispered Skye as she reach out towards her. "I'm so glad you are safe! You don't even know what you've just been saved from."

Skye's arm hugged her sister. "Oh, my sissy, I missed you so much."

Elle was crying as she buried her face in Skye's lap.

"Tank you, Lawd, for bringing both my girls back to me," Aggie whispered heavenward, and then she said to her granddaughters, "Your MawMaw Aggie loves you both more dan you could ever know, and you gone be safe and sound and taken care of from now on." Aggie's arms drew the girls even closer into her as she added, "And dat's just gone be da way it's gone be."

THE END

But the fight to save lives has just begun...

To read the first chapters of the second book in the
Caged No More Trilogy,
go to www.mollyvenzke.com.

NOW IS THE TIME

a message from the author

CREATING SOMETHING FROM NOTHING has always been a passion of mine. Especially if costumes were involved. When I was a little girl, I'd make my sister and brother put on variety shows under our carport in Belleville, Illinois. Convinced of its Broadway possibilities, we'd handwrite invitations for every house in the neighborhood and invite them to come share in our performances chocked full of magic tricks, choreography to Barry Manilow's Copacabana, and scenes with cameos played by Barbie and Stretch Armstrong. What's the craziest thing to me is that people came. And they paid the 10-cent ticket price.

As I grew up, my passion for creativity expressed itself through a career as a singer, actor and even playwright; however, deep inside, I always harbored a desire to go to the "Olympics of Writing" and actually complete a novel of my own. But I kept that ambition on the Someday shelf in my heart. Someday when I'm older...Someday when the kids are all in school...Someday when all my proverbial ducks were neatly in a row. (As if anything in my creative life had ever been neatly in a row.)

When I got the idea for Caged No More, it was a most inconvenient season in my life to write a novel. Impossible, really. My husband and I were on the tail-end of a transitional whirlwind; in a matter of just 4 years, we both quit our salaried positions to begin separate commission-based careers, and I gave birth to 3 gorgeous baby girls (Not all at once, mind you; they're all 21 months apart.) Our hands were more than full, and for me to commit to a project of this magnitude would be completely irresponsible. So onto the Someday shelf the idea went, along with all the other novel plots I currently have standing in line inside my head.

But Caged refused to mind its manners and keep in the queue. I couldn't stop thinking about the 27 million people throughout the world who are living their lives on earth today as modern-day slaves. Of these, several million are young girls and boys whose childhood innocence is raped from them as they are imprisoned in wretched and torturous environments and are forced to engage in despicable sexual acts. Children bought and sold, beaten and starved, daily required to be participants in pornography and earn mandatory wages by having sex with dozens of men every single day. And if they refuse? Then, they'll be beaten and gang-raped again. The images haunted me.

People like Christine Caine, co-founder of the A21 Campaign, continued to open my eyes and heart to this injustice upon humanity. She travels around the world speaking about this, and as I listened to her teachings and podcasts, I found it impossible to turn a blind eye. Then, humanitarians like Lee and Laura Domingue, founders of Trafficking Hope, stretched open my eyelids even more as they helped me to understand the gravity of human trafficking as it happens every day in America.

What?! I remember thinking. *This kind of thing doesn't happen in the United States of America, the Land of the Free!* And I was mortified to discover how terribly wrong I was. In fact, every year in the US, 150,000 youth are thought to be trafficked into the sex trade, and my own city of Seattle is a major portal for it. I unearthed stats that proved SeaTac, WA (a city just 15 minutes from where I live) to be the #6 most popular city in the nation—some sources cite it as #3—for "Johns" to come to and engage in sex with children! Not only was it happening in my nation; it was happening right in my backyard...And I'm sorry if I'm the first person to break this news to you, but it is also happening in your backyard.

As a Christian, I believe in the scriptures that teach us how God hears the cries of the poor and afflicted. So if this is true, then as these millions of people cry out for someone to notice their suffering, what must this sound like in heaven? I couldn't stop imagining the intensity of what God must be hearing. Surely, their voices are breaking the heart of my heavenly Father, and He, in turn, must be calling out to His people to do something, anything, to administer His love and justice to these hurting people, to let them know they have not been forgotten. I knew I could no longer sit in my lovely, blessed life and continue to think, "Someone's really got to do something about that."

But what? Obviously, as a mom of 3 very young children, I couldn't physically become an active participant in the day-to-day needs to combat this injustice. And as I mentioned before, my husband and I were both in the process of building new careers, so giving large amounts of money to the organizations that are making huge impacts in this issue, was also not an option at that particular time. But I had to do something.

It's funny what compassion can do to a person. And when I say compassion, I'm talking about the feeling that compels a person to take action. As compassion for these kids grew in my heart, I became restless to act, and this caused me to see things differently. Excuses were exchanged for strategies, and impossibilities for possibilities.

Caged No More came off the Someday shelf and was moved to the DO IT NOW shelf. My husband and I agreed in the vision for the project; I'd write *Caged* and we'd give 100% of the proceeds to Trafficking Hope, an organization making a huge impact throughout America. As of the date of this 2nd edition release, they've helped bring awareness to millions and have helped rescue and restore hundreds of trafficking victims. It's funny, because when I contracted with Trafficking Hope to own the rights we wrote "Trafficking Hope will own all rights for both the 1st book in this series and the 1st movie in this series." Before one word was written, we were already speaking out in faith.

About a year after the first edition of *Caged,* Lisa Arnold (movie producer and director) contacted us and asked if we'd be interested in making *Caged* into a movie. Are you kidding? We've been praying for you for a couple years now! She asked me to write the screenplay and in January 2016, the feature film was released nationwide.

I share this story, because if after reading *Caged No More*, you too are filled with an urgent compassion to act, I want to encourage you... YOU can make a difference! If I can do it, you can do it. Please don't simply say to yourself, like I did for so long, "Someone really should do something about that" and go back to your safe and happy life. Because that someone is me. And that someone can be you, too. And the time is NOW.

But I am also aware that you might be like most people, and you have no idea what to do. I want to help you. You can join the army of people who are determined to turn the tides of this issue away from terror and bondage towards HOPE and freedom. Here is a list of several things you can do RIGHT NOW to help administer justice to these millions of people:

1. Pray. Everyone can pray. Pray for the victims to be found and rescued. Pray for their rehabilitation and restoration. Pray for the many people who are putting their own lives at risk to save these victims. Pray for their safety, their families' safety, and for them to have the wisdom to know exactly how to strategize and act. Pray for the resources of people and money to be given towards this issue. Pray. Even if you simply think of one girl and pray...pray.

2. Educate yourself. Spend some time on Google, and you'll find an abundance of information on human trafficking, along with all its horrid tentacles. There are great resources out there. Start out with www.traffickinghope.org. Join the HOPE Coalition, which unlocks an abundant supply of resources for you to take action and be busy for a long time.

3. Spread Awareness. Use this book as a launching point. Buy copies of *Caged No More* (remember, 100% of all proceeds go to help stop human trafficking). Facebook and twitter about *Caged No More*, and include the link to www.traffickinghope.org so your friends can buy their own copy. Host a book club with *Caged* as the novel; to make it easy, we've provided discussion questions for your club in the next few pages. Write a review for *Caged No More* on amazon.com, as well as for your local newspapers. Once you start talking to your family and friends, you will see just how unaware people are about this issue, especially with regards to its prevalence in their own communities. Awareness is crucial! Once people know the facts, they will be compelled to act.

4. TAKE ACTION

* Financially support anti-trafficking organizations that you trust, and that you can see are making a strong impact in the arena they are focused.

* Educate yourself about the legislation in your state and government. Write your local and state representatives and senators; tell them to vote for tougher laws to be passed, laws that protect the victims and prosecute the perpetrators.

* Host clothing and jewelry drives, and give all the nice items to a local organization that helps young girls who've been rescued.

* Host an awareness night at your church, school, club, etc. Invite speakers who are on the front lines of this issue and have them communicate the details about human trafficking: stats about your local city, how to recognize trafficking, and where to go to call for help.

* Host a 5k walk/run designed to bring awareness and raise funds to be given to support a great organization.

* Do SOMETHING

Human Trafficking is an enormous problem. Globally. Nationally. Regionally. Locally. I invite you to join the cause and become a 21st century abolitionist. It's going to take a worldwide army, all of us joining forces together, to bring an end to this present-day form of slavery. We must do all that we can to bring justice to these millions of young girls, and also young boys, because they cannot save themselves.

It is up to you and me

to be their voice,

to be their rescue,

to be their freedom.

ACKNOWLEDGEMENTS

THANK YOU TO MY BEST FRIEND and partner in this dramatic improvisation called life. I love you, Jay Venzke. I could not have accomplished even a bit of this without you.

Huge thanks to my mom, Janice Olson, and my pastor, Wendy Treat. No one on earth has influenced my life more than you and you both are extraordinary women who have believed in me and pioneered a path for me (and so many others).

Christine Caine, you are a modern-day William Wilberforce, and I will forever be grateful for you who: #1 talked me into being a writer in the first place, and #2 opened my eyes to this issue.

Lee and Laura Domingue. The Ragin' Cajun and the Texas Firecracker. Quite the world-shaking combination! This novel would never have been written without your support and your belief in this project.

Thank you Jill Cooper who served as my literary mid-wife. Thanks for holding my hand through the contractions of the birth of both the novel and the movie. There are no words. Thank you also to my sisters and friends: Shuie Altizer, Tina Scott, Fahren Johnson, Erica Kelly, and Christian Shook.

Lisa Arnold and Jarred Coates, thank you for picking up the baton of this message and giving your blood, sweat and tears to produce this into a movie. Film Incito has only just begun to become a mighty force in the film industry.

Latasha Haynes and Lisa Garrison. Your support has been ridiculous and I will never forget our midnight scramble to the deadline of the first edition. Lisa, thank you for your work on the design of this edition. Latasha, thank you for your passion to promote this project. Ike & Tash Photography, you have become industry leaders because of your ridiculous gifting and your relentless pursuit of excellence. The best is yet to come!

Merci Beaucoup, mon amies, Floyd and Vee Domingue. You are the human encyclopedia of all things Cajun and Mardi Gras. *Laissez les bons temps rouler*! Your input was invaluable. And Martha Williams, thank you for helping me bring Aggie to life.

Special thanks to the incredible editor Julie Piemonte. You are the needle in a haystack finder. Also: Debbie McCallon and Lynette Clark. Thank you David Bush, for your writing advice. You helped shape this 2nd edition. Caleb Peavy, you are a creative genius, and an idea machine!! Daniella Mark, you are an administrative wizard...even in between baby feedings and naps!

BOOK CLUB QUESTIONS

1. Did the format of this book bring you into an awareness of human trafficking? If so, what are your thoughts and feelings about this issue after reading Caged?

2. Galen was suddenly exposed to an unknown evil...human trafficking. How aware do you think the world is of this present evil practice?

3. The book states, “He (Galen) couldn’t understand why a prostitute would allow herself to be locked inside a room, even if it was for her own protection.” Given the implications of a door locked from the outside, does this change your mind about a possible preconceived notion of prostitutes? What about the young girls who have found themselves caught up in the sex industry? Do you think these girls should be prosecuted as criminals or victims? Why?

4. In Caged, the author presents Jack and Richard as twins. What do you think happened to Jack and Richard that caused the differences in their lifestyles?

5. With which characters’ quality do you most identify? Aggie’s faith? The DuLonde’s compassion? Wil’s determination to succeed? Galen’s courage in stepping into the unknown?

6. At the end of the book, the author lists many options of how her readers can help to fight against this horrific practice. With which option to help do you feel most comfortable?

Molly loves to meet her readers. If your book club would like to Skype or FaceTime her into your discussion, please contact her at www.mollyvenkze.com.

ABOUT THE AUTHOR

MOLLY VENZKE IS A SPEAKER, screenwriter, and all-around word herder. The idea for *Caged No More* was birthed from her passion to not only raise awareness about human trafficking, but also help fund organizations that are fighting to end this modern-day slavery. 100% of the author's proceeds of this novel, as well as the feature film, are donated to Trafficking Hope, a nationwide organization dedicated to the rescue and restoration of trafficking survivors.

In 2016, Molly launched *The Fearless 365 Campaign*, an invitation to any person who will dare to embrace life fearless every day. Fear is a bully that must be silenced in order for dreams to transform into realities. This campaign is a daily challenge to remind us who we really are, and to propel us to become beyond what we imagined possible.

For more information about *The Fearless 365 Campaign*, or Molly's latest novels, screenplays, and projects, visit www.mollyvenzke.com.

Made in the USA
San Bernardino, CA
03 March 2016